Praise for Allaigna's Song: Overture

"Magically unputdownable! JM Landels not only knows her magic, music, and swords, she knows how to weave all these elements into an exciting, enchanting, and uplifting tale. More please!"
— *CC Humphreys, award-winning author of* Plague *and* Shakespeare's Rebel

"An immensely satisfying epic. Landels delivers her richly woven story with both grace and ardor as befits the realm of her tale. Yes, the story includes magic, even beyond the quality of the prose, and the loom is elaborated with line drawing illustrations. This is a fine launch for a promised series — one that seems destined to become a standard! Recommended."
— *Grady Harp,* San Francisco Review of Books

"Elegantly constructed, boasting a subtle and well-thought out magic system based on music, on top of everything else. I'd highly recommend checking it out."
— *Brandon Crilly, BlackGate.com*

"A compelling coming-of-age story that launches a fantasy trilogy to watch for. JM Landels writes with exquisite effect in this emotionally taut, action-imbued book set in a land that battles to come to terms with different forms of magic. Three intriguing women chart their own paths, creating a weave of intersecting consequences for the heroine. There is no shortage of surprises for the reader, in no small part because the characters in this tale refuse to fit into boxes. Good luck putting *Allaigna's Song: Overture* down — I read it in a single sitting."
— *Myst de Vana, Netgalley.com*

"Author Landels knows her stuff. Whether it's horses, sword-fighting, or midwifery, the details and descriptions are well-chosen and convincing. And she makes magic out of music ... or music out of magic. Either way, it works."
— *Sylvia Stopforth, author of* Dragon Rock

"This beautifully-written high fantasy weaves together the tale of three generations of women — grandmother, mother, and daughter — all of whom make very different life choices. It's rare to find a fantasy novel that focuses on female characters and their relationships, and even rarer to find one that does it so well. Magic and knights and swords and horses, yes, all of that is here, but this is definitely not your grandfather's old-school fantasy series.

The story and the relatable characters will hook you right from the beginning, and leave you wanting to know more. I can't wait for the next book in the series!"
— *Five-star review on Amazon.com*

"From the very first page, JM Landels draws me into Allaigna's brilliantly observed world, a land rich in conflict and magic. Landels is gifted with storytelling abilities and gives her readers those greatest of rewards, surprise turns and great character growth and transformation. Subtle and powerful, her writing always pleases."
— *Mel Anastasiou, author of* Stella Ryman and the Fairmount Manor Mysteries

"I loved this novel! The plot is engrossing, the pace is perfect, and I cannot wait for the next in this series. The three heroines are all very different, but beautifully written — they all felt real to me. I laughed and I cried. I don't read a lot of fantasy but this was super enjoyable (felt more historical than pure fantasy — the magic felt totally believable). I liked it so much, I read it twice within a month."
— *Al Do on Kobo*

"*Allaigna* by JM Landels is satisfying fantasy with the emotional grit and depth that could only be written by a mother of girls. It's part romance, part step-family dynamics, part magical coming-of age story, braided together in narratives that have distinct yet overlapping points of view."
— *Susan Pieters*

"Fascinating and well written, weaving the three stories together to bring you to understanding adding layer by layer. Looking forward to the sequel."
— *Five-star review on Amazon.com*

"The compelling plot kept me hooked for hours! It was addictive."
— *Nabila Fairuz, author of* The Chronicles of Captain Shelly Manhar

"Loved, no, LOVED it. Superb."
— *Donna J Saunders*

Find *Allaigna's Song: Overture* at pulpliteraturepress.com/allaignas-song/
ISBN: 978-0-9949565-9-0 (print)
ISBN: 978-1-98886500-3 (eBook)

Also by JM Landels from Pulp Literature Press
Allaigna's Song: Overture (2017)
Allaigna's Song: Chorale (2021)

'Masquerade' *Pulp Literature* Issue 12, Autumn 2016
'Treason's Fulcrum' *Pulp Literature* Issue 25, Winter 2020
'The Shepherdess' *Pulp Literature* Issues 24 & 26, Autumn 2019
& Spring 2020

Allaigna's Song:

JM Landels

PULP LITERATURE PRESS

Pulp Fantasy is an imprint of Pulp Literature Press.

Library and Archives Canada Cataloguing in Publication

ISBN: 978-1-988865-25-6 (paperback) ISBN: 978-1-988865-26-3 (ebook)

This book is a work of fiction. Names, characters, places, and incidents are products of the author's imagination or are used fictitiously. Any resemblance to actual events or locales or persons, living or dead, is entirely coincidental.

The land of the Ilmar and the major political characters therein are the creation of Scott Fitzgerald Gray and are used with permission.

Parts of this novel were originally published serially in *Pulp Literature* magazine © 2017, 2018, 2019, Pulp Literature Press.

Cover art: Melissa Mary Duncan
Cover design: Kate Landels
Edits and interior layout: Amanda Bidnall
Title fonts: Kris Sayer
Map: Scott Fitzgerald Gray & Mel Anastasiou
Printed and bound in Canada by First Choice Books, Victoria BC
International version printed by IngramSpark

Published in Canada by Pulp Literature Press
www.pulpliterature.com

ೊ ಌ

This book is dedicated with love
to the memory of my father
Kenyon Esdale Landels
1934–2011

ೊ ಌ

Principality of Elalantar
The Clearwater
Principality of Hole
Danna River
Principality of Aerach
The
Sandhorn
Aleran (Caranar)
Werrancross
Orey
The Ilmar
Erelin
Rheran
The Clearwater Way
Teillai
Doniver
Sudry
Principality of Brandishear
Nyndenu Wood
Caredry
Kelerin Hills
Hunthad River
Glaeddyn
The Valnirata
Welbirk
Myrwater
The Locurwater
Aldac

Contents

Dramatis Personae

Allaigna's Song
Aerach, the Clearwater Way, the Sandhorn, Brandishear
1587–1598 IA (Imperial Age)

Allaigna Leisana Andreg, runaway daughter of the Duchess and
    Duke of Teillai
Nag, Allaigna's horse
Irdaign, aka Angeley, Allaigna's grandmother and nurse
Tiern Doniver, Allaigna's betrothed, heir to the Doniver lordship
Dog, a mute kennel master
Yannick, 'the Barrel', head of Doniver's boar-baiting operation
Raddick, one of Doniver's stable boys
Eiglin Doniver, lord of Doniver
Edda, one of Dog's two hounds
Morran Rhoan, a travelling singer, currently retained by Tiern Doniver
Fraell Edris, Allaigna's former swordsmistress in Rheran
Garæthiel, Allaigna's liege knight in Rheran
Rhiadne, former huntress at Teillai, now a captain in the Brandishear
    Rangers
Goff, Allaigna's cousin
Talwis, Rhoan's mare
Kîan, a member of the Sage Clan
Duinir, leader of the Sage Clan, Kîan's mother
Gerran, stable master of the Sage Clan
Milask, Duinir's head assassin
Fedorind, a member of the Sage Clan
Dourva, a Leisanmira leader
Glaignen, Dourva's son and Allaigna's friend

Nourd, midwife and seer of the Leisanmira, Irdaign's mentor
Chriani, captain of the Sixth Brandishear Rangers
Chanist, Allaigna's grandfather and Prince High of Brandishear

Lauresa's Chorus and Irdaign's Chorus
Teillai and Aleran in the Principality of Aerach
1584–1598 IA

Lauresa Irdaign Leisana Andreg, Duchess of Teillai, former Princess of
    Brandishear
Irdaign, her estranged mother, former Princess High of Brandishear,
    now the midwife known as Angeley
Allenis Andreg, Duke of Teillai, Lauresa's husband
Einavar, Lauresa's lover and Allaigna's father
Chanist Brandis, Prince High of Brandishear, Lauresa's father
Gwannyn, Chanist's second wife
Dennein, Lauresa's childhood nurse
Glaignen, a Leisanmira boy with the Sight
Carollus, Andreg's vizier
Ceilaf, a Brandishear knight who died protecting Lauresa on the
    Clearwater Way
Seddan, the ostler in Teillai
Vishod, Prince High of Aerach
Allenry, Lauresa's second child, Allaigna's brother
Genissa, Lauresa's cousin
Taerysh, Genissa's mother, widow of Chanist's brother
Peri, Lauresa's courser
Daewen, Einavar's mare
Lauriana, Lauresa's third child, Allaigna's sister
Lady Raen, friend of Lauresa

Darras, Raen's son, Allaigna's foster brother

Julla, second nurse to Lauresa's children

Irdina, Allaigna's middle sister, Branwen's twin

Branwen, Allaigna's youngest sister, Irdina's twin

Wulf, stable boy at Osthegn

Hardin, head groom at Osthegn, Wulf's father

Aster, a broodmare, Peri's daughter

Sir Darien, Andreg's vassal, Darras's father

Eiglin Doniver, lord of Doniver

Fride, head cook at Osthegn

Phillia, Chanist's deceased sister

Girondrey, Chanist's deceased older brother

Goffree, Prince High of Brandishear, Chanist's father

Soot, Allaigna's first pony

Sir Piers, diplomat in Vishod's court

Vardry, Lauresa's youngest child

Baredh, weapons-master at Osthegn

Allaigna's Song:

 Aria

In *Allaigna's Song: Overture* …

Fourteen-year-old **Allaigna** discovered that her family lied to her all her life: her nurse Angeley is really her grandmother and former Princess High of Brandishear, and Allaigna herself is the product of a tryst that occurred when her mother was lost in the Valnirata Greatwood en route to her wedding. Fuelled by hurt and anger, Allaigna stole her mother's only keepsake of the man who rescued her—his Ilvan dagger—and fled from her home and her unwanted betrothal, hoping to find her father by retracing her mother's decade-and-a-half-old route.

Princess High **Irdaign**, set aside by her husband and separated from her daughter, used her power of the Sight to tweak the strings of fate. She returned to her former calling as a midwife, arriving in Teillai in time to aid the birth of her granddaughter, Allaigna.

Lauresa of Brandishear found love for the first time in the unlikely aspect of the wanderer who saved her life on the Clearwater Way. But staying with him and forsaking her intended marriage to the Duke of Teillai would have meant war between the Ilvani of the Valnirata and the four principalities of the Ilmar. Duty overcame desire, and she arrived for her wedding, not yet knowing she carried her lover's child.

Allaigna's Song: Aria

Prologue

Heroism is not in my bones. It is in my blood, certainly. My mother, my father, my grandmother and grandfather: all of them have made heroic sacrifices, taken courageous leaps of faith, risked their hearts and lives for the greater good, or thrown themselves between others and their fates. Some have even made a profession of it.

When I ran away from my home, determined to find my birth father and wounded to the quick by the lies my family had told all my life, I was being brave — or foolhardy — but not heroic. Heroism would have entailed staying where I was, working with my mother and grandmother, and even accepting the hand of Tiern Doniver for the good of Aerach. Instead I left a string of diplomatic incidents, and a trail of blood, in my wake when I fled.

My only defence for the havoc I created in my selfish angst is temporary insanity. I was, after all, fourteen.

Verse 1
Blood and Guts

By the time the sun was halfway to its midpoint on the first day of my hasty flight from Teillai, I realized my error and changed direction. Searching for my father by retracing the route he and my mother took fifteen years ago had a romantic sort of logic, but the road to Werrancross was far too populated for the Duke's daughter, on the run from her betrothal. Several times already I had been seen, and perhaps even recognized. For who wouldn't notice a lone sliver of a girl astride an over-tall, raw-boned gelding, pounding the road in the early light of dawn? So I took leave of the road at the next crossing and spent a few hours slogging through hedge-lined irrigation canals. I meted out the rest of the day along country lanes, losing the morning's gains in a zigzag path eastward. By nightfall, my seat bones were raw, my knees were locked stiff, and I laid out my bedroll in the Eastern forest only a few leagues from where I'd started.

The temptation to turn tail and run home like a chastened hound was strong that night.

The second day ground my seat bones further through my flesh, rubbed the top layer of skin away from the inside of my knees, and made my ankles creak and protest every time I dismounted to lead Nag through thick undergrowth and tangled roots. The sun remained cloistered behind pale, cold clouds, and I judged my direction only by the moss on the trees. At the end of daylight, still less than twenty leagues away from Teillai, I wondered what was worse: being found and dragged ignominiously home; or never being found at all.

The urge to run home the second night was tempered by the small increase in distance and my greater uncertainty that I could even *find* home.

The third morning, I hobbled about like an old woman, shivering and packing up bedding that had been drenched by an icy overnight rain. I dreaded settling in the saddle, sure there was no more flesh left between my bones and my breeks. My voice was thick with cold and disuse, nearly as creaky as my bones, but I sang as I groomed Nag nonetheless.

My body warmed and loosened with the effort of grooming, and so did my voice, the notes finally coming pure and resonant, vibrating between the dandy brush and my horse's sides, filling the air with the Leisanmira magic that was my birthright. I had tried this small charm yesterday, but had only succeeded in mildly scorching Nag's thick black winter coat, making him look as if he had faded in the sun or lain in a manure pile too long. Today, though, I found the right notes, the right sequence. With rhythmic strokes, I brushed the black out of his hair, turning his flanks a ruddy bay.

I stood back to assess the effect. Granted, the pink light of the morning sun heightened the red, but even in the shade his coat was a definite russet brown now. It would be better to continue on his mane and tail, turning him chestnut, but perhaps I would leave that till tomorrow. I had no idea how long the colour change would last; I might have to repeat the song every day. But a different horse each day would go a long way toward throwing off any pursuit, and I wondered how much effort it would take to turn him dun, or grey, or skewbald. It was tempting to try it on myself as well: to go from black hair to blonde, or pale skin to bronze. But with no mirror, I thought it best not to make the attempt. Instead, I used the curved, cruel blade of my father's—my true father's—dagger to hack off great hanks of my long dark hair. I hid the remaining hair beneath a woollen cap and hoped it was disguise enough.

As I tucked the dagger back into my boot, Nag's head shot up, ears pricked. He didn't snort, which meant he sensed danger. If it were other horses, he would have whinnied a greeting. And for a deer, or bird, or other harmless creature, he would have snorted to let me know all was well after the initial alert. That he was still frozen, silent, nostrils flaring and muscles tensed to flee, meant it was likely a predator.

My throat went dry and sticky as I turned to scan the surrounding trees and bushes. Nag flicked an ear at me. He was not yet saddled or bridled. I considered fleeing the invisible threat bareback with just a halter, but getting onto Nag's tall back without stirrups or a stump to stand on was beyond me. I cursed my arrogance in not keeping the beautiful grey pony my father—the Duke, I mean—had given me. That pony I could have mounted bareback. That pony, though no warhorse, was trained to seat and voice commands. That pony was a mare, more likely to defend a fallen rider.

I forced my brain to stop rattling and focus. The forest was almost silent. Not even birds or squirrels rustled or chirped. But there was a distant disturbance, like a windstorm coming closer.

Nag's already tight-wound nerves got the better of him. He bolted, crashing into the undergrowth. I dived for my packs, drawing out my thin Ilvan sword and wishing it were a spear. The thrashing of undergrowth was in both ears now: the sound of Nag's retreat growing fainter, and the other growing louder. Somehow I knew it would be a boar, even before its maddened red eyes and blood-streaked shoulders burst from the bushes. The broken haft of a spear protruded from its thick neck.

The pain-mad creature hurtled at me, and the years of drills with Baredh, Rhiadne, and Edris took over my body. I stepped sideways with a calm I didn't know I possessed, and drove my sword, two-handed, into the beast's neck. It skewered itself with its own momentum, driving the pommel out of my hands and into my belly. The blow collapsed my knees, and the boar finished the job, smashing me to the ground as it tumbled forward.

I lay there for several whistling breaths, listening for the inevitable hounds and riders that would discover me. I am not sure if I was disappointed or relieved when none came. At last I sat up, retched, and fell back again, clutching my stomach. When I did manage to right myself, I spotted the boar, half a dozen paces away. Its sides were heaving, but it was otherwise immobile. My sword was stuck in its neck like a great carving knife, the hilt waving gently with each of the pig's ragged breaths.

If I sat there long enough, would the boar die? I hardly saw how it could live with both a spear and sword inside it. But what if it was just winded, and then it recovered enough to get up and attack? Or run away with my sword?

I stood, shaking, grasping the trunk of a nearby tree. The boar gave a feeble twitch of its feet and tried to raise its head. That's when I noticed how small the tusks were. And the belly, now exposed to me, sported a double row of milk-filled teats. Not a boar: a sow.

A warm rush of anger made me forget my bruises. A sow! What sort of mould-rotted conscience would let someone hunt a sow, especially at this time of the year, with piglets in the nest?

I sidled around her, keeping well away, terrified she would surge to her feet and charge again. Her eye followed me, but she didn't, or perhaps couldn't, move. She would die if left, a long slow death. Noise had returned to the forest, including the commentary of a pair of crows perched above us, waiting.

I slid the dagger out of its place in my boot-top. It had once belonged to the father I'd never met. I'd stolen it from my mother before slipping away like a thief in the night. Like my sword, it was Ilvani-made, but far crueller and uglier, with its dark curved handle and blue-black hooked blade. It was sharp, though, and would pierce a wild pig's tough hide better than my hunting knife.

Continuing my sideways circle behind the sow, I rehearsed in my head what I needed to do. She scrabbled in the leaf mould with her sharp toes when I crossed her field of vision. I took in a breath that sounded nearly as ragged as hers, forcing my heart to calm and my hands to still. With my second breath I lunged, grasping the hilt of my sword in one hand to hold the poor skewered creature still and drew the sharp steel of the dagger across her throat.

Blood fountained as the sow convulsed and rolled; I had to jump backward or be knocked over. Then she lay still except for the slow pulses of blood draining into the forest floor.

My legs and hands were spattered with red. Unthinking, I put a knuckle in my mouth and sucked as if the drops of blood were my own. When I realized what I was doing, I spat, horrified. Then my stomach rumbled, reminding me I hadn't yet eaten. The supplies in my pack were already getting low after only two days on the road. As much as I disliked meat, and the sight and smell of raw flesh especially, I had to admit that the sow's warm blood tasted little different than mine: salty, and really not so bad. There was a lot of food on those bones.

Wishing I'd packed small cords—one of the multitude of things I wished I'd packed—I pulled a leather lace out of my jerkin and used it to lash the sow's hind feet together. At least I had a sturdy rope, which I looped through the hind legs. Tossing the free end over a tree branch, I hoisted the pig off the ground. She was heavier than I, and I would not have managed it at all had I not sung a song to lessen gravity's pull on her. Nonetheless, it cost a great deal of sweat and a number of rope burns before I got her high enough to lash the end of the rope around the tree trunk and leave her swaying above the ground.

I widened the slash I'd already made in her throat and stood back, wrinkling my nose in revulsion while the rest of her veins and arteries drained. Angeley would have chided me for wasting the blood, but I had no hounds to feed, nor any way to make soup or pudding from it. Just because I'd stomached a drop of raw pig's blood did not mean I was about to add it to my diet.

The beautifully sharp Ilvan knife made easy work of the gutting. I could hear Angeley scold me again as the blue-dark intestines slithered to the ground. But I had no use for those either.

"All the more for you, friends," I said to the half-dozen crows watching me with patient intent.

When the sow was cleaned to my satisfaction, I stood back, wiping my blood-drenched hands and knife on a clump of moss. A week ago, I would likely have thrown up at the mere thought of gutting a pig. Today, though I'd taken no pleasure in the task, I felt a gleam of pride in my own sufficiency.

However, I had no time for self-congratulation. I had a horse to catch.

A horse will flee thirty or so galloping strides before it slows and begins to curve its trajectory into a wide arc to see whether it has been followed. It strikes a balance between its need to run from danger and its need to conserve energy and keep the herd together. In a wooded area the flight is shorter, and it was at about fifty of my paces that I saw Nag's track veer east and lose its war-torn look. I angled off the track, scoring a tree trunk now and then with my knife so as not to lose my way. When I calculated I was near enough, I whistled four short notes and a long one, as I did whenever I approached the paddocks at home with a carrot in my pocket.

Sure enough, I saw movement through the scrub and trees, and long ears pricked high above the bushes.

"Nag," I called softly, moving to a clearer patch of ground.

He came, picking his way over dead wood, his nostrils still showing a wary red, but glad enough of my company and the withered piece of carrot I offered him.

"Good boy, goooood boy," I crooned.

He shied away as I rubbed his forehead. The smell of blood must still have been strong on me, but I scratched his poll and breathed into his nostrils, reaffirming our understanding before leading him back to the mess of a campsite.

The morning was almost gone before I tacked up, cleaned up, and managed to sling the sow's carcass across Nag's protesting back. He danced like a racehorse, snorting and tossing his head, and I had to sing him near to sleep before he'd put up with it. It left me almost too tired to move, but I climbed into the saddle anyway, for I was fired with anger.

The penalty for hunting out of season was stiff. Hunting a sow incurred even larger fines, and perhaps a short term in prison for a nobleman. For a commoner, it would be stocks at the least, or perhaps a branding or the gallows. Boar hunting is forbidden in the springtime for good reason. Somewhere in the forest there was now a nest of motherless piglets. And, thanks to the immoral actions of those hunters, I was partly responsible.

The sow's trail was easy enough to follow backward, though I was surprised how far she'd come in her wounded state. Her track broke at last on the verge of forest and rangeland. At first I thought I would lose her trace as the ground became firmer and grassier, but then I saw hoof prints — more than one set — converge where the sow's path had originally left the woods. I dismounted and tied Nag to a tree to avoid further confusing the tracks. Though the prints were harder to see, there were traces of dog as well.

The story was easy enough to read for one who'd spent as many hours at Rhiadne's heels as I had. The horsemen, galloping along the forest verge, had met with the sow who had been driven from her den by hounds. A mix of hoof prints and bark rubbed from the trees showed where the horses had been tied. There had been no pursuit of the wounded sow, except by the hounds; but human boot prints led back into the woods the way the pig had come.

I followed them, and sure enough, they led to the sow's nest, farther back in the woods. There was a mess of human and canine prints where the dogs had rejoined their masters, but not a piglet to be found. No blood either, though plenty of crushed undergrowth showing busy activity. The hunters, it seemed, had left with a sack full of live piglets.

For what? To raise on goats' milk and fatten for the autumn? How a pen full of wild piglets would escape the notice of the bailiffs, I wasn't sure. But these were wealthy folk, for they had hounds and horses. Did they really need to poach newborn marcassins?

I jogged back to find Nag peaceably cropping new grass, accustomed now to the sow's carcass across his saddle. Once back aboard my grubby brown mount, I sent him off at a trot along the return tracks of the horses. We slowed to a walk when the first spiral of smoke became visible. Soon I could hear dogs and voices ahead.

I searched my memory for maps I'd seen, trying to recall the name of the nearest hamlet. By my reckoning, I was west of the city of Doniver. It was a name that made me shudder, being also the seat of my intended betrothed. The largest town nearby was Scrantree, south toward the Valnirata border. I called up those long-forgotten taxation maps Willits had made me study: there were no other settlements in this ward, aside from a few hamlets clustered along the river. There should be nothing here. No farms, no holds. Nothing but forest and rangeland for the game that belonged to Teillai. And yet, above the birches, the smoke from at least half a dozen fires coiled defiantly in the air.

Ride on, my inner voice told me. *What do you care if a band of poachers steals some of your father's game? He's nothing to you.*

The most logical course would be to report them to the sheriff in Scrantree, if it had a sheriff, or at least a bailiff or reeve. And if not Scrantree, then Doniver. But the thought of Doniver called up my parents' promise to its younger lord and one of the reasons I'd left home. Had they already notified old Doniver and his son of my truancy, or were they hoping I'd return quietly, with no one the wiser? Had they sent riders out in all directions, or did the embarrassment of having a runaway daughter curtail any public search? Were they even—I stopped that thought before it went further. Of course they were looking, and therefore I could not make contact with the authorities of any town, large or small.

The light of the short spring day was starting to dim, slivers of gold appearing at the edges of the western clouds. Dealing with the pig had taken half my day, and following her sad trail the other half. My stomach growled. I hadn't the will left to start a fire and cook some of her carcass here on the hilltop. But could I walk into a camp of poachers and demand hospitality? A girl on her own risked much, despite Teillai's harsh view of rapists and molesters. Teillai also took a harsh view of poaching, and what good had that done the sow?

There was one profession safe from interference. I had hoped and counted upon it while packing my saddlebags three nights ago. The unwritten pact with the Leisanmira allows the nomadic people to travel freely, owing fealty to none and protected, if grudgingly, by all. It extends to any travelling entertainer, whether Ilmari, Ilvani, or true Leisanmira, and is a pact of convenience as much as tradition, for the news such people carry is valuable. The written word is lost on much of the population, but songs can make a political career almost as quickly as a bard's tongue sharpened in disdain can destroy it.

To go walking into their camp with the evidence of their crime slung across my saddle would invite scrutiny and hostility both. I slung the sow's carcass from a new tree then spent extra time and effort singing charms to clean the blood from my saddle and clothes. It left me even more exhausted than the efforts of the morning, and I hoped it would not drain my voice too much. I rested a while, eating a precious spoonful of honey from the jar I'd brought for medicinal use, and drinking most of the water in my flask. Once I felt refreshed, I began to softly warm my throat with a few scales and ditties. It was far from its best, but it would have to do. I remounted Nag, steeled my nerves, and rode down into the valley under the blue clouds of dusk.

Lauresa's Chorus

Lauresa blinks, hardly believing it has stopped, that the burning pain is over. On her slack stomach, squirming wetly, is the child. Someone takes her hand, places it on the baby's back, then covers them both with a thick cloth. But no, she wants to see. Lauresa curls over, gathers the baby in both hands and lifts it — or her, for it is a girl — as high as the still-intact cord allows. The infant shivers, mewls in protest, and Lauresa pulls her close again, clutching the greasy, wet, and wrinkled creature beneath her breasts.

Tears start, and it is through these blurry curtains she gazes into the wise and searching eyes of her daughter. Here, in this moment, she could stay forever.

There is a voice beside her, both soothing and annoying, reminding her to push out the afterbirth. It is the midwife, but not the one with whom she began this long labour. Why does it seem like the nagging of her mother? She doesn't have a mother. Except Gwannyn. And Gwannyn never nags.

She finally tears her gaze away from the beautiful stare of her daughter, and is jolted by the face looking down at her. Fractured images like splinters of a broken looking glass stutter and shimmer, layering the midwife's face with long-forgotten memories. She feels like throwing up again, though her stomach was empty long ago. She closes her eyes, and the relief of not seeing is palpable.

They are alone at last, the tiny girl child firmly attached to her breast, those wondrous eyes closed in concentration as the babe works at drawing out scant drops of first milk. It hurts Lauresa—the ferocious toothless mouth feels like it is drawing blood, not milk—but she wouldn't stop it for the world.

All I need is here, Lauresa thinks. For the first time, for as long as she can remember, she feels entire. This child completes her, makes her whole. Whatever lacks or wants she may have had, whatever losses or sorrows, they are irrelevant now. Even Einavar, whose face has haunted her each day and night for the past nine clearmoons, has suddenly slipped back to a pleasant but distant memory. Instead there is Allaigna's face: there when she looks down at it; still there when she closes her eyes. She wants nothing more.

The sound of the chamber door opening disturbs her reverie. Irritated, she wills the intruder away, but knows nonetheless that a face will appear from behind the bed curtains. She even knows which face it will be. She is strong. She can face anyone, anything, now.

The midwife, the new one, pulls aside the curtain and sets a cup of something steaming into Lauresa's free hand.

"Raspberry leaf," she says in a voice at once so strange and so familiar it makes Lauresa want to cry.

Perhaps she is not so strong after all. Instead she summons anger, looking in all the dark corners of her otherwise happy soul to find it. Her own voice, when it comes out at last, is a trembling mix of emotions, but it is as steady as she can make it.

"Thank you ... Mother."

That is all the anger she can summon for this face from the past. There will be recriminations, of course, and long, heated discussions. But today, on her daughter's birth day, she won't voice them. She lets the pain dissolve. It is not gone, and it will precipitate again. But for today, she chooses gratitude.

"Thank you," she repeats, "for being here."

Her mother blinks, surprised perhaps. There are tears in those blue eyes so like her own.

Irdaign reaches out, touches Lauresa's hand, then her hair, her cheek. As if reassuring herself she really does exist.

"Oh, Lauresa, how could I not be?"

You were not for so much more of my life, Lauresa thinks.

Irdaign wipes her eyes on the rough sleeve of her dress. More of Lauresa's memories pour back, sending her stomach reeling again. So many little things. Her mother gathering herbs in the kitchen garden at the Bastion, those same sun-browned hands plumper, less spotted and veined, but just as strong and gentle, picking her up to straddle her hip. Standing regal in full court dress, accepting petitioners, running the castle, the town, the country, while Papa was at war. How could all of those scenes have been forgotten so completely?

Irdaign leans over and pulls Lauresa and the baby together in an embrace.

"There is so very much to talk about, my love. But first, your husband would like to see you and his daughter."

Not his, thinks Lauresa, sure now, as she had not been through-out the pregnancy. "Does he know who you are?"

Irdaign shakes her head. "I think it's best he doesn't."

Lauresa nods agreement but sheds another inward tear for the new lie with which she anoints Allaigna's birthday. But it is a small one compared to the other.

"Send him in," she commands.

Allenis Andreg, Duke of Teillai, her husband, is as gruffly polite as he ever has been. As polite as he was at their betrothal. As polite and relieved as he was when she rode unaccompanied, two weeks late for her wedding and rather worse for wear, through the gates of Teillai. As polite and stately as he was on their hastily re-set wedding day, and as he was on their wedding night, when, if he noticed she was no virgin, he said nothing. As polite as he has been every day since then.

He took the improbable story of her adventure in the forest of the Valnirata at face value. Littered with truth, which was the most improbable aspect, it was as convincing a tale as she could make it. He did not question it, and assured her he would make no redress against the Valnirati, since it was outlaws who had attacked her, and Valnirati who had sheltered her. He expressed (polite) gratitude for her safe return, and then (politely) eschewed the matter to allow her to forget it.

It was not so easy on her part.

Einavar's face haunted her sleeping and waking hours through-out the pregnancy. Andreg performed his conjugal duty on a metronomic schedule: every night for the first week of the mar-riage; every second night for the second week; then every third until it became evident Lauresa was with child. After that, the

Duke's appearances in the bedchamber ceased altogether.

Lauresa both desired and dreaded the encounters. She wondered if it would have been better or worse had not Einavar claimed her maidenhood already. On the one hand, Andreg's perfunctory mating habits may have seemed better without comparison to the heart-stopping passion she had experienced with Einavar. On the other, at least she could close her eyes and pretend it was Einavar's long slim fingers that touched her, his thin and ropy-muscled body that lay across hers, his insatiable thirst for her that held them pinned together. It wasn't easy. Allenis and Einavar were as unalike as two men could be, but her imagination was strong. If she thought about the latter, recalled their passionate lovemaking in the Greatwood, she could work herself into a state of sufficient arousal so that, if she kept her eyes closed, at least it was not painful.

And now ... Now Lauresa's mind is somewhere completely new. The unlikely glimpses of Einavar's face she sees in the chubby features of Allaigna become less and less frequent, until all she sees is the baby girl herself. It is as if the gift of a child sprang from her body by magic. To her it is irrelevant that the babe is not Andreg's and that he seems so much less enamoured of her than Lauresa is. She is blissful when ensconced in her bed with Allaigna nestled under her arm or latched happily on her breast.

It does not last long, this bubble of bliss. By the end of the second day, the milk comes in, finally leaving the child content and sleeping for more than an hour. By the third day, the tears come in as well.

Though Allaigna is still Lauresa's joy, she is her only joy. All else seems awash with bitterness, regret, and anger. Her memories, doctored away behind the spells of her father's mages, now break free and surge forth in tidal waves of feeling. Everything makes her want to cry, from the minor adolescent angst she had all but forgotten, to her bittersweet fortnight with Einavar, to the heart-rending, soul-quelling betrayal of her mother's departure from her life. Even the happy memories — those from before her mother left her — cause bursts of tears, both of happiness and of bitterness at their contrast to the rest of her life.

Her ladies-in-waiting, her husband, and the maids who sweep the fireplace all urge her to pass the babe to a wet nurse, to allow herself some sleep and a break from the child who obviously has tired her so. Only her mother, the woman who calls herself Angeley, insists otherwise. And despite the weight of all those other voices, despite the furious, bitter anger coiled in her chest, she finds that, in this raw and vulnerable state, she is incapable of not listening to her mother. So she keeps the baby with her, nurses her from her own breast, and is grateful to do so. She obediently opens her mouth and lets Angeley place a small chunk of the afterbirth under her tongue as proof against the tears. Whether it is gipsy magic or superstition, she does feel better the following day and willingly accepts the treatment again.

Gradually, like clouds clearing, she reaches a state of near equilibrium: not the rapturous, incapacitating joy of those first two days, but not the crippling sorrow either.

It has been a turn and a half of the clearmoon. The midwinter feast has come and gone, the ashes have been cleared from the great fireplace, and the household is busy cleaning the remains of festivity from the wide stone halls of Osthegn. Lauresa takes a deep breath, enjoying the crisp winter air sweeping through the rooms as the maids open shutters and shake out drapery.

Allaigna has fallen asleep at the breast, a dribble of milk flowing down her fat cheeks. Lauresa heaves herself out of the deep chair, pausing to rock the baby before walking softly to the canopied bed the two of them share. She sets the babe down in the middle and covers her with a small embroidered blanket.

It is one Irdaign brought with her when she arrived for Allaigna's birth, but it is more familiar than that. Memories of her childhood are so soft and inconsistent they melt like fog when she tries to touch one. But this she can touch … and remember. The pictures in her mind are like paintings: static in their time, but immense in detail if she traverses them with her mind's eye. It is there, crumpled at the foot of the small daybed in the solar, sun shining on it, dust motes weaving a pattern above it. Her small-nailed, pudgy child's feet press against the nubbly raised texture of the embroidery, tracing the patterns of leaves, flowers, and stars. Now she does this with her adult fingers in the cold, dim, winter light. The still form beneath the blanket is not one of her wooden dolls with its beautiful painted-wax face, but her own infinitely more beautiful daughter, with skin more pale and translucent, lips more delicate. A pinkish-mauve tinge finer than the finest tints on the royal dollmakers' palettes rests on those cheeks, beneath eyelashes thick, dark, and curved in sweet smiles below the barely-there line of brow. She remembers the doll, her favourite, which slept covered in this very blanket. She once thought she could love nothing so well or so much as that doll. But she has thought that about many things and people. Now she doesn't think. She knows.

A memory flashes. Hot summer sun flooding onto the thick carpet of the solar. Her feet are bare. She digs her toes into the warm woollen tufts of the carpet while she brushes the golden hair of her doll. She takes her embroidered blanket and wraps it around the doll's waist like a skirt. Too big, too bulky. It makes the doll look like old Dennein.

There are voices behind her, raised in argument and grief, but she cannot let the words pierce her understanding. She has a shell, an imaginary armoured egg, around her to keep out such sorrow and anger. The words hit the shell, dissolve, crumble, and flow down the outside so the sadness cannot touch her.

She shakes the embroidered coverlet, spreading its flowered glory out in front of her, and tucks two corners into the back collar of the doll's dress. That's better. The fabric drapes in regal folds, a mantle worthy of a princess, its thickness proof against cold, injury, or inquisitive eyes.

A hand falls on her shoulder. She wants to shrug it off, to stay in this world of wooden and invulnerable playthings, but the hand is insistent, and the voice finds a chink in her armour, slipping through like an arrow.

"Lauresa …"

In past and present, the voice and hand belong to the same person. "Give me a hug," it says. In the past, the voice has a gentle maternal command to it, and an expectation of being accommodated. The present voice does not demand, but Lauresa hears the longing behind it. She turns and embraces her mother.

In the seven weeks since Irdaign appeared at Lauresa's birthing room, they have not touched more than each other's hands. It is the first time in thirteen years, since that sunlit day in the Bastion's solar, that Lauresa has felt her mother's arms around her.

Once the tears begin, they will not stop. Her sobs are muffled, quiet. Even in her grief, she will not risk waking Allaigna, who sleeps, oblivious, her arms above her head, her mouth making tiny sucking, smiling movements in her dreams.

Finally Lauresa breaks away and moves to the diamond-paned window, leaving it open to take in the icy air. She feels her mother move to close the distance, feels the heat of her body stand between the sleeping babe and the cold. Irdaign does not reach to touch her daughter again. Perhaps she senses that this time her touch would be greeted by a blow, not an embrace.

Lauresa turns, the cold wind at her back hardening her. She wants to shout but hisses instead. "How could you? How could you abandon your daughter?" The tears will not stop, even in her anger. "What kind of mother are you?"

Irdaign's face too is wet with tears. "A bad one," she says simply. "A day doesn't go by that I don't regret leaving you."

It is not enough. Lauresa does not want regret or apology. She wants reasons.

"Then why did you?" It is so hard not to scream and rage.

"For you. For her." There is a pause, as if Irdaign questions her next words. "For the Ilmar."

Lauresa fails to notice the hesitation. "For me? How could being abandoned serve me?"

"You grew up a princess."

Lauresa laughs a harsh, barking sob. Surely her mother must know how little that means. "If I were a gipsy, I'd have married whom I chose. I would have grown up with my" —the word is hard to voice— "mother. I'd have proper memories, not this cobbled mess the court doctors have left me with."

Now that the words have started, they will not be contained. "You left me with my father. What use is a damned father?" She can think only of Allenis, who had no part in the making of her child, and of Einavar, whom the child will never know. How unimportant they both are.

"Your father is Prince High of Brandishear." There is a harsh gravity in her mother's voice. "His love for you is more important than you yet know. My love for you, however, will never flicker, never wane, and indeed has only grown stronger with years." She looks over at Allaigna, and her pained expression breaks with a brief smile. "Though when you were born, I thought it impossible to love you more than I did then." And then the smile is gone and the gravity back. "But your father knew you hardly at all by the time we were divorced. He had been at war most of those years. He needed time for that love to grow and not be forgotten in the wake of other heirs."

Lauresa gives another bitter laugh. "If that was your goal, I'd say it failed. He loves me so much he married me to a man twice my age and sent me to live two hundred leagues from Rheran."

"Princes are not always at liberty to do as their hearts dictate. Nor are mothers. Tell me: when you were 'lost' in the Valnirata" — her voice drops and she moves closer to her daughter — "did you not have to choose between your heart, between this child's father, and the greater good of the realm?"

Lauresa puts her hand behind her to steady herself. The cold leading of the window bites into her palm. She has told no one of what happened in those two weeks. How does Irdaign know?

Irdaign guesses her thoughts. "Your secret is safe with me. A mother can guess things others cannot—as you'll learn." That brief smile flickers again. "I don't know what happened in those woods, and someday you may even trust me enough to tell me. I hope you do. But you can't fool an old midwife. That girl has Ilvani blood, and not a drop of any such thing flows in your husband's veins."

Verse 2

Rude Company

I looked down on the enclosure from the slope at the wood's edge. It was more than the simple camp I'd expected. A low wooden palisade, not high enough to repel human attackers but sufficient to contain livestock, circled a collection of rough huts, a lean-to shelter for horses, and smaller pens that I presumed were for pigs.

I rode Nag straight toward the lashed-together gate, willing boldness into my bones. It had crossed my mind to pose as a boy. At fourteen and a half years I was short for my age, barely taller than a ten-year-old. My breasts and hips were not even hints beneath my clothes, and I was still untroubled by monthly bleeding. But being a boy would make me seem even younger. My youth felt like more of a liability than my sex. At least Nag's imposing height would disguise my stature until I dismounted. One hurdle at a time, I reminded myself.

There was no watchman by the gate, so these people were either careless or unafraid. And indeed, with the Valnirati at peace with us, who should they fear? Except the bailiff, of course.

Dogs within the compound picked up our scent and bayed to announce our approach. I shortened Nag's reins and squeezed him forward with my heels, making him flick his ears and dance with more spirit than he normally deigned to show.

"Ho there!" I called, wincing at the pitch of my voice.

A grubby little man with a beard like used straw sauntered out from one of the huts, scratching his sides.

I cleared my throat. "Good evening to you, sir," I began, amazed at the steadiness in my words. "I see you have fires within, and provender, no doubt. But what better cheer than food and a fire is food, fire, and song?" I had rehearsed this pretty speech all the way down the hill and was disappointed to see it fall flat on the blank stare of this clearly dim-witted gatekeeper.

"I'm a travelling singer, good sir," I explained, trying not to sound patronizing. "Would you be good enough to trade a bit of bread or a bowl of soup for a song or two?" I waited an impatient moment and then added, "And with fodder for my mount, I'll sing all evening long."

"Ye're wasting your breath, lad," came a voice like the grumble of a millstone from behind my unresponsive audience. I started at the word *lad*. Apparently I'd disguised myself after all.

The voice belonged to a dark-bearded behemoth of a man, bigger around than a tun and tall enough to look near eye-to-eye with me, even though I was sitting sixteen hands from the ground. I noticed with unease that he wore a padded hauberk and gambeson, torn in places and leaking stuffing, mottled brown and red with various ages of blood.

"Dog's deaf as a snake."

I wondered if he was insulting the small man, or if Dog was actually his name.

"'E can no more hear yer plea than he could enjoy yer song," the barrel of a man continued, unlashing the crude gate. "But come in, lad, and sing for yer supper if ye like." He hoisted the gate out of its trench and swung it easily with one hand.

Once inside the compound, I slid down from Nag's back, giving up my height advantage.

"Why ye're naught but a titch," laughed the Barrel, rudely pointing it out.

"Meagre of body, sir," I grated out between locked teeth, "but full of voice. You'll not be disappointed." I hoped.

Grovelling like that before this uncouth ox of a man was nearly beyond my self-control, but I recalled Garæthiel and her ability to become another person despite her noble breeding and uncommon beauty. And, Angeley had told me, a blend of self-effacement and self-assurance went a long way to endearing the audience before the first notes left your throat.

Barrel laughed, his giant gut bouncing in time. "I'd best not be, boy. I'd best not be. G'wan, Dog. Shut those beasts up," he yelled, referring to the noisy clamour of barks and yips that had played non-stop since my arrival.

He accompanied the order with hand gestures and a push on Dog's shoulder. The little man shuffled off toward the pen that held a dozen or so yapping hounds. The Barrel pointed at a rude corral taking up a third of the camp. "Ye can put yer horse in there."

"Thank you." I cleared my throat in an effort to sound less nervous, less girlish. "But I'll tether him. I wouldn't want to upset your herd." Or rather, I didn't want Nag coming out with the same bites and kicks he'd no doubt deal to the other horses.

"Whatever ye like, boy," Barrel grunted. "Raddick!" His bellow made me jump within my boots.

A youth, older than I but not full grown, loped over, all elbows and knees as if he had more joints than the average human.

"Give this lad's horse some fodder," commanded the Barrel before turning back to me and pointing toward the largest of the huts that leaned against the palisade. "Ye can sing for your supper in there, boy."

I nodded, and busied myself with Nag. Though I knew he'd love a roll, I didn't dare leave him unsaddled. I might have to leave in a hurry. I loosened his girth, replaced his bridle with a rope tied around his neck, and left him to eat the scant pile of hay Raddick brought out. Intent on his food, Nag ignored me as I buried my face in his fuzzy neck, breathing in courage from the scent of him.

"Wish me luck, boy," I whispered, giving him a final pat and strolling off to the large hut with what I hoped was a confident and boyish gait.

As I took that short walk, my eyes went everywhere, mapping the compound. Between the corral with its four horses and the kennel full of hounds was another set of pens. I couldn't see inside, but the grunts and squeals that emerged when Raddick approached with a full bucket of milk let me know there were pigs, most likely wild and certainly immature, within. Aside from these animals, a pair of nanny goats and a handful of chickens roamed the yard, scouring the frozen mud for every blade of grass and root.

As much as this camp appeared to be a hastily-erected affair, it clearly was built to operate for a considerable time. My nerves screamed at me to take my horse and leave while I still could. Everything about the place spoke of illegality, and I doubted the men involved would be tolerant of spies. But why, then, invite me in? Did the Barrel not wonder if I might head next to Doniver to report to the lord there?

Curiosity, and the outrage that had brought me here, would not let me turn away. Might as well be roasted as a chicken than boiled as an egg, Angeley always used to say. I pushed aside the filthy wool blanket that served as a door and was nearly propelled back into the yard by the heat, smoke, and smell.

"Minstrel boy!" bellowed the Barrel, waving me in. "About time! Starm here was just lamentin' the lack of wine, women, and song hereabouts. Don't look like yeh brought the first two, but ye've promised us the third."

I nodded, feeling the heavy smoke from the fire pit clogging my lungs already. I had no instrument. Angeley had taught me the harp, lute, and harpsichord, but I didn't favour them. I wished I'd brought a lap harp, though. An instrument is a shield and a distraction both, giving a singer something to do with her hands and giving the audience something to watch other than her nervousness. Instead I seized an empty cook pot hanging from a peg on the wall.

Sitting on the bench the Barrel had cleared for me, I settled the cook pot upside down between my knees and fanned my tapping fingers over it, searching for sweet spots. It wasn't bad, and would at least provide an almost musical counterpoint to fill the empty spaces.

Only then did I look up to take in the room around me. There were half a dozen men, including Barrel, seated on kegs, pallets, and crude benches. To a man, they were dirty and ill-favoured. Two wore soiled gambesons like the Barrel's, and one had a leather coat with rusted scraps of maille sewn to it. The other two wore what looked like servants' clothing, but grubbier and more worn than any I'd seen on a servant's back before. They were all hard and dangerous-looking men, far rougher than the rowdiest garrison at Teillai, and a universe removed from the knights and squires of Brandishear. Outlaws, I reasoned with a chill, or worse: mercenaries of the poor and desperate sort who'd take any coin for any reason. Did I even know a song that would satisfy their tastes?

I began with the rudest, bawdiest song in my repertoire: a piece of doggerel that had circulated through the pages' quarters in Rheran. It felt mild and childish in this company, but was greeted nonetheless with knee slapping and guffaws. The mood was set, and I was stuck then, dredging from my memory all the humorous songs I knew to keep this rough and reeking encampment happy. The Barrel even added accompaniment, slapping a pair of spoons against his knee, making me sing faster and faster the more he drank.

I ignored the tankard of sour-smelling beer that was set down next to me. I had no head for alcohol, even under the best of circumstances, which these definitely were not. Instead I sipped from my water skin in a vain attempt to ease the rawness brought on by smoke and the need to sing over bawling men's voices that constantly threatened to drown me out.

At last I begged a break and slipped out to find the latrine hole. I took great gulps of the night air and quickly wrapped my scarf tighter round my neck, remembering Angeley's advice to "never drink cold water, never breathe cold air."

A whimpering sound from the sties drew me over to that side of the camp. It was dark now, and I wished I'd taken a look when I first arrived. Even in the foggy moonlight I could see the uncovered pens were packed with bristling dark bodies. There didn't seem to be a piglet older than a few months old, and most were tiny indeed, like the ones I suspected had been captured today.

The smell was appalling. The animals were knee-deep in dung, with no straw for bedding, even if there had been room for them to lie down. As my eyes adjusted, I saw that there were in fact some prone figures. My stomach lurched, and I clapped a hand over my nose and mouth. Those piglets were dead: trampled, and maybe partly eaten, by the others.

I stumbled back to where Nag was tethered, buried my face in his shoulder, and stood there, breathing in his clean horsey smell.

The mooncalf Dog watched me, unabashed, scratching his wretched beard as if pondering supper. I slipped under Nag's neck, away from the disturbing scrutiny, just as a voice called from beyond the palisade.

"Ho, Raddick! Open the gate!"

I peered from behind Nag's shadow as Dog shuffled over to the gate, admitting a rider on a blown, foam-flecked horse. *Not so deaf after all, then.*

"Where's Raddick?" growled the rider as he flung himself from the horse's back.

Dog hurried to the lean-to by the paddock, kicked the boy awake, and returned to attend to the gate while a bleary Raddick took charge of the horse. The Barrel emerged from the dining hall.

"Well?" he asked, handing the rider a mug of the foul-smelling beer.

"I'm going to presume that's your quaint dialect for 'are you well, my lord?'" The horseman took a long swig from the mug and spat it out on the ground. "Disgusting stuff. I don't know how you manage to swallow it. Raddick!" he called over his shoulder. "Bring the skin from my saddle!"

By now Raddick had tethered the horse between Nag and the men, which afforded plenty of cover for me to lurk, unseen and listening.

"Onyssa Red," said the lord as he took the skin from Raddick. "And there'll be plenty more for you and whoever you take with you to drive the beasts to Linæver tomorrow. The ring's set up half a league this side of the Hunthad crossing."

"Hounds?" asked the Barrel.

"All arranged. Everything from ratters for the weanlings to an alaunt and a couple of mastiffs for the boar."

A boar. That was the banging I'd heard from the small covered sty, then. And all those animals were off to Linæver tomorrow for baiting. My stomach lurched in revulsion and outrage. No longer was I merely offended at the poaching on my family's demesne; this was morally reprehensible. And illegal. The treaty with the Woodkin that protected the Eastern forest on our borders forbade animal baiting of any kind.

But how could I stop it?

As I pondered this, Nag was stretching to the end of his tether to sniff noses with the new mare tied beside him. Inevitably there was a squeal, a head toss, and the mare swung her hindquarters toward us. I ducked out of the way just in time to avoid a swinging hoof, and the stable boy, who'd been grooming the mare, did the same. But the noise had turned all eyes toward us.

"Ho!" came the rider's voice. "What horse is that?"

I remembered to bow, not curtsy, just in time. "Mine, my lord."

"And you are?"

"Nalen, my lord. Just a travelling singer, grateful for a roof for the night."

"Aye, m'lord Doniver," added the Barrel. "The lad's got a decent pair o' bellows fer a squit his size."

The name Doniver turned over in my stomach like a vat of tanner's acid. The family was vast, and the name strewn like ragweed amongst the people of Aerach, but still …

"Is that so," mused the man called Doniver. His gaze combed me from head to foot in the faint orange light coming from the crude hall behind him. I tried to stop my eyes from widening like dandelion puffs.

His name, his accent, his age, and the fact he seemed to be nobility: all these led me to a sinking conclusion. This was Lord Eiglin Doniver's son, the potential husband I'd been scheduled to meet just before I'd fled home.

Jrdaign's Chorus

I have entered another prescience-free bubble of time. My energies, my thoughts, my time, are consumed with caring for my daughter and my precious granddaughter. All the scheming steps of fate have led me to this point. I do not want to ask what is next.

I cherish the freedom to exist only here and now. It mirrors the blindly joyful early years of Lauresa's life, and yet is not so simple, so golden, so unadulteratedly happy. For there is the unspoken bitterness that lies between Lauresa and me. She is only beginning to accuse and question me over my long absence from her life and my sudden appearance at her labour bedside. There have in fact been so few words spoken, one might wonder if we have tongues at all. And yet, with the deft way of managing people that she has inherited from her father, she has smoothly fit me into her household, under my assumed identity, with no questions asked.

I cherish each chance I have to care for her: to bring her teas and nourishment that stem the bleeding, bring her milk in, and ease the emotional post-birth turmoil. I try not to assert my motherly authority. I gave up my right to that when I left her to the care of her father and his replacement princess so many years ago. But she seems to listen to me nonetheless. Her own need to be mothered in this raw and vulnerable time leaves open wounds that I can salve. I step gingerly. Each chance to give is a source of joy mixed with regret over the years I forsook.

Only Allaigna can fill my heart with unwatered bliss. I gaze into her eyes shortly after her birth as I did into Glaignen's. I had half-hoped, half-expected, to be met with the worldly gaze of an infant with the Sight. Instead I saw something else. Something strange, and wonderful, and hopeful. I still am puzzling as to what it is, but grand destinies aside, I know this child will let me nurture her the way I was denied with Lauresa.

Fate has not asked me to move, or shift, or influence. My sole purpose in this period is to care. Like any good gardener, I support not just the plant but the soil. Lauresa has done well in the months she has been mistress of Castle Osthegn, but she has endured the trials of a difficult pregnancy in a new home with no retainers of her own. I work to make this hall a home, surrounding us both with kind and cheerful servants, reviving the abandoned kitchen gardens where I can plant healing herbs, brightening the dark cold rooms with hangings, and replacing rushes with carpets. For some of these expenses I draw on my income from Aldac, surreptitiously forwarded by my sister. However, I always make it appear as if the directives come from my daughter. It would not do for anyone to question why a simple nurse wields so much household authority.

My circle of influence spreads outward as Lauresa begins to both trust and forgive me. Soon I have seeded the whole castle, from stable hands to arms masters, with those who will, in time, grow to be the teachers Allaigna will need. This is foresight of a type, but it is practical and useful rather than troubling.

Not all things can be changed to suit my will. For instance, the mage, Carollus, has been with the household since before the birth of the Duke, and it will take nothing short of a landslide to remove his corpulent behind from the vizier's seat. He is not the wizard I would have, but we avoid each other and coexist peaceably enough.

Connections must also be made without Teillai's walls. I cultivate a friendship with the tree priests of the Eastern forest, exchanging plants and remedies with them, rebuilding the strong relationship that the Duke and, I suspect, his father before him let degenerate. Neighbouring noble families are important too. Allenis Andreg's ties with his knights and baronets are strong, but it is the women of those landed families I encourage, inviting them to a gayer, more festive Osthegn than has lately been seen. And lastly, for my daughter's heart, I bring in singers, jugglers, dancing masters, and artists. Osthegn lacks the depth and elevation of the court of Rheran, but it is as close as I can make it, and it seems to help her flourish.

The birthfeast for Allaigna is held later than is usual. She is nearly three months old now, but it is the first time Andreg has been home from the field and court long enough. The delay has allowed me time to arrange things for my daughter.

Andreg dances the obligatory first pass with Lauresa, and one or two more for appearances, but is now deep in conversation with his huntsman. A flagon of port wine is diminishing between them, and the Duke's favourite hounds are curled round their feet at the hearthside.

Lauresa seems not to mind. I watch her dance with Sir Darien, a young and handsome baronet. It reminds me of her own birth-feast, my milk-filled breasts squeezed painfully by the courtly gown. My empty paps ache in memory, and my heart does as well, remembering Chanist's arm about my waist. It is one more source of sorrow that my daughter cannot enjoy the marital happiness I knew for seven years. But then, she did not have the opportunity to marry for love.

My other self, the prescient one, taps me gently on the shoulder and reminds me that her path is not mine, and our joys and sorrows will be different. At least she will have many more years of motherhood, and many more children to enjoy, than I did. I shake my head and order the prescience away. It is too soon for it to come back.

Lauresa returns, out of breath, glowing pink and gold from exertion and happiness, to take the sleeping Allaigna from my arms. I am loath to let go of the warm and content bundle. I wonder if my birthfeast gift will cause my daughter more pain. She seems happy now — why not leave well enough alone? But no, I have set events in motion, and if it causes her pain, I hope it will cause her pleasure in equal measure.

I glance at the Duke, who is still engrossed in his conversation. He won't notice her absence, but I sing a small spell around mother and babe nonetheless.

"Take some air in the garden," I say, my voice low and tinged with music. "By the fish trough — near the sally gate."

She looks at me quizzically but doesn't question. Perhaps I still have motherly authority after all. I watch her leave the hall, my heart in my mouth, as nervous as if I were the one meeting a lost love.

Verse 3

Night Escapes

My knees were turning to marrow. If he recognized me … but how could he? We hadn't met since I was a child, far beneath the notice of a young man of twenty. Since then he would have seen portraits, though, as I had of him. In the dark I couldn't tell if he matched them or not. The relief made my knees more liquid still. If I couldn't see him and knew him only by name, there was no chance he would recognize me either. Not out here.

My head must have twitched toward the makeshift hall.

"Aye, lad," said the Barrel in his ear-bruising voice. "They're waiting for you in there. You've earned your bread but not your bed."

I ducked my head, hurrying off to the large shelter to take my place before Doniver did. I wanted to arrange my seating to avoid scrutiny. *Idiot!* I thought savagely. *How does the evening's entertainment avoid scrutiny?*

There was nothing for it but to hide in plain sight.

I took the proffered cup of beer, as vile as I'd anticipated, and sat half-turned from the room, sipping casually and pretending to warm up my voice. In truth I was casting for tone and resonance, finding the pitches and note sequences to create a glamour. It was risky: a spellsong I'd never tried. The closest I'd come was the charm that changed Nag's colouring. But this was more than altering patterns of light to fool the eye. This was about changing my seeming, creating an illusion that I was not me: like me, yes, but male. No taller, nor broader of build, for I doubted I could achieve that, and it would cause more suspicion than it would allay. It had to be imperceptible enough that none would notice the change, but real enough that those who looked more than casually considered me still a boy.

It was dangerous on so many counts. It might not work; or it might work too well, and those who'd seen me in daylight would notice the difference. And the worst outcome of all would be creating something that drew attention by looking simply wrong. I wished I'd thought of it days ago and had had time to practise. But if wishes were fishes, no one would starve, as Mother often pointed out to me.

When I felt I had the notes and the order, I placed them within a ditty that became the opening number of my second set. By the time I fully faced the crowd, in the centre of which lounged Tiern Doniver, I hoped it was someone undoubtedly boyish they saw.

I avoided meeting eyes, Doniver's especially, singing to the smoke-filled ceiling and the littered floor. As I approached the last of my songs, I laid in a lullaby. Not the kind that would put them all to sleep immediately, for I hadn't the strength of voice left for that. It was only a suggestion that they should find themselves more deeply weary than usual, that their rough pallets call them as if they were down beds, and that they should sleep soundly till dawn.

I was yawning myself as I gave my bow. Magic drew the strength from me faster than a full day at the quintain.

I bit my lips, curled my toes, and suppressed yawns as I made my way to the corner in which I'd placed my bedroll. I didn't dare lie down, for I felt I would sleep instantly. So I propped myself against the bumpy mud-and-greenstick wall, sorted through my things, fussed with my bedding, and tried to hum a counter spell that would keep me awake without spreading to the other bodies settling down for the night.

When snores filled the room and the dim glow from the fire led me to believe that all eyes were firmly closed, I rolled up my bedding, moving with slow and silent deliberation. I stood, shouldered my pack, and took delicately balanced steps over, around, and beside the sleeping figures.

At first, all that was on my mind was escape. I needed to get my horse and flee before Doniver identified me. Even if I weren't recognized, there was a dangerous note in the man's voice when he'd spoken to me earlier, and a pensive stare from his side of the room during my songs, one that made the hairs on the nape of my neck stand up. I felt sure that, having overheard his conversation with the Barrel, I would not be allowed to walk freely from this encampment to spread word that the heir to the Doniver lordship was running a boar-baiting ring.

I stepped outside, smelled the rank stench of the sties, and realized I couldn't just save my own skin and leave those poor animals to their fate. I had planned to bully or sweet-talk my way past Dog. He seemed uninterested enough that some kind of bluff would let me out. But that wouldn't help the pigs.

As I pulled the door-curtain closed behind me, I was greeted by a low growl. The disquieting sound came from just off to my left, and I felt rather than saw the shadowy bulk of a hound coming toward me on great padded feet. My eyes always adjusted quickly to the dark, and I could see it now: a lymer, hackles raised, tail up and aggressive, white teeth a jagged rent against the dark background. It seemed the night watch was left to real dogs.

The hum that began in the back of my throat came out more like a whimper than a note. I forced it lower, praying for the sound to come out true. Now was no time to falter. I opened my mouth to sing, the notes soft but steady.

The hound pricked its ears and tilted its head to the side. The growl shifted to a whine. I persisted, extracting every ounce of effort I had left to make each note clear and low, feeling the magical resonance trickle forth. The lymer shook his head, whined again, then bent forward, like a circus dog bowing, and rubbed its ears with its forepaws.

I crouched, singing out through my bones, and placed a hand on its head, expecting any minute to have it bitten off at the wrist. I let the music flow through my body to his. His back end drooped to the ground, tail lowered, and then he rested his massive head on his paws. At last he rolled onto one side, a position of both surrender and sleep. By now the rest of the pack had gathered around, curious more than aggressive. I couldn't eke more volume from my tired voice, but I held the lullaby steady, moving with gentle slow steps between the dogs, touching each until they all lay down.

By now I was close to the open shelter in which Dog and the horseboy, Raddick, slept. I sidled past, still singing, hoping my lullaby would hold them still as well. I let my voice fall silent as I neared the fence where Nag was tethered. I girthed up my horse by feel and led him across the compound, careful to avoid the sleeping hounds littered on the dark ground.

The gate nearly defeated me. It was held by lashings near the bottom and midway to the top. I had to climb partway up the gate, giving myself scrapes and slivers from the bark-covered wood and making what felt like far too much noise in the process. When that was done, I lifted the heavy bar out of its supports and dragged the awkward structure partway open.

When it was open far enough to let Nag through, I led him back toward the sties. The miserable piglets were snorting and snuffling in their sleep as they scrabbled with their trotters against imaginary ground. I opened their gates wide. With luck, they'd awaken before their captors or the hounds were up. When the last of the pens was open, I paused before the hut. There was a faint rhythmic snuffling from within. Was the boar awake, or simply snoring? It was one thing to free a bunch of piglets, quite another to let loose a mature boar. But I couldn't leave him there, either.

I compromised, removing the bar but leaving the door to his cell closed. I held my breath and backed away, waiting for the creature to explode out. Nothing. With luck, when it awoke and started banging its walls again, it would make its way out of the unbarred door on its own.

Backing out was my undoing. I was so careful not to rouse the boar that I tripped on a slumbering dog. It let out a whimpering bark and rolled over against the wall of the nearest sty, waking up the piglet on the other side. The pig squealed, scrambled to its feet, and stepped on its neighbour, who squealed louder and repeated the procedure until the whole pack of weanlings erupted into a squeaking avalanche through the open gate of their pen. I stumbled out of the way, frightened porkers swarming past my legs, spooking Nag. He bolted, tore the reins from my hand and headed for the compound gate with me at his heels. He snagged a stirrup on the palisade gate, which slowed him down enough for me to catch him, and then we were outside.

He spun around me in frantic circles while I tried to mount. Within the palisade, dogs woke and began barking. Panic gave springs to my legs, and at last I half-jumped, half-climbed aboard Nag. He didn't wait for me to mount properly but took off at a gallop while I lay belly down across the saddle, which was tipping precariously sideways. I lost the one stirrup I'd had my foot in, and my right leg flailed, trying to make it over the cantle, urging Nag faster.

By the time I gained my seat, shouts had been added to the squeals and barks. I glanced over my shoulder. The piglets were scattering across the field in all directions, confusing the dogs, who, it seemed, were chasing pigs rather than me. I hauled on Nag's mouth, slowing him down enough for me to regain my stirrups and wits, then turned him left, skirting the low hill from which I'd first seen the wretched encampment.

I should have taken my lead and run with it, galloping away no matter the direction. But for some stubborn reason, I was unable to abandon the pig carcass I'd strung up in the woods earlier that day. Perhaps it was a sense of misplaced honour to the sow, or just the thought of food going to waste. More likely it was the time I had invested in it: I was not about to relinquish the spoils of that messy and unpleasant effort. So I circled the base of the hill, slowing Nag to a walk as we negotiated an upward path in the parsimonious moonlight. Nag snorted, letting me know he'd caught the scent of the carcass just before its gibbeted shape showed darker against the dark sky.

I would like to say I galloped up, hacked the thing down, and sped away, like Olias rescuing her lover from the gallows in the

Tale of Twelve Crows, but in fact I wasted several tense minutes convincing Nag to sidepass up to the tree, only for him to swing away the moment I dropped the reins to begin working on the rope that held the corpse aloft. Cursing, I dismounted, looped the reins over my arm, and worked the knot while my overexcited horse swung back and forth, bumping and jerking me. I might have cut the rope, but it was the only sturdy length I owned, and I didn't want it shortened. At last, with the rope undone and my fingers as raw and scraped as the sow's skinned hide, I held the rope steady with one hand and Nag with the other as I lowered the heavy body onto his back amid protesting snorts on his part and cursing on mine. Despite having hung for most of a day, the corpse still left gobbets of blood and grease on my saddle as I pushed it into position behind the cantle.

A sounding dog broke through the trees. I scrambled into the saddle, heedless of the mess it would leave on my breeches, and kicked Nag forward.

Nag, bless his dim head, fled like the beast of prey he was in front of the pair of hounds. He could easily have outdistanced them but for the branches and trunks in our way. I would rather have turned back up the crest and farther away from the encampment. But it was more wooded there, and the dogs would have been on us in a moment.

They were barely a stride behind us. By clinging tightly to Nag's neck I managed to avoid being knocked off by branches, though I earned several scrapes on my knees and shins from too-close trunks. But with my head buried in his mane, I didn't see the ditch at the bottom of the hill until he'd planted his forefeet and gathered himself for a mighty jump, up and over the bank.

Nag hit the bottom of his trajectory with me still clinging to his neck. The pig carcass, slung so hastily across the back of the saddle, leaped the cantle and hit me square in the back. I banged my chin on Nag's neck and my hips against the pommel. My feet flew from the stirrups and the next thing I met was dirt as Nag's hooves soared past my head.

The ground was soft with spring thaw, but I was winded, unable to lift my head for the next critical moments. The hounds tore past me after Nag and the more interesting-smelling dead sow. But there were human footfalls thudding toward me. I remember thinking, in the odd dilated time of such situations, how rude it was to shake the ground with such heavy feet. I was grasped by the collar and hauled upright, only to be smacked back to the ground by the back of Doniver's fist.

"Who the hell are you, you little shit?" he was roaring at me. "Who sent you?"

He had me up again. His voice was lower, and he was peering into my rapidly swelling face in the feeble moonlight. "You're not one of my father's. Erelin? Or Andreg?"

My eyes must have flickered at the sound of my family name, and he peered more closely. "Andreg, then."

I was shaking my head as fast as I could in silent protest, my tongue unable to work with the choking hold he had on my collar.

He tipped his head sideways, examining me.

He's not bad looking, I realized, in another of those disjointed thoughts. *If only he weren't a brute.*

"Why do you look famili—" his question stopped, his eyes opened wide, and he fell on top of me.

A muddy boot kicked him off, and I was pulled to my feet yet again, this time by my elbow.

It was Dog, the mooncalf sentry. His already grubby appearance had been worsened by a split and swollen lip, and a jaw that looked like mine felt. He put a finger to his lips, his other hand still holding my arm as I struggled to run. He whistled two short bursts then tugged at me, asking me to follow.

I shook my head, as dumb as he. We stayed there, tugging feebly back and forth until the two hounds that had been chasing Nag reappeared, tongues hanging, followed shortly by Raddick, the stable lad. Dog patted the hounds, who whined and wagged their tails. He waved at Raddick, shooing him back toward the encampment.

Raddick shook his head. "No. I can't go back. He'll treat me even worse than he does you now." He spat at the motionless figure of Doniver. "Unless — Didja kill 'im?"

Dog shook his head and motioned urgently toward the woods.

Distracted as he was, I finally managed to break his grip.

"No!" called Raddick, as I started to bolt. "Wait!" And for some reason I stopped.

"We don't mean you no harm. But we should go together. And before the others come or he wakes up."

My voice was still lost from the evening of singing, the breathless flight, and Doniver's chokehold. I merely stared.

Raddick shrugged. "Up to you, a course, but Dog knows these woods better 'n anyone, and three pairs a eyes are cannier 'n one."

I didn't like it. I didn't trust the filthy kennel master and this glib whipping boy, who were as complicit in the abuse of those animals as their masters. Or were they? I allowed my righteous anger to fade just a bit, to imagine that perhaps they, as much as the beasts they had guarded, were prisoners of circumstance too. It was enough of a doubt to allow them its benefit. I also had to admit that any punishment that befell them after tonight's great pig escape was, in fact, my fault.

Still voiceless, I nodded at last and turned to let Dog and his namesakes lead us up the hill. But something stopped me.

"Wait," I croaked.

Raddick and Dog stopped, already across the ditch.

I turned back to the recumbent Tiern Doniver and coaxed one last song from my exhausted throat. I checked the pulse beneath his jaw as I sang the lullaby, keeping him asleep until I was as sure as I could be he was not dying from the blow to the head. Angeley had never taught me her healing magic, but she had shown me healing tips.

From my pouch, I removed a small stoppered bottle. My skinned knuckles trembled with fatigue as I worked the cork. I held Doniver's chin down and let a single drop of mountain daisy extract fall beneath his lolling tongue before taking a drop myself to ease my bruises and sore throat. Angry and repulsed as I was, I didn't intend anyone to die here.

Still, my generosity only went so far. Though he was only partly dressed, it seemed he hadn't left the camp without his sword or his scrip. I took both and left him sleeping in the grass to the continuing thrum of distant shouts, barking, and squeals.

Lauresa's Chorus

Lauresa shakes her head, wondering that this mother, who had abandoned her for so many years, could arrive back in her life and order her around so handily. Was she using her subtle Leisanmira charms and enchantments without Lauresa noticing? Or was it simply the bond of family? Sharing the river of another's blood creates inseparable ties. Lauresa can understand that now. She bends to kiss Allaigna's sleeping, sweaty forehead. The baby stirs and snuffles, and Lauresa begins to bounce her steps in the automatic pace she, like all mothers, has learned will keep a baby asleep.

When she finally does step into the enclosed garden, she welcomes the shiver of the night air. It sharpens her senses and wakes her from the drowsiness brought on by nursing and the heat of the hall. She walks the length of the long, trout-filled trough to the north end of the garden near the sally port. Here is a corridor of plum trees, their branches crossing overhead to form a tunnel, leafless now, letting the filtered light of the half-moon stray between their budding fingers. Pretty, yes, but defensive as well, allowing castle inhabitants to come and go, unobserved from walls or towers.

At the end of this half-lit tunnel, a figure stands.

Her breath gels in her throat. She knows him, even hooded and cloaked as he is. Is it his posture, his build, or just some scent wafting along the plum-tree corridor, alerting her like a fox to its prey?

Part of her does not want to move forward. If she turns back, returns to the bright and festive hall, she can resume the enclosed life she has lived this past year. She is not yet ready for her attention to stray outside these walls, and until now it has not. But now he has breached the fortress, allowing her thoughts to spill out into the past, and, far more frighteningly, into the future.

In the end she can't not move forward.

"Einavar." The name comes out as a breath of fog in the still, cold night.

If it bothers him that she calls him Einavar and not his true name, it doesn't show. He might be a dark statue here in the garden but for the cloud of white breath pluming in the moonlight.

She feels awkward facing her erstwhile lover and protector, with whom she shared a passion so intense and yet so brief. Should she greet him as if they are the strangers they agreed to be to one another? Or fling herself into his arms once more?

They are no longer lovers, and she is the protector now. She is conscious of the sleepy weight of Allaigna nestled in her arms. Allaigna is all that matters now, and to protect her, Lauresa will deny all other passions. But this ... This is Allaigna's father, whether he knows it or not.

In an impulsive acknowledgement of the Ilvani blood in her daughter's arteries, she lifts her hand, palm up, in the greeting of his people.

His palm meets hers like a shot of witchfire. She expects his hand to be cold, but it nearly burns her with its heat. They stand thus, feeling the pulse in each other's hands for uncountable heartbeats, until at last he twists his hand beneath hers, grasps her fingers, and brings them to his lips.

It is a deferential, proper salute to one of her rank; except that his lips linger too long on her knuckles, his grasp of her fingers is a hair too tight, and though he lowers her hand, his fingers stay, stuck to her own. She is not sure whose hand is trembling, his or hers.

"Your Grace," he whispers, his voice cracking and flaking in the cold air. Not 'Princess', not 'Highness', as it used to be. He has deliberately reminded her of the change in their relationship.

It is too much. Longing she didn't know she'd suppressed these past months rushes to the surface. Her fingers grasp back, pull him closer by a step. She may not be his princess any longer, but she still wields power. She leans forward, across the head of their sleeping daughter, and kisses him. It is a long, sweet, gentle kiss at first, until his large black cloak opens and enfolds them, pressing her against his horse-scented travelling clothes and the heat of his body. Her breasts ache, and she feels milk start to flow. Allaigna senses it too, or perhaps simply objects to being sandwiched between two bodies, and lets out a crow-like squawk.

Lauresa struggles out of the embrace and rearranges herself, jiggling Allaigna into a more upright position, fussing with the swaddling blanket.

Einavar is solicitous.

"I'm sorry … Forgive me. I didn't mean …"

Lauresa shakes her head and smiles, turning the babe out to face her father. Dark, almond-shaped eyes in a pale moon of a face are all that is visible in the dim light, but Lauresa shows her off proudly anyway.

"This is Allaigna."

He nods almost curtly, his head jerking as he recognizes Aerach's patronymic custom of naming firstborn children.

"Your daughter," he states. He reaches out, gingerly, as if the creature might bite. "She will be as beautiful as her mother."

His voice is courteous but flat.

"Thank you. But I think she takes more after her father."

He winces as though wounded, and she can't help but laugh softly.

She lifts the cap the babe always wears and traces a finger around the tops of Allaigna's ears.

He still doesn't seem to understand, even when she runs a finger around his own.

"She has your ears. And eyes," she whispers with a laugh. "Don't you recognize her?"

He catches her wandering hand, kisses it again, almost absently, his eyes never leaving the wise and curious ones of the baby.

"Truly?" he asks at last.

"Why would I lie to you?" she asks sadly. "It would be better for all of us—for me, you, her—if she were Allenis's. And he must never think otherwise."

She shudders, thinking of wild beasts and princes. Both have been known to dispose of children they believe to have been laid, like cuckoo's eggs, in their nests.

Verse 4
New Friends, New Enemies

As unkempt and ragged as Dog looked, he was fit enough: fitter than Raddick and I, who struggled to keep up as the older man trotted through the ill-lit woods, a hound at each heel. The fall from Nag, the bump I'd given myself on the chin, and Doniver's blow to the face compounded to make me both light-headed and lead-footed. My condition was made worse by lack of sleep, and the bone-draining exhaustion of having used so much magic. Finally, after half a bell or so of rough jogging up the ridge and east along the tree line, I fell to my knees, retching but desperate not to vomit.

Raddick stumbled to a stop beside me and called to Dog to halt his steady pace. As I kneeled there, shaking and heaving, I felt a tentative, friendly hand on my back.

"You hurt?" he asked, his voice no more than a pair of gasps.

I shook my head, even though it made the nausea worse, and sat back on my haunches, brushing leaf mould from my hands and knees.

"My horse," I breathed. "I need to get my horse back."

It wasn't just that I was fond of the beast, or that I needed him to carry me over the leagues I planned to travel in search of my true father. It was that he carried too much of me with him. My sword, the one I'd trained for, then lost, then won again in Rheran; and my bow, the one Rhiadne had given me that had been fashioned by her father: both these weapons hung from Nag's saddle, along with all my provisions, that cursed pig carcass, and my spare clothing. More important than all these were the little things I'd taken from home, such as one of Mother's thimbles, a pair of herb scissors from Angeley's workshop, a scroll of Ilvani text from the archives that I had only begun to translate, and letters. The letters Mother and Angeley had written to me during my stay in Rheran two years ago were the greatest liability. I had been foolish to bring them with me, for they told far too much about who I was. If I retrieved my horse and my belongings, I resolved to burn those missives.

Dog shook his head and made a series of hurried hand gestures accompanied by whistles and clicks. He was mute, I realized at long last, not deaf as the Barrel had claimed, nor the mooncalf I'd taken him to be. Raddick seemed to understand him, though.

Raddick nodded and said to me, "It's too dangerous. Lord Doniver'll be in a killin' mood." That much I understood without translation as Dog slid a finger across his throat.

I shrugged. "You don't have to come." I stood, turned, and began trudging off to the forest edge, where I hoped I could pick up Nag's tracks by morning. They couldn't be that far off.

After a hundred yards or so, the brush crackled behind me and the hounds caught up, followed by their master and Raddick.

I turned back. "No, really, you don't have to." I was beginning to wonder if this was some subtle play to recapture me. Then I remembered the blow to Doniver's head. That was no ruse.

Dog whistled the pair of hounds to heel and stood beside me, pointing at my calves. I froze while the pair of them sniffed my feet and lower legs, and flinched as Dog grasped my wrist and held it out, knuckles forward, to the questing canine noses. Of course, my hands were covered in Nag's scent, as were my legs.

Dog made a sound almost like a bark itself and pointed ahead. The hounds surged forward, muzzles to the ground, tails high, weaving through the woods for a trace of scent.

When we emerged from the woods at last, they sounded. Dog silenced them with another yelp then pointed again, this time in the direction indicated by the turf torn up by Nag's shoes. The questing pair loped away, the rest of us struggling to keep up. The tracks, unfortunately, curled back toward the camp. The beast could not resist the company of the other horses there.

The half-light of dawn was upon us now, and I could see the palisade clearly. The gates were open, and a single dog sniffed around outside. My heart dropped into my aching feet. Nag was back in that compound, which to Raddick, Dog, and me was as safe as a bear trap. Across the tussocky field was the place we'd left Doniver. There was no way to tell from here whether he still lay in the dirt, had risen on his own, or had been carried away.

"I've *got* to get my horse back," I hissed at Raddick, hoping somehow this stable-lad no older than I would have some clever plan for doing so. "And my saddlebags."

"Yer lucky to have yer skin right now," he hissed right back at me. "There's no way you can walk in and back out of there with that, never mind the horse."

Dog made some gestures and clicks, which Raddick seemed to understand.

"We'll get the horse." He nodded agreement at Dog. "Doniver doesn't know who beaned him. Maybe he never will. If anyone has a chance of getting past the other hounds, it's Dog. Maybe they'll be too busy still to notice us or stop us." It sounded as if he were talking himself into it.

If I were an adult, I would never have allowed it. But for all my fierce independence, I was still a child of fourteen, used to bowing to the authority of age, at least when uncertain of myself. I was a daughter of nobility, accustomed to having people at my disposal and unused to asking why. It didn't occur to me that that same deference shouldn't extend to the ragged and bloodstained travelling singer I appeared to be. It wasn't till many years later that I fully comprehended why this odd pair decided to align themselves with me, and risk their own necks in doing so. At the time, I accepted their allegiance without question, and without the sense of responsibility that should have gone with it.

All I did was nod, and wish them luck.

Stretched belly down behind a low hedge of rock and gorse, I was hard-pressed not to fall asleep as the morning sun crept up behind me and warmed my back. Despite the worry that gnawed at my gut, my exhaustion from the sleepless, terror-filled night was overriding. I didn't drift off entirely, just far enough for my mind to make up strange daydreams. When the sound of hoofbeats broke my reverie, they were the stampede sounds of a full cavalry charge. In those in-between seconds Teillai — or was it Rheran? — was stormed by a vanguard of ancient Imperial troops aboard grey chargers.

My eyes snapped open to reveal only Nag, and not two, but a dozen hounds coursing beside him. Raddick and Dog clung to his back. I scrambled to my feet as they skidded to a stop. Dog flung himself out of the saddle and offered me a leg up behind Raddick. I wasn't too proud to take it. Dog practically flung me over, and I had barely grasped my arms around Raddick's waist before he kicked Nag forward.

There was a hue and cry from the encampment, the second that day, and two men emerged, hurtling after us on foot.

"The others'll be out soon on horses," Raddick panted, as if in answer to my unvoiced question.

Dog was waving us on, and Raddick turned Nag toward the trees.

It was then I noticed that I was sitting right on the saddle's skirts, behind the cantle. The pig carcass was gone — good riddance — but so were my saddlebags.

"Back!" I screamed at Raddick. "We have to go back!"

Whether he heard me or not I never knew, and Nag continued to thunder on.

Irdaign's Chorus

He is already at the prescribed rendezvous point, where Cloth-market meets with the New Road. The tavern beside the well is always crowded, though never with castle folk. Seamstresses, tailors, merchants, cordwainers, glovers, and haberdashers gather here for small ale, fresh water from the fountain, and gossip.

I set my bag, heavy with goods from the apothecary and spice merchant, down between my feet and begin to work the pump handle. It is our prearranged signal and he crosses to the fountain, gallantly taking over the chore of pumping up a bowl of water.

"Your Highness," he says, proffering the bowl.

"Not anymore," I say sharply then smile to soften the sting. I drink deeply — it is the best well in town, better even than those within the castle. "Here and now, I am merely Angeley, and you are Einavar."

"It is a better name than my own." His voice is cool and liquid, like the water. Not emotionless, just smooth as the surface of a deep pool hiding jagged rocks beneath. "It's . . . an honour to meet you."

"Oh, we've met before, young man." I flash a merrier, more wicked smile at him, making him start. "One day I may tell you about it. But let's sit, shall we? The beer here is excellent, thanks no doubt to the water."

Once we are equipped with tankards, there is an awkward pause through which I wait, allowing him to break it.

"I must thank you, madam, for . . ." He clears his throat and a pale purple tinges his cheeks. I feel a surge of fondness for this almost son.

"No," I interrupt. "You must not thank me. Your gratitude would make a procuress of me." I smile again to show I am at least partially teasing.

His return smile flickers, nervous and brief, then disappears again. Oh, how serious and worried he is!

"Einavar." I take his long-fingered hand within my own two. It is strangely smooth for one who has spent so much time rang-ing. "I love my daughter above all else —"

It is his turn to interrupt me, his free hand covering our other three.

"As do I. But . . ." He swallows, breathes, continues. "Because of that I would not bring dishonour or pain upon her. I . . . we . . . did not —"

"Please!" I exclaim, pulling my hands out from his. "Do not tell me what you did or did not last night." The mauve tinge on his cheeks spreads and reddens. "Dishonour is within my skill to prevent. Pain …" It is my turn to sigh. "She has suffered much already. I would have her gain what joy she can."

His own brow is creased in that same pain. "Wouldn't it be better for her to … to simply forget me?" The suggestion is agonizing to him, but he offers it nonetheless.

I shake my head. "If she gives her heart to her husband, it will be worse." As I say it, I realize the Sight has returned and settled on my brow. I blink, forcing away the things I hope won't come true. "Love is a rare and precious commodity, Einavar. Cherish it when it finds you, and never relinquish it." Another shake of the head brings me back to the present. "I would not accept your gratitude, but I will accept your troth. Ceilaf bound his to me when I was Princess still. He recommended you to me, and you saved Lauresa's life on the Clearwater Way. More than that." I smile once more. "You've given me a granddaughter any prince would be proud of."

I watch the emotions flicker through his pale, pale eyes: grief, equal to my own, at the mention of Ceilaf; pride nowhere equal to mine at the mention of Allaigna. But that can and will be nurtured.

"I need eyes and ears within Brandishear. For this I can pay you." I've already noticed the wear on his boots, the fraying on his sleeves. "I may even still have enough connections to secure you a commission. Rangers, I think? Through indirect channels, of course."

He is about to protest, but I stop him. My plans have no room for false modesty and polite demurrals.

"Meeting here is not safe, though. I will show you a place in the Eastern forest, and give you a token that will allow you to contact me through a scrying pool there." I can see he is about to protest his ignorance of magic. "It is a simple enough trick. I can teach you.

"And I will, when it can be arranged, show you glimpses of your daughter ... and mine."

The gratitude hidden beneath those frost-grey eyes nearly staggers me, and makes me hope I am not making an error.

Lauresa's Chorus

He is gone again, and Lauresa is left raw and aching once more, the wounds she thought healed bleeding freely.

They have agreed it is best for him not to come near too often. But it is impossible for him to never return. He has held the child in his arms and fallen in love with her sweet breath. However cruel it is to Lauresa to have him reappear at sparse intervals in her life, it would be infinitely crueller to deny him precious glimpses of his daughter, who is growing and changing so fast. Whatever her burdens and sorrows, his will be harder to bear.

She doesn't know whether to curse or thank her mother, who arranged this meeting. The childish, still-adolescent part of herself is indignant, outraged that her mother has even the knowledge of Einavar, and worse, that she can procure him as if she were a common panderer. And yet, now that it has happened, and the pain of saying goodbye is even worse than the first time, she wouldn't have it any other way.

With her heart reawakened, she is more conscious than ever of the cuckoo she has brought to her husband's nest. As Allaigna grows, she looks more and more like her natural father. The child wears a linen cap to cover the straight black hair that is neither Allenis's dark brown curls nor Lauresa's golden ones, and to disguise the Ilvani cast to her ears and forehead. As the years go by and the baby fat falls away from her high-planed cheekbones and delicate limbs, the differences become harder to hide.

So Lauresa takes to hiding the child herself, keeping her away from Allenis's scrutiny when he's at home, which thankfully isn't often. And in trying to protect Allaigna, she makes her a stranger to her supposed father.

Verse 5
Bare Necessities

Dog clicked and whistled. The bitch, Edda, came and settled her hoary grey head on his knee, looking upward with pointed eyes while he scratched beneath her collar, around her ears, under her grateful chin. They were a matched set, I thought: Dog with his bristly thatch of mouldering straw for hair and beard, his eyes as kind and soft as Edda's. They both watched the sleek, brindled male patrol our rough campsite with his inexhaustible bladder.

It reminded me of mine. I'd put it out of mind all morning and most of the afternoon, but now that we'd lost the pursuers and their hounds and stopped to rest, it was impossible to ignore.

Raddick and Dog, like the hound, had simply unlaced in front of me and wet the tree trunks. Dog, praise Brandis, had at least turned his back, but Raddick had barely moved away from where we sat. I had to pretend to have a coughing fit to avoid the sight and account for my red face. And now how could I, pretending to be a boy, find any pretext for haring off into the bushes for some privacy?

I untied Nag from the tree and cleared my throat. "I'm just taking him off for more grass." Which was absurd, as the patch he was currently grazing was ample.

Raddick appeared about to say as much, but Dog clicked and motioned to him. I led Nag off, grateful for the distraction, not waiting for Raddick's translation.

I stayed a long while away from the others after relieving myself, the numerous developments of the day skirmishing in my head while I tried in vain to quell and sort them. My overriding worry was the saddlebags and the letters. Those stupid letters I should have left at home were now in Tiern Doniver's hands.

Raddick broke through the undergrowth and into my thoughts. He had his ugly, dirt-coloured cloth hat in his hands and was wringing it without mercy.

I looked at him clearly, in daylight, for the first time. He had brown curls that made a matted carpet over his head; wide-set, perpetually astonished brown eyes, at this moment more astonished than usual; a high, broad forehead, bisected top and bottom with a line of dirt from his cap; and no chin to speak of. He was short but, I realized from the down of fuzz on his upper lip, at least as old as I.

He gave the cap another vicious twist as a delicate tide of pink rose up his neck and over his cheeks.

"Dog … He says …" He gulped like a perch in the fish trough at feeding time. "I'm really sorry, miss. I didn't know … I didn't know you're a *girl*."

I wondered how Dog knew. *Probably has a nose to match his name,* I thought bitterly. I drew myself up to my full height, which, surprisingly, was on par with his.

"I don't see how it's any business of yours, but is that a problem?" I asked, once more the daughter of a duchess speaking to a stable hand.

He shook his head miserably. His colour, now bright red, reached his broad and grubby forehead.

"No, miss, I …" He floundered, no doubt wondering as I did how anything in the last half-day might have differed had he known.

And then I realized he was as embarrassed as I had been about unlacing his breeches beside me. I laughed. It was a bit cruel, but I couldn't resist.

"Don't worry, Raddick," I said. "I didn't look."

I handed him Nag's rope. "Bring him back to the other clearing when he's done here, would you?"

With my saddlebags gone, and Dog and Raddick having left the compound in a hurry, we had no food. But at least my precious sword and bow had still been attached to the saddle when Raddick and Dog rescued Nag.

I unwrapped and strung the bow. Fatigue-haunted as I was, sleep was not in the cards yet.

"I'm going hunting," I announced to Dog. "Please keep the hounds close so as not to scare the game." Really I would have liked one with me, but I doubted they'd leave his side anyway.

The low sun was almost gone behind the hills by the time I returned without so much as a single squirrel or sparrow and nothing more than a handful of winter-dried hawberries.

We chewed the bitter things in silence for a while, until Raddick cleared his throat.

"Miss." Another throat clearing followed this timid address. "Is Nalen your real name?"

"No." I looked him in the eye and lied. "It's Merri. But you can continue to call me Nalen."

"Ah." He nodded, misled comprehension lighting his eyes. I felt terrible about lying to these two, who had been nothing but kind. More than that, they had put themselves directly between me and harm. But with my letters most likely in Tiern Doniver's hands, the fewer who knew my name the better.

"Your saddlebags, I'm real sorry we couldn't get them. Yannick had already taken them off—"

I stopped him. "It's all right, Raddick." Another lie, but this one for him. "It doesn't matter, and I am truly grateful."

That last, at least, was true.

It was a miserable night, with only water, berries, and the winter-skinny rabbit Edda caught and deigned to share with us. It was cold as well, and my two blankets had gone the way of the saddlebags. As I shivered myself to sleep, I wished I were brave enough to snuggle up to Raddick, Dog, and their bookends of furry hounds.

Though the loss of the letters proved a more serious problem in the long term, it was of less immediate concern than the loss of my supplies. I hadn't had much food, but what I did have would have lasted me another week or so, and much longer if the wretched pig carcass were still with us. More important was the wooden mazer, and the small open kettle I had been using to cook porridge and heat water. I still had my hunting knife and my father's wicked-looking dagger, but the spoon and the flat metal plate I'd been using as both trencher and skillet would be missed. There were more personal items as well: a bar of Angeley's rosemary-scented soap; my brush and comb;

a dandy brush and rag for rubbing down Nag, as well as one or two more feeds of grain; a second pair of breeches, a spare linen shirt; and, most embarrassingly, underclothes that were not remotely clean.

After spending some time brooding and sulking over these losses, I realized it had only sped up the inevitable. I still had my purse, and we would have to brave a village and do some shopping.

I hadn't set foot in a town since my flight from home. Was it only six days ago? The smartest course of action would have been to send Raddick in with money to buy provisions. Though he risked recognition as a runaway servant, he knew the towns better than I and was less likely to wander into the wrong place. But I didn't trust him that far yet, nor was I about to have him purchase small-clothes for me. The choice of town was difficult too. We were, all of us, wary of Doniver's seat, but it was the only city of size within two days' ride. The smaller surrounding villages, though less likely to contain Tiern Doniver, were also less likely to contain the goods we needed in any quantity or quality, and more likely to have residents who might remember the odd sextet of persons and beasts we comprised. Anonymity was far easier in a populous place.

Like Osthegn in Teillai or the Bastion of Rheran, Doniver's castle, White Tooth, rises above the town, dominating it. The towering central keep for which the castle earned its name is taller than anything on Osthegn or the Bastion, though. A huge cylindrical chimney, it is windowless until at least thirty yards above the ground. Soaring high beyond that, its white stone seems to pierce the sky. It is rumoured the dungeons beneath run as deep as the tower is tall. As Raddick and I entered the lower gates of Doniver with the morning traffic, the White Tooth felt like a sword waiting to fall upon us.

With little sleep, less food, and my head starting to ache from the combination, Raddick and I battled the crowds entering Doniver that day.

"Food last," I said to Raddick, denying the complaint of my own stomach as my companion veered toward the market. "It'll be heaviest, and we don't want to pack it around." As I said it, my belly made dragon-like grumbles, causing me to avoid Raddick's pitiful stare. "But maybe we should eat something first," I amended, feeling a pang of guilt for Dog, who, with the hounds and Nag, awaited us in a covey well past the commons.

Across the road was a tavern spilling noisy patrons onto the cobbles and sending forth the aroma of stewing meat amidst the beery air. I grabbed Raddick by the elbow and dragged him across the teeming foot and cart traffic to the open door of the Gosling. Such an innocent name belied the tavern's contents.

It was the first time I'd ever been to a drinking house, and I tried not to let my unworldliness show as I peered around the massive shoulders and backs of patrons. There was no place to sit, so we elbowed up to the bar, both of us so short as to barely catch the taverner's attention. Raddick had been making strange embarrassed noises all this time, and finally, as we waited for our bowls of pottage and cups of beer, I asked him what was wrong.

"I haven't any coin," he hissed at me.

"I know that." Was he embarrassed at not being able to gallantly treat me to a meal? "Luckily Tiern Doniver is paying for this." I patted the purse I'd taken.

As a rule, I never touched meat and seldom fowl, but today I gobbled the stew, with its sparse and unidentifiable lumps of brown matter, as if it were pudding. The beer made my headache worse, but I drank it nonetheless, fearing to hazard the water, while Raddick told me a little of himself.

He was from here, or rather Donwych, the village just northeast. His family had been farmers till his father died after being trampled by spooked oxen and dragged by his own plough. It had been a lingering death, and Raddick, though only five at the time, remembered it well. Lord Eiglin, Tiern Doniver's father, had retaken the leasehold, asserting that Raddick's mother and older sister were unable to work the fields. Both of them landed as scullery maids in White Tooth, and Raddick in the poultry pens. When he proved diligent at that, he was moved to the kennels, and then to the stables. It didn't seem so bad to me, the way he described it matter-of-factly, but as I thought more, it began to bother me.

"But … your family were tenant farmers?" There were very few serfs in Aerach: serfdom occurred only when a farmer was unable to pay his rents. Even then, the condition was not hereditary. No one could force a family into generational bondage.

"Aye."

"And not in debt? Your rents were paid up when your father died?"

"So Ma told us."

"Then Eiglin Doniver had no right to seize your land!"

I became aware my voice had risen, turning the nearest few heads in the noisy room. I hunched over my beer.

"But with Da gone," Raddick said, "we couldn't work the land."

"Was that proven?"

He looked at me with a blank expression.

"Did they give your mother a chance? To try? To hire hands for the harvest and sowing?"

He scowled defensively. "I dunno. I was only a wee lad."

I leaned across the empty bowls, feeling like the older sister I never was to my own siblings. "Raddick, if they didn't give her the chance to farm it, then the seizure was illegal. Your family could still have the right of leasehold."

He slumped over his beer. "Don't matter," he said. "Ma died two summers back."

There was such a bleak look in those usually soft eyes I didn't press him for details, nor even offer sympathy.

"Chessa," he said, his look even more hopeless, "she wouldn't want to be no farmer. Not now. And me ... after all this"—he waved his hand around, indicating our shared predicament—"it's not like I'll ever get it back from Doniver, will I?"

I dropped my eyes. "I'm sorry, Raddick," I said, then offered words even rarer and more painful for me. "It's my fault you're homeless."

"No. No!" He straightened. "I couldn't bear it there at the camp anyway. I woulda left soon—soon as I could figure a way." His face was as twisted as his cap, which was back in his hands and being slowly tortured. "I couldn't do it, keep tending them poor creatures and sending 'em off to fight to death. I just ... just weren't brave enough to figure a way to stop it. An' here you did it in just one night—" He broke off, giving the cap another violent wrench.

"M'lady." He made a pair of bobbing dips, and I thought he was about to go down on one knee here in the barroom. Fortunately he possessed the discretion, or lacked the courage, to finish the motion. "M'lady, I'd rather pledge myself to your service. If you'd have me, that is."

"Hst! Who says I'm a lady?"

"You do, miss. When ye speak. The things ye know, like."

I couldn't help glancing around the room, though it seemed no one was interested in the conversation of a pair of ragged boys.

"Stop it. Stop calling me that. I'm just … I've been more fortunate than most. I'm nothing. Nobody." Panic had begun to well up in me. I didn't want him even speculating on my heritage. "And remember: I'm a boy, like you."

This time he looked around the room, then hunched over in so obviously furtive a gesture it was lucky indeed that no one seemed to care about or even notice us.

"Look," he said. "I don't know why you're running away from home."

I hadn't told him that. Was it that obvious? The panic turned to a ball of ice in my gut.

"But you've bought my bread, and I've done you a service. If ye don't want me, I understand … I … I'd just rather serve a … a minstrel boy like you than the finest lord in the land."

As much as I was touched, I was also worried. I needed to work on my disguise. It was one thing dressing as a common boy, but sounding like a duke's daughter was giving me away. I could alter my voice, that much I knew, and having Raddick around as a model—well, that would make it easier. I had to admit I liked the thought of an extra pair of eyes, hands, ears, and a body at my back.

But in return?

"Look at me, Raddick. What you see is all I have, all I am. I've got no lands, no funds past what's in this purse to support a vassal."

"You've yer voice," he said so softly I barely heard it amid the din of the tavern. "That's worth gold and land and horses and armies right there."

A sudden warmth washed through me at the compliment. But I wasn't about to let pragmatism be swept aside with pretty words.

"It barely puts a roof over the head for the night and a meal for the day. How many wealthy musicians have you seen?"

"None. But I've never heard any with a voice like yours, either." He was blushing now too, defensive. "But that's not here nor there. Point is, you oughtn't be travelling the country with none to look out for you." I forbore from raising an eyebrow at the thought of this skinny, weaponless boy, no bigger than I, protecting me. "I'm offerin' my service in return for no more than a roof when you have one, and a half-full belly so long as yours is full. You've every right to turn me down, but only if you think I wouldn't be of aid to you."

"I'd be an idiot to turn you down." I was trying for a casual tone, but my voice was rough with unexpected emotion.

I took a long swig of the wretched beer. In return, I thought, I was going to see what could be done about the decade-old injustice that had been done to his family. How, I didn't know.

The more I learned of the Doniver family, the less I liked them, and the more I thanked fate for the childish outrage that had caused me to run away from home before the betrothal could proceed any further. If married to Doniver, though, I could probably effect reforms in the land: stop the illegal beast-baiting; maintain widows' rights. If only I could stomach it.

I remembered the brutal, ugly look on Tiern Doniver's face. I wouldn't change him, and I couldn't change his policies any more than Mother could change Father's. Was that what she had hoped when she'd agreed to marry him? Or had she simply preferred marriage to a Duke to a pauper's life with my real father? I would not fall into that trap. But those problems were in the future.

LAURESA'S CHORUS

Allenis never makes any accusation that Lauresa came to him already pregnant. She almost wishes he would, so she could build a lie and use the stories she's created to defend herself and her cuckoo child. His absolute silence on the matter is unnerving.

Allenis doesn't share the bedchamber she, Allaigna, and Angeley sleep in. He did, during the first months of their marriage, but since the baby's birth he keeps to his bachelor rooms and study on the eastern side of the keep. When he is at home, that is.

Tonight, though, he steps into Lauresa's room, softly pulls back the bed curtains, and watches as Lauresa finishes nursing the child to sleep.

Lauresa tucks her breast back under her disarranged chemise and pulls the coverlet up to Allaigna's gently rising chest. She starts slightly as she sees Allenis and puts an admonitory finger to her lips, warning him not to wake her.

He nods. He's had this warning many times. He offers her a hand as she rolls off of the bed and oddly does not let go once she's standing. Puzzled, she follows him as he leads her out of the chamber, wondering what household crisis now needs her attention.

They walk widdershins around the gallery, conversation made impossible by the tumult of evening noise coming from the great hall below.

She has been in his study four, maybe five times in the three years since coming here. Most of their conversations about the castle happen in her study.

There is wine on the sideboard, and a pair of goblets. He pours and hands her one.

"She's beautiful, our daughter," he says, as if he's appraising a mare or a hound. Though perhaps then his voice would be more animated.

He clears his throat, as if to say more, but stops. Lauresa can see colour creep up his throat. With a bolt of realization she discovers his voice is flat, not because he is dispassionate, but because he is nervous, and it melts her heart.

She nods, suddenly shy in front of this stranger of a husband.

"Nearly as beautiful as her mother."

It's not what he was going to say originally, she is sure. Now it is her turn to blush.

He holds forth his chair for her and takes the smaller stool himself.

"I have been ..." The throat clears again. "Less attentive to you than a husband ought."

She's glad she's sitting down as he continues.

"I ... I confess I didn't want this marriage. And I suspect you felt the same. And perhaps you still do, with cause. Nonetheless, you have fulfilled your duties as chatelaine and mother beyond my expectations. And if your duties as wife have been small ... that is my fault, not yours."

She is both flattered and wrong-footed by this speech, and dreads what will come next. Although the marriage is, in all practical senses, non-existent, she is happy with that. She manages the juggling balls that keep her secrets and her duties in careful balance, and she is afraid he is about to toss her another one. Can she juggle them all without dropping some?

She feels she should speak, say something to prevent that happening. But even that may send them all flying.

He must see the fear in her eyes, and he takes her hand, becoming paternal.

"My dear, I'll not ask for my marriage rights tonight. That would be sudden and ... unchivalrous.

"But perhaps, since we had no courtship, nor have I been home long enough to be a proper husband, I thought we should simply start by making closer acquaintance."

He raises his goblet, the question lingering in his hazel eyes.

Tentative, terrified, she accepts the invitation and raises her own.

It is the strangest sort of courtship. Allenis is all solicitude and chivalry, which makes Lauresa nervous. Where has his change in disposition toward her come from? She feels as if she is being led into a trap, and thus guards her tongue and feelings more closely than ever. It only seems to make him try that much harder.

He takes meals with her and Allaigna in the small hall, or even in the octagonal room off the guest chamber. He dandles Allaigna on his knee, which fills Lauresa's heart with terror. The girl, though wary of most other adults, takes the attention in stride.

Under the loving eyes of two parents and a grandmother-cum-nurse, Allaigna flourishes. It is this, more than kind attentions, gifts, and sweet words, that opens Lauresa's heart to Allenis. For the first time they feel like a real family, and it brings back the gentle memories of her own childhood in Rheran. Were it not for the sharp sweet bursts of pain she feels when Allaigna's small face turns solemn and inscrutable like her true father's, or when the pupils in her grey eyes shrink to unreadable pinpricks in the pale field of her face, Lauresa feels as if she would be entirely happy.

It is a warm, late summer morning when the marriage is reconsummated. Lauresa and Allenis have been taking their breakfasts more and more in the octagonal room, far from the heat and noise of the kitchens. Allaigna, who eats little and unenthusiastically, has already left them for the company of Angeley and her garden of enticing smells, tastes, and textures.

Lauresa is warm already, but still she languors in the heat of the morning sun, never as hot here as it is on Brandishear's arid shores. Allenis has seated himself on the shaded side of the table as usual. Today they linger longer than normal, and the travelling sun now kisses the tops of his dark brown curls. There are more grey hairs than there were at their wedding, she notes, but in the sunshine they glint like silver.

She finds, to her surprise, a fondness in her heart when she looks at the man she accepted only out of duty three years before. And it is with fondness and gratitude that she stands and reaches a hand toward him, aware of the sun glinting off her own hair and the shoulder exposed by the loose fall of her morning dress. He takes the hand, kisses it.

It is not the whisper-dry kiss he bestowed the day they met, or the equally absent ones of their betrothal and wedding ceremonies. Nor is it the rough perfunctory embraces of their marriage bed. It is warm, hesitant, and lingering. He doesn't let go, but allows her to lead him out of the small bright room into the cooler depth of the guest chamber. The bed there is made in preparation for a visit from the Duke of Therein tomorrow. Lauresa parts the curtains and slips her body backward between them, leading him like a tame bullock. But the hand that reaches through her hair to clasp the back of her head is anything but tame, and the kiss that lands full on her mouth, parting her lips, is as passionate as any she's felt. With a shock that sends a shiver through her belly, she realizes she is aroused.

She arches her back to curve into him, appalled by her unreined appetite but unable to resist it. What began as an act of fond kindness on her part has become the satiation of desperate need. He is not Einavar. They are as different as midnight and noon. But the need is satisfied, nonetheless.

After that morning, when they hastily straighten the bedclothes of the guest chamber and put their own clothes in order before going their separate ways for the day, Lauresa finds herself tormented by contradictory feelings. One minute she is languorous and content, relishing the still-warming tingle of intimate touch after so long; the next she is aching with bitter guilt and longing for Einavar. It is absurd: she didn't feel any guilt when she and Allenis first shared a bed. But she hadn't enjoyed those early encounters. This time … This time she can hardly wait till the next opportunity to avail herself of her husband's body. She may long for the cool yet burning touch of Einavar's fingers, the intoxicating scent of his pale smooth skin, and the enigma hidden behind his silver-grey eyes. And yet Allenis is, in his coarse but gentle passion, in the weighty strength and maturity of his body, if not equal to her distant lover, enticingly different—and, more importantly, closer.

But Allenis is oddly distant after the fact. He sends his page with regrets to the small dining room at dinner that night, and Lauresa doesn't see him at breakfast either. When they are both in attendance at the arrival of the Duke of Therein and his retinue, Allenis barely glances at her. It is as if these last weeks of their relationship have evaporated like the morning mist. By evening it has aroused her ire. No one treats a princess of Brandishear, even a former one, like a cast-off plaything.

When Allaigna is in bed, and the guests have retired, she strides to Allenis's study and enters without knocking.

He looks up from the pile of parchments scattered on the desk, startled then ... what? Guilty? Annoyed?

"Husband," she says, without waiting for him to speak. "Have I offended you?"

He blinks, a mix of emotions rippling through his reddening face as he stands.

His stammer as he replies annoys her further. *You are the Duke of Teillai,* she thinks with scorn, *not some bumbling country oaf, some unwashed boy. Speak with authority, whatever truth or lie you have for me.* But as that thought flashes by, she sees some genuine pain cross his face. It doesn't matter the cause, it is enough to soften her mother's heart, if not her newly reborn lover's one.

"My ... my dear wife. What — what possible offense can you have caused me?"

She is struck by how dangerous their questions are. Her daughter, the thing most precious in the world to her, is, by her mere existence, cause for offense.

Lauresa's own tongue trips in the country manner she's just scorned her spouse for.

"I ... I..." She grits her teeth, irritated beyond belief at her inability to voice her complaint, realizing she cannot do it without seeming a lovelorn supplicant or a whining cupboard wife. She can't even turn on her heel and flee the awkward and dangerous question without appearing a petulant child. There is no choice but to bare some part of herself. She takes a deep breath.

"Your affections, husband," she says softly, demurely even — anything but strident, she hopes — "seem to ebb and flow like the tide. What heavenly body exerts such pull on them, I wonder?"

He blinks, blushes. Blushes, even! "My lady." He steps from behind the desk, takes both her hands in warm square-fingered ones, but cannot seem to look her in the eyes. "Please … forgive my inattention. Other affairs … matters of state … weigh heavily on me. I meant you no insult."

She extricates one hand, and with it gently lifts his chin as if he were a shame-faced child.

"My name is Lauresa, husband. I would that you called me by it."

She leans forward—they are nearly of a height—and plants a delicate kiss upon his lips before pulling away.

"My chamber door is open, for whenever you need to set such weight aside for a time."

She turns to leave, hears him release his breath in half sigh, half groan. She smiles to herself, knowing it will not be long.

Thus the happiest era of her marriage begins, and when her next child is conceived, she can truly say he was born, if not of desperate passion, at least of comfortable accord between his parents.

It is a far easier pregnancy than her first. Her mother's body knows this road now, and perhaps, she admits to herself, the absence of Ilvani blood within the child's veins makes it easier as well. Her mother claims that half-blood pregnancies are often more difficult, and now she is willing to attest to it personally.

Spring burgeons around her: calves in the meadows, the lower yard littered with downy morsels of infant fowl, spring grass and flowers dressing the dull grey stone and winter-tired fields of Teillai. She is burgeoning herself. Her hair, always thick and golden, is too dense and curly to draw a brush through. She gives up trying to tame it and wears it loose down her back like a maiden's. Her skin is pink and fresh, her belly and breasts round like melons. Allenis finds her so attractive he can barely keep his touch from her; even at state occasions, his hand will steal to her belly or to the soft nape of her neck beneath its curtain of pink-gold hair.

Her gravid beauty does not go unnoticed by others, either. The local lords, young and old, pay her court as they never have before. She accepts their gifts and compliments with demure smiles, her hand resting comfortably in her husband's warm grip. She is secure, loved, admired — she could ask for no more.

The spring air is glorious, full of the scents of moist earth, new grass, and blossoms. The sun warms her back; the breeze off of the fish pond cools her front. The temperature is ideal, the air clean and fresh, and yet she can hardly breathe. She is gasping; stifled, frozen to the core; and burning with indignation, humility, and pain she must not let show.

Allaigna is trotting toward her, something cupped in her tiny hands. At three and a half, she has lost so much of the pudginess of babyhood. The realization is an ache within her, beneath the other, sharper pain she's feeling. Her baby is a baby no longer, and will soon be usurped by another. Lauresa rubs a hand across her belly, pushing back at the insistent kicks, trying hard not to resent the life within her.

I cannot, will not, love it as much as I love her, she insists to herself.

Allaigna has reached her knee, the worried crease between her dark brows breaking Lauresa's heart once more. A pale blue egg lies cupped in her daughter's tiny hands.

"Look what I found, Mama."

Lauresa nestles her own hands around Allaigna's.

"Where was it, love?"

"Under the plum tree." Allaigna looks back over her shoulder at the blossoming plum. She turns back to face her mother, her grey eyes clouded with worry.

"Angeley says eggs that fall out of their nests don't hatch. That … that the mama birds push them out …"

Lauresa interrupts the worried tumble of words. "Let me see."

She takes the fragile blue orb into her own hands. It is warm, perhaps from the heat of Allaigna's hands, perhaps from the sun. Or maybe it hasn't been on the ground that long.

"Show me where you found it."

Standing on the spot Allaigna points out, she can just see a nest between the pink and white flowers.

"If I put you on my shoulders, do you think you can reach it?"

They try, but Allaigna's arms are not quite long enough.

The little girl is in tears.

Well, thinks Lauresa, feeling the weight of her seven-month belly, *I hope the branches will hold me.*

"What is this?"

The voice booms up at her just as she is reaching toward the nest. She gives a jerk, nearly dropping the egg.

The mother bird, who has been screeching at her from the neighbouring tree, falls silent.

Lauresa holds her breath, stretching her arm out as far as it will go, feeling the branch creak and groan beneath, then lets the egg fall the few inches into the nest. There is no sound. She has no way to tell if it's the right nest, if the egg is still alive, or if the mother bird will push it out again, but she's done the best she can.

She inches back down the branch as, from below, Allaigna babbles at her father.

"Mama saved the baby bird, 'cuz it felled from the nest, and its mama couldn't get it back, 'n' I couldn't reach it, so Mama climbed the tree, so the baby will be born now."

Strong arms reach up and lift Lauresa down from the lower branches, as if she weighed no more than an egg herself, and was just as fragile.

Allenis is frowning. "My dear, is this wise in your state? What of the child?"

Lauresa's glance falls on the excited, radiant face of her child — the only child she'll ever love — and the tears she has held back all morning burst free. She breaks out of her husband's arms and crouches, wrapping Allaigna to herself, as if to bring her back within her body once more.

Perplexed, Allaigna wipes at the tears with inefficient starfish fingers. "Don't cry, Mama. The baby's home now. Its mama will look after it now."

The serious solace coming from this three-year-old throat is almost enough to make Lauresa laugh. Or it would be if the hurt wasn't blocking the way.

Hiccoughing, she wipes her nose on her shoulder and sends Allaigna off to play with the new litter of puppies in the kennel, though letting her out of her arms seems the hardest thing she's ever done.

Her husband's hand is on her shoulder, his voice soft and apologetic. "My dear, I didn't mean to chastise you."

She shakes her head, wipes her nose again, and forces a smile. "You're quite right, husband. I'm in no shape to be climbing so high."

In that moment she is resolved. She will make no accusation, nor admit to her discovery.

Her knowledge of the letters, hidden so carefully beneath the floorboard of Andreg's study, will remain her secret.

They date from long before their marriage, it is true, and she would have no quarrel with them if the correspondence had stopped then. From the rough, untutored hand, it is clear the author is of lower birth—no doubt an unsuitable match for the Duke of Teillai. And it is clear the relationship is old and well-established. There are references to a son as well, though it is unclear from the context whether that child is Andreg's or another's. Lauresa supposes she could piece that together with a careful study of the missives, but that is too painful a task, at least for now.

It is also clear that her husband's absences over the past four years have not entirely been spent on the campaign borders or at the capitol. The more she thinks on it, the more resentment grows in her heart. It is true she brought another man's child to the birthing bed, but she has been faithful since the wedding vows were spoken. Her husband, it seems, has not been so restrained.

Anger bubbles up, and she is tempted once more to throw this in his face, along with whatever other objects may come to her raging hand. But she won't. Her pride will not allow her to admit out loud she has been made into a fool. And more, beneath that pride, is caution.

For if accusations of infidelity start flying through the air, that dreaded accusation, the one that could endanger her daughter, may also spread its ugly wings.

So for now, perhaps forever, she will contain her pride, her outrage, her hurt. Even if it means never admitting that she had come to love her husband.

Irdaign's Chorus

Oh, how I wish I could take my daughter's pain away, take it as my own, the way I can ease a birth or heal a festering wound. Why is healing the heart beyond my skills?

Of course I knew of Andreg's lover, have known since … Well, I can never remember how long I have known things. It is one of the many reasons I brought Einavar back into Lauresa's life, that knowing. But even still, I haven't been able to prevent or salve the pain.

I have watched helplessly as she tumbled into love with her husband, my attempts to warn or steer her away interpreted as a manifestation of animosity between myself and Andreg. And that, as in any mother-daughter-husband triangle, could serve only to push her faster into Andreg's arms.

"I told you thus" would be worse than useless.

For now, all I can do is love her and feel her pain as if it were my own.

Einavar has not visited her in over a year. Whether he sensed her heart's division, or whether Fate has simply caused his duties with the Brandishear Rangers to keep him away, the effect is the same. Lauresa is doubly bereft, both of her husband, whose lack she had never felt before, and of her lover.

But then I smile and recognize Fate's wisdom, if such a force can be said to have so human a quality. Husbands and lovers are not what she needs, but a mother and daughter. Between the sudden doting attention she bestows on Allaigna, and the motherly care I can wedge around her when she isn't looking, we bookend her, shelter her from the outer world, and remind her that, more than a duchess, a wife, or a lover, she is above all a mother.

Unlike what I feel for Lauresa, I have no aching desire to take away Allaigna's pain. Perhaps it is because there is a gap between our generations — a buffer that allows me to see her with no less love but with less involvement. Nourd told me once that a mother already carries all her babies within her, even before she is born. In that sense, I carried Allaigna and Allenry and all Lauresa's other offspring within my belly all the while I carried her. It is a surreal yet comforting thought. It is not that my love for my granddaughter is any less; it is simply that I am far enough removed from the type of pain she suffers that I can see it for the transient, necessary, character-shaping anguish it is.

And for all that — maybe because of it — I am able to hold her hand and support her through the first awful trauma of her young life: the birth of her baby brother.

I am happy, delighted, and selfishly joyful to be able to give myself so entirely to her. If there is any thought that my motherly attentions should be turned to my own daughter, I realize my gift to her is to assuage her own guilt and allow her to give herself fully to Allenry because Allaigna is taken care of.

Lauresa has matured as well. She is no longer a lost child of nineteen in a strange land, new to the ways of motherhood. She is a seasoned mother, more experienced than I by twice the children, with an easy command over servants and nobles that I never achieved, not being born to the role. I am so very proud.

I feel the tingling in the back of my skull that tells me someone is trying to reach me. I pick up the heavy basket of plums I've been gathering, push the sweat-stuck bits of hair back under my kerchief, and head indoors to my workshop. Normally cool in the worst of summer, today the muggy hot air has even penetrated this sanctuary. It is like swimming in a cauldron.

I take down my silver bowl from the high shelf, wipe the dust from it with my plum-stained apron, and fill it with tepid water from the bucket by the hearth. While the water settles, I wash my face in the plain stoneware basin and dry it on a clean corner of my apron. Sometimes I'm surprised I have such vanity left.

I clear my mind, gazing into the still water of the silver bowl, opening the back of my brain to the buzzing. I let it percolate through my awareness for a taste, a flavour of the caller. It is not a practitioner of the art, that much is clear, which leaves only one likely candidate.

"Einavar."

The taste comes to me as I breathe on the water, rippling its surfaces. The wavelets fold and crease, reshaping themselves until his face appears in the bowl, reflected in place of mine. It is shiny with sweat, creased with anxiety, and the eyes are dark and troubled.

"Einavar. It's been some time. What's the matter?" I try to sound light-hearted, ignorant of my almost-son's distress.

"Angeley," he croaks, his image wavering. "I must see you … I'll come to the sally port tonight.

"No. Andreg is home. Stay where you are." I run through my day's schedule, seeing where I can make time. "I'll come to you tonight."

I leave Lauresa to put Allaigna to bed. It is still high summer and the sun sets late, so I must bide my time while the household settles. I let myself out the main gates just before dusk. The castle retainers are used to my comings and goings on various errands, so my departure causes no stir.

I walk downhill to Werrancross gate, where a smithy stands, attached to an ostler's. Here I keep Yannina's second filly, the offspring of a Sandbred stallion I left with my Vanner mare one spring five years ago. The young mare is bay like her mother but swift and delicate like her father, and the perfect size for me. I keep her at the ostler's for occasions such as this, when I want to move quickly without anyone in the castle knowing I've gone farther than the town gates.

I don't bother with a saddle, just bridle her and slip onto her comfortable back.

"She may be a bit fractious, mistress," Seddan the ostler reminds me. "She hasn't been run in a good while."

"I'll be sure to let her run, then." I wink at Seddan. "I shall be back tonight, all being well."

The youngster is jittery at first, but as promised, I allow her a gallop across the commons. I've sung a charm that makes us less noticeable. Not invisible by any stretch, but unremarkable, unlikely to draw comment or remembrance.

Night has fallen by the time we reach the edge of Werran Forest. I leave my mare tethered by a charm at the foot of the scree slope, and climb up the noisy shale that announces my arrival. As I reach the top, a dark figure blacks out the moon, offering me a hand up.

We embrace hurriedly. I can see the worry etched between his thin brows.

"It is Chanist," says my son-in-love without preamble or greeting.

My heart stops. Why, after all these years, can thoughts of his safety make my otherwise rational heart trip?

And why hasn't my Sight warned me of this?

But it has, I realize. I simply had not thought the moment would be so soon.

"The tinctures …?"

"Are losing their effectiveness. I am less and less in the capital, and have less access than ever to His Highness."

I look up at him, my eyes sharp. "Why?"

"The mages. And the Princess. They are always at his side."

I pace back and forth, worried and frustrated, then kneel at the shallow spring-fed pool that surfaces on this plateau, the same pool Einavar called me from. It is an ancient spring, steeped in old, deep magic that was here long before Ilmari, or even Ilvani, came to this part of the world. The crystalline waters call me. I wash my face, soaking my eyes in the cold, clear water.

Einavar comes near to see what I am doing, but I hold up a hand. For this, I need all my concentration.

The water drops from my face as I bend over the pool, my reflection haloed by the light of the risen moon behind me. I sing to the water, slowing the drops to a rhythmic pulse, turning the air thick and gelid around me.

The wards in and around the Bastion are stronger than ever. I push, forcing each drop of water through the surface, imbued with my will.

I can feel him, distant, but drawn closer. I can smell him. At first it is the familiar odour of leather, smoke, horse sweat; then newer ones of perfume, spices, and something—someone—else. But underneath it is still him.

And yet there is another smell, sharp, burning the back of my nostrils, and sickly sweet at the same time. I recognize the scent of madness. Sound begins to filter through, slowed and garbled by the sticky slow time. He is murmuring, distressed, but I can't hear the words.

Sight remains elusive. I push harder but find only darkness. It is not the natural darkness of night, or of a windowless room, just black nothingness. And then, like a knife in the brain, is another set of eyes, normally soft and doe-like, burning across my vision.

I slap my hands into the pool, breaking the contact, reeling back, dazzled by flashes of light and careening stars before my eyes.

Einavar is at my side, helping me stand.

"He must come here," I gasp. "At least get him away from the Bastion." My chest is heaving, my breath scraping hard and rough down my throat.

"How?" begins Einavar.

"I will give you a missive. Signed by Vishod. A stop in Teillai on his way to Aleran would not be amiss. And he will come without his court." I grip Einavar's hands. "He still must not know I am here, though. I will have Lauresa administer the treatment."

Einavar frowns, a familiar pain flickering across his face.

"Does she know?"

"That he forfeited her life in exchange for a war? No. He was not himself when he sent her on the Clearwater Way, and she must never know."

"But if he is not himself now …"

"He is still himself, but not for long. We will see he stays himself. You must ride tomorrow. I'll bring the message.

"I'm sorry," I say, looking at the pain in his face. "There will be no time to see her."

I do not add that she is busy with her baby and has little need of him right now. That is a pain he doesn't need, just as she does not need his distraction.

As I ride back to Osthegn, a pair of thoughts circle endlessly in my head like battling crows. *Gwannyn is a mage.* And, *how did I not know?*

Verse 6

The Bard's Bail

The sun was unseasonably bright and cheerful, I thought, given my mood.

I couldn't fathom what had possessed my self-appointed squire, Raddick—despite the one and a half eagles' worth of small coins I'd given him to complete his shopping errands—to attempt instead to steal a leg of cured mutton hanging from a butcher's stall. I learned the reason later: it was his pressing sense of obligation to me, his desire to save me a few coins and lessen the burden he made on my purse.

Of course he was already in the stocks by the time I'd spotted the commotion across the market square and pressed my laden way through the crowd. All of his purchases and his purse had been confiscated by the guard, and, after I bought Raddick's freedom, I had further negotiating to do to release his possessions. They were lighter by at least a third than they ought to have been, but I had no way of proving it.

I loaded him up with my shopping as well, and sent him, shamefaced from my scolding, back to where Dog camped a league outside town. The reason we had separated in the first place was so I could buy new underclothes, and that task was still unfinished.

I set off, head down, grumbling at the inconvenience and cost of being liege to even one dim lad. I had only made fifty disgruntled paces when a large firm hand settled itself on my shoulder.

"Hold up a bit there, lad."

I came to a slow stop and gave an even slower quarter turn of the head, just enough to see my interlocutor. It was one of the city watch: not the thick-jawed clerk or the hoary veteran I'd dealt with for Raddick's release, but the one who'd been sitting at the back of the guardroom, whetting and oiling his sword.

Some rusty instinct began screaming at me to run, but I didn't pull back from the hand, which I felt would only tighten if I did. I simply stood, knees bent, weight on my toes to see how this new development would hinder me.

He walked to cross in front of me, that enormous hand never letting go of my shoulder as if in some strange madrigal. He held me at arm's length, studying both me and a sheet of parchment in his other hand.

"Nalen, is it?" he asked. It was the name I'd used to sign Raddick's release; but it was also the name, so foolishly close to my own, that I'd given at Doniver's camp. He must have felt the involuntary quiver that ran through me, for his grip tightened. "Ye'll need to come back to the guardhouse wi' me," he said, not unkindly.

My feet were glued to the cobbles, resisting the gentle pull on my shoulder.

"Naught to fear, lad," he encouraged. "A simple misunderstanding. Ye'll not be punished."

Fear warred with curiosity. What could that parchment say, and what did it reveal about me? With practice borne of many sibling battles, I dropped down out of his grasp and twisted up again, snatching the parchment from his other hand as I hurtled off across the public square. The curiosity had hurt me, though. The twisting motion I'd used to reach the parchment had sent a twinge of pain through my knee, not to mention costing me a heartbeat of time. Sometimes I still wonder what difference that fraction of a second might have made.

As it was, I only just missed escaping down an alley as a drover backed his oxen into it. I tried anyway, hitting the cobbles with my already sore knee, and scrabbling like a lizard between the cart's moving wheels. I was almost home free when that large muscled hand clamped down on me again, this time on my ankle, and pulled me out like a load of washing against the washboard cobbles, not nearly so gentle this time around.

"I said, lad," he puffed, once he'd pulled me upright by the collar. "Yer master don't plan to punish ye. But make me run like that again, and I might do it for him."

Thus I found myself in the holding room of the city watch, eyeing the window dubiously and waiting to find out my fate. I pulled the crumpled parchment from under my shirt. I'd had the presence of mind to stuff it there as the sergeant of the guard had retrieved me from under the cart. Crowding close to the window, I turned my back to the door and smoothed the sheet out, peering at the words in the stingy light.

. . . forsworn apprentice, Nalen by name, though he may give another . . .

Apprentice? Why was I being painted as a runaway tradesman's pupil? There followed a description I found most unflattering, particularly in regards to stature, but sadly accurate. How had anyone even seen my face long enough to note the mole below my right eye? And then I knew. The paper described my hair as black, but two days ago it had been a dirty blonde. I'd let the colouring charm fade, feeling it was safer to be my own colour once more, and indeed, my hair was now largely black. But Tiern Doniver had his own description, from the portrait he'd been given. Which meant he'd read the letters in my saddlebag and guessed my identity. I leaned against the wall, my knees no longer solid enough to support my weight on their own.

Would he send me home in disgrace? Or—I shuddered—simply wed me here and now? He couldn't. He wouldn't. The grants of land and titles in my dowry would not apply if we were wed without the formal consent of the Duke. But what if he had consented already? Two days was time enough for a messenger to have gone and come from Teillai, bearing word of my appearance nearby, bearing permission to marry in return. That would certainly solve the Duke's errant daughter problem.

The words on the crumpled paper sprawled and squiggled as I imagined another notice:

Runaway daughter. Reward for capture. Lands, titles, hand in marriage . . .

I shook my head to clear it of these flights of painful fantasy. That was absurd. No matter how angry the Duke was, he wouldn't resort to such fairy-tale theatre. I was, at least, mostly sure of that.

But he could quite easily have already granted permission to Doniver to marry me if he should find me. Doniver's own reward notice was real enough, and proof he knew my identity, though he'd chosen not to reveal it. It would be embarrassing to have his bride-to-be picked up in the street like a criminal. Perhaps he was no longer interested in me as a marriage prospect, especially after the havoc I'd caused to his illicit pig operation. Did he seek to capture me for revenge? Or did he intend to gain some political leverage from my family? A queasy heaviness settled on me as I began to think what implicit demands could be made of my family, of how I had just handed more power to the person who least deserved it.

My miserable thoughts were interrupted as the guardsman who'd captured me opened the door and beckoned me forward. I stuffed the paper back under my shirt and followed him out of the tiny room.

"Yer apprentice?" he asked as we entered the main room.

A tall, thin man dressed in slightly crumpled velvet and silk stepped forward and grabbed me by the ear.

"That's the young rascal!"

The guardsman handed over to this stranger a bundle that looked like my possessions. The tall man tucked them under his arm while he shifted his pincer-like grip from my ear to my shoulder.

I took the opportunity to twist away.

"I'm no apprentice!" I shouted. "I've never seen this man in my life." My voice came out high and girly in the panic of the moment.

The large guard was blocking the outer doorway with his casual bulk; the clerk looked at me with only the mildest of interest, and the stranger, chuckling, closed the third side of the triangle around me.

"Tell them another one, lad. Your parents paid hard-won coin to settle you with me, and it's coin I'd rather spend than have to give back to their disappointed hands if I return without you. And think how sad they'll be when you come running home with your pockets and your head still empty, having squandered their hopes for naught."

His voice was musical, almost as hypnotic as Angeley's, though I sensed no Leisanmira magic beneath the words. I almost didn't notice that he'd grasped my upper arm in that firm grip again and somehow silenced my protest.

He turned to the clerk. "The lad's a touch homesick, see. Though I have a suspicion it's not the charms of his mother's kitchen he misses, but those of the sweet barley-haired lass who kissed his cheek when I led him away."

He gave a broad wink, which somehow seemed directed at me as much as the clerk. I felt my cheeks burn with indignation, but a small part of me couldn't help but admire how he strung out these lies for his audience. In the end, it was curiosity that bit me and let me walk out unprotesting. That, and the thought that it would be easier to cut and run from a single man out in the crowded streets than it would be to dodge him and the constables from within the guardhouse.

He tipped the guards and bade them a grateful farewell, his long-fingered hand still wrapped like a manacle around my bicep.

Once clear of the guardhouse door, I wiggled a bit, testing his grasp. It was implacable. He pulled me in toward himself, curling his long frame down so his voice was in my ear.

"I don't know who you really are, lad," he said in that low, musical voice, "but the one truth is I'll be paid well to bring you to Caer Doniver. Alive, yes. But no one said anything about conscious. Now walk nicely, or I'll knock you cold and sling you over my shoulder like a sack of onions. Your choice."

"You've got the wrong person," I hissed at him.

"Oh la, I know that! But young Lord Doniver seems to want you to be a runaway apprentice, so who'll argue, eh?"

I could feel panic welling.

"Who are you?" I asked, hoping to distract him into loosening his grip.

"Why, don't tell me you don't recognize the Lark of Aleran? Morran Rhoan at your service." He gave a mocking hint of a bow without loosening his grip a hair. "Though it's you who's at mine, isn't it?"

And then of course I did know him. A travelling minstrel, one who'd passed through Teillai many times when I was younger. He wasn't coiffed and kitted out as usual for those appearances in the great hall, but I should have recognized him nonetheless. He was one of Mother's favourites.

Should I reveal my identity? Appeal to him for help? But that would still hand me back to my family, and I wasn't feeling trusting. Instead I made a bluff.

"How much were you paid? I'll more than match it."

He laughed, loud and long enough to make the crowds we passed turn and look before resuming their business.

"I doubt that, young thing. Besides," he said, hefting my bundle of possessions, "I already seem to have all you're worth right here."

I opened my mouth to argue that my worth was more than my possessions … but that would lead to a discussion of who would pay for me.

I stumbled over the cobbles as I kept up with his long stride. The White Tooth of Castle Doniver loomed far too close. Desperate, I tried another tack.

"I do recognize you," I gasped. "I saw you sing in …" I couldn't say Teillai, or he might recognize me too. "In Aleran, at the fair." I hoped it was true. Even the most popular court singers would not turn down the easy silver of market fairs.

I trolled my memory for one of those long-ago heard tunes my mother always requested, and sang, warbly, faintly, with lack of breath,

And rose in summertime
Blooms not so fair as thee
But flowers envy thy return
Lest thou come back to me . . .

He stopped and stared at me, his head turned at an odd angle.

"I spoke true without knowing it. You ought to be my apprentice. Where did you learn to sing like that?"

"My gran," I said, turning from his gaze. It was true enough, and farther than I wanted to go.

"What a shame Doniver seems set on having you. No, don't worry, lad." He didn't loosen his grip on my arm, but placed his other gently on my shoulder. "Tiern Doniver's tastes don't run to boys as far as I know. And he did ask for you unhurt. So I'm sure he means you no harm."

I was not nearly so sure.

Lauresa's Chorus

If her husband notices a chill between Lauresa and himself, he doesn't remark, perhaps attributing her distance to her increasing gravidity.

Lauresa keeps Allaigna close to her in the next two moons, seldom letting the child from her sight. Her daughter warms and thrives, basking in Lauresa's undivided attention. They spend time in her mother's garden, picking the season's first strawberries, their lips and aprons stained pink with this earliest foreshadowing of summer. They do puzzles and play cards together, Lauresa ever marvelling at the mathematically precise mind of her three-year-old daughter. They sing nursery rhymes, Lauresa's patchy memory pulling forth tattered threads and pieces that Angeley, when she overhears, joins in to weave together. The three generations of voice mingle to the delight of each and the enjoyment of anyone else within earshot.

Lauresa's joy is marred only by the foreboding urgency that causes her to glut herself on her daughter's presence and enjoy her to the full while she can. It is a buffer against the wedge she knows will come between them: that other life harbouring in her belly. For now, she ignores it as best she can.

But ignoring can last only so long, and as the days approach midsummer, she knows this babe will be denied no longer. Shortly before the longest day of the year, Lauresa brings into the world a bawling, ruddy, nine-pound boy, changing her world once more, and her daughter's forever.

She is astounded, befuddled, and enraptured by the love she feels for this new baby: the one whose existence she tried to deny for the past months; the one who came, not from her lover, but from her husband; the usurper who arrived to take her precious daughter's place not just in her arms but in her inheritance as well.

She thought it was impossible to love another as fully, as unreservedly as she loves her first child. For how could her heart possibly hold any more? And yet she does. Despite the fact she doesn't want to, she loves him just as much. And because he is newborn and vulnerable, because his need is greatest, she appears to love him more.

She sees the pain in Allaigna's eyes and wants to take her in, hold her close in that sheltered world that once contained just the two of them; but her arms are full of Allenry. The constant strain of this double pull on her heart makes her irritable, prone to tears and angry words. She snaps at her husband, her mother, and, even though she hates herself the moment it happens, her daughter.

Allaigna is angry too. Once a model child, it seems she has suddenly found a streak of venomous mischief within herself. A kiss delivered to her baby brother somehow makes him cry. The tiny hand so helpfully rocking his cradle moves faster and faster till the passenger slews about and wakes, while the grin on Allaigna's face stretches wider. The admonishments she receives from Lauresa and Angeley do little to stop such behaviour, and Lauresa suspects she knows why. No longer the centre of her own universe, lacking the attention she's had for the first three years of her life, Allaigna will attract attention from her mother and nurse any way she can, no matter the end result.

Lauresa tries to find time to spend with her daughter while the baby sleeps or is tended by Angeley. But she is so tired herself; what moments she finds are brief and hardly enough.

Allaigna is not the only one sensitive to the direction of maternal affection. Lauresa has heard that second babies are easier, less needy, than the first. But whenever she finds time for Allaigna, and Allaigna alone, Allenry awakes with uncanny promptness and demands to be fed, or changed, or simply carried. It is as if he is trying to make up for being ignored throughout the months of his gestation and is demanding his due now. And it is the guilt Lauresa feels for the months she ignored, resented, or even hated this baby that tips the balance.

Fair enough, she thinks. *Allaigna had me all to herself for three and a half years. She has been steeped in love. It will have to serve. She has her grandmother~nurse, and Allenry will have me. Not because it's what I want to choose. Because I have no choice.*

Andreg is enamoured of his boy. If he suspects this is the only legitimate issue of their marriage, he still makes no mention of it. Perhaps it is simply that he has a male heir to secure the patrilineal succession common in Aerach. Lauresa seethes whenever she thinks of her adopted nation's barbaric laws, which will deny her daughter a title or holdings except by marriage. And yet, when she looks into her son's slate-blue newborn eyes, she wants the world for him. She wonders if she has become two people—Allainga's mother and Allenry's—and whether the two are reconcilable.

Angeley holds baby Allenry, rocking him while his eyes droop and then snap open, fighting sleep. The birthfeast has been held in the courtyard, the hall being too stuffy and dark in this beautiful summer weather. The sky is fading to teal, darkening overhead.

Lauresa leans over her mother's shoulder, passing a refilled goblet of wine to her.

"You shouldn't be playing the serving girl at your son's birthfeast, Lauresa," says Angeley.

"My castle. I can do what I want," Lauresa laughs. "And don't forget to address me as 'your Grace'," she adds in a low voice.

"There's hardly anyone close enough to hear me, but fair point, your Grace."

Lauresa's glance passes over the wine-soaked lords and ladies lounging tipsily against what solid stone furnishings the lush garden provides. From where she stands, they seem leagues away.

"Is Allaigna asleep?" asks Angeley.

Lauresa nods. "She was asking for you, but I told her a story and sang a lullaby, which eventually was enough."

"Better than enough. She needs you more than she needs me. Especially tonight, with all the fuss over this one."

Lauresa looks down at the sleepy baby in his grandmother's arms, at the eyes so desperately trying not to succumb to night. "They seem to be getting darker, not lighter—his eyes, I mean."

"I think they'll be brown, like his father's," agrees Angeley.

"Why don't my babies have my eyes?" Lauresa half complains.

"They have plenty of other things of yours. Allaigna has your stubbornness, your sharp mind, your sense of justice. Though she'll look more like her father, I think she'll have something of your beauty as well."

"Her father's beauty would be enough," murmured Lauresa. "And what of Allenry? What will he have?"

"A sense of entitlement. Oh, and many other things as well." Angeley's voice had taken on its prophetic tones.

"And Allaigna? Won't she feel entitled as well?" Lauresa's heart cracks at the thought.

"No, she'll have to earn that, I'm afraid."

It surprises Lauresa that she needs to learn to nurse a baby all over again. So many things came back without effort: the automatic bouncing rock of her hips when she holds him; the comfortable way he fits wrapped against her chest in a shawl, scandalizing the notions of the other court ladies, who have nurses or cradles to attend their babes while they tend the affairs of their keeps; her recognition of the subtle cues he gives to let her know he is about to soil his swaddling, which gives her time to whisk him over a chamber pot or privy hole; the instinct that tells her he is about to wake from a nap. At all these she is so much more confident and proficient, so less worried by the trivial.

So why do her breasts not remember the sandpaper grating of a poor latch as he clamps her nipple between his gums and makes fruitless, clicking sucks? Again and again she breaks the latch, starts him over, and his round little face goes from turnip to beetroot, his mouth becomes a brick-shaped hole, and he clenches his fists like a prizefighter. At this point Allenis invariably wanders into the nursery and makes some proudly obtuse comment about his son's lungs, causing Lauresa to want to scream louder than Allenry.

He never spent so much time in the nursery when Allaigna was a babe, seethes Lauresa, tallying up the slights against her firstborn while resenting her husband's interest in this one. *He is mine,* she wants to tell him. *Just because he is a boy does not mean he is any less mine.*

But there is still that other reason that makes him more Andreg's: the reason she won't mention anymore, even in her thoughts. It is not that she wants Andreg to love Allenry less —she simply wants him to love Allaigna as much. And if he did, she wonders, would she feel jealous and possessive of her daughter as well?

It is on such a morning of frustrated, interrupted nursing and ill-tempered musing that Angeley comes into the room, leading Allaigna by the hand.

"The painter is ready," her mother-cum-nurse announces.

Allenis scowls, though it was his idea to commission a portrait. Perhaps it is the fact that the painter is one of Angeley's people that irks him so. Her husband and nurse can barely tolerate one another.

"He must wait till the maids have had time to dress my wife." He glances down at Allaigna in her worn tunic, rolled-up breeches, and grubby bare feet. "And daughter," he adds with evident distaste.

Angeley curtsies, not meeting the Duke's eye, which is fortunate for both of them, given the ice Lauresa can feel coming from Angeley's averted gaze. "Your pardon, your Grace, but the tinctures are highly sensitive to the air. Once mixed, they will not last long before losing vivacity. Every minute wasted will dull the final portrait."

And with every minute, Lauresa can see the Duke's good temper waning. Breaking the latch that has only just succeeded, Lauresa stands, tucking her wet breast back into her bodice.

"Husband," she says, handing him the objecting child. "If you would be so kind as to take your son"—there is ever so slight an emphasis on the last word—"we ladies will clean up and meet you in the hall." She leans across the bundle of baby and kisses Allenis on the lips, a feather-light touch with a hint of promise.

His shoulders relax, and he smiles and takes her hand with his free one, kissing the fingers as he takes his leave, unperturbed by the increasing, fussy squalls from the bundle in his arm.

Lauresa's tense back releases as well, and she lets out a long breath. Whatever her failings as a mother and wife, she has not lost her charm.

"Come, my darling," she says to Allaigna. "Let's wash our faces, brush our hair, and put on our best smiles for the painter."

Verse 7

Doniver

It was my feet that gave me away. They had fallen of their own accord into a trotting double-time rhythm to Morran Rhoan's long strides, but as we passed under the rusty, half-lowered portcullis of the keep, they faltered. Rhoan's grip had been loosening on my arm as we progressed, but the hesitation in my legs made those fingers tighten, noose-like, on my upper arm again. I looked over my shoulder as my last chance to escape disappeared behind me.

I wondered whether I'd be taken to a dungeon or a high tower, clapped in chains or locked behind doors, but it turned out to be none of these. Morran Rhoan led me to a small office adjoining the solar, and without pausing to demand audience, strode in.

Tiern Doniver was seated at a counting table, and Yannick—the Barrel—stood at his shoulder, both of them engrossed in documents spread across the table. Yannick looked up first, a large unfriendly grin spreading through the black bristles of his beard.

"It's the little troublemaker," he rumbled, causing Doniver to glance up as well. A sharp, equally unwelcoming smile grew on his face.

"Bring him here," he commanded Rhoan, beckoning with a roll of sheepskin.

The bard had to tug harder at my rapidly numbing arm, for my feet had glued themselves to the floor. He jerked, and I stumbled forward, fetching up against the table, scattering rolls of parchment in the process. Doniver seemed not to care about his papers. He reached across and grasped my chin in his cold fingers, peering at my face, nodding.

"Yes, that's the one."

He let go of my chin, reached beneath the table and procured a neatly tied bag that dropped on the table with a heavy clink. If those were eagles, there must have been fifty in there: a small fortune.

"Thank you, Rhoan."

The singer reached over my shoulder to pick up the sack. In its place he left the bundle of my possessions. As he left the room, I glanced back at him, and he at me. I put a hand on top of the bundle.

"You too, Yannick."

The Barrel looked surprised. "Are you sure?" he rumbled.

"I think I can defend myself from a ragged, unarmed boy," was Doniver's mild reply. He snatched the bundle from under my hand and unrolled it like a card sharp fanning out his trumps. From the meagre pile he removed my hunting knife and the curved dagger, placing them beneath the table, out of sight.

"Yes, Yannick, I'm sure," he snapped when the Barrel had still made no move to go.

Finally the immense man left to the sound of tapping from Doniver's fingers.

"So, Allaigna," he began. I didn't blink, certain as I had been already that he'd divined my identity. "Your family must be worried half to death about you. I was just composing a letter to tell them you were in such a hurry to be wed that you ran here to my arms rather than wait for the tedious betrothal to end."

He was lying. I didn't know how I knew, but I realized with certainty he had no intention of writing any letter … yet. It was both a relief and a worry. Any threat he might make, then — to send me home, to formalize the betrothal — was an empty bluff I could ignore. The worry, though, was what he did want from me, and why it was worth as many eagles as he'd just paid Morran Rhoan.

What value could I have to him? As a hostage, I had none if no one knew I was here. As a bride, my value was in alliance, which was also worthless if I was anonymous. And if he wanted from me what could be had from any dairymaid or courtesan? Well, I was hardly worth fifty eagles in that regard.

"But come," he said, standing. "You are tired and hungry, no doubt. You'll pardon me if I don't take your arm, dressed as you are." He flashed a quick and almost charming smile.

The elaborate courtesy was an utter contrast to the beastly fury I'd seen on his face when he'd struck and nearly choked me two days ago. I tried not to let it disarm me. But I was hungry.

He motioned to the door.

"Don't run," he murmured as he led me out of the counting room and across the solar. "You wouldn't get farther than ten yards."

It was likely true. Morran Rhoan had led me past at least a dozen men-at-arms in the courtyard and within the castle, and Doniver could alert them all with a word.

There was a small dining room across the solar from the office, and it was here, again with grandest courtesy, he offered me a seat. When the serving maid he called had come and gone, leaving bread, cheese, cold meat, and curious glances, he poured us each a cup of wine.

"Your health, my dear." He raised his goblet. When I didn't respond in kind, he looked hurt. "Come now, I hardly brought you here to poison you."

I had yet to open my mouth in his presence, but drinking seemed preferable to explaining that I didn't tolerate wine well. I would not show him even that weakness, so I took a sip, held it in my mouth, and swallowed slowly. At least it was well watered.

At his insistence, I helped myself to bread and cheese, and waited, still silent, for him to explain himself.

"Make no mistake," he said. "I am extraordinarily angry still for the mischief you caused. Though had I known who you were …" He paused, reached out, and tried to touch the fading bruise on the side of my face. "You must accept my apologies for striking you."

Must I? I dodged his touch.

His look of sincerity didn't sway me. It was fine to strike boys, by his reckoning, but not girls? Or just not highborn girls he might want to marry?

"Nor do I know the true reason you left your home." He offered a pause for me to enlighten him, but it would take more bait than that to draw me out. "But I suspect that if you'd left with your parents' blessing, you would not be dressed as a boy and travelling on your own. Though you're not really on your own now, are you? How are my kennel master and stable hand?"

I kept silent still.

He shrugged. "Whatever your reasons, I imagine your identity has a price. What, I wonder, would you do to keep it to yourself?"

Anything, I thought. *Everything.* But there were many, many things I would not do. I would buy his silence, but I would drive a hard bargain.

My voice was hoarse, as if it had been silent for weeks, not minutes. "You obviously have some price in mind." It was a childlike whisper, not the wry adult sound I'd hoped for.

"Ah, the little bird can indeed sing."

I flinched. Edris used to call me that. It was wrong, fouled, coming from his lips. But the thought of the strong and stubborn swordsmith lent me a spine of iron. I thought too of Garæthiel, with her smooth and easy tongue, her courtly, graceful manner that oiled the subtle wheels of intrigue. I would be both, I thought: sweet and subtle, with a centre of steel.

I gave a slight smile, inclining my head, my silence soft and inviting this time, waiting for him to take the first step into it.

"Well, sweet bird. Negotiation must begin with a certain level of trust, must it not? To start with, I'd like a tale. Not just any tale. I'd like to know why you're here."

I lifted my eyebrows. "Did you not order me brought here, my lord?"

The 'lord' was a gift: a free offering to sweeten the mood. As Andreg's daughter, I outranked him. In fact, I could command fealty in Andreg's name should I choose to play that card. He knew that too, but accepted my gift with either grace or arrogance. My reading of his expression wasn't profound enough to tell which.

"Are we going to dance this out then, Allaigna? Very well, let me rephrase. What were you doing in Doniver? And before you reply 'shopping', you should know I mean in Doniver in the company of my stable hand. With whom you seem to have been in collusion when you admitted yourself to my encampment under false pretences and proceeded to ruin what would have been a very profitable venture, not to mention a lot of entertainment for the masses."

"That's a very long question, Sir Doniver." I took a minute sip of wine to compose my answer. "I was indeed shopping. To replace the things I lost when my saddlebags were stolen. And I believe you still have them … my lord?" I shot him a look.

It was his turn to raise eyebrows.

"For how else did you know my identity?" I continued, throwing his phrasing back at him. "And before you claim to have recognized me from portraits and our few meetings, consider that you hardly saw me long enough, or in full daylight.

"And since, as you say, negotiations are based on trust, I trust you to return those effects in full."

He inclined his head but said nothing. I took that to mean assent. Point to me.

I gathered another deep breath. "As to what I was doing at that camp, I had come across evidence of poaching in the common woods, which, as you know are part of my father's demesne. I was investigating."

His look chilled somewhat, but his smile stayed in place. "And finding it was I who has a legal right as liege regent of Doniver to hunt these lands, you must have decided to leave well enough alone, no?"

Instead of fixing a false smile to my face to match his, I left my features as mild and dispassionate as possible. "Perhaps you have lost track of your calendar? It is, I believe, still the month of Ranis, and as you must be aware, the taking of game is prohibited for another five clearmoons. Even for those of us with rights of the hunt."

"*Killing* is prohibited, indeed. But all those piglets were rescued. It has been a hard winter, and many sows have not fared well. We cull their litters, lessening the burden on the sows and ensuring the ones we take are raised and fed."

"And yet your humane culling process seems to leave wounded sows behind."

He shook his head. "Only in the most unfortunate circumstances. Our hounds draw out the sow, and a few of our men keep her away while others take half the piglets. The sow that you found — and thank you so much, by the way, for skinning, gutting, and bringing her to us — was intractable. My men had no choice but to kill her, which is why we took all, not just some, of the marcassins."

It was almost plausible, and he seemed so regretful I just about forgot my outrage. But the lie was there.

They didn't kill her. They left her wounded and mad with pain. But surely he knew that — otherwise it would have been his men, not me, who brought the carcass in. I decided to hold the fact in reserve in case I needed it later.

"In that case, my father will be relieved and grateful to know you take such care with the management of the wildlife in these forests. I will be sure to commend you to him should I happen to see him soon."

And there it was, my threat to counter his own. Send me back to my family, or alert them to my whereabouts, and I would spill his secret. "After all, animal baiting is illegal all year round."

My small thrill of triumph was undercut by fear. It was a high-stakes game I played. I had just let him know that to send me back home or even admit my presence here to my family was to let them know of his highly questionable activities in the woods. I had increased his incentive to simply dispose of me. My safety depended on my having read him aright: that there was something he wanted from me that would ensure I'd be kept alive. I only hoped it was not what he had already been promised.

"It would seem, my dear," he said, eyes hard now, "that you have no wish to be reunited with your family."

I swallowed. Had I overplayed my hand? "I am in no hurry," I responded as calmly as I could, though in fact, what I wanted now more than anything was my mother's and grandmother's arms around me.

"They are looking, you know. And are offering to pay not just for your safe return, but merely for word of you. Oh, not to worry," he added with a patronizing pat on my sleeve. "Word hasn't gone out to the commons. Only to the noble and friendly families. The fear of ransom demands prevents them from making your absence known to the rabble."

I was not reassured.

"So you might wonder," he asked, "why have I not already sent word?"

I didn't respond.

He took a sudden change of tack. "Why did you run away? Some secret beau you're planning to meet? It can't be Raddick!" He laughed. "No? The life of a duke's daughter is just insupportably hard, and you thought grubbing in the woods would be easier?"

He reached for the flagon and refilled his goblet without offering to refill mine. "Or were you jilted, perhaps? Broken-hearted by some young swain? That's not it either. The prospect of marrying me, then?"

My face must have given something away.

"Aha," he said. "Am I so repulsive? Sorry to hear it."

He didn't look sorry, but I responded anyway. "Not you. Anyone."

"You prefer maids, is that it?"

I felt my skin fill with hot blood. "No—"

"So you do have a swain somewhere."

"No!"

"It's all right," he continued, ignoring my interruption. "I would certainly allow you your lovers, providing you allowed me mine."

My face, my whole being, was burning with shame, embarrassment, and outrage. I didn't want this knowledge, or to be having this conversation. But my outrage was causing me to lose what control I had over this conversation. With a deep breath, I mustered myself.

"Sir," I said between my teeth, "I'm no sighing romantic with thoughts of marrying for love. I simply have no wish to be a pawn—or even a queen—on the chessboard of our nations."

"Despite your father's reliance on you as such?"

"Because of it." I held up a hand. "Before you jump to conclusions, I bear the Duke no malice. I simply refuse to accord him the right of disposing of me to suit his aims."

"You don't believe closer ties to Doniver would benefit us all: Teillai, Doniver, Aerach … and you and me?"

"Perhaps they may. But they will have to be bought with other coin than me."

"Your sire has the right, by the laws of the land you were spouting at me a few minutes past—"

"Then those laws, in this respect, are wrong."

"And you intend to challenge them by removing yourself from the equation?"

"I intend to remove myself to somewhere the laws are more just."

He was looking at me differently now, the smug superior arch to his brow replaced with what seemed to be genuine interest. With his face so changed, I could almost see him as attractive. "And what will you do in Brandishear, since that must be where you're heading?"

I started back in my seat, my mind spinning frantically. I'd said too much, been lulled by this conversation of almost equals.

"Brandishear is not the only principality that keeps the old ways."

"It's a long way to Elalantar on that bony nag of yours …"

I blinked slowly, letting him follow his own conclusions.

"… and all the ports are in the other direction. No. It seems to me you're heading to the Valnirata borders."

I held on to my blank look, puzzled though I was at the direction this was going.

"You spin a pretty tale, little bird." He shook his head, chestnut hair swinging in the sunlight. "Allenis Andreg is too careful of all things to allow something as obvious as a daughter to slip through his fingers."

Does he even know? I thought. I had been gone but five days, and he was in Aleran when I left. Had Mother sent word to him? I had no idea. And if he knew, would he even care? Still, Doniver was right—even if he cared little for me, his pride would not want me to be here now.

Doniver's voice burbled over top of my musing. I only half paid attention to it.

"The more interesting question," that voice interrupted my thoughts again, "is why he'd use his daughter as envoy to the Ilvani."

I started, blindsided by the question, which had come from nowhere in my horizons. It must have made me look like he'd hit upon my secret.

"Obviously not an official ambassador," he continued, "or you wouldn't be stealing my stable hand to serve as your retinue." He reached inside his doublet and pulled out a flattened roll of parchment.

My eyes widened, and I nearly laughed as I recognized it.

"So what message could be so secret only a member of the family, dressed in rags and alone, could be trusted to deliver it?"

My mind was racing furiously, clicking over and over like a waterwheel in a torrent. He was no skilled interrogator, I realized. Instead, he was so proud of his own erroneous deductions he needed to boast of them. He had laid out the whole story he'd constructed for me, and now waited for me to step into the shoes he'd cobbled to size.

Should I do it? I wondered. He was so caught in his web of clever deductions that the simple truth—that I was a common runaway, angry at my parents, in search of my own history and destiny like any other truant child—would be unbelievable to him. But following his line of thought could be hazardous, and difficult. Could I even pull it off?

The paper he held was one of the copies I'd made of Ilvani missives from the Teillai archives, dating back to my grandfather's wars. I'd brought them along to study the language: if my real father was of that race, knowledge of his tongue might prove necessary. That Doniver took them for current missives meant he'd either not shown them to anyone else or he had no one close to him who could translate them.

I maintained my passive silence as he unrolled the parchment. "But surely your father has many messengers. Why you?"

He peered at me over the paper. "He couldn't possibly be offering you as hostage. What could require that huge a surety?"

I raised an eyebrow. I didn't want him going down that track—he might begin to consider ransoming me himself. Time to speak.

"*Espaegh dhi Yllvaeni?*" I asked. *Do you speak Ilvani?*

His blank look was my answer—and my bargaining chip.

Irdaign's Chorus

Allaigna is still rocked back on her heels, her world pulled out from beneath her by the birth of her brother. No matter how a child likes the idea of a baby brother or sister, the reality is impossible for her to anticipate or adjust to easily. I comfort her small yet great hurts as best I can, assuring her she'll someday love her brother, hoping to plant the seeds that will grow to truth.

But I am preoccupied with preparations for the visit of my former husband. The urge to linger in Osthegn is nearly overwhelming. I could stay out of the way, remain ignored in the background, just to see him again. To see if he really has changed so much. My heart contracts, though I'd thought it had long since ceased to do so for him, especially after what he did to our daughter. But the mark of true love is that it can be smothered, forgotten, blinded, and waylaid, but it is impossible to extinguish. And for that reason, if no other, I must not stay at Osthegn. The risk of discovery is too great.

Lauresa is ambivalent regarding her father's impending visit. She is agitated, unable to sit. Her sudden rise from the chair by the fire wakes Allenry, but that merely provides her the excuse to pace back and forth, jiggling him.

"But why now? He's never felt the need to come before. Not for my wedding, not when …" She glances over at Allaigna, who is lining up wooden chess pieces on the hearth like a choir, or perhaps rows of soldiers.

I motion to Lauresa to follow me to the window seat on the far side of the great curtained bed. We can see Allaigna through the open curtains, but the quiet chatter of her monologue is muffled by drapery.

"He was ill for a long time after your wedding, Lauresa," I murmur, "both in body and mind. The guilt——"

"Guilt?" breaks in Lauresa, louder, I think, than she wanted. She glances at her daughter, but Allaigna still plays blithely by herself. "Over what?"

I weigh my reply before it escapes my lips. "He married you off to a foreign lord, sent you on a journey that nearly killed you. For more than two weeks, he thought it had. How might you think that sits on a man's conscience?"

"If it was enough to make him ill, he might have reconsidered before actually sending me." Lauresa's voice is brittle. "What sort of illness, anyway?"

I turn my eyes toward the window so as not to have to look at my daughter. "An illness of the mind, my love. You must not judge him too harshly. It is likely he was suffering from it long before you left home."

"How long?" I can hear from her voice that Lauresa is taken aback.

Chanist showered her with affection when he was around. And when he was not … he simply was not. Had her memories not been clouded, she might have questioned his absences. But then again, she had been an adolescent, with all the self-centredness that implied.

"Still." She pulls back to the original subject. "Why now? Is this truly the first need he's had of a diplomatic visit to Aerach in five years?"

"Perhaps it is the first in which he'll have the time to stop and see you." I raise a hand to silence further argument. "In any case, it is imperative he not encounter me, so while he is here in Teillai, I will be in Aleran. There are many supplies I can't find here, and this is as good an excuse as any to make the trip."

Lauresa will not be silenced, though. "Why must he not know? What harm could possibly come now? And don't you want to see him again?"

I feel my eyes water despite myself. "I will see him again, but not now." I refocus. "And do you think Gwannyn would allow him to visit you if she knew I were here?"

Lauresa's head jerks back as if slapped. As if the thought has never occurred to her before. "Could she stop him? He is Prince of Brandishear!"

"Oh, I think she could quite easily," I reply. "But you tell me. You know her better than I do."

My daughter's frown increases as she realizes, for the first time in her life, who truly rules Brandishear.

What I have told Lauresa is true: there will be a time when Chanist and I meet again. It may even be within these walls. But the details of that future encounter are still unclear to me, hazed with a worrying sense of peril and change. I can do nothing but wait. I can see the present at will, regardless of distance, but the future only comes to me when it wants to.

Back in my workroom, I deride my wandering thoughts and continue to prepare the ingredients. The tincture I make for Lauresa to administer to her father I have made once before. It was when Lauresa was sixteen, not long after the birth of her cousin Genissa's baby, when the shutters of Chanist's mind first began to swing in the breeze of madness. I am still unsure what caused that loss of reason, for it was well covered up by Gwannyn and her advisors, and not a breath of it reached beyond the walls of the Royal Apartments — except for the words dear Ceilaf gave his young squire to carry to me.

I prepared this potion then, and Ceilaf ensured Chanist received it. It worked. It slaked the Prince's madness for a time, and, as Einavar later told me, perhaps saved a life or two. Now I have no insider within the Bastion. Ceilaf is dead, and that pain still burns when I think of his sacrifice. Lauresa's old nurse Dennein has been dismissed now that the last of Gwannyn's children have grown. So Chanist will have to come here, to my demesne. Where, if I cannot tend his sanity myself, I can at least leave the task in my daughter's hands.

Verse 8

Morran Rhoan

"The lad is in my employ," Doniver informed Rhoan as he handed me back to my original escort. "But I prefer it if he appears to be in yours. I understand he can sing a bit—you might find him useful."

"The message, my lord," I reminded him.

"The message?"

I scowled as much as I dared.

"Ah, yes," he recalled. "You're to carry word to a pair of vagabonds—the boy will tell you their location—and inform them I hereby lift all burden of obligation and debt. They are free from service, and I will press no charge upon them."

"And the papers, milord."

"Of course, of course." He reached into his doublet with a lazy gesture. "Give them these as well."

He passed Rhoan the two squares of parchment I had carefully read as he'd drafted and sealed them. Neither Raddick nor Dog could read, but if they kept these papers safe, they would hold Doniver to his word.

I was not a prisoner—not exactly. I had the run of White Tooth and most of Castle Doniver. I imagine I could even have left if I wanted to. However, I knew the moment I did so, messages would go out to Teillai, and rangers would be on my trail by the time I walked through the city gates. I was a prisoner of unspoken threats.

Morran Rhoan delivered the message and the papers, or so he said, and the words he carried back to me from Raddick gave me cause to believe him.

"The scruffy gentleman said nothing but clicked and gestured. I suspect him to be mute," said Rhoan, slinging his gloves and riding cloak carelessly over the bench and stretching his long legs out before the fire. Though the day had been warm, the spring nights were still cold. "The slightly less ragged lad babbled confusedly for a bit."

I was surprised at the warm rush of relief I felt at hearing Raddick had indeed made it safely back. I'd only known him and Dog three days, but our brief and intense sojourn in the woods had made me oddly protective of them, and of Raddick in particular.

Rhoan continued. "When he finally began making sense, he commended himself to you." He paused with a performer's flair. "Let me see if I can remember the words. 'Oi'm indebted to … er … 'im, body and soul.'"

It was a great exaggeration of Raddick's rural accent, but Rhoan delivered it with such an accurate portrayal of the boy's hat-twisting hands and perpetually surprised eyebrows that I couldn't help but smile.

"And he sent me back with a jug-headed, sway-backed creature he claims is yours."

My heart jumped.

"I left him in the stables, but you'll have to pay his board, I'm afraid. Favours only go so far."

I hadn't dreamed of getting Nag back. I'd assumed Dog and Raddick would simply take him as theirs, and I was prepared to let them have him with my blessing. That Raddick had returned him with no thought to his own gain both warmed and saddened me.

"And ..." I hardly dared ask. "My tack?"

"In the stables as well, of course. Oh, and I suppose you want these." He reached behind the settle and pulled out the bundle he'd dropped there upon entering.

I turned to the bundle of my belongings: my bedroll, my bow wrapped in waxed cloth, my quiver. Rhoan reached over my shoulder and picked up the green- and gold-scabbarded sword. He drew it halfway, peering at the ripples of watered Ilvan steel.

"Where does a poor apprentice singer get a pretty little pig-sticker like this?" he mused. His choice of the word 'pig-sticker' made me wonder what exactly he had learned from either Doniver or Raddick about my adventures of the past week. "None of my business, I'll be bound," he concluded, though I could tell already that his was a personality which would leave no mystery unearthed for long. He clacked the blade home in its scabbard and tossed it to me. "This may be none of my business either," he said as I caught the sword, more grateful than ever to have it back in my hands. He leaned forward in a swift motion, like a bird targeting a worm: poised and ready to strike. "But tell me, does the young Lord Doniver know you're a girl?"

I jerked back, fumbling in my head for an answer.

If I told him yes, what did that indicate about my relationship with Doniver? More than I wanted known.

"No," I lied, hoping to deflect further inquiry. "How did you know?" Maybe asking would flatter him. I was so deeply embroiled in lies, what was one more?

He laughed. "I'm not as blind as all that. Not as blind as you think Doniver is either. But rest assured, I did thoroughly rifle through your saddlebags to be sure."

He laughed again despite the mounting fury that must have been growing on my face. "Just so we both know where we stand. Or sit."

Although ostensibly Morran Rhoan's apprentice, I really had little to do during the day. My keeper slept till the noon bells most days, spent his afternoons I know not where, and appeared back in the great hall in time to sing and tell stories for the evening.

He surprised me one afternoon when he strolled into the archery yard as I was sinking goose-feathered shafts into a butt with a dull rhythm born of boredom and frustration.

"You're a fair shot for such a slight g — I mean lad," he whispered behind me, making my shot go wide and rattle across the ground, scattering hens who'd wandered out from the kitchen coops.

I glared at him and ran to retrieve the arrow. He twisted the others from the straw of the butt and handed them to me with elaborate courtesy.

"Where did you learn to shoot like that?"

I pretended not to hear him, busying myself with examining the fletch on the mis-shot arrow.

"And where did you get such a lovely bow?" He took it from where it leaned against my thigh and turned it over, testing the pull and eyeing the wood. "Elalantar work, if I'm not mistaken."

I snatched it back. Rhiadne had given me that bow. I hadn't seen her since she'd taken a captaincy in Brandishear, and thinking about the woman who'd taught me to hunt and track like a ranger, and who'd treated me like a younger sister rather than a duke's daughter, put a lump in my throat I could do without.

"Interesting," Rhoan continued. "I had one very similar, once. Harwen Elsing. They're very rare. His daughter gave it to me." His face looked different somehow. Sad, almost. "I lost it not long after I lost her."

On the base of the grip of my bow, right below where one's little finger sat, were the initials *H* and *E*. They were entwined with plants and a pair of chasing hounds, making them hard to see unless you knew where to look. I remembered Rhiadne showing them to me the day I shot three bull's-eyes in a row, and she gave me that bow.

"There," Rhiadne had said. "My father's mark. He's famous in Elalantar — and across the Ilmar. One of the finest bowyers and fletchers outside the Valnirata. Or at least he was."

"Was?" I asked. "Is he dead?" Back then, at the age of nine, I had very little in the way of tact.

She shook her head, a bitter look crossing her face. "You can't make a bow with only one hand."

I waited for her to explain, but she said nothing.

"It's pretty," I said, to break the uneasy silence.

"It's more than that," she agreed, her eyes seeming moist. "It's exquisite. It's the first one he ever made for me. It doesn't have the range of this" — she stroked the pale wood of her five-foot-tall longbow — "or even that." She pointed to the curved cavalry bow leaning against the stone wall. "I've not used it in years, yet still I carry it with me.

"But a bow should be used, Allaigna. The wood grows stiff and cracks if it is not. And a tool not used for its purpose is a vain and wasteful thing. I want you to have it."

I took the well-loved wood from her hands, hardly aware at that tender age of the great gift she'd given me.

Back in the present, I eyed Rhoan. I wanted to ask how he knew Rhiadne, and if it was before or after I had. But those sorts of questions would reveal far too much about me. I unstrung the bow, gathered my arrows, and bid good afternoon to Morran Rhoan.

Later that afternoon, I sat in the quarters I shared with Rhoan, running an oily rag back and forth across the carved shaft of the bow. The whorls and lumps of the pattern were as familiar and soothing as the turned posts of my bed back in Osthegn or the cracked and dimpled wood of my mazer.

That Doniver allowed me to retain my weapons seemed to say I was no prisoner. And yet I was not free to walk out of White Tooth. How long, I wondered, was he planning to keep me here? How good was his promise not to advertise my presence? And what would he extract from me in return?

It was all I could do to sit and calmly clean my weapons rather than bolting for the stables and riding out, no matter the pursuit. But doing so would only ensure I would become a prisoner in fact rather than in theory. I needed an ally, and the most likely, drunken dilettante though he was, was Morran Rhoan.

Before I could decide to trust him, I needed to know more about him, and to do that, I had to befriend him. It wasn't in my nature, but it was something I'd learned from watching Garæthiel, and, I realized with an old stab of pain, from Goff. Those two could make friends of almost anyone. A shared confidence, a point in common, some small form of connection was all it took.

Until now, there had been no connection I could make with Rhoan. I knew nothing about him other than that he slept late, drank late, and was a musician of at least moderate skill. My ability to sing was far too personal, and too linked to the talent I didn't dare advertise, to serve as common ground. But the bow … that was my way in.

Using a silvered glass I'd 'borrowed' from the Dowager's lady's maid, I adjusted my appearance. It was a fine balance between maintaining my current boy's guise and allowing enough girl-ishness to come through. I brushed my hair thoroughly for the first time since leaving home and washed my face more carefully than I had in nearly as long. I had only the clothes I'd left home with, but I sang a small ditty, whitening the stains on the shirt cuffs and generally making myself presentable. This alone didn't make me more feminine, just less grubby and offensive.

I bit my lip as I regarded myself in the glass, wondering if I should find some rouge to pink my cheeks and lips. But I wasn't trying to seduce him. I wanted him to feel sorry for me. Protective, even. Still, I loosened the laces at my collar more than usual. I didn't have cleavage to expose, but my blue-veined, too-white skin was vulnerable and young looking. I considered singing a glamour over myself to enhance the effect, to make him want to help me. But though I knew in theory how such enchantments worked, I lacked the skill, as well as the knowledge of men's minds to be sure of myself. As a final touch, I swept the rushes out of our apartment and replaced them with fresh ones, adding generous handfuls of dried rosemary and lavender for remembrance and love.

Nothing remained to do but sit and wait until he made his inebriated way back upstairs.

Lauresa's Chorus

"Yes, Angeley. I know." Lauresa rolls her eyes at her mother, taking the bottle of brown liquid. "A dram in his cup at least once a day. Preferably twice."

Angeley sighs and wraps her arms around herself, nodding. "Yes, you've got it. But it's not just the tonic. It's what you say and do that will affect the cure."

Her mother untwines her arms, taking Lauresa's hands in her own. "Be the loving daughter you once were. Smile, and be gentle with him." Her mother deliberately relaxes her brow, trying to erase the frown on her daughter's by example. It won't work, determines Lauresa.

"I know you have so much anger left." Angeley takes one hand and places it on her daughter's chest just above the milk-heavy breasts.

As much as I had toward you, Mother, Lauresa thinks.

"As much as you must still have for me." Angeley echoes her daughter's unspoken words uncannily. "But withhold it for now. If you must … If you must release it, don't confront him till he's been here at least a few days."

Lauresa nods. "I understand. Allow your magic time to work."

Angeley shakes her head. "Not my magic," she insists. "Yours."

And before Lauresa can ask her what she means by that, her mother has enveloped her in a swift embrace and stepped out of the workroom en route to Aleran, leaving Lauresa truly alone and in charge of her castle for the first time since her daughter was born. It is a frightening yet heady feeling.

Chanist, Prince High of Brandishear, arrives in Aerach under the guise of a knight ambassador, insignificant enough not to be known widely, but important enough to have a retinue. If anyone remarks on how unusually large and well equipped the retinue, they assume Ambassador Ceilaf, as he calls himself, to have a fat purse from long years of campaigning followed by long years of royal service. Which would have been true, Lauresa thinks, her chest contracting, if the real Ceilaf had lived so long.

It shocks and angers her to have the memory of the man who'd died in her service sullied by a convenient charade. It makes practical sense, but it only adds to the confusing mix of emotions battling for supremacy in Lauresa's heart as the herald announces his arrival.

Chanist leaps down like a man of fewer years and strides across the yard, leaving the stable boy to catch the reins of the stallion.

"Lauresa ..." His arms spread wide, as if for an embrace, before he recalls himself. "I mean, your Grace." He bends, sweeps off his hat, and kisses her hand. There is a mischievous glint in his eyes, and none, that she can see, of the madness her mother spoke of.

Still, she is wary. Not just because of the alleged madness, but because she still does not know how she feels about this man who sold her off to Andreg in return for power. Time has not healed all the wounds. But she can play her part.

"Ceilaf." She reaches her arms out, returning the embrace he stopped himself from giving. "It is so very good to see you again, my old friend." The statement is made for the benefit of the onlookers, but for the most part, it is true.

"**Lauresa,**" calls Chanist, just as she's about to leave her father and his squire to sort out their baggage in the guest chamber.

He crosses to the door, out of range of the squire's hearing, and leans against the lintel.

"When might I see my grandchildren?" He's not a very tall man, and his eyes are level with Lauresa's, his bearded face and slightly beery breath a mixture of familiarity and uncomfortable distance. The jug of ale that was brought up when he arrived has been drained already, and only a small portion of that was taken by the squire to slake the dust of the road.

She leans away from his breath, wishing she felt happier about seeing her father for the first time in five years. Still, the watery blue eyes before her don't disguise the longing.

"Soon, Papa," she promises. "Allenry is still napping, and Allaigna should be, though she's probably playing with the litter of pups in the kennel. Why don't you rest and change from your travelling clothes" — *and let that beer settle,* she thinks — "and I'll bring them to you when they're both awake and clean."

And hope you are the same is the unspoken addendum.

She gives him a dutiful daughterly kiss on the cheek and closes the door after herself.

Her first destination is straight to the buttery to ensure that only very well-watered wine is sent to the guest chamber. Her next is the nursery, where, as she can tell from the ache in her breasts before she's halfway back up the stairs, Allenry is waiting for his lunch.

When the junior nurse brings Allaigna, filthy from the kennels and disgruntled at having been interrupted at play, Lauresa is still wrestling with her dilemma. Allenry has fallen back asleep at the breast, so Lauresa has to lean over him to kiss her daughter. The child squirms out of the embrace, prickly and put out.

"Allaigna, love, I need you to wash and put on your best gown."

Allaigna twists her face into a deeper scowl. "Why? I don't like it. It's itchy."

"There's someone I want you to meet."

The scowl twists deeper still, and the child glares at her mother but eventually complies.

The decision is still not made when Lauresa heads for the guest chamber with a shiny yet surly child in her train and a dozing baby in her arms.

She holds her breath, hoping her father is respectably awake. She sent a page to warn him of his family's imminent visit half an hour ago. That must have been enough time.

The held breath partially escapes as his voice, clear and loud, responds to her knock. There he is, in the large armchair by the hearth, clothed in fine court garb, as regal and yet welcoming as she remembers him from childhood.

She releases the rest of her breath and takes a long, slow one back in. The windows are open, the air is clear, and her decision is made. There have been enough lies surrounding her family. She will not add more to the burden, nor deny her children at least one honest relationship. Bad enough Allaigna knows her grandmother only as a nurse; bad enough she'll never know her father.

She touches her daughter's shoulder and whispers, "Curtsy," out of the corner of her mouth. The girl is still learning that skill and accomplishes it unwillingly, but with enough childish charm to widen Chanist's smile and bring one to Lauresa's lips as well.

"Allaigna, love, this is your grandfather."

Allaigna cocks her head to one side and stares at Chanist. "My grandfather is dead," she declares. "And the other one is the Prince of Bandi ... Brand ..."

"Brandishear," supplies Chanist, chuckling. "And since I'm still more or less alive, old though I might be, I must be the 'other one.'"

He rises from his chair, makes a deep obeisance, and takes her small soft hand in his large square one, kissing the fingers.

"I am delighted to meet my only granddaughter at last, your Grace."

Lauresa is impressed with his charm. Any attempt at hugs or kisses would have instantly estranged her thorny daughter.

He straightens with a hand on his back. "Oof. Alas, I'm out of practice — or perhaps too old — for such courtly manners." He winks at Allaigna, charming her all over again. "Shall we come to an arrangement? We shall not bow and curtsy to one another, and you may call me 'Grandpapa' if I need not call you 'your Grace'."

Allaigna solemnly weighs this offer and nods with a dignity beyond her years. "All right … Grandpapa." The last word rolls out slowly, as if she tasted it first.

"Wonderful! And will you introduce me to your brother, your Gr — I mean, Allaigna?"

Her tiny shoulders slump a little as she remembers she's not the sole centre of attention. But she dutifully stands on tiptoe as Lauresa lowers her arms to reveal the now wide-awake face nestled in them.

"Grandpapa, this is Allenry." She can't help wrinkling her nose a little at the name. "You don't need to call him anything special. Allenry, this is His, um, Royal Highness, the um, Prince of B … Ba … Brandrishear." This time Chanist lets her struggle with the word on her own. She leans close to the baby then, and whispers, though both the adults can hear.

"You must bow to him, or you'll go to prison."

I'm glad you told her who I am," says Chanist to his daughter, as Allaigna, done with grown-ups, hurries off to the busy life of a child.

Lauresa watches her go, her mind wandering its own paths. "Mm," she finally agrees, shifting her gaze to her father. Her mother's words come back to her. *Do not push him, accuse him, confront him until he's been here a se'ennight.* She allows herself only the softest wary scrutiny of him as she responds. "With Allenis's parents dead, you're the only grandparent she's met." A lie. The only grandparent she knows she's met. "The only grandfather she has. How could I deny her that?"

"She's only three. Can she keep my identity a secret?"

"She's nearly four. But of course not." She lifts a hand to forestall any argument. "And it will be impossible to maintain this charade of your presence within the walls of Osthegn at any rate."

He frowns at the knuckles of his hand. He is struggling with the instinct to fight with her so soon into their reunion.

To his fingernails, he says, "Brandishear's Prince cannot spend time as a guest of House Andreg. It would upset the balance of power between Aerach's duchies — and between Aerach's throne and Teillai as well."

She sighs, exasperated, and breathes again, fighting the urge to fight. Old habits always come to the fore in families; she knows that. But why is it their stormy relationship from just before her marriage that resurfaces rather than those long, golden years when he was the ideal father and she the loving child?

Perhaps because he is no longer the ideal father. And she no longer a child.

"Of course I know that, Papa," she says in the gentlest voice she can muster. "I live here, remember? But it is only important that you are not *seen* to be visiting here. Outside these castle walls, it's known that Ambassador Ceilaf is here — my old bondsman from girlhood. Those who notice that I feel for him as I do a father would not be wrong." She catches a flicker in his eyes and hurries on. "But I trust my household. It is unfair to them to keep your identity from them. And unfair to the children."

"It's your house, my dear, and I bow to your wisdom within it." Before he dips his head in mock courtesy, she catches a glint in his eyes but is unsure whether it is one of admiration or criticism.

Lauresa grits her teeth. She wants to, but doesn't dare, kick her husband's ankle beneath the small table. Andreg has hoisted the pitcher yet again and is refilling both his and Chanist's cups. The wine is strong, unwatered, and — worse — untainted by her mother's tincture.

Her father has been unwittingly consuming the tincture for only two days, which is not enough time, according to Irdaign, to make drink intolerable. How she wishes her mother were here now. But of course, the web of lies must remain. Andreg must not know Angeley is Irdaign, and Chanist must not know his former wife lives here and not at Aldac.

His initial reaction to the taste of wine is overcome soon by the masculine camaraderie engendered by great draughts of the stuff and the constant replenishment of his cup. After the first cup he forgets he dislikes the taste, and after the third he cannot taste it at all, fine Myrwater red though it is.

The chatelaine in her also balks at this guzzling of expensive cellared wine, imported at considerable cost from the south of Brandishear. But of course her husband has his insecurities, and it will not do for him to serve her father any less a vintage than he would find at the table on a Rheran feast day. Never mind that it is Lauresa who has chosen this wine, fit it into the butler's budget, arranged its shipment, and overseen its delivery. Never mind that at this rate half the cask will be gone by tomorrow and none left for the autumn feast. Lauresa is no more than sipping. Red wine gives her a headache, and more than a glass will pass her hangover to Allenry. The last thing she needs is a cranky, dry-mouthed baby waking her in the early hours of morning. Especially with Angeley gone.

Her reverie is smashed by a roar of laughter which awakens Allenry from his nap in Andreg's bed. They are having this private dinner in Andreg's chamber, and Lauresa has placed the baby on the bed rather than take him up to her own rooms. She stands, scoops him up, and begins the bouncing sway now ingrained in her bones.

Chanist opens his arms.

"Here, give him to me, Resa."

She hesitates, but deems her father still sober enough to hold a baby. At least if he's sitting.

"No, don't get up, Father." She leans over and places the wuffling Allenry in Chanist's arms. The baby will want feeding soon, but for now he keeps the cup out of her father's hands.

Chanist leans back in his chair, a smile of contentment on his face. Allenry, miraculously, doesn't fuss but relaxes against his grandfather's chest. *Maybe he's been knocked unconscious by the fumes,* Lauresa thinks uncharitably.

"Ah, I've missed this," murmurs Chanist. "I love a sleepy baby … and babies love me … I could always get you to sleep on my chest when your mother was exhausted by your demands." He smiled and patted his chest. "Babies know they can't get anything but a warm place to sleep from this."

Lauresa glances at Andreg, who has been puzzled into silence. As proud as he is of his male heir, he generally prefers to show him off in the arms of his wife, as a matched set. He's probably only held Allenry half a dozen times in the boy's life. He is having a hard time reconciling the Prince of Brandishear with the delighted grandfather who rocks the babe back to sleep, looking for all the world like a grizzled nursemaid.

A swell of unleashed tears brims up beneath her eyes, both for the father she no longer has and the father her children will never have. At least they have a grandfather for now, however long that lasts.

Chanist echoes her thoughts. "I'm so sorry I never got to hold wee Allaigna like this." His eyes are wet, as if the quantities of wine he's consumed are leaking out.

"I'm sorry too, Father," she murmurs, though even those few words clog her throat.

Andreg looks more and more uncomfortable. Family intimacy is not his strength, and he has become the intruder here.

Chanist reaches out with his free hand and touches Lauresa on the cheek. "You look so much like your mother. Sometimes I wonder if I left any mark on you at all."

It is a dangerous statement in Andreg's presence, with mention of Allaigna still hanging in the air. She catches the hand, holds it to her cheek.

"Your ears," she says with a smile, "and your temper."

He looks at her in surprise, pulls his hand free, and lifts the curtain of blonde curls that hangs over her shoulder. "My ears? Really?"

He drops the hair and feels his own ear — small, compact, and flat to the head like a seal's. "By Fingal, girl, I do believe you're right!" He laughs. "But just in shape, I hope … not my tone-deafness?"

"Not quite as bad as you, Father," she laughs in reply. "I can carry a tune with a lot of other voices and instruments. But not like——" She hesitates, knowing she should not remember her mother well.

He finishes for her. "No one in the world has a voice like your mother's," he says softly.

She lets that lie, grieving for the first time for the wife her father has lost.

Allenis has taken the opportunity created by his exclusion to refill his cup and his father-in-law's. Lauresa shoots an angry scowl at him across the table. He half-closes his eyes, smiles languidly, and ignores her. Of course, he has no reason not to: she hasn't told him of her father's condition, and not only because she doesn't want to hand Brandishear's secrets into Aerach's hands. She can't bear to see her father's dignity reduced in her husband's eyes.

Chanist raises his hand, refusing the refilled cup. "Not while I hold such precious cargo." He pats the wheezy Allenry in the back, swaying from side to side. A tuneless humming emanates from his chest.

As if he's forgotten he's already said it, he repeats his earlier statement. "Such a shame, such a shame I missed so many of Allaigna's early years."

"Then you will have to do double duty, Father, to make up lost time. This is your first visit here since I've been wed. I hope it won't be your last."

This time it is Andreg's turn to look daggers at his spouse.

Verse 9
Faces Past

Even in his drunken state, Morran Rhoan paused on the threshold of the apartment, his eye sharpening momentarily as he took in the subtle changes I'd wrought in the room and on myself.

"Glad yer up, boy," he slurred, dropping his heavy wooden harp into my lap. "Y'can oil and restring that now, 'stead of lettin' it sit till morning like you usually do."

Though I resented the work and his incrimination, I was glad enough for something to occupy my hands. And the muted burr of the harp strings as I turned the instrument over would be useful as well.

He dropped his long form into the large, leather-lined chair by the fire, limbs sprawling as if to occupy all of the small anteroom.

"Stroke of luck finding you, boy-girl." He laughed at the angry look I shot him. "My small room wasn't nearly so nice as these." He waved a loose-boned hand about his head, indicating the three rooms that made our apartment. "Lucky for me he seems to want a close eye kept on you."

I forced a wide-eyed expression, and though I knew full well the answer, asked, "What do you mean?"

He lifted a lazy eyebrow at me. "Why move me from a poorly furnished room next to the great hall to these rather pleasant chambers unless he needed to keep you high in this tower?"

I could barely breathe. Rhoan was leading the conversation exactly where I wanted with no help from me at all, and I was now terrified a wrong word would send it off course.

"Unless ..." He glanced sharply at me, eyes clear through the fog of wine. "You said he doesn't know you're a girl?"

My eyes went as wide as I could make them. "I never told him," I whispered. It was true enough. "Why would I?"

"Why? Why ask me?" His voice slurred once more. "I don't even know why you want to dress as a boy, so I'm the least-informed person here." He leaned over the arm of the chair and peered at me foggily. "Why *do* you pretend to be a lad? I'm sure you'd be a much prettier girl."

My hand jumped to my throat, pulling the neck of my shirt together. This was not where I wanted the conversation to go.

"Do you think he knows?" I pleaded, begging him to take the bait back to the intended trail.

"Well ..." He wiped a hand down the length of his face as he did when thinking, closing his eyes and drawing his long features down farther still. "Why else put you far away from the prying eyes of the hall?"

Because I'm his fiancée, I couldn't help thinking, hoping the thought wasn't as plain on my face as it was in my head.

"What did he tell you?" I asked.

I withstood the foggy gaze again. "That you are a runaway apprentice from Erelin. That he heard you sing one night and took pity on you. Rather than delivering you back to your old master, he delivered you to me. Out of the goodness of his heart.

Though I've always suspected young Doniver has very little of that beneath his ribs.

"But," he continued, sagging back into the chair, "if he knows you're a girl, why … why …" He fell quiet, staring at me with the unnerving clarity that swept in and out of him.

It set me wondering myself. Surely Doniver would expect Rhoan to see through my disguise sooner or later. So was his promise to maintain my secret empty? Was he deliberately trying to expose me second-hand?

I had to know more about Rhoan before I could decide. I dropped the oily rag in the rushes and set his harp upright in my lap. Picking a string at random, I plucked it, testing the sound. No … not that one.

Morran's gaze was still pointed toward me, but not at me. As if he were staring through me.

I plucked another string, felt its resonance: yes, that one was part of it. Before the sound died I added one more string, but it was major. I muted it with my wrist, cursing inwardly. Angeley had trained my voice, and I'd taught myself to sing small spells, but I'd never learned to play the harp well enough to know from sight which strings could make the spell I needed.

Two more strings, plucked together … Ah, these were right. I could feel the harmonics blend and intersect, waves colliding and multiplying. This would be so much easier if I could use my voice, but I needed to speak.

"The bowyer's daughter," I said, my voice so soft it barely rose above the rhythmic tapping on the two strings I'd chosen. "Was her name … Rhiadne?"

He blinked, his gaze sharpening again. I kept my fingers moving, a metronomic alternation between minor third and root, the fifth coming in like a drone every twelve counts. It took enormous concentration to keep it constant while talking and listening, even more to keep it soft and subtle, no more than the twiddle of idle fingers.

All signs of drunkenness were gone as the man focussed his dark eyes on me.

"What makes you … ask that, lass?" he said.

In the end, I didn't need to sing a spell to gain his trust. The mention of my old tutor unblocked some latent torrent within him. Their relationship dated from before Rhiadne had left Elalantar and crossed the *Brôna Cæbann* to sell her sword to House Andreg.

The Kingfisher Queen, as Elalantar's Princess High was known, had summoned Rhiadne's father to court. Rhoan, besotted as only young lovers can be, had followed, playing his lute and composing maudlin ballads, while Rhiadne, scarcely older than I was now, occupied her time helping her father teach the young ladies of the court to shoot. One of these ladies had overheard a proclamation of Rhoan's adoration and mistaken it for something directed at her. That the lady was already enamoured of Rhoan helped her to this conclusion. The comedy of mistaken intent led to Rhoan being chased from Caella with the hired swords of the girl's father on his heels, and Rhiadne close on theirs. Where poetry could not warm her heart, his plight could. They fled together, taking ship for Brandishear. Their misfortune wasn't over, however, for the carrack was attacked by pirates. Rhoan was struck unconscious, stripped of his belongings, and left for dead on the wallowing deck of the ship. What happened to his lover, he never found out, though he returned to Elalantar and went by foot to every town between Farwiel and Sudry in search of her.

I knew the end of her story, though Rhiadne had never mentioned Rhoan's name to me. With her rich clothes, she had been taken hostage. She maintained the pretence of noble birth for some time, knowing it might save her from rape at least. But when the pirates learned at last she had no ransomable value, she threw her lot in with them, her skills with the bow unprecedented among the ranks of most mariners. But she was no sailor and longed for the firm feel of land beneath her boots. So she left them on the Isle of Orey, from where she joined the first militia she came across. Her rise to lieutenant of the Duke's rangers was almost inevitable from there.

What coincidence, what strange confluence of fates had thrown Rhoan onto my path? I wondered darkly if it was the meddling of that self-styled Queen of Fates, my grandmother, extending her long arm yet again. I put that thought out of my head for the time being. Dwelling on her could drive a person mad.

Rhoan, though, wept for joy upon hearing Rhiadne was still alive, and from then on, he was mine.

Now I needed to get around Tiern Doniver. Each day since he'd stationed me in his keep, he called me to his study sometime after the noonday meal. Still convinced I was on a diplomatic or espionage mission sanctioned by my father, he questioned me daily about the situation in the Valnirata. I truly knew nothing — less than he, in fact — but with a skill learned from Garæthiel, I turned his questions around, letting him suppose I'd given him answers. I was continually astonished it worked, yet I had little idea what else to do. Our discussions went something like this:

"My scouts have reported unusual activity on the eastern borders."

I would raise an eyebrow, leaning forward with interest. "Did your scouts identify their clan markings?"

He might shake his head.

"Dress, then? What marks did they wear?" It was a senseless question. I knew next to nothing about the clan tattoos or manner of dress.

He would reply, "They didn't report on such details."

I in turn might roll my eyes at such ignorance, secretly frustrated, for I wanted the information for myself as well.

"Is it Oskaniia, do you think?"

"How can I speculate without more details?" But my glance let him think he was right. And why not?

And so this cat-and-mouse game went: me pretending to know something and him pretending to have only Aerach's good at heart. But on the ninth day, the game changed.

"I tire of this, Allaigna," he said, provocatively using my real name.

Suspicion froze my face. I waited, wondering what new snare he had set for me, but he simply stared, thumb and knuckle pulling at his lower lip, his eyes burning into and past mine, forcing me to ask.

"Tire of what?" As soon as I'd spoken, I realized my mistake. Our relationship had changed. I was relaxed enough to question him, and that familiarity meant he no longer had to step with care around me.

"This charade. This game of telling me nothing every day. Either you're a better spy than I would credit possible for a fifteen-year-old, or you're nothing more than a runaway I should send packing back to her parents."

There was nothing I could say to these twinned accusations, for I had worked hard to keep his assessment of me balanced between these thoughts. To tip the scales either way seemed precarious, and I had no idea which side held the greater peril.

"And also," he continued, "I'm tired of sitting face to face with a grubby boy. He waved toward a bundle of cloth sitting on the bench by the fire. "That ought to fit. Put it on, and we'll continue this conversation over dinner."

I moved to the bundle and unrolled it. It was a dress, used but fine, in House Doniver's colours of gold and vair. It probably belonged to one of his sisters. Or mistresses.

I crumpled it to my chest and spun back to face him.

"You swore to protect my anonymity," I hissed.

"In exchange for your cooperation and information. Do you feel you've fulfilled your end of the bargain?"

"As best I can." It was true, in a way.

"Well, your best, in this case, seems inadequate. I require more. And as lord of the castle in all but name, that is within my power to attain."

"What are you threatening?" I asked through clenched jaws.

"I'm threatening nothing, Allaigna. Only requesting your presence in a more amiable situation, over a meal, and with your true face."

"This is my face." As I said the words, I realized they were true. I was more at home in my boy's guise than I would be in any dress, no matter how fine.

"But not the one your father sold me, I'm afraid. Don't look so affronted. You came with a dowry of certain powers and privileges, but your bride price is as high as any in Aerach, including that of Vishod's bastard daughters."

I didn't want to ask, but couldn't stop myself. "Why?" My voice sounded despicably meek.

"Why indeed? Looking at what I have before me"—he drew his hands through the air, presenting me to myself—"I'm hard pressed to answer that."

I felt the blood rising in my cheeks, half in embarrassment, half in fury.

"It might be your valuable heritage as daughter of Aerach's rising military star or as granddaughter of Brandishear's well-established one. Oh, I know that part is not widely advertised, but you don't buy a mare without looking at the pedigree first."

The heat in my cheeks was all fury now.

"Or it might just be that your parents value you. Not beyond price—but nearly."

How wrong you are, I thought. That chilling thought slowed my rage, let me remain silent for three long breaths. At last I spoke.

"So you would trot me out in borrowed finery, assess my gaits, check my teeth?" *I warn you, though*, I continued in my head, *they are sharp.* My fingers twitched, wanting the sword that lay safely stowed in my room.

"I would have a better look at the *girl* I've agreed to marry, yes." His reply was mild, but the threat still felt present.

And if you don't like what you see? I thought. *Or worse, if you do?*

What was to stop him consummating the marriage early? It would ensure I'd not be married off to anyone else. And it might lower the bride price my father could still demand.

Terrified, but determined not to show it, I folded the gown over my arm.

"And what if anyone sees me in this?"

"Wear a cloak and hood. There is a back stair that runs from the tower base to my apartment. I'll leave the door unlocked."

"And Rhoan? Will he not wonder where I am?"

Doniver looked at me, suddenly taken by a thought.

"Does he know who you are?"

"No."

"That you're a girl?"

I shook my head. Lying seemed so much easier these days.

"How unusually thick of him. If he spent less time in his cups, perhaps he would have you figured by now. But don't worry. I'll send notice I've put you to work in the library. He'll never miss you."

I nodded and left, my curtsy hardly hinted at.

This must not happen, I thought. The next thought was, *Tonight. It must be tonight.*

Irdaign's Chorus

Though I miss my daughter and grandchildren, I am glad to be in Aleran. There is a freedom to wandering the market stalls of the capital unknown and unfettered, for the time being, of responsibilities. It is not so grand or varied as Rheran, but near enough. It makes me feel almost young. For all that I have lived I'm not so old, I remind myself. Only forty-two, and thanks to Leisanmira lore and a varied and active life, not nearly so worn in appearance as many women of my years. I laugh to myself at this spark of vanity. And what good does my lingering beauty do? I have no husband or even admirer for whom to display it. I am no longer a princess, whose loveliness is needed to reflect the state of the realm. No, it is for me and me alone that I take pride in still being able to turn heads as I walk down the street. How many grandmothers can do that?

It is a shame Chanist is not so well-preserved.

The thought sobers me as I reach the inn where I've taken a room. I lay my bundles of herbs, packets of spices, buttons and coloured threads, steel needles, and bottles of oils and essences on the small table. From my pack I draw the scoured brass bowl I travel with and fill it with water from the ewer on the nightstand.

It takes a while for Chanist's image to form on the surface of the water, possibly because it so little matches the face from my memory. True, he is six years my senior, but he has aged far more than that. The sandy brown of his hair has been replaced almost entirely by white, and his beard, sparse when I married him, is clipped short but covers his chin and jaw in a dense thicket.

His eyes, his lovely soft blue eyes, are the same, though they are watery and red-lined and set in flesh that pouches below and creases above. I want to see hen's feet of laughter, but instead I see lines of anger. The jaw is still strong and square, squarer perhaps, with a stubborn cast that wasn't always there. Or was it? Is my memory touched with a golden glow?

Yet despite the disservice time and care have done to this face, it still stirs me. Not with the passion of youth that made me cast my nets upon it, but with a tender desire to care for it, to nurture and heal it.

And I could. I could easily restore his looks. We Leisanmira cannot turn the hourglass upside down, as some think we can, and restore lost youth. But I could heal what damage sorrow and drink have done, and bring him to the health a forty-eight-year-old should have. But only in person. And that I cannot do. By the terms of our divorce, we are allowed no contact but by written word. Breaching the terms of the divorce would allow the Lords to remove him from the throne and replace him with one of his daughters or son, or with Gwannyn, even.

Tears fall, shattering the image in the scrying bowl. For his sake I would do it. Not just for his health, but for his heart. The taste of happiness he and, I admit, I would earn if he were no longer Prince is sweet but deadly, and I will not indulge. The Ilmar needs him still.

The next time I see him in the bowl, he is in a full rage. A carafe of wine hurtles across the room, trailing pink droplets as it lands squarely in the hearth. His aim, at least, remains good.

His squire, still cowering, skulks over to mop up the mess. Sound fades in slowly, as if approaching from afar.

"... mind that! I said leave it, boy!" The squire jumps to his feet. "Are you a drudge or chambermaid? I said I want some decent wine, or damn it I'll have that butler striped."

The squire scurries from the room, and I am tempted to follow him with my Sight to see what gossip ensues amongst the servants. But it takes a more skilled farseer than I to split one's attention easily, and I do not want to lose track of my former husband.

He paces the room in a stumbling, uncoordinated way, then throws himself down on the armchair. One might think him drunk, but I'm sure these are instead the signs of withdrawal.

A knock comes on the chamber door, and it opens without pause for a reply. My daughter steps in, regal, poised like the water-bearer of legend, a new pitcher in her hand.

"Lauresa, darling." Chanist rises with difficulty and comes toward her, stumbling as he negotiates the bedpost. "I don't know what's the greater treat for these tired old eyes——your lovely face or that pitcher you're holding."

She turns a cheek for him to kiss, still elegant and composed. "Well, father, I hope you treat daughters better than pitchers." She nods toward the mess in the hearth. They stare at it, both aware that he in fact treats daughters much the same.

He puts a gnarled hand on her shoulder.

"I think you should have a word with that butler of yours, dear. The swill he sends me is dreadful. I think he's watering it."

Without responding, she crosses to the sideboard and pours him a small amount from the vessel she carries. It is dark, ruby red, and unwatered. And, I hope, it contains my tincture.

"Ah, that is so much better …" He takes an appreciative swallow, draining the small cup in one gulp.

The tincture is flavourless, and he doesn't notice its presence in the wine. But when Lauresa refills the cup, he merely sips. The third, he refuses altogether.

I hope the fortnight he is there will be enough time for the spell I sang into the tincture to work. Though it doesn't affect the taste of a drink, it affects the desire for it. If Lauresa offers him wine, mead, port, and brandy during these days, he should leave Teillai with the taste for none of them. It won't last forever, but it will help; and for now it is the best I can do.

When Chanist is gone on his way to Aleran, it is once more safe for me to return to Osthegn. I feel uneasy, a stranger in this castle I've made my home for the past four years. I tread lightly, like a cat ready to flee, and for the first time in years I feel the pull of the road, the urge to return to my travelling lifestyle. It is because things have changed here.

Lauresa is different. Sadder, more thoughtful, but also more content and more in charge. She has at last grown into her role as mistress of this demesne. But it is not just Lauresa. It is him: his ghost, his scent, still in the air of the guest chamber he vacated only two days ago. The aroma has changed but holds elements so close to the remembered scent of him it breaks my heart all over again.

I smell hers as she enters the room, that dear scent, closer even to my heart than his. But it is the sound I hear, the raindrop-like tattle of bare feet on warm stone, that roots me here.

"Jelly!" cries Allaigna as she tumbles into my arms.

"Oh, how I've missed you, my darling." I scoop her up, her tiny body settling itself comfortably astride my hip. "You will have to tell me all about your grandpapa's visit."

Verse 10

A Dangerous Dinner

I knocked on the door at the top of the narrow passage, my fingers plucking at the waist and bodice of the ill-fitting dress. The blue-and-grey velvet was fine enough. And the garment was well made. But it was made for a figure other than mine. Though Doniver had judged my height well enough, the whole dress hung shapeless on my peg-like frame.

"Enter," he called at last, and I pushed open a door so small even I had to duck to enter.

The scent of roast meat and decanted wine reached my nostrils before my eyes found Tiern Doniver in the softly lit room. The sideboard was already laden with food and drink; there would be no visits from servants tonight. The thought should have relieved me on account of my new appearance as a girl, but instead it made me nervous.

Doniver had just been washing his face. His reddish hair was damp and pushed back from a shiny forehead. He wore no doublet, only breeks and an unlaced lawn shirt. He was at least wearing boots, but those too were unlaced, sagging about his ankles.

As inexperienced as I was in such matters, I was in no doubt the setting was designed for seduction of one kind or another. And if that failed … would he truly force himself on me when all he had to do was wait? I was certain my charms were insufficient to cause a man to lose his judgement so.

He closed the distance between us, scooped up my cold rigid fingers, and kissed them. I snatched them back but refrained from wiping them on my skirts. Openly insulting him would probably be a bad idea.

"Welcome, Allaigna." He took me by both shoulders, held me at arm's length, and turned me back and forth. "You make a pretty boy, but an even prettier girl."

I snorted, as indelicately as possible. I would not give in to his pretence of courtesy. "What is it you wished to discuss? I haven't had time to do more translation since this afternoon."

He smiled, undeterred, and pulled out a chair. "Sit. Please share the board with me."

I did sit, arms crossed, legs akimbo, still as ungirlish as possible.

It seemed to amuse him, for he chuckled while he brought over the flagon of wine, the platter of quail, and a loaf of bread.

I accepted a glass of wine but barely let it wet my lips. I could tell from the touch on my tongue it was an excellent vintage, velvety and rich, tasting of honey and oak. It would have come from the warm south of Brandishear, not our cool and rocky vineyards here in Aerach. I wasn't at all hungry, but I took some bread and one of the bony little birds. I might be glad of a full belly later.

Later. How much later? I had hoped to be gone by now, before having to dress in this unwieldy costume and dance this dangerous galliard. Had I been wrong to put my trust in Rhoan?

He had convinced me to wait till night to leave the castle, but every nerve in my body wanted out of here now.

Doniver was saying something, and I'd missed most of it. I pretended to be focussed on extricating slivers of meat from the twiggy bones of the quail. It seemed it was just more pleasantries, at least until his had reached across the round table and grasped my wrist—not hard, but not gently either.

He was leaning forward, eyes sharp and menacing. "I asked, do you know how much you cost me?"

I blinked, unsure how to answer

"You haven't been listening, have you?"

There wasn't much I could say to that without proving it true. "You mean the pigs?"

Apparently, yes, that was it. He leaned closer. He must have been drinking before my arrival. His breath was rank with it, and his pupils were dilated.

"If you weren't such a useful little catch, I would send you back and collect the reward."

I leaned away, narrowing my nostrils against the boozy, animal smell of him. "I thought my information was barely helpful to you."

He laughed, dropping my wrist. "Yes, you're rather useless as a spy. But your worth as a wife will seal the fortunes of this house. How old are you?"

"Fourteen."

"Old enough to be married by the old laws."

I set my jaw and pulled a drumstick off of the quail, perhaps more violently than necessary. "Sixteen is the legal age of marriage in Aerach."

"Common law allows for marriage younger than that, if the parties are in agreement."

Agreement he would never get from me.

"A messenger arrived from your father today."

I froze, the quail drumstick partway to my lips.

"It seems after only two weeks, they've given up on you. They returned the bride price and annulled the betrothal."

My heart soared, then crashed, fluttering to the ground as he continued. "No one is looking for you anymore, Allaigna. You could rot in my dungeons, and no one would be the wiser."

His hand was on my wrist once more. He plucked the half-eaten bird leg from my fingers and dropped it on the plate.

"Such a tiny hand," he said. "Worth so much, and so little. It seems to me, Allaigna, you could stay as a guest in my prison, or marry me now."

I pulled back, but he held my wrist firm. "I'll never agree," I hissed, standing.

He followed me, brushing half the food from the table with a clatter.

"Sorry, but you owe me too much to deny me now." As I retreated, he followed, till my back was to the sideboard. "The old laws will also allow for marriage if you're with child."

Terror stopped my ears, filled my head with rushing blood. His voice was an odd tonal buzzing, too close yet high above me, a distant droning of wasps. The hand that grasped my jaw, forcing my face up, was sweaty, hot, and implacable. I could feel his meaningless words vibrate through his bones and into mine.

I caught the buzz in my throat and enlarged it, letting it swell, tuning the distant drone into a note so large it filled my head and ricocheted off the bones of my jaw, my nose, my brow, propagating subharmonics and overtones as it grew.

His other hand still held my wrist, but now it was wrapped around my back, crushing me against him so he had to bend me backward to bring his face near mine.

As his mouth, still moving in meaningless pantomime, met my lips, I released the sound. It wasn't a song I'd practised or planned: just a raw explosion of panicked energy that ripped from my throat.

He hurtled backward as if hit by a cannonball. His hand nearly snapped my jaw as it went, and the other one, still holding my wrist, dragged me with him.

I landed on top, staring down into unblinking eyes. I struggled to my feet warily, ready to dash for the door if he rose. As I stood, his head rolled to the side, and from a hole no bigger than an arrow shaft in the back of his head, a small puddle of blood began to grow.

Lauresa's Chorus

Lauresa feels furtive, like an adolescent once more, sneaking out of her home. It's not that anyone would stop her. She is mistress here, after all. But they would try to accompany her. Andreg, bless his rediscovered tender concern, does not want her travelling unescorted, even into Teillai. But her mother understands at least that every once in a while she needs some time alone.

Peri nickers and comes to the paddock gate when Lauresa passes.

"I'm sorry, old girl. Not today." Lauresa scratches around the grey mare's eyes and ears with a lingering moment of regret.

Peri has mellowed and matured. She's no longer the flighty creature she was — *and nor am I*, thinks Lauresa — but she is simply too tall for Lauresa to mount from the ground with a four-month-old strapped to her chest. Instead Lauresa orders the groom to saddle a sturdy little gelding, barely bigger than a pony. She longs to do it herself, and fidgets with irritation as the groom misses a patch of manure on the hock and bumps the horse's teeth while bridling. Picking hooves and heaving saddles are not easily done with a babe in arms either.

She runs her fingers through Allenry's sleep-damp curls and kisses his biscuit-scented head. Patience is a gift, she decides, not easily acquired.

When she has finally escaped through the eastern gate, she can breathe again. The sun is warm, but the late autumn air is chilly, and mist still clings to the wet ground. Trotting is uncomfortable, sitting aside as she is with the burden of a baby, so she gives the gelding his head and lets him meander at his own pace across the commons. Happy to be free of the stuffy confines of Osthegn, she is reluctant to reach her destination too soon.

A spark of resentment has kindled within her, and she toys with the idea of not making the meeting, of leaving him there, waiting. But that wouldn't be fair — she's not angry with him. Only with … Where does that little flame of anger come from? Andreg? Her condition? Her mother?

In fact, she doesn't make it to the spring. She has barely entered the woods when her gelding stops and lifts his head. Three heartbeats later she sees the familiar dark-cloaked shape astride a shadow of a horse.

She stays where she is, in the sunny verge of the woods, letting the shadow move toward her.

"I thought you'd be at the spring," she says, her voice barely louder than the rustling of leaves, knowing he can hear anyway.

"I didn't want you to have to ride so far," comes that voice, so strange and so familiar. His thin-lipped smile breaks the ghost-pale face. "And I was impatient."

She nudges her horse forward now, into the shadows with him. Daewen and her gelding blow and snort, introducing themselves, while Lauresa reaches her hand up toward him. Before, when she rode Peri, they were of a height. Now he towers above her.

His hand is as cold as hers, but his lips are warm on her fingers.

There is a long moment of saying nothing before their hands fall apart. Neither one seems willing to break the silence, but Allenry, noticing the change in temperature, or perhaps the change in his mother's heartbeat, stirs and snuffles. Her hand goes protectively to his head, and her heart stops for a moment, struck suddenly by the inverse side of the coin. All these years she has been wary of Andreg and her other-man's-daughter. Does she now need to protect Allenry from his sister's father as well? It is an irrational thought — they are men, not beasts prone to eating the young of others — but her maternal heart is fierce, not rational.

She quells the thought.

"I need to feed him," she says shyly, apologetically.

Einavar leaps from his horse with embarrassed haste and helps her down from the sidesaddle. She could dismount by herself, but part of her enjoys the awkward way he has to disentangle her from the saddle forks and lift her without squashing her son. The other part of her enjoys the feeling of his hands on her waist, and wishes she didn't.

He averts his eyes while she, sitting on a fallen log, latches Allenry to her breast. She laughs quietly at this discomfort from one who has seen, felt, and tasted every inch of that bare breast.

That memory sends a tingling rush of milk that makes Allenry cough and splutter. She bends over, relatching him, letting the shadows cover the blush creeping up her face. This is going to be so much harder than she anticipated.

When Allenry is finished and dozing happily in her arms, Einavar at last sits down beside her.

He clears his throat. "He's a fine boy," he says, though she can tell he'd say that regardless of the baby.

She nods, stroking the downy russet curls on Allenry's milk-drunk forehead. She wonders if he had thought she'd come alone, if this was a lovers' tryst. If she had come alone, well, perhaps it might have been. And that … that would have made things worse.

She wishes Allaigna were here, that Einavar's restless gaze could fall on his own daughter. He's only seen her a handful of times, but if there is one thing of which she is sure, it is the protective light of adoration in his usually masked eyes. It is the light she has felt fall on her own shoulder, the top of her head, her turned back, but never directly on her eyes. When their eyes meet, Einavar's and Lauresa's, the gaze that flows back and forth is rippled and confused: a mixture of too many said and unsaid thoughts.

They avoid each other's eyes now, he looking out through the bright and shaded autumn woods, she staring at the chestnut down curling around her son's ear.

At last, he murmurs into the silence, "I have a commission … from your father."

She nodded. "I had heard. Congratulations."

"Your mother has the most amazing web of connections. How she secured me the offer, from here in Aerach, not even from her alleged place of exile … imagine what she could accomplish if—"

"If she were still Princess High?" Lauresa's voice sharpens. "Yes, she is a mistress of manipulation, a puppeteer of politics, and a weaver with a finger on every thread in the weft of the Ilmar. But she couldn't prevent her own exile, could she?" And the unspoken words continue: *she couldn't contrive to mother her own child.* It's a speech Lauresa has made in her head so many times, wrestling the questions of Fate. Would Lauresa be wed to Teillai now, would she even be wed yet, if her mother had remained at Rheran? And yet … without that marriage, there would have been no detour upon the route, no encounter with Einavar. No Allaigna. Without this marriage there would be no chubby boy asleep in her arms. Before these thoughts can dull her growing irritation, she voices the nagging question that keeps resurfacing. She knows the answer, has known it for years now, and yet wants to hear it from another's mouth.

"It was she, wasn't it?" she asked, "that put you on my road. How did she know?"

He shakes his head, blinks. He has been far away in thought also.

"How do the Leisanmira know? That's something you'll need to ask her."

But that's not the answer she really wants.

"Why you?"

Did she know … was her mother's Leisanmira Sight plotting Allaigna's heritage like some studbook manager?

Einavar looks almost hurt. "Do you not think I've asked myself that so many times? Why me? How could she trust a disgraced squire like me with such a duty … such a precious charge?" He blinks again, and she realizes there are hints of moisture in those cold grey eyes. His voice is hoarse when he continues.

"And I failed."

She puts a hand up, in protest, ready to assure him otherwise, but he catches it.

"Oh, certainly, I delivered you from death, but I hardly left you in the condition I found you."

She jerks her wrist back, the skin burning and pinching. She welcomes this pain.

"I was involved in that choice too, if you recall," she snaps.

It's almost as if he hasn't heard her. "And yet she trusts me still. The only explanation is that, somehow, she knew that no one could love you more. And now she's trusted me with looking over your father."

Lauresa is caught for a moment on the phrase 'no one could love you more'. She holds it for a moment, relishing, wishing that and only that could shape the rest of her life, make what needs to come next less painful. But it can't.

She diverts. "He needs care," she says softly. "Prince of the strongest state of the Ilmar he may be, but he is wounded, broken inside."

Einavar's next words are harsh. "I am not watching over him out of concern for him. Only to ensure he does no harm."

"Will you ever forgive him?" she asks.

"For deliberately placing you in danger?" His voice is soft, but it is a knife wrapped in velvet. "For gambling your life for his dreams of power? Never."

So final, that answer.

"It was my life. And I forgive him."

"Then you have a larger heart than I, your Grace."

"I'm a mother," she replies. "I have to have."

There is another silence, not awkward any longer, just thoughtful. It is as if her statement, the verbal reminder of her new role, has eased tension between them in a way that all the visual evidence had been unable to do. She inhales the fresh wooded air and lets her body expand, soften, and lean to curl gently against his side. It is a bold move, a proprietary one, that refuses to acknowledge the distance that has grown between them and, after today, will grow larger still.

She lingers in this comfortable domestic moment, unwilling to let it end. He slips an arm around her shoulder, no longer embarrassed or hesitant or formal, but not passionate or demanding either. Just close.

She doesn't have her mother's gift of the Sight, but if she did, she would say this moment transcends the ordered progression of time. Regardless of the passion they have shared, despite the barriers of distance, marriage, the other man's child nestled in her arm, and beyond what may occur in the unforeseen future, in this moment their true selves, their inner cores, touch one another and share an understanding that will last forever.

It gives her the strength for what must come next.

She takes a long and slow breath that fills her ribs, pressing them against his arm and side, maximizing the contact between them, gluing her bones to his flesh. But a breath can't come in forever. As she lets it go she sags, melting into him, her perfect moment of contentment gone, replaced by a hungry sadness gnawing at her from the inside. She must speak before it hollows her entirely, leaving her without will.

"Your posting," she says to the woods beyond them. "It will keep you in Brandishear." It is not a question, merely a preamble.

His arm tightens around her, and she feels his breath warm her scalp as he answers her hair. "Yes."

"I want you to forget me." Her voice is so small she wonders if it has escaped her lips at all. But the sharp cold intake of breath across the top of her head tells her he has heard.

"Lauresa" — not 'your Grace' or 'Princess' — "I could be as old and addled as a moon bear, and I would forget my own name before I could forget you."

Silently, she agrees. She has forgotten more of her life than she can remember, and even still she knows there are some things that are eternal. Including the pain of separation.

Irdaign's Chorus

When Lauresa returns from her outing in the forest, she is wreathed in a cloud of sorrow that is almost palpable. And yet, though it floats around her, it is no longer within her. There is a quiet, airy freshness behind her eyes, a calm emptiness that lets me know she has released him from the corral of her heart. Despite the cloud of sadness, there is a small core of relief. The burden of a forbidden love has been lifted. She loves him still, and he her, there is no doubt. And neither is there obligation. Perhaps now she will have the space and breath to afford her children, those born and those yet to be.

She has found us in the herb garden, Allaigna dutifully following me with a withy basket, nearly as wide as she is tall, into which I drop my harvested bundles.

Lauresa passes Allenry to me with a sad wordless smile and scoops Allaigna into her arms. The child drops the basket, which tumbles its fragrant contents onto the gravel path.

"No-ooo," howls Allaigna, kicking her tiny legs. "Put me down!"

Lauresa laughs and swings her daughter onto her hip. "No," she says, kissing the girl on the nose. "I've got you, my beauty, and I'm not letting you go."

Allaigna squirms some more, all sharp toes and knees, leaning as far from her mother as she can, but she settles nonetheless, finally realizing a cuddle from her mama is a treasure indeed these days. Her upper body keeps its distance, though her legs cling as comfortably as a squirrel on a branch.

"Angeley," my daughter says, "Can you put Allenry to bed for now? My daughter and I will finish gathering herbs."

I nod obediently, covering my smile with a downturned gaze.

Already the cloud of sorrow is drifting away, dispersed in the cool air of late Tarcia.

Later that evening, when Allaigna has gone to bed and Allenry is back in his mother's arms, Lauresa brings up the topic that has lain dormant for four years.

"I don't want to lie to her any longer. She doesn't know her father. She should at least know you."

My heart shudders to a groaning, painful halt before limping on again. I focus on my needle rising and disappearing through the thick cloth of Allaigna's tunic. She grows so slowly, our little one, that she wears out clothes most children would simply outgrow.

"She does know me." I say this to myself as much as to my daughter.

Lauresa is scornful of my evasion. "As a nurse, not a grandmother."

I raise my eyes, weary of the argument I've already lived a dozen times. "It is still me, Lauresa."

"But it is not the truth."

It hurts that my daughter is so right in this. And I, though I know better, know also that I must take the wrong — and I must win, at least for now.

"Would you place that burden of secrecy on her?" As I put words to it, I feel its weight press down on us all, forcing the air from the sultry summer night. "She's not yet four, Lauresa. She can't keep that kind of secret."

"We let her in on her grandfather's identity."

"That's a secret she only has to keep from the outside world. Not from the household. Nor from her father. Something would slip out. I am around her all the time, not just on an occasional visit. A four-year-old can't manage to call me grandmother when we're alone and nurse when we're not." I take a few more stitches, allowing the silence to breathe for me. "And," I continue at last, "this is even worse: if she could keep that secret, would you truly force it upon her? It gnaws at your heart, Lauresa, and that's why you want to share it —"

"No," she shakes her head. "It's not for my sake. It's for hers. My daughter deserves some truth in her life." I can tell, though, from the falter in her voice, that she is coming around to my side of the argument.

"Then for her sake, my love, let her have a normal child-hood — with a mother, a father, and a nurse — for as long as she can." I don't say, *It won't be normal for long.*

Moisture clouds Lauresa's sky-blue eyes and she nods, acquiescing, her heart breaking for the second time that day. I want to gather her in my arms and rock her as I did when she was a child. But she has her own babe at the breast, and I have in my lap a jumble of torn fabric, thread, and pins.

Hers is not the only heart breaking. Inside, I weep for her, my long-lost child, and for myself, whose greatest joy right now would be for Allaigna to sit upon my knee and call me Grandmama.

And so life ripples on. Lauresa, it appears, has conceived again, a mere nine months after Allenry's birth. I chide her for not nursing Allenry enough. It seems she has hired a wet nurse to see Allenry through the night. It hasn't harmed him, for he is a robust baby, but the unintended consequence of another pregnancy is draining Lauresa.

Andreg is delighted, of course, so much so that he hasn't visited his mistress since Allenry's birth. I am not all-seeing, but of this I can be fairly sure.

But Lauresa … Lauresa is so drawn, exhausted beyond exhaustion by a new pregnancy and a new baby all at once. She doesn't need my chiding. She realizes the effect her small holiday from maternal care has had. I can almost see the blood drain from her face as she guiltily nurses Allenry. She is so thin her belly begins to show at barely two months, a strangled lump between her belt and her bony hips. How can Andreg not see it? Why must he insist on banquet after banquet, parading his beautiful yet rake-thin wife and chubby son before his vassals? I could almost wish the borders were less quiet, to draw his noisy, overbearing presence from the household and let my daughter rest.

And Allaigna, poor Allaigna, suffers the most. Her mama has gone from her, no matter Lauresa's wishes. She hasn't the means to afford Allaigna more. At least I am here to fill in the gaps, pick up the morsels Lauresa lets fall from her plate of care. It is second-best to a mother's love, but it can be no other way.

That hard little shell Allaigna is growing around her tender heart will serve her later on. She will never find it easy to love or to trust, but she will also find it hard to be hurt … and that may be the bitter gift she needs.

I am busier than ever, taking care of Allenry, Allaigna, and their weary mother. Every morning I see Lauresa come down the stairs, paler, weaker, and larger of belly but narrower of wrist and face. I curse myself for not foreseeing it, for being taken unawares and letting this happen to my daughter. I will not lose vigilance again, I swear.

Lauriana is born easily, though: a bronze and ruddy fair-haired baby, fat and content as a piglet. I sequester Lauresa and Lauriana in their chamber for the month, allowing Allenry in only to nurse once or twice a day. He is busy crawling and has lost most of his interest in the breast except when sleepy. He is too young to remember the loss of his mother to a sibling the way Allaigna does, but he feels it nonetheless. Although he never had the privileged years as elder sibling, he knows he has lost something, and is cranky and ill-tempered much of the time.

Allaigna takes her new sibling with much more equanimity this time. She is happy to have a sister, and keen to induct Allenry into the responsibilities of being an older sib. Whether a small part of her delights that he has now been shut out as she has, I will not comment on.

It is easy to keep the children from their mother's door. It is less easy to keep Andreg from his wife's. As with the first two, he eschewed Lauresa's bed during her pregnancy, but his interest has awakened with the desire to reclaim his wife's body from the child who now owns it.

In the end it takes a small charm, laid at her doorstep every morning and night, to discourage him for the next year.

What damage might that charm be doing, I wonder, to their marriage? It will endure, this much I know, for I have seen enough glimpses of the future to envision yet more children growing here in Osthegn. But will it be happy? And if it will, or if it won't, is it any business of mine?

VERSE II
THE LOST BRIDE

Morran was in the stables as promised, with Nag saddled, my bags packed, and the change of clothes laid out for me.

The shaking arms and legs that had propelled me down the back stairs of Doniver's tower suddenly gave way, and I hit the floor of Nag's stall, retching into the straw bedding.

"What, too much wine?"

Rhoan's bemused voice filtered into my head, the first words I'd truly heard since I fled the tower room.

"Did your song not work, and you had to drink him under the table?" Rhoan continued. "I'm surprised you can still walk, girl.

"Lass …" his hand fell on my back, patting uneasily. "Are you all right? Did he —"

"He's dead," I gasped out, and vomited again.

There were some more unanswered questions from Rhoan while I continued to squeeze my now empty stomach dry.

Finally he handed me a stable rubber and a canteen. I sat on my haunches, trembling, wiping my face, trying to stomach the water, trying to make the words come out properly.

"He's dead, Morran," I said in a voice flat enough to squash the terror. "I killed him." The last came out in a whisper, and helpless tears started.

Rhoan took me in his arms. I tensed, nearly convulsing again as I recalled the dead man in whose arms I'd been only minutes before. But Rhoan's embrace was brotherly … fatherly, even. I shuddered, breathed, and let him shield me from the world with his arms while I told him what happened.

It seemed like an age we sat there in the straw, me sobbing into his chest. But it was probably only a few minutes. The implications of what I'd done began to outweigh the sheer horror of it, and I pushed myself to my feet.

I began stuffing my change of clothes into Nag's saddlebags. I'd have to ride in the dress—there was no time to change.

"I've got to go now," I said. "It won't be long … before … before someone finds him."

Morran caught my wrist and I flinched, feeling Doniver's grip once more.

"You can't leave. Not now!" His whisper was hoarse.

I began to struggle, panicking again.

"Sh, sh, sh. Stop, lass! Think!" His hands were gentle once more, holding both of mine as if they were glass. "If you disappear now, everyone will know it was you. Who saw you?"

"A … a serving girl."

"And did she recognize you—Nalen, my apprentice?"

I paused and looked down at the borrowed blue and grey finery.

"Probably not," I admitted.

"And if she did recognize you, it is her word against yours. And mine. And I, for one, know you spent the evening restringing my harp."

He put a gentle hand under my chin, and I flinched like a head-shy foal. Why did he have to do the same things as Doniver … and yet so differently?

"Can you manage to maintain that story?"

I nodded. Avoiding the truth wasn't hard. But to stay here, after what I'd done … The urge to flee was strong enough to set my whole body shivering.

He must have seen it in my eyes. "I will get you safely away, lass. I promised, and I'll keep that promise. It will just be later than we planned. But easier too. After all, what is keeping us here?"

The realization was yet another cold shock to the stomach. Indeed, the man who'd kept me here was dead. And he'd given me an identity that would allow me to simply walk away.

Morran interrupted my sudden relief. "There will be an inquiry, of course. No one will be allowed to leave the keep for a while. But after they conclude he was killed by one of his many courtesans—"

My self-interest wavered. "I don't want one of them accused."

He gave a twitch of his mouth. "Not to worry, lass. The courtesan who did this, I think they'll find, already disappeared mysteriously.

"Now change out of that soiled dress and get back to work on my harp strings." He waved long fingers at the chaos of Nag's stall and the patiently waiting horse. "I'll deal with this."

Sure enough, the blue-and-grey dress turned up several days later, torn, soaked with blood, and buried in a midden heap. Rumours circulated under the masterful, invisible hand of Morran Rhoan, caulking together a tale of a pair of travelling entertainers, husband and wife, who had applied to the castle for a commission. It was amazing to watch Rhoan work. He would approach a guard or a porter, saying, "Do you recall the fair travelling singer? The one with hair as rich as polished bronze and eyes like pools of amber ale?" His rapturous description of the imaginary woman and her matching, very real dress soon had the listener believing he remembered her and her silent, dark husband. All manner of varied speculation would take wing from there, with no further prompt from Rhoan.

So pervasive were the rumours, I could almost convince myself to believe them. At least when others were around. In private, or with Rhoan, my only ally, accomplice, and perhaps friend, I writhed in an agony of despair and self-loathing over the murder I had committed. I allowed myself to crumple with the weight of guilt, emptying my stomach at least every night into the chamber pot. Each time, Morran would hand me a cloth and water and, in a patient drill, I would drink, waiting for the inevitable headache to come. Just punishment, I knew, for my crime.

"It's ..." he began one night.

"I know," I snapped. "It's all right. No one will connect me to the deed." *I see that. I see how right and clever you've been.* "But maybe I deserve to be ... to be ..."

"Implicated? Accused? Tried? Hanged?" I flinched at each word, gentle as they were in his slow, drawling voice. "How often must I remind you, you were defending yourself?"

"He wouldn't have killed me. I should have just ..."

"Let him rape you?"

The word grated like a knife in my already aching head, and I retched, ready to empty my stomach again.

"I would have lived," I said between clenched teeth, holding back nausea.

"And I would have killed him anyway."

He said this with such dark measure in his normally easy voice it took my breath away. I felt at once flattered, protected, and uneasy. I wanted no attachment, no father figure save the one, the true one, for whom I searched.

I shook my head. "No. I would have." It was probably a lie. Would I have taken revenge with a knife or sword? Strange that the thought repelled me less than the murder I had actually done. If I'd killed him with the sword, that I could comprehend. But that my voice, so unintentionally, so easily, could steal a life—I could not come to grips with that.

My face was wet with tears.

"Look at me," I snapped, wiping my eyes. "I make a terrible boy."

Rhoan handed me a lace-edged handkerchief. "Boys cry. Especially when they kill a man for the first time."

"Have you ever …" I couldn't finish the sentence.

He looked at the floor, shook his head. "No," he said softly.

"Then what do you know about it?" I hissed at him. I balled up the handkerchief and threw it at the hearth. It fell short of the flames and lay there, crumpled and drying. I stomped off to the sleeping area and threw myself onto my trundle bed, not bothering to undress.

Rhoan stayed where he was, but I could hear him pick up his harp and begin to tune it.

"Rhoan?" I asked at last, my voice weak and timid.

"Mm?" he asked.

"Play something."

The tune was not one I knew, but it was oddly familiar. There was a Leisanmira lilt to the phrasing, and a resonance in the bone that both thrilled and comforted. My headache was too fierce for me to hear the words, but they left half-conscious images within my brain as I fell asleep, clutching the fine bright flowers of my eversweet posy.

I dreamed of my mother that night, and of my true father.

When I awoke before the cockerel, I couldn't sort my dream from the tangle of words Rhoan had left lying in my head.

I used the pot, dressed, washed my face, and then paced the chamber until my fretting steps caused a stirring from behind the bed curtain that contained Rhoan. Since the death of Tiern Doniver, the keep had been in mourning, and there was no call for musicians in the evening. This by itself kept Rhoan's drinking down, as did a prudent need to keep a wise head and a close tongue. But hungover or not, Rhoan was not an early riser, and his waking was slow and owl-like.

"Sing it to me again," I demanded when he at last emerged.

"What?" he mumbled.

"The one you sang last night. 'The Lost Bride'. No ... don't sing it." I still hadn't stopped pacing, and his owlish stare followed me around the room. "Just tell me the words."

"What, now?" he yawned.

I stared him down until he began:

Fierce winter frost still gripped the ground,
The air was bright and sere
When from the crownèd Bastion hill
Rode forth the princess fair.

I shook my hand at him, as if waving off midges. "No, never mind, not the words," I said, though that was what I'd demanded. "Just give me the plot."

"I can't believe you've never heard it," he said grumpily, dropping the coverlet that still rested on his shoulders and moving to the basin to wash his sleep-disordered hair. "Where did you say you grew up?"

"I didn't," I snapped, burning with impatience that quickened my pacing to a near trot. "The plot. Please?"

He yawned again, wiping his face dry. "Princess sets forth on a journey to marry her beloved, is captured by bandits, rescued by faeries, and lives as one of them for fourteen years before returning from the Otherland, nary a day older than when she left. Her beloved, now twice her age, sets aside the wife he took in her stead and weds his true love, ending the war between their countries."

My pacing had stopped, and I sank into Rhoan's usual chair by the hearth. "Not fourteen years—a fortnight," I whisper to myself. "And not the Otherland." I look accusingly at Rhoan. "The Greatwood. Not faeries. Ilvani."

He raised his eyebrows. "Most ballads, even the fantastical ones, have a grain of truth."

"The bride," I say. "She's Lauresa of Brandishear." *My mother.* I stop myself from saying it out loud.

Lauresa's Chorus

With the birth of Lauriana, Lauresa's already thin and taut attention is stretched to the breaking point. It is not the physical demands of mothering three children. Her mother and the second nurse help her juggle these needs easily enough. It is the emotional burden.

She thought she had settled these inner conflicts when Allenry was born, and had learned to divide her attention fairly. But two is not three. She longs for a third arm, so she can hold all her children at once, but like a set of juggler's batons, one must be in the air at all times or else be dropped.

She has the hardest time with Allenry. Though he is but a yearling, only just walking and talking, he has become a large and lumbering inconvenience who still needs his swaddling changes, who still wants to be at her breast, but who seems to dwarf and threaten her fragile newborn. She hates herself for thinking of him like that, but she can't stop herself. It is natural, her mother explains. All mothers want to, need to, protect the youngest and most vulnerable, even at the expense of the elder ones. That's easy enough for Irdaign to say. She only ever had one. She never had to divide her love. The fleeting thought winks in her head: the tiny wish that she'd only had Allaigna. But then her heart fills with love for the other two, and for a while it seems she loves them more.

Allaigna, at least, seems happier since her sister was born. Her brother, while no playmate, is at least entertaining to her now, and is filled with adoration for his older sister. His large brown eyes follow her around the room, and, when he has learned to crawl, he launches himself after her like a fat puppy. When he can walk, he bumbles after her like a duckling. His third word—after *no*, and *mup* for milk—is *Layna*. The sibling adoration thrills and warms Lauresa, though she wishes it were reciprocated.

The late summer air is heavy with the smell of cut hay and plums ripening on the tree. Lauresa is bathed in sweat, and so is her baby—reddish-brown curls plastered against her sleep-serene forehead.

Lauresa slowly eases her into the cradle beneath the plum tree and adjusts her bodice, hiding the evidence of a recent feed as the junior nurse announces the arrival of Lady Raen and her retinue. Lauresa takes Allenry from the nurse's arms for a cuddle before Raen is shown in, but he squirms free and crawls to the long rectangular fish trough. It is the perfect height for him to pull up on, and he begins to cruise sideways around it, chubby bare legs wobbly but enthusiastic as he sidesteps its perimeter. That will keep him occupied, at least.

Raen is shown into the garden with her maid, her nurse, and her two-year-old son Darras.

She and Lauresa give each other the customary kiss on both cheeks and the usual polite offering of conversation and compliments on each other's children before sitting to drink goblets of iced punch and nibble fruit pastries.

The ice house is dangerously low this summer, but Lauresa has used it nonetheless, out of self-indulgence or a wish to impress her friend, she is not sure which. Raen is not what you would call a close friend, but she is the closest thing Lauresa has to a friend, even after all these years in Teillai.

Despite their stations in life — one a duchess, the other a highborn lady — they speak as any two mothers would: of teeth and toddler talk, of both ends of the digestive system, of baby steps and large tumbles. Lauresa is the expert here, with five years of mothering experience to Raen's two, but Raen knows more of boys, and it is a relief and curiosity to watch Darras in his busy toddler preoccupation, and to try to predict Allenry. They are so much more alike, these two, than Allenry is to his elder sister. It is only now, when she has other children to compare her to, that Lauresa realizes how different, how out-of-the-mould Allaigna is. It makes her worry yet again.

"Where is Allaigna?" Raen asks, as if reading her thoughts.

Lauresa frowns. "An excellent question. I had asked Angeley to bring her by now."

She shoots a look at the junior nurse, who is hovering a step behind Allenry, ready to spring into action should he stumble in his circumnavigation of the trough, all the while casting nervous glances at Lauriana's cradle, for Darras seems about to wake the baby.

"Go on," Lauresa says. "I'll watch them while you fetch Allaigna."

Darras's nursemaid escorts him away from the sleeping baby, pointing out the trout swimming in the trough. Darras leans over, harnessed by his nurse's grasp on the back of his tunic, and lunges for a fish. A splash and a shriek ensue, waking Lauriana anyway with both noise and water. Lauresa rushes to pick up the baby and rock her back to sleep while Darras is scolded and dragged away from the water.

She turns back in time to see Allenry, entranced by the noisy, wet audacity of the older child, step away from the security of the stone wall and take his first unsupported steps, not toward her, but toward the giggling Darras.

Lauresa claps her hands as if she's no older than the children, brimming with vicarious delight at the accomplishment of her middle child.

His balance doesn't last, and he tumbles onto his hands and knees in the gravel of the yard. Lauresa is there in an instant, balancing Lauriana on her hip while she brushes away the tiny stones embedded in Allenry's pudgy bare knees. His tears are short-lived, and he struggles out of her arms, determined to assay his pursuit of Darras once more. Lauresa gives him the compromise of a finger to hold and follows him, one wobbly step at a time toward the older boy.

But Darras's attention has been taken elsewhere. Angeley and Allaigna have come into the garden, the latter dragging behind her nurse in evident reluctance.

Lauresa can't stop beaming. "Allenry just took his first steps!"

Her smile spreads to Angeley's face like a mirror, though Allaigna is clearly unimpressed.

"Aren't you proud of your little brother, darling?"

Allaigna, nonplussed, disdains an answer.

"But come, I'm ignoring my guests. Allaigna, do you remember the Lady Raen? And Darras? You haven't seen him for a very long time."

Allaigna shakes her head. Lauresa gives her mother an imploring, embarrassed look, as if to say, "Teach my daughter some manners, please."

But Raen comes to the rescue. "I'm sure she doesn't, your Grace. A year is such a long time in a child's life. And adults are so dull." She gives Allaigna a winning smile, but the girl is not so easily wooed.

Darras, on the other hand, has come trotting up to Allaigna, hands outstretched.

She recoils, retreating farther behind Angeley's skirts, but the visitor is undeterred in his quest to show Allaigna the handful of dripping duckweed he's pulled from the trough.

Raen walks to Lauresa and takes Lauriana from her arms, letting her console the now mewling and woeful Allenry, who can't hope to keep up with Darras.

Lauresa shoots darts of irritation at her recalcitrant elder daughter, who is both fending off the attention of her suitor and resenting the accomplishments of her brother. And while Lauresa holds the hand of her now howling and frustrated son, she feels her milk start down at the addition of lusty cries by her baby.

"You are so fortunate, your Grace," Raen says, "in all your fine children."

Oddly enough, despite a damp bodice, crying baby, soggy toddler, and scowling child, Lauresa feels it is true.

Verse 12
Release

My eventual reprieve from the White Tooth, scene of my crime, was as prosaic as my first attempted escape was catastrophic.

Morran came whistling into the apartment. "Pack your bags, lass. Again." He grinned.

I jumped to my feet, alarm coursing through my body.

"What is it?" My voice croaked as it came out. I couldn't trust the verity of his smile. "Am I found out?"

He laughed, swept his arms around me, and scooped me off the floor, kissing the top of my head. "Not a bit of it. Breathe easy, lass."

He put me down, ruffling my hair with a familiarity that annoyed me far more than the hug or kiss. I backed away, smoothing it down and straightening my shirt, exasperated.

"Well tell me, then!"

He was still grinning. "I'll tell you, lass, I've never been so happy to be let go."

"You mean you've been dismissed?"

"We, lass. *We've* been dismissed. Young Tiern Doniver, not his father, was my patron. It seems House Doniver has no need of entertainments, especially in this period of mourning."

The sick guilt that twisted my stomach at every mention of my former betrothed now torqued even harder, knowing I'd cost Rhoan his commission as well, and it choked any relief I felt.

"And further," Rhoan continued with unwarranted cheerfulness, "House Doniver's treasury is a bit lean at the moment. It seems young Doniver made more than a few investments that haven't yet paid off——"

"And won't," I spat, the guilt lifting for the space of a breath as I thought of the cruel beast-baiting project I'd foiled.

"Oh, that wasn't Tiern Doniver's only illicit venture," said Rhoan, guessing my thoughts. "Whether you intended to or not, you've done your father a great service by disposing of a considerable thorn in his side."

My first blinding thought was fury that he would marry me to such a thorn. My second, falling over that immediately, was, "My fath ..." I gasped, open-mouthed. "How ... who do you think my father is? Did *he*," I said, meaning Doniver, "tell you?"

Rhoan was busy packing his things. "I'm a troubadour, Allaigna." I jerked at the use of my name, glancing at the open door to our chambers. He kept his voice low. "I'm used to taking small bits of information and stringing them into a story. It didn't take much to guess your identity. And," he added, "just because I make fast work of guesses doesn't mean others can't follow my thoughts. Which is why I'd say you've lingered overlong in Aerach. If escaping your family is truly your wish."

Was it still? I thought. I no longer had an unwanted betrothal to run from. But that wasn't the real reason I'd left home. It was the lies, the layers and tangled strands of them, twisted about me since childhood, that I could no longer support.

"It is," I said. "I've been packed forever."

I have taken other lives — too many others — since Tiern Doniver's. Some were more deserving of death, perhaps. Others less. But who am I to judge? I cannot peer into the minds of others and see what actions come from malice and what are true regrets. I cannot see the hidden good or ill many might have done, nor can I scry the future like my grandmother and see what conse-quences may follow this deed or that.

But no other death haunts me as Tiern Doniver's has. I did not mean to kill him — had no idea my voice could even do that. But, as my grandmother would have said, ignorance is the coward's excuse. I should have known. I should have stayed at home where Angeley could have schooled my voice further. I could have taken the geas never to use magic upon another — and after Doniver's murder, I nearly did — or simply used my wits rather than my unproven, unharnessed gipsy magic. I have many regrets, and many deaths upon my head, but this one remains the greatest.

Jrdaign's Chorus

One morning, near Allenry's fourth and Lauriana's third birth-days, I am stirring my thoughts like the infusion of raspberry and nettle leaves simmering over the small charcoal burner on my worktop. Allenry's nurse comes waddling in, a child on each hip.

Allenry is screaming fit to raise the dead, and Lauriana is giggling, fingers in her ears, enjoying Allenry's pain far too much.

I relieve Julla of half her burden, scooping Allenry's bulky weight into my own hip.

"Shh, shh, shh," I start crooning, letting my voice tinge with music. "Tell Angeley what's the matter, then?"

I am only half paying attention, the other half of my brain flipping through vignettes of future memory, trying to determine whether I've seen this scene before.

I unconsciously put my hand on the back of Allenry's head to comfort him, and his howls escalate once more into a screech of pain. My hand pulls free of the matted curls on the back of his head: red and sticky.

Julla's eyes, frightened and distressed, are already stretched, large as gold eagles. "It was that wicked, wicked sister of his. She pushed him out the hayloft. It's a miracle he's not—"

"I highly doubt that!" I snap, silencing her babbling. "Now take Lauriana for her nap, so I can tend this wound."

I should have harsher words with her over the inadvisability of picking up an injured child, but I can see the girl is frightened enough for her job already. When she is gone, I sit Allenry on the workbench and sing a charm to ease his pain while I wash the bruised cut on the back of his head. There is plenty of blood, but the cut itself is small—a thumbsbreadth, no more. I hold it closed and sing another charm to speed the healing. No stitches will be needed, I think.

When he is calm and drinking a cup of warm milk sweetened with barley sugar, I get as coherent a story as is possible from a four-year-old.

And finally it hits me, when he mumbles something about the 'lubba-bye'. I know where I will find Allaigna, hours later when the furore has died down.

Lauresa's Chorus

Lauresa is surprised to find herself content. Her life as chatelaine of Osthegn and mother to three small children keeps her unforgivingly busy despite her two nurses, two ladies' maids, several chambermaids, cooks, butler, and footmen. How do farmers manage, she wonders, with no servants and with families twice or thrice as large as hers? But then, they have smaller houses to maintain, and no dignitaries to entertain. Milking cattle and hoeing fields every day would be hard work, but undeniably easier on the brain. On philosophical days, she guesses that the work of motherhood is the same in the end, whether you have one child, five, or fifteen; or twenty servants, ten, or none. On worse days, she longs to take her three away and live in a cottage. She could cope with feeding, changing, and maintaining a house and garden if her audience were but three. On good days, though, which are most, she realizes she is blessed. There seems no more important task than bringing up these children; and if she no longer dances at balls under the glittering evenlamps of the Bastion's great hall, she is at least far from the tangled threads of court politics. The land here in Aerach is temperate and lovely, if not as warm as Brandishear, and the people, if she avoids Vishod's court, are honest and likeable. And though she has no husband in her bed eleven moons of the year, she wakes to the warm and sleepy bodies of her children, curled like cats about her, every morning.

The passion Andreg once felt for her and she almost felt for him never returns, but there is an amicable agreement that leads them to share a few nights together in the guest chamber whenever he is back from the field or the capital. The infrequency of these visits delays but does not prevent the inevitable quickening when Lauriana is two.

She attributes the increased nausea and fatigue this time to being pulled in three directions by her adventurous band. While Allaigna is old enough to be helpful some of the time, she is no replacement for the nurse who was fired when Allenry fell from the hayloft.

So when Angeley makes the offhand remark, sometime in the last month or so of pregnancy, that there are only half the number of swaddling cloths and infant clothes ready, Lauresa is taken off-guard.

"What do you mean? Two dozen is what I've always laid in—unless you're predicting a laundress or two leaving us?"

Angeley puts her hands on her hips and tilts her head in the way that always makes Lauresa want to laugh, such a parody of a mother hen that it is.

"Surely you've noticed, your Grace." Lauresa never knows when Angeley is using the honorific sarcastically or not, but since a chambermaid is with them, airing out the linen, she guesses not this time. "Mag, take these down to the laundry." Angeley hands the maid a basket of baby clothes. She then reaches to the top of Lauresa's wardrobe, where her midwife's kit has resided for the past month.

"Noticed what?"

"How big your belly's grown this last month."

Lauresa makes a face. "I know. I'm just hungry all the time, it seems. I've probably gained a lot of weight."

Angeley nods. "You have, but none of it is yours. Lie down—it's time I listened again."

Lauresa sighs, but there is no point arguing. She lifts her overskirts and loosens the laces of the undershift, baring her enormous belly.

"Look at your wrists, Lauresa. They're nothing but a pair of chicken bones. You are practically wasting away …"

Lauresa stares in disbelief at her mother-cum-nurse-cum-midwife over the monstrous belly between them. "Hardly!" she snorts.

Angeley places the bell of a long wooden trumpet on Lauresa's abdomen, and her ear on the small end. "Shh!"

After trying several places, she stops and listens for longer.

"There's a heartbeat. Nice and strong."

She feels with her hands, palpating the belly and causing the inhabitant to squirm and kick in protest, and then listens with the horn again, higher, and on the other side.

"And there's the other."

There is a prolonged moment in which Lauresa can hear nothing but the beat of her own heart, rushing in her ears. Or is it the baby's heart? Or babies'?

She shakes her head. "No. Twins? It can't be!" She bursts into tears.

The life which had seemed so manageable, so amiable, is now spinning out of control. One baby is so much work, but it is work she knows. But two? The horrible sound of the reins snapping out of her hands, the carriage wheels bouncing free, and the axles of her carefully managed life breaking to splinters echoes in her ears.

"How long have you known?"

Angeley shrugs. "Oh, sometime before you were born I knew I'd have twin grandchildren" — the remark makes Lauresa want to scream — "but I didn't know it would be this time."

"*This time?* How many more times are there to be?"

Angeley looks sympathetic, which aggravates Lauresa all the more. "I can't tell you that, my dear."

"Because it will change the future?" Lauresa wants to shout, but keeps her voice to a hiss, conscious that the maid could return at any moment.

Angeley laughs. "Nothing so melodramatic, my dear. Because I don't know. I don't know anything for certain till it actually happens."

Lauresa senses this is not the whole truth, but she lets it pass. "And you didn't tell me till now that I'd have twins, because ...?"

"Why? What could it change? You would only have fretted and worried for the last eight months. Now you only have another three or four weeks to worry—which is plenty of time, for instance, to order extra swaddling cloths. And," she adds, running a hand through her hair, "to hire an additional nurse."

Verse 13

Hiding in Plain Sight

We had been on the road together less than a day, Morran Rhoan and I, before we had our first argument.

"Absolutely not!" I pulled Nag up hard, causing him to toss his head in annoyance.

Rhoan turned and leaned a hand on his cantle, but didn't slow his bay mare's walk. "The sun's getting low, lass. The Bend and Bow's a fine inn, but the best beds will be gone soon."

I would have yelled back at him not to call me 'lass', but an ox cart had appeared at the turn in the road ahead, and a loud discussion on my sex and identity was out of the question.

Nag fidgeted and danced, impatient to catch up with the other horse, but I stubbornly held him in place, spinning small circles on the muddy road while Rhoan made a resigned turn back to us.

"Be reasonable, lass——"

"Lad!" I hissed, now he was close enough again.

He let his laconic gaze roll up and down me, and sighed heavily. "Have it your way ... lad," he said. "But a girl posing as a boy is bound to draw more questioning looks than simply a girl."

"Are you saying I can't pass as a boy?" I scowled contemptuously at him. Of course I could. I still had no chest to speak of, and I had the build of a ten-year-old boy, not a fourteen-year-old girl.

There was a sad little quirk at the corner of his mouth. "Maybe," he said without sounding like he believed it. "Until you speak."

"What's wrong with my voice," I growled, lowering it. "I can talk like a boy."

He laughed. "A boy your size has the voice of a reed pipe, my dear. You've a lot to learn about disguise and misdirection before I can put you in front of the public like that."

"Which is why we are *not* going into that town!"

The ox cart was rumbling nearer, and I nudged my horse off the road to let it pass. Our conversation halted for the long slow minutes it took the beasts to trundle past. Nag was fully agitated now, as was the bard's horse, by our lack of forward momentum.

The drover gave a friendly smile and wave as he moved past, calling out to Rhoan. "That's a fell beast you've mounted that wee slip of girl on, sir. Red Anders at the east side of the village has some nice cobs in his stable. He's an honest trader—ye'd make a fine deal."

Rhoan lifted his hat. "Thank you, good sir! Most grateful indeed."

He said nothing to me as he waved the drover off, but the expression on his face was insufferable.

"*That* is why we're going nowhere near any towns," I spat when the cart was far enough away.

"Don't be absurd, Allaigna." He used my name just to irritate me, I was sure. "Look at the sky. We're in for another soaking like we had this morning, only this time with no sunshine to dry us off. I'm still damp and have no intention of getting damper when there's a perfectly good inn just over the hill there, with a fire, hot food, and a mattress with only a few fleas in it."

"You've seen yourself—in fact, you've been at pains to point out—just how inadequate my disguise is, and you want me to go into a village?"

"As a boy, no. As my daughter, I think it's perfectly plausible."

"As … your … daughter?"

He bowed from the saddle. "I know my humble origins don't match your noble bloodlines, but really, do we look so different?"

His hair was wavy, but as black as mine. His eyes were brown, not grey, but his build was thin and gangly: much more similar to mine than Allenis Andreg's was. In fact, he looked more like me than either of my parents did.

He caught my wondering look. "No. I'm not. Really. But it's not such an implausible thing."

I followed him down the muddy road to the village, devastated by the tiny moment of hope that had dashed through my heart and fled.

It was, in fact, easy for Rhoan to pass me off as his daughter, Merri. As Morran and Merri, we sang for board that night. The strain of singing ordinary notes and words, letting no hint of magic creep into my voice, made me hoarse and tense. If it hadn't been for Morran's practised ease, I'm sure we would have earned no bed at all.

I hadn't sung since the night I'd killed a man with my voice, and the terror of it strung my nerves tighter than Rhoan's harp strings. By the end of the evening, my head throbbed with the worst headache yet. I fell into bed without eating the supper for which I'd sung, and spent the night with my dreams of terrified guilt and the empty eyes of Tiern Doniver.

My head still pounded when I awoke, and Morran couldn't drag me from bed till well past the breakfast hour.

"Faith, lass. If this is your aspect after a single mug of watered cider, I'd hate to see you recover from a real drunk."

I growled something unintelligible at him and filled my stomach with prunes and water, not daring to brave the noise of the tavern below for warm porridge. We packed our saddlebags in silence, till at last Rhoan cleared his throat and tossed a handful of bronze and silver coins onto the bed.

"Not too bad a turning for last night, it seems."

I looked at the coins in puzzlement, unable to comprehend.

"That's from the punters," he explained. "They liked us enough to throw some extra coin our way. That's your share."

I thought about refusing it. I hardly felt I'd earned it. But I was in no position to be turning down silver. The metallic clink of the money as I dropped it in my pouch sounded like the snip of scissors … or knives. It was ominous, but liberating. It had been over a month since I'd left home, but only now did I feel free of it.

It was, as Rhoan had promised, a fairly good inn. But the horses' accommodation was better than ours. Each of our mounts was bedded down in a roomy box with a generous layer of straw on the floor and good hay in the manger. I relaxed as I entered the stable. My gut, knotted since we'd left Doniver and even since I'd left home, unclenched at last in the soothing beams of the thick morning sun.

Which is why I was completely off-guard when, after opening the bottom half of Nag's stall door, I was bowled over backward by a pair of grizzled paws planted on my chest.

It only took a fraction of a panicked second to realize the creature, a large gazehound, was not snarling but smiling, with its slobbery grin, tongue out, dog breath filling up my face. As I heaved the beast's paws off me, I recognized it.

"Dog!" I exclaimed, not at the beast but at its master, who also stuck his straw-coloured head out from under the top door. "What are you doing here?"

He couldn't answer me any more than I could understand his tongue-less clicks and whistles. The bitch sat politely behind her master, thumping her tail on the ground, while her mate busily circled me, sniffing my boots and legs.

"Is Raddick here?" I asked, half hoping he wasn't — that he was settled back at his family's farm.

But sure enough, up out of the manger popped a sleepy, hay-prickled head.

"Did someone say my name? Mistress Merri!" He scrambled out of the manger, tripping as he did, and threw himself on bended knee at my feet. "It's so … so very good to see you safe, my lady Merri!"

His head was lowered, but I could tell from the bright pink tips of his ears he was blushing. Nag, who still hadn't received his morning grain, was unimpressed by all this human and canine traffic in his stall. He gave me an impatient nudge with his head, sending me tripping over Raddick, to the embarrassment of us both.

"Get up, Raddick," I snapped, sounding like Angeley. "There's no room in here for courtesy. What are you doing here?"

Rhoan, who had been settling the account with the landlord, appeared at this moment and stuck his head under the stall door.

"A party! And no one asked me!" he exclaimed. "Why, 'tis the little lad to whom you had me deliver those deeds. Boy, you scarcely look better now than when you were living rough — did you not reclaim your farm?"

Raddick was hastily straightening his tunic and picking chaff from his hair. "No, sir … I mean yes, sir. The farm is mine in name and deed, thanking your good selves."

"Oh, the lady, ah …" He paused. "The lady Merri here, she did all the work. I was just the errand boy."

I frowned. "If you got the farm back, why are you here?"

"Well." He shrugged. "Um … It seems your, uh, intervention gave me more than my ma ever had, like. Y'see, we were leaseholders before. The deeds you sent were for a freehold."

"Yes, I know." I was rather proud of that, negotiating more from Doniver than Raddick had ever had.

"Well, so, I can't farm that much land on my own … and it didn't seem right to toss out the farmer and 'is family of seven who work the land now."

"So you're a homeless landlord, is that it?" laughed Rhoan.

He nodded, blushing again. "They're building a new house for me in exchange for this year's rents … but until it's finished, well, Dog and I have nowhere to live."

"So you've come to ask another favour of the lady who's bettered you already," said Rhoan in his sternest voice. I knew he was mocking, but Raddick shook in his boots.

"No, sir. Of course not, sir. It's just …" He turned to me, pleading, and dropped to one knee again, narrowly missing one of Nag's piles of droppings. "I swore my oath to you, lady.

That hasn't changed. And since I've naught to do on my lands … well, I thought I'd be of service, like."

It was my turn to be embarrassed now. I looked at Rhoan. "Didn't you convey the whole message? I released him from his oath."

Rhoan looked amused. "It seems, lady Merri, the young swain has declined to take it back. That's his prerogative, I'm afraid."

"Raddick, I … Oh, Fingal's balls!" I swore. "I'm flattered. Truly. It's just … we're travelling fast and light, Rhoan and I." I looked over to him for cues, but he was impassive, and still amused, damn him. "We haven't any other horses, and—"

"Oh, m'lady, I did not expect to *accompany* you!"

I breathed my relief.

"Though it would be an honour beyond my worth." He looked at me with those giant hazel eyes, reminding me more and more of the two hounds also staring me down. "I merely came to see if I can do you some boon."

"How did you know I was here?" I asked, with a cold lump starting to form in my gut.

"Happenstance, m'lady. Dog heard you singing last night. But the room was full, and he couldn't catch your eye."

Dog gave a series of quiet clicks, and Raddick jumped.

"Oh … I nearly forgot!" He pulled a crumpled handbill from his shirt and passed it to me. "I can't read it, of course, but it looks like …"

And of course it was: cleaner-looking than I was now, but unmistakably me.

Why now? I wondered. Why had it taken so long for my family to start papering the countryside with my face?

Rhoan looked genuinely sad when he saw the handbill. "Your parents must be desperate with worry, Allaigna. Would it not be better to simply return home? Your fiancé is no longer … a concern. What have you to fear?"

Fear? Nothing. Not even my parents' or Angeley's anger would give me pause. Pride—now that was another thing. And anger. The anger was still there.

"Oh yes, Doniver's gone. But I'm sure they've notified the next on a very long line of suitors already."

And then I realized why the handbills had appeared only now. They had thought I was safe at Doniver—he had broken his word, no doubt—and I almost wondered if they'd been depending on him to keep me there. Fury boiled up inside me again, as fresh and new as it had been that early morning I'd left home.

But Rhoan persisted, insisted that I at least send word. And so I wrote a letter on the back of the handbill to Mother—not Angeley or Father—informing her of my good health and my lack of intention to return home. Also instructing her to reward the messenger well. Dog, being both unlettered and mute, could not be questioned, making him the perfect messenger. I would have sent Raddick with him, at least as far as Teillai city, but Rhoan had other advice.

"Lad, your tenants may be glad to be no longer beholden to Doniver, but that makes them anomalies in their neighbourhood. You would do well to maintain a presence. Rent a room in town, do odd jobs for your keep, but visit your farm regularly. And if you can't afford a horse, hire one and learn to ride it when you inspect your farm. No matter how good your tenants may be, you are now their landlord, and they need to be reminded of it."

So easily, I thought, a careless word of mine had changed Raddick from peasant to gentry, and thrown the responsibility of land onto his shoulders. Would he thank me for it? Would he rise to his new station or be forever outcast, a true member of neither class? That sense of responsibility almost did make me want to take him along. To relieve him of his duties and take him under my wing. I could tell he would jump at the chance. But my wing was too thin and frail to shelter myself, never mind another. The best thing I could do for Raddick was say goodbye to him.

I surprised myself with the depth of my feeling. He had been so loyal, so helpful, so eager to please beyond the debt of the small and questionable service I'd done him. I didn't know how to respond to that sort of fidelity.

"You've changed my life forever, mistress," he said, his wide-set eyes glazed in water. "Whatever you need, wherever you need it, you've but to ask. I'm your man." He seemed a bit embarrassed at that last: he was no more a man than I was a woman, and we both knew it. He covered his awkwardness with an attempt at a courtly bow that became even more awkward. I shot a glare at Rhoan, demanding he not laugh. His eyes were merry, but his mouth stayed neutral.

I offered Raddick my hand, wondering if he knew what to do with it and wishing I could teach him the courtly skills I'd learned at Rheran. He did know what to do, though he did it as awkwardly as all else, taking my fingers and kissing them rather too firmly and too long. No, I decided, he wasn't a courtier, and I wouldn't want him to be.

I raised him up and wrapped my arms around him. It felt odd, and I was as awkward as he, embracing someone my own age.

I allowed hugs, reluctantly, from my mother and grandmother, but never gave them. This was a gift, pure and simple from my heart to his, and when I broke away I felt, rather than giving, that I had received.

Jrdaign's Chorus

Although I am always stern and full of cautions when I teach Allaigna control of her voice, I am inwardly delighted. It is all I can do to play the strict task-mistress when locked within the music room. What I long to do is revel in the joy of Allaigna's perfect, budding voice.

I never dared to teach Lauresa the art of spellsong, not when her gipsy blood caused trouble enough amid Rheran's court. But then, Lauresa never found her talent by accident. Or perhaps she did, after I left. Was that, more than grief I wonder, the reason for those wizards to wrap her mind in clouded spells?

Anger surges within me once more, at what I allowed Chanist and Gwannyn's mages to do to my daughter. But I can hardly cast blame about without laying the larger portion at my own feet. My heart, which I thought healed, bursts its scars and bleeds again. But I will not indulge in grief and self-blame. Allaigna needs me, and I will not fail her as I did her mother.

"Again," I repeat. "Do fa so fa do ..."

I will guide and shape Allaigna's voice, firstly to safeguard her, and anyone else, from the unattended effects of power. Secondly, to avoid the attention of the mage guard, for I will not have her taken to one of their dreadful academies. But most of all, so it is honed and ready for her when she finally grows into her power. Allaigna, more than Lauresa ever did, needs my talent in this.

And Lauresa—well, if I cannot serve as her tutor, she at least can benefit from my more earthy talents.

The tingling sense nudges the back of my skull. It's not the back-of-the-brain flutter of the Sight, but that more common intuition given to all mothers.

"Enough," I say, clapping the harpsichord lid closed. "Your sisters will be born soon."

There are perfect moments in my life: scenes that, when they finally occur, I realize I've seen over and over, that I've been waiting for all my life. The birth of my twin granddaughters is one of these. Allaigna is at my elbow as the untrained yet, unusually for her, responsive and obedient assistant. I feel assured, finally, that I have an heir. She will follow in my footsteps. Not as a midwife, for I have always known her destiny lies elsewhere. But she is my spiritual successor. Her sensibilities, her sense of duty, and, in her own way, her motherly care of others: all these are fledgling, underdeveloped, and hidden most of the time. But I know now that whatever childhood rebellions might grip and sway her, these strong and giving fibres will remain rooted in her being.

When she takes her mucky, birth-wet sister into her arms, I see her cradling the world. I would cry, but I am busy encouraging Lauresa to ignore her two new babies and finish pushing out the enormous conjoined afterbirth.

As I deal with the bloody mess at the foot of the bed, I look at my Lauresa with envy. There she sits, sweaty but radiant, with a baby in one arm, her eldest daughter snuggled against her, a baby in hers, and two other children peacefully asleep outside the curtains.

Does she know all I have sacrificed for this moment? I have given up my husband and titles, missed her childhood, missed my chance at other children—and oh, how I would have loved a family as large as this—but she doesn't know. She probably has never forgiven me, and maybe never will.

I wash my hands in the basin then pull an extra blanket up around Lauresa's shoulders.

"What are their names?"

"The first born," she replies, smiling at the babe Allaigna holds, "is Irdina."

Every once in a while I am taken completely off-guard. It is an unusual feeling for me, for whom the future holds so few surprises. I blush like a little girl, so pleased and honoured am I to have this child named for me. Perhaps I am forgiven after all.

"And this one," Lauresa murmurs as she bends and kisses the head nestled between her breasts, "is Branwen."

My breath catches, and I seem unable to draw it back in. I feel the flushed pleasure drain from my skin. She is named for her grandfather, and is the first of Lauresa's children to make that public claim. She is named not just for Chanist, but for Brandis, for the whole line of Brandishear princes. It is bold, and politically unwise in Aerach, but that is not what stops my heart. Not only has she forgiven me, she has forgiven him as well.

And if she can, then should I not be able to? She doesn't know the worst of him, but then, no daughter should have to. And I won't be the one to tell her. Instead I smile and kiss the top of her head. The maid has gone from the room, and I count Allaigna as too preoccupied with her new sister to notice how motherly a kiss it is.

"One for your mother, and one for your father," I say. "Very elegant, your Grace."

Lauresa's Chorus

For some reason, the weepy period lasts longer after the birth of her twins. Her mother explains it as twice the babies, twice the tears. But it doesn't seem to be the babies that make her sad. When she has one or both at the breast, which is almost always, she is as content as ever. But because there are two, she always needs Angeley, Allaigna, or one of her maids to take one infant down the stairs while she carries the other. The utter dependence on others makes her feel as if she's drowning. Those few times when both are asleep, and the other children occupied elsewhere, she is restless and unable to fix on what to do. There are so many activities in which she could partake—sleep, read, catch up on the accounts, write long overdue letters—that she can't choose among them. She longs to saddle Peri and escape, but the twins' naps are not yet long enough for that, even if her full breasts would let her enjoy more than a sedate walk.

The birthfeast draws near, and she is unable to even begin to plan it. She leaves it all in Angeley's hands, feeling once more like an incompetent mother and irresponsible chatelaine. But what can she do? Her life is being guided by others again. Like an old workhorse, she is more comfortable between the yokes of duty than without them.

She has never heard her daughter sing before, other than her childish tunes and aimless ramblings as a toddler. In fact, it seemed as if Allaigna had given up on singing altogether. But now it turns out Angeley has been tutoring her for some months. How did that detail of her daughter's life escape her? The way so many others seem to, she supposes.

The girl is shaky and white-knuckled as she stands up before the small crowd in the great hall. Lauresa feels for her to the extent she is trembly herself, causing Branwen to squirm and fuss in her arms. She wants to comfort Allaigna, to rescue her from her tormented embarrassment, and yet she wants her to succeed. Her stomach clenches, and she feels nauseated.

The girl opens her mouth, and though the first notes are wobbly, they are birdlike and pure, soaring up to the oak beams of the hall.

It is so beautiful, she can't stop herself crying. It is not the oppressive weepy feeling that has weighed in her chest these past weeks, but a torrent of tears, shed for the inexpressible beauty of the moment.

Allenry gives her a puzzled look, and Lauriana toddles over with a grubby handkerchief that she solemnly hands to her mother.

"I'm all right, love," she whispers to Lauriana's curly ginger head. "She's just so lovely, isn't she?"

Allaigna will hardly meet her eye when she next sits down, her pale cheeks turning to hot pink.

Lauresa reaches over and catches her daughter's thin hand. "Thank you, my love," she says, and adds, with all honesty, "That was the most beautiful thing I've ever heard."

It takes a while for the hall to recover from the hush in the wake of Allaigna's song. Through her tear-spangled gaze, Lauresa sees her friends and acquaintances shift in their seats, dab at the corners of their eyes, and turn dreamily toward their neighbours to talk in murmurs. There is a movement from the gallery overhead, and Lauresa's glance is drawn upward in time to see a dark figure shift back and melt into the shadows. Her mother, she notices, disappeared shortly after Allaigna's song.

She wishes Andreg were here. If he could hear Allaigna sing, would some spark of love, or at least pride in the girl, grow in his heart? Does he somehow know Allaigna is not his own? Is that why he shows no interest in her? But then, he's shown little in Lauriana, and even less in the twins. He has seen them but once, on an overnight stay between Aleran and the southern border. He has not even bothered to come home for their birthfeast.

As a politician's court-bred daughter, she understands this. His role as warden of the Clearwater Plains is to oversee the peace, and the peace has been fragile of late, with more hostility between the border hamlets and the Ilvani to the south than she can remember since her wedding. But ... surely his captains could manage on their own for a day or two?

She feels the bile of resentment in her throat, and she unlatches Irdina, who has fallen asleep at the breast. She doesn't want to feed her that sourness. But no sooner has she done so than Jura is there with Branwen. She wishes she could retreat to her chamber and sit in her nest of a bed, feeding the two of them at once. Here in the public space of the hall, when she can only manage one, she is chained the whole time.

The smoky, mead-scented air is busy again with high-pitched chatter. Lady Raen is here, but not her husband. He too is at the borders, as well as many of the men of the city and surrounding villages. She would feel insulted by their absence if she didn't know better. Men only attend birthfeasts for the political connections they can make. Most are entirely uninterested in the subjects of the festivities. With Lauresa's husband absent, most of the lords won't see the point in attending. Women, on the other hand, don't dream of turning down an invitation, even if the political pickings are slim. No one would risk making the slight. And, she concedes, most are happy to coo over a new baby or, better yet, two.

When Branwen also is settled, Lauresa looks around for Angeley. At last she catches sight of her grey skirt in the unlit shadows of the upper gallery. There is someone with her: a darker shadow that slips away toward the upper stair.

Lauresa passes her youngest daughter into the somewhat reluctant arms of her eldest, and excuses herself on the grounds of needing some air.

Angeley meets her on the stair, and she knows, before her mother opens her mouth, what she's going to say.

VERSE 14
MISERY

Now that Rhoan had convinced me it was safe to appear in towns, and now that the first enticing jingle of coin rattled in my pocket, I was entirely dispirited to have to revert to my original plan of sleeping rough. But the handbills were out there, and even though I cut my hair as short as I could bear, leaving just enough to cover my hated ears, I wouldn't risk being spotted.

I handed Rhoan back my share of the silver from the previous night and demanded he acquire supplies. He did this while I nervously groomed our horses over and over. It was just before noon when he returned with his purchases: a waxed canvas tent, ropes, two new woollen blankets, plenty of flatted and milled oats, salt fish and beef, a large loaf of dark bread, a wheel of cheese, currants, prunes, and a few withered apples and onions that had survived winter storage. To my disapproval, he had also bought a skin of wine and a flask of whisky. Since the death of Doniver, he'd ceased his evening debauchery, and I had hoped he wouldn't recommence. He assured me it was only to flavour the stews and warm the limbs on cold nights.

"Besides," he added, "a dash of whisky's always good to have for cleaning wounds or numbing the bones. Or making friends. And when you're sleeping rough, you need to make friends of all you encounter."

The rain started when we were only an hour out of Cranhold. By the time we camped for the night, my woollen cloak was soaked through and Rhoan's leather hood and cape were stiff and sodden. In the morning, our clothes were hardly drier, having shared the damp air inside the tent with us. Our boots, at least, were still dry.

The next few days were even more miserable. The spring rains set in with spite, turning roads to byres, streams to rivers, clothing to sponges, and tempers to bonfires. It was a pity we couldn't warm ourselves on our smouldering, crackling, blazing arguments. Instead we huddled, sodden and chilled, under the only partly waterproof canvas of our tent, chewing on hardtack and jerky, or stomaching cold gruel soaked overnight in the absence of a cooking fire.

Rhoan refused to take his harp out of its case even at night. The air was too moist, he said, and he trusted the oiled and waxed leather more than the soggy canvas above our heads. So we passed the time by singing: ditties, rounds, drinking songs that made me blush, love songs that made me blush even more, and sagas that stirred something deep and restless in me. It was always disquieting when I recognized relatives within a ballad, some as close as Grandpapa, some as distant as Brandis himself, who of course was my great-however-many-greats-grandfather. It was odd how I'd always known the facts—that Mother and Grandpapa are descended from the line of Brandis—but had never made the connection that it is his blood, however many generations diluted, that flows in my veins. Rhoan knew one or two songs about the distant heroes of Aerach, but none of them hooked my imagination as they once might have. Even if they were ancestors of Allenis Andreg, or his cousin Prince Vishod, I knew now they were no blood of mine.

And then there were the Leisanmira songs: not spellsongs, but the ones sung about the campfire. I knew them, for I had heard Angeley sing them many times. But now, knowing they too were part of my blood made me ache with the thrum of those notes. The only gap in this family history of song forming around me was my father. I asked Rhoan if he knew any Ilvani songs. He cocked his head to one side, as if listening for them in the heavy spatter of rain upon the cloth over our heads.

"I know one or two I can sing by heart. But I only know a few words of Ilvani, so I may not be singing this right."

He launched into a ballad. At least that's what I guessed it was, though the progressions were strange — so full of semitones, minor sixths and seconds — that I had a hard time parsing it. But it vibrated with that same recognition in my bones. *Yes,* I thought, *this must be part of my heritage too.*

My Ilvani was a bit better than Rhoan's. Partway through, I began to piece together enough lyrics to recognize the plot.

A chill ran through me that had nothing to do with the dampness of my clothes.

"Wait," I said, halting him mid-stanza. "This is about Wellbirk, isn't it?"

He'd sung the familiar, Ilmari version earlier, but this … this was its mirror. Where the song I knew told of the tragic nobility of High Prince Goffree, my great-grandfather, in the face of insurmountable odds, this one sang of the courage and cleverness of Caradar of House Halobrelia, and how he had defeated the evil tyrant encroaching on the last of the Valnirata lands. I laughed at the cruel irony. All this time spent searching through scarce Ilvani records to learn the other side of the story, and all I really had to do was listen to some old songs. It was no longer so easy to take sides. I didn't know for sure whether my birth father was full Ilvani or a mongrel like me, but in whatever amount, the blood of both peoples mixed uneasily in my veins.

I woke up when cold drops of water from our sodden tent fell onto my head. I heard the sound of water pouring and hoped it was one of the horses, rather than Rhoan, relieving itself so near the tent.

He stuck his head back in. "Wake up, lazy-guts. The rain's stopped for now. It's as good a time to strike camp as—" He stopped and sniffed. "What's that smell?"

I grimaced. "Don't blame me. I wasn't the one breaking wind all night."

He flicked my toes. "Don't be rude to your elders, little girl. I mean the smell of flowers. I know that scent … Eversweet."

I sat up, releasing another waft of scent from the posy that hung around my neck.

He inhaled again. "But it doesn't grow here."

I fished the little bundle of herbs out from beneath my shirt. "You mean this?"

His eyes widened. "Where on earth did you get that, lass?"

"I've always had it. Well, since I was little."

"You still are little," he said absently, gently fingering the bundle. "But where did it come from?"

I shrugged and hid it back beneath my shirt. What could I

say? From a peasant woman, who was no doubt *not* a peasant woman. "It was a gift." I was beginning to become irritated by his probing tone. "I've always worn it. You just noticed now?"

"Enclosed air space," he said, tapping the canvas ceiling, causing another shower to fall on my head. He grinned as I scooted backward, knocking my elbow on the tent and wetting it even more. "That must be why I like you. You smell like home."

He moved aside as I crawled out of the tent and shook my wet head. My boots were still damp, and as I struggled to put them on, hopping on one foot, I used some of Ormé's favourite curses.

"Such a mouth on a high-born lady."

"What do you mean, 'smells like home'?" I growled, before he could mock me any more.

"Well, you must know eversweet grows only on the high mountains in the north of Elalantar. Where the Sîul Ilvani live."

"And you're from the south, like Rhiadne, you said."

"No, I only said I met her there. I grew up west of Ysevan, in the lower slopes of the Bywirn range. My mother used to take me once a year to visit my grandfather's family in the alps. I'm one-sixteenth Ilvani, on my mother's father's mother's side, you know."

"I thought Ilvani didn't breed with Ilmari," I said, trying to sound casual, knowing full well I was proof they did.

"Every rule has its exception, lass. But as far as that goes, you should know the Sîul are less hostile to Ilmari than the Valnirata clans are. They live and trade under Elalantar's rule quite peacefully."

He sounded proud, which made me prickle in defence of my nation and my grandfather, but I suppressed it. I needed to know more about these Ilvani.

"What are they like, the Sîul?"

As we moved about, breaking camp, shaking out and rolling up our rain-soaked shelter as best as possible, feeding and towelling off the miserable horses, he told me.

They were from the Valnirata originally, exiled long ago. Some say it was for collaborating with Ilmari; some say for intermarrying with them; others say for political reasons that had nothing to do with the Ilmari at all. Most of the Sîul have dark hair unlike their fair-haired cousins, but they still possess the violet eyes and white-pale skin that set them apart from the bronze-skinned Ilmari.

I looked self-consciously down at my own pale wrists, so different from the honey-gold skin of my sisters and mother. Even Rhoan, with his proudly confessed titration of Sîul blood, was far darker-skinned than I.

My mother had told me so little of my father, when she had at last told me anything. He was Ilvani, or at least partly; he had been a squire in Rheran; he had hair and eyes like mine.

I remembered the stranger in the garden the night of my twin sisters' birthfeast: the pale cool hand, the thin smile in the narrow white face. I thought of the smell I had noticed then, and realized it had been with me for years. Did the posy come from him? It was a longing both cold and warm: to be watched over and cared for, and yet to be spied upon, shadowed.

If my father was Sîul, as my colouring seemed to suggest, was there any point pursuing him in the Valnirata Greatwood? Or in Brandishear? But those were the two places my mother knew him, and it seemed a closer place to start than across the sea in Elalantar.

It took four days in total of cross-country riding to reach the edge of Aerach, three of them spent soaking in the rain and the fourth spent shivering in the late Ilia wind that dried our clothes but froze us to the bone. By the end of that fourth day, though, I didn't feel the cold, because I was burning from within with the fever that visited me, along with a throat too sore to talk or swallow and legs that ached with every jolting step Nag took.

By late afternoon, I no longer noticed the road. It was all I could do to keep my eyes on the rump of Talwis, Rhoan's bay mare. Long before dark descended, I'd ceased bothering to keep my eyes open at all. Twice I nearly fell off: the first time jolting awake when my chin hit my chest, the second saved only by some simian reflex that made me clutch Nag's neck as I started to roll out of the saddle.

For all I know, I may have indeed accomplished falling off in the end, for I don't recall anything between that last near miss and waking up in a bed. Not a particularly clean or soft bed, but after soggy, stony, tree-root-ridden ground, it might as well have been the softest feather bed in Osthegn.

Alarmed, I sat up like a released trebuchet, making my head swim and pound at the same time. It knocked me back into the bed as quickly as I'd sat up.

My pillow, I noticed as I readjusted to proneness, was Rhoan's velvet jerkin, the one he hadn't worn since we'd left Doniver. My own clothes — just my shirt and breeches — were still damp, but whether from rain or sweat I didn't know. From the mildewy, sour smell that rose from me, I guessed both. The single high window was unglazed and missing a shutter, by grace of which omission a block of chilly daylight relieved the simple room of utter darkness.

I must have slept the entire night, I reasoned, and I began worrying again. We'd agreed to stay out of towns and inns, so why were we here? Had Rhoan decided to ransom me back to my family? Anger warmed me again, and I threw the thin blanket off and struggled to my feet, delusions of complex plots feeding my still-feverish brain. My feet tangled with the blanket, and I only just managed to twist my flailing body around to fall on the prickly straw-stuffed mattress rather than the wooden floor, my head now pounding. The temptation to lie there was too great, and down I stayed till Rhoan came in.

I was confined to the straw-stuffed mattress for the rest of the day and the following night, while Rhoan coddled and fussed over me like a nursemaid. Prickly as the mattress, I resisted at first, trying to dress and vacate the bed every time he left the room; but every time I sat up, the blinding headache would slam me back down. By the time he had returned with a midday meal of beef broth, soft bread, and wine-soaked currants, I had resigned myself to my marginally comfortable prison. And once resigned, I relaxed and found the mindless boredom a soothing respite from constant tension.

Since I'd left home — nine weeks ago, though it seemed a lifetime — not a moment had passed without some anxiety twisting through my mind. Even my sleep had been full of worried dreams. I had made friends and enemies, found my life in peril more than once, and caused a death that haunted me. But here, in the dull stillness of the inn room, the cords of tension snapped and released me, and I was able to surrender my care into the kindness of a man I'd known for less than two months.

Strangely, his paternal concern didn't make me long for the father I was seeking, or at least no more than usual. Instead I thought of Mother, and even more of Angeley's cool hands and calm comfort in the face of any illness. At last, I allowed myself to cry for them: not homesick tears of wanting to return, but tears of apology, knowing how much pain I was causing them and wishing in my heart to say sorry. And when I realized I had at last begun to forgive them, there were tears of relief.

Lauresa's Chorus

The long spring dusk has settled over the garden. Nonetheless, she feels exposed. There are many windows that look down into this courtyard from the west hall, the stable loft, the granary and dovecote. But there is one corner that is virtually free of overlook: beneath the plum tree, sheltered from the sight lines of the parapets by a buttress flanking a small wooden door. It is no doubt a risk, if a small one, to the defensibility of the castle. Lauresa is convinced it is only by dint of his spending so little time in the courtyard or solar that her husband hasn't noticed. Otherwise, she's sure, he'd order the plum tree Angeley planted when she first arrived cut down.

The dark-cloaked figure is there, as she knew he would be. It has been nearly three years since she's seen him. Then she had two children and another on the way. Now she has twice that number. With each of Andreg's children that she has carried and nursed, she has felt her attachment to the father of her firstborn grow thin and weak. She senses more than sees him: a veiled piece of darkness revealing no more than a thin pale chin and knife-like line of a mouth. His breath, warm in the cool night air, is a palpable thing. It erases that thin distance, replacing it with a longing as fresh and strong as the day she first felt it.

A small sound escapes her lips. To call it a moan or a sigh would be to enlarge it beyond its measure. It is a tiny sound, of protest, relief, denial, and surrender, but his sharp ears catch it nonetheless, and he answers not with voice, but with movement. A tiny ripple shivers his cloak like the breath of wind in the plum blossoms.

These two signals, the sound and the movement, are as loud as a shout, stronger than a blow, to their audiences, and for four long liquid heartbeats, there is no more sound or movement from either.

"Your Grace," he says at last, just as she reaches a hand toward him, puts her fingers over that thin mouth, and stops any more words.

They are frozen, noiseless, for four more heartbeats before she replaces her fingers with her lips.

It is a long, still kiss, not of passion, but of remembrance. Her body, heavy with a mother's curves, melts into his as if they had never been apart.

"You shouldn't be here," Lauresa says at last. It is stating the obvious, but she has to say something, do something, to prevent herself from dragging him up to her chamber.

"Agreed," he murmurs, his face buried in her hair. He draws in a long, starving breath and releases it, sending warmth through the crown of her head. His arms have not loosened their hold, and she has to curve her spine backward to see his face.

Before she can speak again, he stops her with a second kiss, this one more insistent, more urgent than the first. Never mind her chambers: she is in danger of spreading that cloak of his right here in the damp gravel of the garden. His arms become tighter than she thought possible, as if he would crush their bones together, their ribs inextricably tangled and laced like the skeletons found in joint graves, their remains forming the frame for a strange, two-headed, eight-limbed beast. And she would happily perish in that twined embrace. That is, until her breasts, doubly full with the task of feeding two babies, ache and remind her of her other loves, and her other duties.

She lets out a yip of pain and struggles free, adjusting her squashed bosom within her bodice once more.

He steps back with a jerk, the heat of his body replaced by a chill breeze.

"Forgive me, your Grace. I didn't mean to hurt you."

She laughs. "They've seen far worse treatment." The flash of anger that passes over his face makes her laugh again. "From my babies. They've been bitten, grabbed, scratched, elbowed, and even kneeled on." She is babbling, and also giggling like a twelve-year-old at his appalled puzzlement.

She relents, strokes his face, so familiar and yet so forgotten. "You didn't hurt me."

Except with your absence, she adds silently. *And now, your presence.* She is not sure which is worse. Absence is a dull longing, an empty hole in the landscape of her heart that she covers over and steps around, pretending it isn't there. His presence is fire, wounding and delighting. The pain is like a hot southern spice that burns the tongue and upsets the stomach but makes her long for more.

"I am glad you're here," is all she says aloud.

He catches her roaming hand, brings it to his lips, and holds it there as if he would inhale her all, beginning with her fingertips.

"Your daughter's voice is exquisite," he says at last.

"Our daughter's."

"You are still sure of that?"

"More and more every day. How did you hear her?"

"Your … Angeley brought me to the gallery to wait for her."

How thoughtful of her mother, to plant him where he could hear her sing. But …

"Wait for her?" Einavar was here to see her mother?

"I had news for her—from Brandishear."

It more than irked that he had come all the way here to see Irdaign and not her. Was she just a side visit, then?

He sensed her anger. "It was both urgent and sensitive in the extreme. Believe me, nothing less could induce me to break my word to you and return."

Break his word? *Of course.* She made him promise not to seek her out again. But that oath, she knew now, was one she'd always in her heart hoped he'd be unable to keep. She pushes away the irritating thought of her mother using her lover as a messenger, determined not to ruin these stolen moments.

"You are forgiven," she says, planting a playful kiss on the bridge of his nose. "But what news is so urgent from Brandishear that my *nurse*"—she spreads deliberate emphasis on the word—"needs it?"

He opens his mouth, closes it again, struggling for the right answer. "I haven't laid eyes on your face or heard your voice in three years. Do we need to talk of that?"

"What else would you talk of?"

"You." He leans forward to kiss her again, but she retreats.

"Me? That's hardly an interesting subject. I have babies. I nurse them, wipe their noses and their bottoms, and toss them like jesters' clubs between my hands and those of my nurses, hoping none of us lets one fall." As she talks, a sharp bitter note edges into her voice. "I order the household, keep records of the number of sacks of rye versus barley in our storehouses, the candles we use and the cost of evenlamps, which barrels of wine and which of ale should be broached each night. It is an army of small details, and I am its general. A more boring life you cannot imagine."

He catches her fingers again, tangling them this time in his own. "Then run away with me." He smiles.

The sudden brief thought of it leaves her breathless for a moment, before it slaps her face.

"You cannot be serious," she snaps, then softens her reply. "When you first asked it of me, I wouldn't trade peace in the Ilmar for my own happiness —"

"Are you saying that peace still hangs on this marriage of yours, eight years on?"

She laughs, a sharp humourless sound. "Not in the least. I am utterly unimportant to the current chessboard, I'm sure. And no doubt Allenis would hardly miss me. Or his daughters either, at least until they're of an age to marry. But his son he'd miss, and I would never leave one of my children behind. For anyone."

Einavar looks over her head, up toward the towers of Osthegn. "For that, I could almost hate him."

Hate whom? she wonders. Andreg? Does he not already hate Andreg? She hopes so. But Allenry? He could not possibly mean Allenry, for then she would have to hate Einavar, and her heart couldn't stand that. She doesn't ask for the clarification. Better not to know. This is not the conversation she wants to have.

"What of you? I thought you had rejoined the Rangers."

"I have. I am." He is startled out of his thoughts.

"And yet here you are." She eyes him, and before he is forced to explain, goes on. "One of the loyal Brandishear Rangers my father puts so much faith in. And yet you really work for my mother."

He lowers his head in acquiescence.

"I work for both. And above all, the Ilmar."

"But what happens when the demands of your masters conflict?"

He doesn't meet her eyes. "They have not, so far."

"So far."

There is another silence. Lauresa feels the weight of his words settle on her. The temptation is so strong to test that loyalty. Find out where his true allegiance lies. If she were to ask him to reveal her mother's business — ask him directly — would he tell her? Most of her hopes not. And yet the small, childish part of her that wants proof, and proof again, of his love for her can't help but wish it, ever so slightly.

But she will not test it, not tonight, and perhaps not ever. For she too is beholden to duty.

The euphoria of Einavar's visit lasts nearly a month before the endless stream of bookwork and accounting, the minutiae of mothering five children and a castle full of servants, retainers, and guests, pushes down on her shoulders and her feet drag on the solid ground again. Summer's bounty, and easy days with children playing in the garden, give her some buoyancy. But the suspicion of political undercurrents passing just beneath her nose, and the uneasy feeling her mother knows more about the affairs of her domain than she does, wipes some of the bloom from her happiness. She would delve deeper, try to investigate, if only she had the energy.

She looks back to her time growing up in Rheran and wonders that life was ever so uncomplicated. She wonders too how she could have been so casually oblivious to the politics of court when she had all the time and energy to engage in them. Perhaps if she had been involved, her life would have been different. She might have had a say in whom she married. But then she would not have met Einavar. Allaigna would not be Allaigna, and neither would Allenry, Lauriana, or these two half-sleeping cherubs nestled under her arms, nursing themselves to sleep, their matching fuzzy heads pressed against each other.

Irdina shifts, opens her eyes. Lauresa strokes the bridge of her nose until the blue eyes are hidden again. Branwen stirs as well, eyes still closed, but her tiny hand reaches for her sister's face. Lauresa intercepts it before a finger up the nose awakes Irdina. The minute fingers wrap themselves around her long one, and both babies settle into a deeper sleep.

No, she would not trade it for anything.

Irdaign's Chorus

I follow the bobbing track of Wulf's lanthorn through the dark castle and out into the sharp black cold of a spring night. The warm smell of the stable is both cloying and comforting after that. Ten-year-old Wulf leads me with an air of urgent self-importance to one of the two broodmare stalls at the far end of the stable, where Hardin, his father and chief groom, has draped himself uneasily over the stall door.

He has been a groom here since before my arrival in Teillai, and has been head groom almost as long. He often comes to me for advice on ailing horses, but he must be worried indeed to send his son to wake me on the far side of midnight.

He doesn't say a word, but motions me to the stall. I signal Wulf to raise his lanthorn and shine it into the loosebox. Disturbed by the light, Aster heaves herself to her feet, ears pinned back, snaking her pretty dappled head into a ferocious, wild-eyed vision. She is Peri's daughter, a gift from Lauresa to her husband. It is typical of Andreg that he scorns to ride her and keeps her as a broodmare only, to improve the blood of his warhorses. Peri is of the finest pedigree of Brandishear coursers, and Lauresa had to look far and wide to find a sire to match her. A lot of eagles have been invested in this mare, who now bears a foal by Andreg's huge-boned, chestnut stallion. No wonder Hardin has woken me.

"She's up, she's down, and then she's up again, pacing around." His low calm voice does not fully disguise the worry I can smell on him.

"Colic?" I ask.

He half shakes his head. "Don't think so. She's eatin' and drinkin' fine. It's her time, I'm sure of it. Plenty of show." Indeed, there is a sticky rivulet down one elegant, black-stockinged leg. "I'd check, but she won't let me near."

The mare has never been backed, and hardly ever handled. Andreg may value her for her bloodline, but he has little other interest in a fine-boned courser. 'Mares are worth more with foals in their bellies' is his theory. He only rides stallions, and the vast bulk of his mares spend most of the year pastured above the commons.

I curse him for his false logic. Both Hardin and I know that a mare that's been a riding horse has manners and a known temperament. For more than blood goes into the making of a horse. A mare that loves and is loved by humans teaches her foal the same; a mare that is ridden shows by example there is nothing to fear from saddles and bits and a person on her back. And a mare that trusts her handlers is far easier to help while foaling.

All these thoughts pass unspoken between Hardin and me. We've had such discussions many times before.

I nod to him and start to sing. Aster flicks her ears back at the sound, then turns them forward again and seems to find it pleasing rather than not.

I sing until her neck relaxes, her head drops below her withers, and her tail stops its irritable swishing. Hardin and I enter the stall slowly while I continue to sing.

Hardin slips a halter over the mare's head. She barely twitches, and then, resigned, rests her forehead against his chest while he caresses her poll. I ease myself alongside her, running my hand over her distended flanks, waiting for her to react as I come to rest at last on her dock. The tail stays still, and her ears remain drooped sideways as I lift her tail and stroke the sides of her well-muscled rump.

There is the barest bulge in her vulva, the tip of a foot just showing. I drop her tail and wash my hands up to the elbows in the bucket of water standing by the stall door. Hardin follows my movements, asking with raised eyebrows whether I need help. I shake my head and return to Aster's hindquarters, feeling for the feet.

She shifts her weight but doesn't otherwise flinch as I slide a finger around the protruding forefoot, with its soft, leathery hoof, searching for its twin. Nothing. Only a single hoof presenting. No wonder Aster is restless.

I slide my hand in farther, standing well to the side in case Aster snaps out of the dozy trance I've sung her into and lets fly with a back foot. Still only one baby hoof, and no sign of a nose either.

I sing a few more lines, increasing Aster's drowsiness so much that she spreads her forefeet wide and leans into Hardin to hold herself up.

My wrist, my forearm, follow the foal's leg all the way up to my elbow when my fingers finally reach something else: not a nose or another hoof, but an ear.

This will be long and difficult. I will have to push the flexed head of this baby back, working against the mighty force of a horse's womb, bring the nose forward, and try to find the second foreleg, no doubt tucked beneath the foal's chin.

I look over the mare's hindquarters at Hardin. Again, my eyes tell him most of it. The rest I illustrate with my free arm, crooking it to mirror the flexed head of the foal. He nods his understanding. We both know it will be a long night.

Hardin and I lean on the stall door, our arms crossed under our chins like a pair of children at the fair, unable to stop beaming idiotically at the sight of the newborn filly's curly brush of a tail flicking up and down against her wet rump.

Aster sniffs her daughter, her own ears flicking a quizzical counterpoint to the flapping tail as she experiences the new sensation of a foal at the teat. Like they always do at the thought of any suckling babe, my own breasts tingle in memory, and I think of Lauresa.

What a fine creature Aster is, and what a waste to keep her as a mere broodmare. Her legs are smooth and straight, her nostrils large, her shoulder long and sloping to a broad deep chest. This mare could run like the wind if given the chance. I long to take her on, train the mistrust and sour habits out of her, and turn her into a fine hunter. But Andreg barely tolerates my influence over his wife. He'd never allow it over his horse.

Aster's eyes have lost their white rings, and her sides move contentedly in and out. She pricks her ears and fixes me with a stare that is only partly trustful, and maybe a little bit grateful.

"I think she likes you," murmurs Hardin.

A small chuckle escapes my throat, causing Aster's delicate ears to flick again.

"*Like* may be too strong a word. She may have just come to the conclusion she need not totally mistrust me."

"A waste of a fine mare," Hardin says, echoing my thoughts. "The mistress might have done better by her than to gift her to his Grace."

I glance in surprise at Hardin. It is bold talk from a groom to speak so against his master, never mind his implicit criticism of Lauresa. I should respond with caution, but he has struck a chord within me.

"It was a gift of the heart, not of the head. Nonetheless, as much as our lady may regret it, she cannot ask for the mare back."

I see in his eyes he cannot understand this. He could never weigh subtle marital politics against the well-being of a horse, and for that I respect and warm to him even more.

Verse 15
Running

By the following morning, I no longer wanted to leave the womblike confines of the inn room. My tears, which had continued on and off all night, were somehow soothing, an indulgent relief from action, and illness was an excellent excuse to avoid questioning myself.

However, my large appetite when Rhoan brought in a tray of breakfast gave my health away.

"Are you well enough to ride?" he asked.

I hunched down in the bed, wriggling muscles stiff from unuse.

"I'm not sure ..." I began feebly.

"Because the weather is fine, and I'd hate to lose a good day's riding waiting for the rain to come back."

He had a point. I had no desire to ever sit on a wet horse under dripping trees again, nor did I relish sleeping in that mildewy sodden tent. Since none of my family's soldiers had come knocking on our door, perhaps inns were a better option after all.

"How long a ride till the next town or inn?" I asked, thinking I could probably tolerate no more than three hours in the saddle.

"A full day at the trot and we can make Rhercyn if we start now. If we don't, we'll only get as far as the Nyndenu troop station — and I doubt you'll want to stop there."

My mind was ticking over geography. "Rhercyn — that means we're in Werrancross now?" I nearly yelled, then glanced worriedly around at the thin walls, which suddenly seemed to be hiding ears. "Of all the places they'll look for me," I whispered, "they'd look here first. Why did you bring me here?"

"Would you rather I'd let you perish in the woods?" he replied drily. "I could have spent a few days vainly looking for a Wood-kin camp — they're reputed to be so easy to find. But I thought an apothecary would be faster and safer."

"But here? In Werrancross?"

"Apothecaries don't set up shop in wayside inns or farming hamlets. And besides, a pair of travellers is far less noticeable in a city of ten thousand than a village of a hundred."

I could see his logic, but I was still nervous. "Have you been out and around? Are there …?"

"Yes, your lovely face is still displayed on handbills at every tavern and merchant's in town. Luckily you weren't looking much yourself when I brought you here, and the landlady paid little attention. But it wouldn't do to stay too long."

"The road between here and Caradry …"

He nodded. "Will be full of Aerach and Brandishear patrols. We'll keep our heads down and seem no more than any other travellers till Caradry. At which point we will be in Brandishear. And presumably out of reach of your family."

My family's arms are long enough to stretch all the way across the Ilmar, I thought, but merely nodded.

Could my short hair and meagre disguise fool all those eyes

on the Clearwater Way? And if not, what alternative? Cross the Sandhorn desert? Enter the Valnirata Greatwood? Take ship at the highly controlled port? Or turn back and go home.

The worst that could happen, I kept reminding myself, is that I would be recognized and returned home. After all, the handbills were only the effort of a loving family to see their daughter safe. Not a portrait of a wanted murderer—no matter how close to the truth that was.

Though not a lord's seat, Werrancross is larger than either Teillai or Doniver. Its position as the entry to Aerach from the Clearwater Way, and the nearest port to all points west, has made it swell its original walls in a spill of ever newer houses. It is a situation I had heard my father—the Duke—grumble about before. He despised settlements that outlay curtain walls, and I'm sure he would have walled in all of Aerach if he could. He had a point, especially here, so close to the Valnirata and the sea, where one attack could drive all the inhabitants within the old city walls, crowding and starving the current inhabitants, while goods and lands would lie vulnerable without. There were at least two places where new outer walls had been begun, but the growth of houses and shops had outpaced wall construction, and these segments lay unfinished, serving as back walls to buildings on all sides.

The city council set itself in opposition to direction either from Aleran or its direct liege, Teillai. While princes and dukes of Aerach commanded fortification, the merchants wanted trade. Nonetheless, a new hill fort had been begun opposite the old motte and bailey inhabited by the governor. It was in the new style, large and star-shaped with rammed earth behind stone walls. Rather than being a home for nobility, its centre housed troops both permanent and temporary, as well as stables for horses, barns for livestock, sheds for the new horse-drawn artillery and, if I guessed correctly, an arsenal of reserve weaponry.

Under the looming glare of this mile-long outpost, we nervously set our horses upon the Clearwater Way. I would have been far happier if I could have sung a charm to change my hair colour and Nag's coat. But my throat was still stopped with the memory of the last magic I'd sung. All I could do was keep my hat low and my head down despite the warm spring sunshine.

The road was busy, merchants and other travellers having also delayed their journeys for the weather. Many of the wagons streaming from inns and hostels were headed for the port. An equal number, laden with Aerach wool, barley, wheat, and sugar, or with finished goods like whisky, porcelain, copper, and tinware, were setting their drays toward eastern Brandishear. Towns there were too far from seaports to acquire goods easily, and were more than happy to put gold and silver into the hands of those traders willing to cross the Sandhorn.

The four-oxen teams were wide and lumbering, and we rode past them where the muddy verges of the road allowed, but all around was cultivated farmland through which we dared not ride in the face of farmers out sowing their crops. When we finally passed the last of the caravans, the morning was already gone, but the road was clear and straight ahead of us, with no traffic in sight.

I looked across at Rhoan. "Race you to that tree," I challenged, pointing to a lone oak at least two furlongs away.

Rhoan's middle-aged eyes crinkled into pure boyishness. Without even a breath to ponder, he kicked Talwis and sent her springing forward in a startled scramble.

I was launched backward and hit the cantle as Nag burst after her. The half-dozen strides in which I slewed in the saddle, regaining my seat and reins, gave Rhoan and his mare a sizeable lead. But though Nag wasn't one of the fine-boned coursers my mother bred, he was long-legged and deep-chested. He stretched his jug head forward, and his body dropped beneath me as he flattened into a ground-eating gallop.

Rhoan's mare was fast too, with a densely muscled rump built for comfortable collection at the walk or trot and good for powerful bursts of speed in the short distance. Nag was gaining on her slowly, but he'd never catch her in the distance left between us and the tree.

I sat up straighter. No need to spend my horse completely in a friendly and unwinnable race. But as I raised my eyes and eased his pace, I caught sight of a glint on the horizon: a flash that was neither water nor glass but the unmistakable flicker of sunlight on steel.

I yelled at Rhoan, urging him to stop, and hauled on Nag's none-too-soft mouth. Rhoan didn't hear me. His form stayed bent over his horse's neck as she kicked up rounds of half-dry mud.

Nag fought me, leaping sideways and giving a crow-hop of protest, his neck twisting and jaw gaping, incensed at being left behind.

Finally Rhoan looked over his shoulder to see how far ahead he was. He pulled the mare up when he spotted me spinning Nag on the spot. Talwis dutifully rolled back on her haunches and returned to us in her floating trot, ears pricked, pleased with herself after the exhilarating gallop.

At Rhoan's puzzled look, I took a hand off my reins long enough to point at the flash of helmets and armour on the horizon.

"You don't want to run straight into a patrol, do you?"

He shaded his eyes and peered down the road. "Are you still feverish, lass? There's nothing there."

I sighed, frustrated with the poor eyesight I'd always recognized in adults. Now I wondered if my sharper eyes and ears were not due to youth but to Ilvani blood.

"Trust me . . . there's a patrol up ahead. Three or four helmets."

He squinted, shaking his head. "Going or coming?" He still looked doubtful.

"How can I tell?" I snapped. "*You* can barely see them." I paused, watching for a bit. "Going, I think." I let out the half breath I'd been holding.

I let Nag walk forward just to stop his restless shifting, and Rhoan's mare fell into step beside me.

"Should we leave the road?" I asked, looking around. The countryside was fairly flat: easy to cross, but lacking in cover.

He shook his head. "That would certainly call attention to us. We stick to the road, like all other innocent travellers."

"But . . ." I began to protest.

"And if we're going the same direction, we won't need to cross paths at all."

That was a good plan as far as it went. I kept my eyes on the road ahead, holding Nag to a pace that never gained on the sparkling glints of armour ahead of me.

The sun rose and crossed the sky's axis while we kept our uneasy distance behind the armoured riders. It was up to me, with my better vision, to maintain the space. Between the glare of the sun in my face, the heat of it on my head, and the strain of staring at the horizon, my head was pounding.

"We should stop now. Let the horses graze," I said. "And we can rest in the shade of those oaks."

Rhoan shook his head. "Wait till they break."

"Why? If they get farther ahead, that's good — we'll catch up when they do stop."

"And if they break for longer than we do, do we stop again? I'd rather keep them in our — your — sight."

"What if they don't break at all?"

"Then we're sure to make Rhercyn by nightfall."

That was little comfort to my aching head. I returned my eyes to the road ahead and breathed my relief.

"They've stopped."

He peered down the road. "Are you sure? There seems just as much dust in the air."

"Of course I'm sure," I snapped. "You can see the horses milling about. That's why there's more dust."

I kicked my feet from the stirrups, ready to dismount, but something about the cloud of dust made me look again. Was it just that some of the horses were turned sideways or ...

"There's more of them!"

Rhoan was already on the ground. "What do you mean, more?"

"I mean there's more horses, more riders ... at least twice as many. And they've stopped up ahead."

"Brandishear Patrol." He frowned, thought a second, and swung back into the saddle. "I guess we find out now how good your disguise is, lass."

I opened my mouth, but my throat was dry. Sure enough, the Aerach patrolmen we'd been following turned their horses back, having exchanged reports with their Brandishear counterparts.

"I can't." The words came out a barely audible croak.

"You look little enough like the handbill these days."

His encouragement merely dribbled off the wall of fear I felt growing around me. Another thought had struck. There was a chance—quite a good chance—the Aerach patrol contained riders from Teillai, any one of whom might know me, with or without a handbill.

The flashes of sunlight off armour were growing larger and brighter with each constricted breath I drew. Senseless panic overwhelmed reason. I yanked Nag's head around, jumped the grassy roadside ditch from a standstill, and cantered toward the stand of oaks on the right hand side of the road.

I could hear Rhoan's curse above the pounding of blood in my ears and looked back, relieved to see him mounting up to follow.

The oak trees were not nearly as densely spaced as they had seemed from a distance, nor so far from the roadside. Without checking to see if Rhoan followed, I wheeled again and sent Nag at a gallop toward the ravine between two low foothills.

The footing at the bottom was both rocky and muddy from spring rain, forcing me to slow to a trot, and then to a walk. When at last I pulled up, Nag was huffing and snorting at the impromptu workout, and Rhoan's mare was slowly picking her way up the gully. From here the tops of the oak trees were still visible, but the road was hidden until it meandered into view farther east.

"They shouldn't be able to see us here," I panted when Rhoan caught up.

He was scowling. "Not from the road, no. But what if they turn off to find out why two riders went haring off into the hills? Which I'd certainly do if I were on patrol."

"You think they saw us?" I interrupted.

"By the time you made your mad dash, *I* could see them with my dreadful eyes. So yes, I'd say so."

The walls of fear pressed tighter, squeezing the breath from me. "What do we do?" I whispered, feeling tears start.

"Sensible option: we ride back down. If they ask when we meet them, which we will do, I tell them my *daughter's* horse spooked and bolted. And we carry on our way."

"But we can't ..." I shook my head, trying to chase away the tears that wouldn't stop. "I can't. There may be ... probably will be soldiers from Teillai. They'll *know* me."

"And then what, lass?" he asked and reached over to put a gentle hand on my knee.

Nag was taller than his mare and standing upslope from her, so Rhoan had to look up to see my water-filled eyes and crumpled chin. "They'll take you home, where your family loves and cares for you. Is that so bad that you'd risk fleeing through the Kelerin hills with me instead?"

I couldn't answer. I couldn't tell him that I no longer *could* go home, with Doniver's death on my hands, to face Mother and Angeley. That I was no longer sure they would still love me. I only nodded.

He sighed, patted my knee, and pushed past Nag, leading the way up the gully.

Irdaign's Chorus

There is a new light in Lauresa's eyes, a floating swing to her step that reveals the lightness of her heart. She is softer and warmer with the children, kinder to the servants. I do not know what occurred in the garden that night — though there was time for little more than talk — but whatever it was has revitalized my daughter.

I shake off the image of myself as the matron of a bawdy house, arranging assignations. Whatever the risks to her marriage, to peace in the household, the refound joy in Lauresa is worth it.

I only wish the news Einavar brought with him was as happy.

Chanist is in his cups again. I should have known that even without hearing it directly, just by learning of his actions. Scouting parties of Rangers have been sent to the Valnirata territories. Small, unobtrusive no doubt, but not unobtrusive enough to avoid the watchful Ilvani eyes. What could he be thinking? But then thinking has little to do with it, I know. If he were thinking, he would value what he has over a revenge that will never satisfy him. More disturbing still is what Einavar has learned from connections within the Mage Guard, of experiments taking place in the high fourth floor of the Bastion, the heart of Rheran, his own home. That bit of recklessness alone astounds me.

I have provided Einavar with more tonics, though it is harder and harder for him to deliver them to his prince, stationed as he is on the outskirts of Brandishear. No, it is time for another visit here from Chanist. I sigh in frustration, thinking of the days I will have to absent myself from home once more, never mind the number of subtle wheels and cogs I must put into motion to bring him here.

Life was so much simpler when I was a princess. But I wouldn't go back to it for anything.

Coming home to Teillai after being away for one of Chanist's visits always seems like visiting a new province altogether. Or another world, just like this one, but altered in unidentifiable ways, as if turned a fraction of a degree on its axis. I have never been entirely sure how the gift of precognizance works. That I can see things before they happen does not mean that all our lives are preordained. For if they were, what use would be the Sight? Events would roll out on the carpet of history and future with never a snag or dropped thread. Some things I have seen have never come to pass, as if by seeing I have altered the weft of history. And yet others I see are terrible, and I am powerless to prevent them. All I can try to do is soften the blows they have on the lives around me.

Did I save Chanist from death at Welbirk? I did not see his death as I did the deaths of the other three of his family, only felt a presentiment of danger that made me call him home before his sister, brother, and father died, all within a week of one another. And did I save him for the good of the Ilmar, or for my own selfish reasons? If I had not, what other world might I be coming home to? How can I ever know?

I sometimes feel that time is merely a construct and all that ever will happen already has, in its infinite possibilities. So perhaps the Teillai I left is not the one to which I come back, for something small has changed. A tiny, unforeseen choice has moved me from one future to the next one over. Why does this make me so uneasy? Does the need to hold the shuttle that weaves my family's threads grip me so tightly that any small loss of control causes me worry?

I take a long measured breath as my carthorse slows to a stop in front of Osthegn's great gates. The stakes are high, yes, but surely I am not so important in the grand tapestry that I cannot allow other hands to cast a pass or two. Not all the times life has surprised me have been bad. Surprises, on the balance, have been as many parts pleasurable as otherwise. I wonder what surprises await me this time.

Hardin and his son are sitting on overturned buckets, cleaning harness by the sunny south wall of the stables. Hardin jumps to his feet with a jangle and clatter as the leather and brasses tumble to the ground.

He hands me down from the cart with such alacrity and deference I wonder for a moment if he has guessed my true relationship to the lady of the castle. No, I decide, it is merely the respect so many stablemen have for Leisanmira.

He holds my hand for a tiny instant after my feet have touched ground.

"It is good to have you back, Mistress Angeley."

"It's good to be back, Master Hardin," I reply, smiling at his kind and honest face.

"Wulf," he calls over his shoulder. "Quit dallying and unhitch Pashu." He swings up onto the buckboard, reaching out the cases and bags I have brought back from Aleran.

"Are these all going to your workshop, mistress?"

"Yes, but don't trouble yourself with them. The porter can deal with that."

"No trouble at all, mistress." He grins, tossing a sack over his shoulder and grasping two bags apiece in his great hands. "I'll take them straight over."

"And how goes it in the stable yard, Master Hardin?" I ask, slowing my usual stride to match his easy gait. "How's the filly doing?"

"Growing hand over hand." His smile stretches to his ears, crinkling the sun-cured skin around his eyes. "Aster's a good mother in spite of her snarly nature. Her Grace has ta'en an interest in them both."

"She has?" There it is: a complete and unforeseen happening. It is nothing of import in the grand weaving, just a thread I hadn't expected or seen before.

"Aye, the Duchess has a canny way with the pair of them—she's the knack of horses, no doubt."

"She's of the royal line of Brandishear. Horses run in her blood."

"Well, I'd swear there was Leisanmira in that touch of hers as well …"

My heart does a trip and double beat.

"… not just from her golden hair and sea-blue eyes."

I breathe, my thoughts scrambling around in my brain for the correct response. What is he implying? The breath calms me, and I realize truth is my friend here.

"Did you not know, Master Hardin? Her Grace's mother was Leisanmira."

He frowns. "I thought she was some small royalty of Brandishear—not that I know the noble families, 'specially not outside Aerach But still—Leisanmira? Are ye sure?"

I can see he is both pleased and puzzled. Puzzled at the incongruity of gipsy blood running in the veins of nobles, and pleased that he'd spotted her bloodlines like any good purveyor of horseflesh would. I am amused more than insulted. Proud, in fact, of my daughter's ancestry shining through.

"Her mother," I say softly, "was the Princess High Irdaign, first wife of Chanist of Brandishear, and quite fully and firmly of the Leisanmira."

He whistles, impressed perhaps at the height of her royal

lineage, not widely known in Teillai. Or perhaps it is the other half of her blood that has his attention.

"Well, if that doesn't beat a dead donkey to life. No wonder she's such a beauty. Why, you could even be related."

My heart does its stumble again. That is too close to truth for comfort. I'm so preoccupied I nearly miss the compliment he's handed me. He places the bags at the door of my workshop and turns, asking where I'd like them put.

I let the question drift by, gazing at his honest, sun-worn features, and he is forced to ask again. I am utterly unaware of my answer, for I am caught up in the look he gives me.

Verse 16

Into the Wasteland

The ravine between the two hills narrowed before long, becoming clogged with small trees and undergrowth that forced us onto the hillsides. No longer able to stay in the middle, we were forced to choose the left- or right-hand path. Rhoan looked back at me, leaving the decision resting on my saddlebow. The right-hand foothill was slightly less steep, with easier footing. But if we took that, we'd be keeping the gully between us and the west.

"Left," I said, without a trace of the hesitation I felt. "The vantage is better," I added in an attempt to hide my real motive, which was to increase the distance between me and Aerach.

Rhoan didn't argue, just nodded, riding his mare across the rivulet of water that ran along the ravine floor and heading up the rocky bank to the tuft-covered slope on the left.

The horses were lathered and puffing from the climb when the hill finally levelled out to provide us a vantage. To the north loomed a larger hill, a mountain almost, though dry and brush-covered, not lush and forested with a snowy head like the mountains of home. To the east was a lower hill, the one we didn't climb; and to the west, a ridge skirted the larger mountain like a curtain wall around a massive keep, leading off to the maze of the Kelerin range.

The horses couldn't puff for long.

"Look." I pointed down the hill behind us.

That now-familiar and awful glint of metal in sunlight winked out of the tree-lined gorge. It was a single rider, thankfully on the eastern slope.

I heard Rhoan let out a whooshing breath. "Not so good a tracker, then," he breathed. "But let's move before he spots us."

I squeezed Nag's reluctant sides hard. He snorted, almost, but not quite, masking the distant shout. I looked back again. A rider on the opposite hill was pointing and calling … and someone answered. I had to know. I dragged Nag's head about and forced him back at a trot in the direction we'd come, just until I could look over the hillside. Sure enough, a second rider was on the same hill as we were, and moving as fast as his burdened horse could lunge upward.

I spun Nag back and kicked him into a canter, surging past Rhoan on the narrow ridge. "There's two of them," I yelled.

Cursing, Rhoan spurred his mare to catch us.

I leaned low over my saddle, one hand holding the reins as far forward as I could, giving Nag his head over the uneven ground; the other hand twisted in his mane, expecting a stumble or jump at any time that could spill me from the saddle.

The ridge was long and tortuous, rising and falling like the back of a dragon. At several points Nag had to slow to a trot to negotiate the wild game trails that wove their way along it, and at many of these I caught sight of our pursuer flashing over the horizon and disappearing again. However, each time he appeared he was farther away. He was only lightly armoured, but it was enough to slow his horse.

"Hold!" Rhoan shouted at last, slowing to a walk. Nag was only too happy to comply, despite my desperate urge to push on.

"Their horses can't keep the pace of ours," he said. "We can slow, at least for a bit."

I nodded with reluctance, acknowledging the truth of the statement and the need to rest our blown horses.

After walking two full sets of switchbacks, Rhoan allowed us to move faster. "Trot only," he said. "It's fast enough for this terrain, and they'll last longer."

"Should we head down into the trees?" I asked, looking nervously at the ever steeper shoulder that led into the thin pine forest now between us and the road.

"Not a bad idea—next down-ridge we get. Better than heading into that." He motioned with his head toward the badlands of the Sandhorn, which stretched out below us to the north.

Soon enough, a side slope did lead down into the forest. Rhoan led the way, his mare cautiously zigzagging down the scree-strewn slope. The shoulder levelled for a bit, and widened, taking a gentler, almost road-like track as it entered the sparse but welcome shade of the pines.

The bay mare had just slipped into that shade when Nag's head shot up. At the same time, I heard the clink and jangle, saw the terrible telltale flash again.

"Rhoan!" I hauled back on Nag, causing him to scramble for footing and almost slide off the shoulder. The gelding didn't want to go back up the hill, never mind at speed, but I pounded with my heels till he did. I couldn't even spare a glance backward as he lurched in great rock-scattering leaps up the hillside, me clinging to his neck like a burr in his mane.

I heard a horse behind me as we crested the hilltop, prayed it was Rhoan, and started off along the western track, only to come to a skidding halt. Coming toward us, in Brandishear blue and silver, was another horseman. And our first pursuer, in Aerach colours, was clearly visible to the east. They must have sent riders back to the Brandishear patrol.

Without asking, without waiting, I took my last open direction, sending Nag skidding down the steeper northern slope, straight into the badlands.

The air felt different almost the instant our horses' hooves started down the northern shoulder. The wave of heat, like a smithy furnace, rolled over us as the horses slid and scrambled down the rocky decline. Even when we entered the shade of the ravine bottom, there was little relief.

Shouts were audible from the ridge top, and I could clearly see both Brandishear and Aerach colours on the patrolmen who gathered there. Rhoan pulled up behind me in the shadowed side of the ravine, and we peered at the soldiers. Their horses' ears made a row of points against the horizon, mirroring the feathered treetops. The patrolmen weren't following us or stringing their bows. Nor were they leaving. It seemed they were content to leave us to the mercies of the desert and the bandits who lived there.

I wanted to apologize to the bleak look in Rhoan's eyes. Instead I said, "We could wait till they leave?"

He shook his head. "They won't. Oh, for certain some will report back to their way stations. But at least four will camp on that ridge — and patrol the ones on either side for the next several days."

"So where do we go?"

He looked north into the rutted and wind-blasted desert ahead of us. "Into that."

The dry hot air wrapped itself around me, drinking the last traces of moisture from my skin, my nose, my eyes. The horses, once lathered and sweaty from our frantic chase over the hills, were dry now, their coats bristly and caked with hardened dust and foam. They walked slowly, their heads low, stumbling on the cracked and rocky desert floor. Rhoan's part-Sandbred bay suffered less than Nag, whose black coat soaked in all the shadowless heat.

By all rights, the water-laden air from the sea should have made this peninsula greener and more temperate than the land south of the mountains. But the immense forest of the Valnirata creates its own climate, which gathers moist air and recycles it over the Greatwood and its environs. Prevailing winds from the Clearwater send the sea air scudding past the Sandhorn, slipping sideways over the Kelerin hills and into Aerach's south-western reaches, leaving the northern stretches of Kelerin and the Sandhorn a region of bare red and grey rocks and swirling sand beneath clouds that withhold their rain. It is inhabited by strong desert plants, hardy beasts, and people who have no better place to live.

Nag stumbled yet again, throwing me against the saddlebow. I took this hint at last and slid to the ground, feeling the oven heat of the sand and rocks through my boots. The air was even hotter this close to the ground.

One step, two, three, four … I counted in time to my footfalls. Any distraction to keep my feet moving. It was boring, but it was all I could think of.

Rhoan, riding ahead, noticed me falling back and dismounted as well.

He didn't speak—just raised a questioning eyebrow at me. I nodded assurance that we were fine, and he turned north again, leading Talwis. No need to waste breath on talk.

The dark shadow of a large rock we had chased all afternoon was growing at last, though perhaps that was just the lowering sun stretching it. I looked back at the Kelerin hills behind us, with their taunting fringe of trees. They seemed smaller, and were so far off I could no longer smell the pines or taste the cooler breezes that trickled off of them.

By the time we stumbled into the lee of the great rock, its shadow stretched across the ragged desert floor to three times its height: a welcome black blanket on the red-gold glare of late afternoon. A family of stunted, scraggly trees—no more than bushes, really—huddled at its base. Grooves etched in the rock showed where rainwater had converged and collected year after year, the channels carving a hollow side to the otherwise loaf-shaped mound. It was in this protected hollow, where trees thrived, if barely, that we found water.

It was no more than a puddle, two large strides across, shallow but clear, with a muddy border indicating it had been larger than this at dawn. Beyond the mud was cracked, dry clay, and beyond that bunches of hardy, deep-rooted grass.

The numerous small animal tracks indicated the water was sweet. Moreover, it was the sweetest thing I'd tasted in all my life. Rhoan held the eager horses well away from the water, letting them graze while I refilled our four water skins. When at last we let the horses drink, they widened the muddy verge by a good foot.

"It wasn't always like this, you know." Rhoan used his shirt to wipe his wet face.

I looked at the arid land around us, relieved only by the tall upshoot of rock and the straggly bushes that survived in its lee.

"How do you know?"

He stretched his long legs out in front of him and began unlacing his boots. "Ancient legends say people lived here once — that the land had trees and crops. There are even traces of buildings out here somewhere."

I frowned. Willits had been excessively diligent in stuffing Ilmar history into my head, but this was not familiar.

"You mean Ilvani — before the arrival of Ilmari?"

"No. Before the Ilvani."

"But they were here for thousands of years before the Ilmar migration."

He had his boots off and was splashing water onto his feet. I looked askance at the waste.

"Don't you think we should conserve the water?"

He shook his head. "This is a rainwater puddle. It ran off this miniature mountain during the rains we suffered from last week. From the size of it, it will be gone by tomorrow anyway. Our canteens are full — enjoy it while you can."

I lifted a disapproving eyebrow but decided I'd take my own boots off as soon as the horses were groomed.

"What happened, then, to those people? Did they move? Was there a war?"

He shrugged. "We don't know. They might have warred with the Ilvani. They might have moved when the land became barren. Or maybe some other calamity struck."

It irritated me, this uncertainty over something so vast as the disappearance of a civilization.

"We may never know," he added, only making it worse.

I untacked Nag, brushing the dried sweat out of his coat as best I could, and began picking the stones out of his feet. I let out a wail as I held up the gelding's off fore. "Look," I said, my chin quivering embarrassingly as I tried not to cry.

The hoof I held was still shod, but barely. Of the three nails that held the left side of the shoe on, one was loose, another was missing entirely, and a third had worked itself halfway out and bent over, so its square head pushed into the sole of Nag's foot.

Rhoan whistled, shook his head. "Damn me, I should have had him re-shod when we were in Werrancross. I'm so sorry, lass."

I dropped the hoof, and my tears began in earnest. Part of me, the childish part, wanted to latch onto Rhoan's self-recrimination and blame him; but I knew I had no one to blame but myself. I counted the weeks since I'd left home — too many. Nag's feet were far longer than they ought to have been, the hoof wall growing out over the shoes, and it was a miracle he hadn't cast a shoe before this. No wonder he'd been stumbling all day.

I grabbed one of the plentiful rocks and lifted Nag's foot to bang the one straight nail flush with the shoe once more. The hoof around the clinches was dry and crumbly, and there was no way I could re-clinch the nail I'd just re-driven, but it might hold a day or so. I slipped my knife under the bent nail, noting how Nag flinched when I dug the head out of his sole. It had created a bruise for certain, but at least it hadn't punctured the sole.

There was no way to salvage the nail, so I wiggled it with the crossbar of my knife. It came out far too easily. That left one nail, badly clinched, holding the left side of the shoe on.

"Do you have nails?" I asked Rhoan, knowing already what the answer would be. His mare went barefoot.

He shook his head. "No, but we'll make something."

"Out of what?" I could feel an edge of hysteria creeping into my voice.

Rhoan rested his hand on my back between the shoulder blades. It was hot and uncomfortable, pressing the sweaty clothes to my back, but it was also oddly reassuring, an echo of Angeley's touch.

"Something. We'll work out something. But for now, we need to rest."

Lauresa's Chorus

Summer passes, and when the animals begin growing their thick coats again, Lauresa feels an itch as deep as theirs. As much as she loves her family, this sweaty summer spent in a bed with five children has nearly suffocated her.

She is drawn outdoors—not to the gardens, where Angeley is harvesting late squash and laying down mulch for winter, but to the stables, where restless fuzzy horses chafe in their paddocks and long for the fields now denied them.

Today she is dressed as a stable hand. Already filthy from grooming Peri, she turns to her mare's daughter, Aster, and the still unnamed granddaughter.

Aster is a cranky and mistrustful creature who was never backed—she has lived her whole life a broodmare. That ought not to happen to her daughter, Lauresa decides. The mare flattens her ears and swishes her tail when Lauresa puts the headcollar on her. Her filly watches warily, curious and interested in the carrot Lauresa gives Aster, but still staying on the far side of her dam. Lauresa ignores her and proceeds to groom Aster, keeping her own wary eye on the mare's ears and hindquarters. Despite her show of protest, Aster relaxes at last and enjoys the thorough grooming.

Just when the mare seems to be entirely content, her head snaps up and her ears plaster back again.

It is the head groom, Hardin, and Allenis, walking down the stable aisle, discussing conditioning for Allenis's new destrier.

Lauresa scratches the mare's mane, cooing to her until the head droops once more; but up it goes again when Allenis stops at the stall door.

Allenis wrinkles his nose at the cloud of dust and hair that floats in the sunshine streaming through the back window. Or maybe he's wrinkling it at her in her trousers and dirt.

"Lauresa? Whatever are you doing, working in the stable?" He turns to Hardin, his mild distaste sliding into the beginnings of anger. "Are we so short of grooms that my lady wife must soil her hands?"

Lauresa lifts a stray lock of hair out of her eyes with the back of a dandy brush. "Master Hardin. Husband," she begins, slighting Allenis by addressing him second. "Peri seems to be in excellent weight to face winter, as does Aster here. I haven't yet had a chance to check over the filly. Has she been halter broken?"

Hardin looks at Allenis, allowing him to reply, but when he doesn't, clears his throat and answers, "Aye, your Grace. She's good for the farrier too. But she's had little handling aside from that. I understand ..." He glances back at Allenis. "She's to go to auction soon?"

Lauresa raises her eyebrows and gives Allenis a 'we'll discuss this later' stare. Auction, indeed! No filly of Peri's line will be sold as a carthorse.

"Well, you've done a fine job with her, Master Hardin."

And with that she turns back to Aster, dismissing her husband and stableman at the same time. The day is waning, but tomorrow, she determines, she will ride.

The moment Lauresa steps into the stable the next morning, the horses begin to nicker, some deep and throaty, others high and soft, but all of them eager and impatient for their morning grain.

With a sigh, she places her saddle pommel down against the wall and turns back to the feed room. Now they have been woken; if they aren't fed soon, they'll wake the whole castle with their snorting and banging on stall doors.

The light is dim in the feed room, and she has to put her hands in the bins to feel which is barley and which is oats. For that matter, she has no idea how much each horse gets. The stable boys must know it all by heart, as none among them can read or write. Hay should be easier, so she climbs the ladder to the loft, wincing at the increasing cacophony from the animals below, and begins tossing them sweet-smelling fodder through the holes above each stall. The ruckus below eases in measured increments as each horse begins to eat.

When she climbs back down, Master Hardin is standing in the feed room, hands on hips, glaring up at her. As recognition dawns, the glare turns to surprise, and he removes his hat with a worried air.

"Your Grace," he begins, offering her a hand for the last few rungs of the ladder, then withdrawing it at the presumption of offering his hand to a Duchess.

She can tell he is desperately concerned: wondering why she was in his loft, what error in management he committed to bring her there, or worse, what impropriety may have occurred and who might still be waiting above.

She smiles to put him at ease and extends her hand, allowing him to help her off the last step.

"I apologize, Master Hardin. I didn't mean to disrupt your feeding schedule." She brushes wisps of hay from her breeches and sees he is slightly scandalized by the sight of her out of her usual clothes. "I came for an early morning ride, and of course your charges all asked me for breakfast."

She can hear voices in the main corridor, and guesses Hardin's son and stable hand, Wulf, has also emerged from the groom quarters at the far end.

Hardin fidgets with his hat. "Thank you, your Grace. You should not have ..." He pauses, wondering no doubt how not to criticize his mistress. "... have had to do that. I'll discipline the lad for not feeding them earlier."

Lauresa's eyes widen in alarm, and she puts a hand on Hardin's arm.

"Please, don't! It was my error, not his, in coming here too early."

He shakes his head. "That is kind of your Grace, but we will make sure they are ready for you next time. Would you like me to saddle Peri for you now?"

Lauresa sighs. Is there nowhere she can be alone, unnoticed, unwaited-upon?

"Thank you, Master Hardin. That would be pleasant. But let her have some breakfast first."

While she waits for Peri to eat, she leans over Aster's stall and watches the big chestnut foal flick its tail as it drinks. Aster plasters her ears back and snakes her head toward Lauresa.

"That's hardly necessary," she admonishes the cranky mare. "I'm not after your food or your baby."

At that moment, a cheerful "good morning" echoes down the breezeway. Lauresa turns, astonished to see her mother, clad like her in riding clothes, striding down the aisle. Even more astonishing is the mare's reaction. She pricks her pretty dark grey ears and nickers, coming to the stall door despite her nursing foal, who trips over herself to stay latched on to the teat. Aster cranes her head over the stall door, ignoring Lauresa, evidently eager to greet Angeley, who scratches the mare between the eyes and croons a greeting.

"What are you doing here?" Lauresa asks.

Irdaign raises an eyebrow, makes a show of curtsying for the benefit of the staff mucking out stalls, and murmurs, "The same thing you are, by the look of it."

"I didn't know you rode."

"There are many things you don't know about me ... your Grace." She adds, under her breath, "You don't think your love of horses comes just from the Brandis side, do you?"

Lauresa can't take her eyes off Aster. The mare, so witchy at the best of times, is confidently closing her eyes and allowing Irdaign to scratch behind her ears and under her chin.

Irdaign opens the door and slips in, running a hand down the mare's neck, picking up each foot in turn. She then turns to the foal, who allows the same without a hint of protest from her mother.

"Have you charmed her?" Lauresa is dying to know.

Irdaign glances up. "Not in the way you mean."

Lauresa can hear the heavy echo of Hardin's boots clumping toward them.

"Peri's ready, your Grace."

Lauresa thanks him and then turns to Irdaign. "Would you like to accompany me, Mistress Angeley?"

Her mother smiles. "Why yes, your Grace. I think I would."

Lauresa walks back to where Peri stands waiting, held by Wulf. She takes her mare outside, accepts Master Hardin's leg up, and suggests Wulf help Angeley tack up a horse.

"No need for that, your Grace," Master Hardin replies, turning to face the stable.

Lauresa turns as well, in time to see her mother vault onto Aster's back with nothing but a bridle for tack.

She trots up, the foal at her heels. "Where shall we ride?"

Irdaign's Chorus

We say little at first, my daughter and I, as we ride out the gates of Osthegn and into the wider world. But my heart is warmer than the vernal sun that shines in our faces. Peri is old now, the hollows above her eyes profound, the blue grey of her coat faded almost to white, and yet she still carries Lauresa easily, with a spring in her step, a fast single-foot that Aster has difficulty keeping up with.

I wrap my legs around the younger mare's barrel, encouraging her to lengthen her stride instead of breaking into a jigging trot. Her back may be young and round, but my seat bones are less so, and I have no wish to sit her trot with no saddle beneath me.

I am reluctant to start a conversation yet. For now I merely enjoy the new experience of riding with my daughter. It shouldn't be new. There ought to have been so many rides together as she grew up. I admire her seat, the way her hip bones swing in smooth serpentines to Peri's long stride. I didn't teach her to ride, much to my regret, but she has a seat to rival the finest horsemen of the Sandhorn. *Blood will out,* I think, mine and Chanist's, though I allow some grudging credit to whatever riding masters she had at the Bastion.

As we reach the open fields of the commons, my centaur daughter turns to me with a rebellious glint in her eyes. "Do you feel up for a canter?" she asks.

I give her a measured look. I know she expects me to say no because we haven't warmed up at the trot, because I am riding bareback. But I am done with caution, for this day at least.

I smile, nod, and squeeze Aster into an easy canter. She is still unschooled, and heavy on the forehand, so I let her pick her own path, checking her every so often. Beside us, Peri is springing in a bouncy rocking-horse pace, fighting Lauresa's tight rein. Aster feels the competitive pull from her dam and stretches her neck, shifting from canter to gallop. I let her stretch. It's easier to sit than her heavy canter, and I enjoy the sting of wind in my eyes.

Peri will have none of it, however. As soon as Aster has overreached her by a length, she takes the bit in her teeth and flattens, dropping long and low. She is ahead of us in a single stride. Lauresa must have raced her as a girl. The thought flicks through my head as the older mare cuts off our path with a dropped shoulder—a typical courser move. But there is no time to dwell. Aster responds to her mother's challenge, ears back, neck straight out, hooves thrumming across the tussocky grass. She's not yet trained enough to listen to me when the urge to race is on her, so I simply lie low over her neck, grab a handful of mane, and let her fly.

The tree line stops our race, and Peri at least has enough sense to come to a bouncing halt well before it. I fear Aster will head straight into the forest, but once Peri has stopped, her daughter regains enough sense to listen to my legs and hands as I wheel her in a slowing canter.

The mares are dancing, fractious, nostrils wide and ears pricked, not yet willing to settle, and I can see the same look in my daughter's wild grin as she pats Peri's damp neck.

"We've got a good long walk ahead of us to cool them out, at least," I comment.

She shrugs, the smile still stretched across her face. It's the happiest I've seen her in a very long time.

"I've got time."

We skirt the forest, soaking up the warm sun rather than entering the chill of the woods. It is Lauresa who seems to want conversation first.

"She's as fast as her mother, it seems." She nods to Aster, who now has no trouble keeping up with Peri. "I can't believe how much you've done with her in so little time."

"Good old-fashioned gipsy horse charming," I reply, surprised at how much my daughter's praise means to me. "I could teach you, if you like."

Her bright face closes like a shutter, and I wonder at the nerve I've hit. Peri snorts and tosses her head irritably, feeling her rider's tension. "What?" I urge.

She looks at me, frustrated, exasperated — angry? — then away. "You know that's a talent I don't have."

I'm shocked at the resentment I feel coming from her, and ashamed I'd never noticed it before.

"It's not spellsinging," I say, feeling like I'm approaching a skittish, mistrustful foal. "Nothing you couldn't lear—" I break off, my normally eloquent tongue at a loss. How do I say it to her, when she should have learned this years ago?

"But the other ... the singing. I could teach you that too."

When she looks back at me, her eyes are bright, glassy with unshed tears. "Don't you think it's too late for that, Mother?" The last word comes out like an epithet. "If I'd had that talent, it surely would have shown by now. Allaigna certainly didn't need to be taught."

"And where did Allaigna's gift come from, if not through you?"

"Her father is part Ilvani."

"And that is why it comes naturally to her — she has the gift from both parents. Which means it's yours as well."

"I have sung for years and never a glimmer—"

I lift my hand to stop her. The pain of what has been done to her memories, to her talents, by the mages of Rheran is a wound still too fresh beneath the surface to even talk about.

All I can do is apologize.

Verse 17
The Sandhorn

I woke up with the first change in light, my body cramped from shivering. I had argued with Rhoan about the need to set up the tent in this hot, parched desert, but he was right: the heat from the ground had long since vanished, and the dry air held no warmth. I stuck my nose back under the blanket, breathing back my warm breath, and shifted closer to Rhoan, ignoring the nagging from my bladder.

There was a small square of canvas missing from the corner of the tent flap, sacrificed, along with one of Rhoan's bootlaces, to improvise the slipper that held on Nag's shoe. Through the hole, I watched the sandy ground turn from black to blue to grey.

Just when I thought I might fall asleep again, Rhoan stiffened and then stretched, shaking cold droplets of our condensed breath from the tent.

He peered out the flap at the grey pre-dawn and swore. "We should have been up an hour ago." Tossing off his blankets, he crawled out of the tent. I followed, shivering, a blanket still wrapped around me.

Rhoan was already pulling up tent pegs, and I scrambled to retrieve our packs from inside before the tent collapsed on them.

"Why the hurry?" I yawned. "If the patrol didn't catch up with us yesterday, then they're not following."

"Patrols are the least of our problems, my girl. There's a reason they didn't follow us. The climate here does in most travellers if the outlaws don't."

Was there an accusation in that statement? If there wasn't, perhaps there should have been.

The waterhole had diminished overnight to an arm-span across, our tracks from yesterday already hardening in the drying clay. New tracks of desert fox, mouse, small bird, snake, and toad adorned the fresh mud beside the larger hobbled prints of our horses. I could hear birds, invisible and distant, but of the other small night creatures, there was no sign. How could they disappear so thoroughly in this treeless desert?

There was no time for breakfast. We needed to ride while the morning chill was in the air. I splashed a handful of muddy water on my face, wincing as it stung my sun-scalded cheeks.

A flash of kingfisher blue caught my eye, glowing and out of place in the dawn grey. It was a spot no larger than an eagle coin, but it promised something larger buried in the clay. I scraped back the mud, revealing a larger and larger smooth blue surface. At no other time would I have been able to discover it: yesterday the water had covered it, and by this afternoon the clay would harden over it.

The surface rounded and went deeper into the dirt. Rhoan was urging me to finish packing the tent, but I was compelled now to unearth my find. At last he came to help and, with both of us scraping away at the sticky mud, we exposed the object: a pitcher of opaque blue glass, etched round the rim with unfamiliar patterns of script, and miraculously unbroken.

Rhoan whistled, shaking his head in admiration as the first rays of sun creased the horizon and set the jug aglow. I took it from him, wiping bits of clay from the incised script. It was writing—of that I was sure.

"It's not Ilvani," I said. "Where do you think it's from?"

He shook his head. "I wish I knew." There was an odd, hushed quality to his voice. "It's not Kavatir either, or from any of the outland nations I know of. And it's old."

"How do you know?"

"Look inside."

The inner surface of the jar, once cleared of the thick darker mud inside, was marked by criss-crossed black patterns.

"That's from decaying plants," Rhoan pointed out. "Water weed."

"So?"

"This little puddle couldn't sustain water plants. I doubt it has for centuries. The Sandhorn has been a desert like this as far back as recorded history shows."

"So ..." I added up the dates of the calendar: 1600 from Empirical dates, and nearly as many in the pre-Empire days beyond it.

"I could be wrong." There was that odd quality to his voice again. "But if I'm not ..."

"This jug is worth a lot."

"Much more than a lot. Something like this ... proof of people living here that long ago ... clever people, to make something this beautiful ... No, that is priceless."

I quickly put it on the ground, terrified of dropping something that had survived at least three millennia.

We stuffed it with an empty grain sack, wrapped it in one of Rhoan's best shirts, and nestled it in the remaining grain sack, hoping the oats would cushion any shock. That sack went across Nag's pommel, and I rode with a nervous awareness of our treasure resting just in front of my hand, which stole down to check on it every few strides. Nag's trot was rough enough at the best of times, and with his unevenness from the improvised canvas shoe and the rocky, trackless desert footing, I was in a constant state of worry that the bundle would come untied, or that his jolting trot would smash the vessel to dust.

Our shadows, stretching long and blue in front of us when we had started, had shrunk to small puddles of black. I begged Rhoan for a halt. It was an even more barren piece of land we were now in. The foothills to the south were hazy bumps on the horizon, separated from us by a long gorge that had started as a small rift between the rockier ground and the smooth desert. Now it was the width of a river and the depth of a lake, with none of the longed-for moisture of either.

Nag was limping badly, and when I slid off I saw that the canvas boot had worn straight through and the shoe had disappeared somewhere behind us.

"We can't rest here," Rhoan insisted. "No water, no shade, no wind."

"But he can't go on," I protested, holding the unshod hoof, which now sported a large chip out of the left wall and two spreading cracks on the right.

"Then we'll head there." Rhoan pointed to the gorge. "There may be a way down. Or at least some shade." He looked down into my despairing face. "You lead him halfway there, then we'll switch."

That journey of maybe half a league in the midday sun seemed to take longer than the four or five leagues we'd travelled since dawn. I felt nearly as lame as Nag by the time Rhoan took over leading, and I mounted his mare at what was probably far less than the halfway point. I ended by sliding off and leading the mare, walking in what little shadow she cast long before we reached the lip of the gorge.

And there, any hope of shade was dashed—as it would have been before this if we'd paused to think. For the gorge ran east-west, and the sun was still high overhead. Even when it descended, it would continue to shine on the northern face: the small slivers of shade lingering in the rock outcroppings of the southern wall were separated from us by the precipitous ravine.

Rhoan's face was now as desolate as I felt. For the first time it occurred to me we could die out here in this desert, with little food and less water. Or the horses could. This latter thought was the one that brought guilty tears to my eyes, and I leaned my head against Nag's too-dry, salt-stiffened hide.

We poured some meagre water into our mazers for the horses to sip and allowed ourselves a precious mouthful each.

I couldn't even voice the question "Now what?" though my face must have said it for me.

Rhoan's skin was red and parched despite the white cambric shirt he'd used to cover his head. The creases around his eyes and mouth were darkened with the dried muck of sweat and dust. My guilt expanded to include him as well as the horses.

All this was my fault. So immersed was I in my self-pity, I barely heard him.

"Allaigna?" he repeated, shaking my shoulder. "If you can't see anything, we'll put up the tent here and wait till the sun lowers."

And what about the horses? Or when the sun travelled west to shine straight in our faces?

I shook my head and peered down the length of the canyon, scanning in both directions for a way down. There were trees at the bottom, and every once in a while the ghost scent of moisture drifted up, making me hope for a river or at least a spring. But the edge at our feet was unrelentingly steep for as far as I could see westward. To the east, though, the canyon rose and the cliff edge melted somewhat. And was there, perhaps, a ledge sloping crosswise down?

Even if it wasn't a trick of the light, I didn't know if the horses could manage it. It would mean another half league of travel back in the direction we'd come. It was so much more tempting to simply sit here, waiting for darkness to come and save us. But then tomorrow we would be faced with the same choices, and even less water.

Rhoan couldn't see the hope that shimmered on the eastern horizon. Which left the decision on my shoulders. I rolled them back, feeling sand and dry sweat creak and scratch against my neck. I'd put Rhoan in this situation, and I would get him out.

"East," I pointed. "Half a league." My heart fell even as the words escaped my lips. "Maybe a bit less," I added to encourage us both.

At least as we turned our faces east, the sun now had to settle for our backs, and our dwarfish shadows led the way.

The shadows lengthened as slowly as our progress, footfall by limping footfall, back in the wrong direction. With each painful step my heart lurched, pulled by the green shores of Aerach — which I could now see as a distant smudge on the northern horizon — and repelled still by the desperate sense of flight that pushed me toward Brandishear. The dual forces left a void between my ribs, an ache so empty I would have filled it with tears if only there were enough fluid left within me to cry.

At last we approached the breach in the canyon lip. It was no more than a crumbled edge where the steep walls gave way to one that was gentler, but treacherous with scree. There was no safety there, or shade.

My parched eyes discovered a few last drops of water that muddied my vision. I sat down, head in hands, too dry to cry outright, too despairing to do anything else.

I had led us all this way back for nothing. The relentless sun still beat on us, but now our shadows stretched long, and we would spend another night in this desert, this time with no water and no shelter from the nighttime wind and frost.

I could feel Rhoan's hand on my shoulder. His tall form shaded mine, so I didn't shrug him off.

"The land is more broken farther on, Allaigna." His voice was cracked and caked with sand. "We may simply need to go farther."

Farther? I couldn't possibly go farther. But then … all this was my fault.

I grasped his elbow in an unusual acceptance of support and allowed myself to be pulled upward. I nodded and limped onward.

Lauresa's Chorus

Lauresa walks with hurried, nervous steps across the gallery to her husband's study. Her breath feels shallow and high, reaching only to her throat and back, as if breathing deeper would unlock the emotions hidden below. She is so distracted, so removed from herself she almost knocks at the door. Her hand has begun to curl and rise before she stops herself and simply turns the handle.

Allenis is standing, leaning on the table with arms wide on each side of him. Sir Darien, commander of the western garrison, and Eiglin Doniver, his vassal to the east, are all poised to pore over the same map.

As Lauresa enters, Allenis looks up, and the corners of the map he's been holding curl together with a snap and a rustle. He is startled to be interrupted, but he knows only one person who would walk into his study unannounced.

"Lauresa," he says, and then, as if in afterthought, "My dear. How can I help you?"

She swallows the knot of nerves in her throat. She has chosen this time to broach the subject precisely because she knows he doesn't have time for it.

"Forgive me, my darling. My lords. You'll think me remiss as a hostess for not bringing you refreshment here. But the day is lovely, and a lunch has been laid out on the terrace. I thought you might enjoy the air, and a break from these dusty parchments."

Sir Darien moves into the beam of sunlight coming through the leaded glass of the window, his white-gold hair sparkling like platinum. "You are graciousness itself, Lady." He bows, kissing her hand.

Lord Eiglin performs similar gestures in his stiff, reserved way.

"Husband," she says, as Allenis comes third to kiss her hand. "Might I have a word with you before you join your guests for lunch?"

She draws herself close, so that when he releases her hand, the backs of her fingers slide gently down his cheek, over the wiry greying beard, landing lightly on his chest, just where his shirt laces lie open.

The other two men are watching, she knows, and she sidles even closer to her husband, looking over her shoulder at them.

"You'll forgive me, sirs, if I steal my husband back for a moment?"

They both bow again and leave, a look of amused admiration in Lord Eiglin's face, and envy in Sir Darien's.

"Lauresa," Allenis begins, annoyance and interest mingling in his voice. He knows his wife's beauty, charm, and courtly skills earn him respect amongst his vassals: a respect that has just been reinforced. But she can feel he is itching to get back to his planning. "Could this not have waited till evening?"

"Alas, my dear, I'm afraid this," she kisses him lightly, teasingly, on the lips, "must. But there is an urgent matter I would discuss with you now. It won't take long, I promise."

He sighs, sits in his chair, pulling her by the hand till she perches on his knee where he can slide his hand around her waist.

"I wish to engage another tutor."

He frowns. "What's wrong with the one we've got? Brother … whatshisname? Willits."

"Nothing. He is quite sufficient for most of Allaigna's studies. I don't want to dismiss him. It's an additional tutor I require."

His frown deepens at the thought of spending more money to educate his daughter.

"Allenry will be beginning his studies soon, and then Lauriana, and Willits will need to teach all three. But there is a bard—"

"A bard?" Now the frown is formidable.

"Yes. The one who performed in the hall last night."

"You want a music teacher? I thought the nurse did that."

Here comes the selling point. "Folk tunes. Gipsy songs. I want her educated in the music of the court—to dance, to play the harpsichord. And more, this man is learned in the ways and politics of all the Ilmar states. He could teach her to be a proper courtier, and"—this is the tricky part—"he has a licence from the College."

"A what?" Allenry's hand, which has been running distractedly up and down her back, stops suddenly. "He is a mage?"

She nods, leans a little more against her husband, returns her hand to the V in his shirt.

"A minor one. Not so skilled as to be registered. But he could teach her to control the talent she has …"

Allenis grabs her by the hips and pivots her to face him. "What talent?" he growls.

She blinks, taken aback by the bristles he is raising. "You know my mother was Leisanmira—"

"What of it? You're no mage."

"The talent sometimes skips generations." She is stammering, cursing her nerve and cool demeanour for leaving her now.

"Are you saying my daughter's a mage?"

"Of course not! Not yet. But she has talent—"

"How do you know?"

"Little things. She can see arcane aurae—"

"And how long have you known this?"

Lauresa shakes her head. "Not long. It only starts to show in children around seven …"

"She's nine!"

"And she's secretive. She's probably just not told us before. But she needs a tutor. Otherwise …"

"No. We're not hiring some travelling singer to teach hedge magic to my daughter."

She can see the violent distaste for magic in his expression.

"But the danger … She needs tutoring."

He stands, dumping her off his lap, and strides across the room, pacing. He has always disliked and mistrusted mages, the colleges, gipsy spellcasters, and mere tricksters alike. It is only because he must have a vizier that he tolerates the fat old spider who has been sitting in the north tower since before Allenis was born. Of all the options, he is Lauresa's last choice.

"Carollus can tutor her," he says. "See that she starts tomorrow."

Verse 18

The Sentry Stone

Rhoan's tall back and the black tail of his mare were wavering twin gateposts ahead of me. The rest of Talwis's dust-covered body faded into the red brown of the late afternoon light. I didn't know if Rhoan was aware of how far behind I'd fallen, but I hadn't the voice or energy to call for him to wait. It didn't matter. He'd stop eventually, and I'd hardly lose him in this vast plain.

Keeping my head up was too hard, and the glare of sun on sand hurt my eyes, so I let my gaze fall, focussing only on the tracks Rhoan and the mare left behind. His feet were so much larger than mine, I mused, and his stride so much longer, that I took three steps to his two. I played a game for a while, matching my right foot to his, then my right foot to his left, counting how many man-strides I'd made.

I stopped, nearly staggering against Nag, and slid down his leg to peer at the ground. Beneath the tracks of Talwis and Rhoan were more hoof prints. I stood to call Rhoan, but my voice could do no more than croak. And the black tail and tall dark form had vanished in the heat haze ahead.

My heart did triple time. Where was he? Had he found a way down? Torn between his safety and Nag's foot, I paced in circles for a moment before urging my feet and my poor horse into a bobbing trot. I loosened my sword in its scabbard, following the bay mare's tracks as well as the smaller sets of hoof prints beneath them.

A minute or two of our pained, stumbling trot brought us to a rock about four feet high and half again as wide, standing on the canyon lip like a sentinel. That must have been what Rhoan was heading for. I dropped Nag's reins, hoping his fatigue and unsound hoof would keep him ground-tied.

The sets of prints were those of Rhoan's mare, Rhoan's human feet, and at least two smaller horses, all leading around the corner of the rock.

It was indeed a sentinel, or a marker. A narrow path wound down the side of the ravine, and the hoof prints followed for at least a few paces until a sudden confusion of marks marred the trail and another set of human prints joined in.

I flattened myself against the ravine wall, glancing around for other eyes, but the canyon seemed utterly empty of life except that of a bird—eagle or vulture, I couldn't tell which—circling high above.

The other human tracks were smaller than Rhoan's but larger than mine, and soft-shod. Someone watching here had waylaid Rhoan. If the meeting had been friendly, Rhoan would have waited for me. So I had to assume it was not. But where had they gone so quickly?

I was just about to set foot on the downward path when a faint grumbling reached my ear. I dropped to the ground and flattened myself against the rocks.

A figure, clad in grey and tan to match the desert sands, appeared seemingly out of nowhere on the trail below. The person had a clump of brush in hand and was sweeping the path with a grudging motion.

Luckily she or he was looking down at the path, not up it, and didn't seem to react when I slid back behind the curve of the tall rock. I had already cursed my dark garments for the heat they drank in and trapped near me; now I hated them for their contrast to the pale desert earth. At least the long shadow of the rock was dark enough to soak me up, and a heavy layer of dust had brought my blacks and russets closer to the grey of sand.

The figure proceeded slowly with their brush, giving me time to think. It seemed as if they were going to sweep the whole trail free of tracks — but if that were the case, why not start at the top and work down? Unless they weren't planning on going back down?

I examined the shadowed ground around me. There were tracks other than those made by feet, implying that someone had rested here, sat in the dust, stretched their legs, and even, I realized, dropped tiny crumbs of bread or hardtack. All this musing while the sweeper inched closer only served to delay the decision of what to do when they finally got here. My sword was still strapped to Nag's saddle. That thought reminded me that Nag's tall withers would soon be visible to the advancing figure, even if I would not. It forced my decision.

I slipped my father's dagger from its home at the back of my belt. I was less sure with the hooked blade than I was with my straight and simple hunting knife. But the dagger looked more threatening, and I felt bluff could be as important to my next move as prowess.

"Worry about the weapon first," Edris had always told me. "It's no good landing a killing blow if your opponent delivers one at the same time."

While the sweeper didn't seem visibly armed, there was no telling what lay beneath the sand-grey robes, and the makeshift broom could certainly cause me trouble on the narrow path.

So instead of jumping down behind the sweeper as I'd first planned, I launched myself in front of them, landing with one foot on the brush. I snapped the broom handle away with my right hand, while my left shot forward, hitting them in the chin with a warding arm. The dusty figure reeled backward on the narrow path, slipping, rolling, and sliding off the edge. I lunged forward and grasped their wrist. I was yanked to my knees as my victim's weight nearly dragged me down the steep-sided slope with them.

It was an idiotic impulse: I should have just let them fall instead of risking my own skin. But I was grateful, too, for the thoughtless instinct that made me react. I wasn't ready to have another death on my conscience yet, or ever.

Slight though they were, they were heavy, and it felt as though my shoulder would rip right out of its socket in another breath or two. The broom I'd confiscated was in my other hand. I held it high over my head in a clear threat and looked my opponent in the eyes.

It was a girl, I decided, not much older than I, her brown eyes wide with fear as she scrambled with her toes and free hand to gain purchase on the crumbly bank.

"Up or down — your choice," I barked with more conviction than I felt, hoping the message was clear. Either I gave her the broom to pull herself up, or it was a weapon and down she'd go.

"Please," she gasped, reaching for the broom.

The motion cost her toeholds, and she slipped farther, pulling me flat onto my stomach, her wrist sliding through my grasp. I flung the broom forward just as her fingers left mine, and had to hold onto the brush end with both hands as her weight dragged us both closer to falling. She inched upward, hand over hand, until our whitened knuckles nearly touched. We looked in one another's eyes again.

"On three?" I said.

She nodded. I counted and I coiled myself to curl backward as she launched her midriff onto the path.

The sudden release made me roll backward. She let go with one hand and was scrabbling to her knees, so I rolled, jerking the broom away from her.

I was back on my feet, and so was she. I had the broom, but she now had the high ground, as well as a natural hand-span in height on me. But I'd grown up fighting taller and heavier opponents. I eyed her stance, trying to assess if she was a fighter or not. I calculated that my best move would be to go low and thrust the broom between her legs to trip … if she attacked.

She was inching up the slope, crouched with her weight over her back leg, her eyes raking me up and down to assess my threat. She wasn't completely green, but her look was wary, unsure.

"We could do this all again," I threatened, pitching my voice low, but amplifying it with Leisanmira resonance, making me seem stronger, more assured, than I really was. "Or you can talk to me."

Her eyes narrowed, thinking, and she straightened a bit. She nodded her head ever so slightly and her shoulders relaxed, which put me on guard again. I took a backward step, broom extended in front of me, and a quick look down the path. No one else was visible. Her relaxation wasn't due to the arrival of allies.

But she tensed once more in response to my defensive move.

I raised one hand in a sign of peace and dropped the tip of the broomstick to the dirt. I still didn't like being on the low ground, so I stepped up onto the higher bank—the plateau was still more than a man's height above me—and motioned for her to approach.

She came uneasily, inching below me on the narrow path, our eyes nearly level. This was risky. She could easily grab me and throw me over the edge. My higher ground only made this simpler. But somehow I knew, I hoped, that because I hadn't let her fall, she would save me too. As we completed this watchful dance, I realized I had just fought my first real fight: not a practice match or even a tourney bout, though those seemed real enough sometimes, but an actual life-and-death contest of skill. And I'd won. So far.

When she passed, I slid back down the path, and we faced each other once again. Now the slope made us of a height.

"Where is he?" I asked, using the same resonant voice.

She motioned with her head to the path below. I could see nothing but the grey dirt against the grey bluffs. I raised the tip of the broom, couching the brush under my arm like a spear and wishing my sword were not still slung on Nag's saddle.

"What's there?"

"Upper chamber," she said, in a voice as quiet and dusty as the desert air.

"And how many others?"

Her eyes flashed defiance. I cocked my head and took a step closer, within striking distance.

"I need more words than that, or it'll be back over the side."

She spat on the ground, raising a tiny puff of dust. "That won't get your friend back. There are three dozen armed men and women down there. Are you going to hit them all with my broom?"

Sandhorn bandits, I realized, who live in this hot and barren land by preying on travellers along the Clearwater Way. And there was a nest of them below me.

I rethought my decision. Wouldn't it be better to throw this one over the edge after all, return for my sword, and attack with better odds? Except those were still no odds I'd survive.

I drew my father's dagger from my boot top. Her eyes widened further as its cruel curved blade flashed.

"This way." I motioned her toward me, backing up the hill, knife and broom both trained on her. "Here's what we're going to do …"

Lauresa's Chorus

Lauresa shuts the door to the guest room — the sickroom — behind her. She leans against the carved wood panels, small fingers of acanthus leaves poking into her back with each large and shuddering breath she sucks into her ribs.

The corridor is gloomy, and she is grateful that the guards stationed at each end can't see her face twisting to hold back tears.

She straightens, brushing her skirts smooth, tucking a stray piece of hair back into its pins and leaving behind the closed chamber with its sickly sweet smell of illness and impending death, with her father lying pale and fevered and Allaigna shut in to watch him die.

By the time she reaches the kitchens, her face is, she hopes, once more a mask of cool, efficient authority.

The regular staff has been joined by family members, chambermaids, grooms, and craftsmen working feverishly to prepare enough food for the sudden influx of soldiers from Brandishear. Every area of the household has donated hands to the cause, save for the guards. Those have been doubled on the walls, the gates, the doorways, and even the town, each one standing double or triple shifts.

Lauresa has to squeeze sideways to fit into the kitchen, and it is a testament to how busy everyone is that no one seems to notice, bow, or make way for her.

"Have we enough, Fride?" she asks the cook. "Meat, barley, and hands to prepare it?"

"'Twill do, 'twill do, your Grace," Fride answers, bobbing a half-curtsy as she inspects the cauldron of soup hanging over the fire.

"The broth can be thin for the wounded. And you may add plenty of porridge to spread that out for the well."

"Aye, mistress — so Angeley's said," replies Fride as she bustles off between pages laden with turnips and beets from the cellar, checking the baking ovens on her way.

Normally Lauresa would feel a flush of irritation at her mother usurping her role as chatelaine, but today she feels only relief, and an unbidden welling of tears she forces back.

"Where is Angeley?"

Fride calls over her shoulder. "Most like in the hall with the wounded."

Lauresa turns to make her way out of the room, but Fride is at her elbow once more, directing traffic with unconscious pushes and tugs on the helpers who jostle past them in the kitchen doorway.

The cook lowers her voice so Lauresa has to bend over to hear her. "Who are they, these soldiers we're harbouring, your Grace?"

The rehearsed lie slides easily from her lips. "Troops from Erelin and Doniver."

"And is it war?"

Lauresa shakes her head, swallowing the dire feeling in her throat at this stickier lie. "No. No, they encountered an Essaruk encampment in the mountains."

The older woman's eyes stretch wide in fear. "Essaruk?" she whispers, no doubt reliving the terrifying tales every child in Aerach hears in her cradle, of barbarians and madmen who steal infants for their dinner bowls.

Lauresa places a calming hand on her cook's shoulder. "They were driven off, and the mountain pass closed. Aerach is in no danger from the Essaruk, Fride." The last bit at least, she thinks, is truth.

But how much more injury might this lie cause? The truth—that Brandishear's Prince lies wounded and perhaps dying in Osthegn's guest chamber—must not escape to damage the fragile Ilmar treaty. But to shift the blame to Essaruk, who haven't crossed the mountain passes in two lifetimes ... could that not cause even more panic? And should the public know that the so-called peace of the Valnirata is as firm as pond ice on a warm spring morning?

These decisions, these lies, are ones she has concocted in collusion with her father's captain and her mother. Andreg is away at the moment. Would she even have consulted him if he were here? Oddly, for the first time in years, she wishes he were: that she could defer her decisions, and let him comfort and protect her. But it has been months since they've shared an embrace, never mind their feelings.

Instead she moves into the hall in search of her mother.

Angeley is there, of course, ordering healthy soldiers to tend the wounded with the authority of a general. She is harsher, more strident than usual, and Lauresa can see the twin furrows of worry fixed between her brows.

After so many years of concealing her nurse's identity, she nearly slips and calls her mother as she reaches out to touch her elbow.

"Angeley." She clears her throat at how foreign the name suddenly sounds. "A word, if you please."

Angeley nearly slips as well. "Not now, Lauresa," she mutters, before correcting herself at volume. "Certainly, your Grace. Hold this," she tells the wounded man she is tending, pressing a wet cloth into his hand. "Keep squeezing water over the wound until the doctor comes. She'll stitch it for you."

Mother and daughter leave, stepping over and around the pallets scattered on the rushes of the hall. They stop when they reach the open window of the gallery, where cool blue twilight and fresh air still breathe into the hall.

"I'm worried," Lauresa begins, "about the rumours we've created. Surely people will piece together ..."

Irdaign shakes her head, impatient. "We have no choice." There are blue circles beneath her eyes, and her voice is ragged. "It is too soon — war must not restart with the Valnirati yet."

Lauresa realizes her mother is speaking not from reason but from that place of foretelling that is incomprehensible to others. The strain is written clearly across Irdaign's face. It is as if she is trying to hold the lines of present and future together by force of will alone. And all on top of the love and fear she carries for her former husband.

Lauresa had wanted her mother to hold her, to soothe her fears. Instead, she wraps Irdaign in her arms and whispers words of meaningless comfort.

Irdaign's Chorus

I busy myself with the needs of the wounded, pushing the thought of that one, most wounded out of my head. Chanist's troop was not large: less than twoscore, including farrier, cook, clerks, healer, and vizier, along with knights and their squires and pages. A number of those were killed in the attack, and a half dozen or so died en route here. Of the remaining two dozen, more than half are wounded, and most seriously.

If they had stopped near the borders, at Werrancross perhaps, more might have lived, or saved limbs.

But Osthegn was the only castle in Aerach where Chanist could maintain anonymity, so he pushed on here at the cost of life and limb … perhaps his own.

It is the simmering anger over this, and the need to know why, that keeps me occupied, prevents me from sinking into despair at the image of my once-beloved husband lying across death's threshold in the guest chamber upstairs. The Sight is worryingly absent, giving me no clues, no flashes as to the outcome of this dreadful happening. I search my memory for further future events, and though I feel he must live for the destinies I've seen so clearly to unfold as they ought, I have no promise of this.

I focus on the present: the political, practical concerns. Why is he here? What has drawn Chanist with a force, not large, but no small party either, from his seat in Rheran to Aerach? And why through the Valnirata, and not by sea?

Part of me does not want to know. Part of me is only happy to see his face again, not through the shifting waters of a scrying bowl or the tatters of an incomplete vision, but in person — haggard, asleep, and deathlike though it may be. To be so close and not touch it tenderly, or kiss those eyes awake, requires force of will beyond measure. But he must not open his eyes to me. A vision does flit through my head, of Chanist, Lauresa, her children, and me: a group portrait like the one that hangs at the foot of the great stairs, but happier, glowing with the bond of a family. But it is a false vision, built of longing, and I know it will never be. Our family is scattered, fragmented, and steeped in lies. That it could someday come together does not appear in any of my true visions.

When I at last go upstairs, I leave behind the wounded Brandishear men and women in the best condition I can, feeling once more, as their former souveraine, I have done some good by them. My steps are slow and measured, fatigue and thought tempering the speed at which my heart wants to fly to the sickroom.

The guard at the corridor nods to me with a note of obeisance that I never receive from Teillai's guards. This household soldier of Rheran can have no idea I was once Princess High, and yet, as one of the two allowed past him to tend the Prince, I have gained a measure of respect. It is a sign of loyalty to Chanist, and I admire once again the charisma that allows him to draw such fealty, and even love, from his men.

It is late, and Allaigna has extinguished the lamps, leaving only moonlight to guide my steps. I cross first to her pallet near the window. She is asleep. The white light picks out her features in stark contrast: black hair, a curve of dark lashes against smooth white skin, and eyebrows for once relaxed from their perpetual half-frown. It makes her look younger, even more vulnerable, and my heart aches with the burden we have placed on her, though I know it will strengthen her for those yet to come.

I will have to remind her, I think, not to frown so much and permanently crease that beautiful forehead.

I leave her sleeping and draw the bed curtains aside. The smell of sickness washes out, but beneath that is the scent of him, so familiar and yet so far in the past. I feel tears pushing up beneath my eyes and blink them back. There is no time for sentimentality. I have work to do.

I begin to sing, quietly at first, the notes squeezing past the lump in my throat. As my breathing deepens, I am able to relax, to allow the song, though quiet, to fill the curtained chamber of the bed.

Chanist's shallow breath deepens as well, and I settle myself beside him, his head cradled against my hip, my hand resting on his still-fevered forehead. It is a familiar pose, so reminiscent of the times he would come home exhausted from campaigning and sleep in my lap like a babe. It nearly chokes the song in my throat once more. I let the moment pass, let the feeling dissolve without indulgence, and keep the song going, reverberating through my chest, down my arm, and into the skin beneath my hand. When the song is there, the notes vibrating between us like the strings of a lute, I let my mind follow.

I find him in the battlefield. No surprise there. His sometimes young, then aging face is wet with tears as he picks his way over bodies. There are so many. Amid the bloodied corpses, faces appear that both of us know, eyes staring wide at the thunder-purple sky. Phillia, Girondrey, his father Goffree, Ceilaf, and so many other knights. But there are other faces, worse ones to see: Lauresa's and mine.

He stumbles to the ground, gathers Lauresa's limp body in his arms, and howls. His guilt is a palpable swamp that begins to suck at our feet. I will not let him wallow in it now. Taking hold of his dream version of my corpse, I slide in, lift its stiffened limbs and sit up.

His dream is so vivid I can feel the gelid deadness of the flesh in which I've encased myself. It makes my mouth slow and hard to open.

As I say his name he turns to me, clutching our daughter to his breast.

"What have I done?" he asks, his eyes as young and helpless as a child's. "Irdaign, save her. I know you can."

His faith in me would be touching if it were not so misplaced. But in dreams, all things are possible. I touch my dream-daughter's head.

"Lauresa, you can go now."

She smiles, stands, and fades like mist.

Chanist is standing on the bright green grass. All signs of battle and death are gone, and the sun is warm on our heads. He wraps me in an embrace. Even though I know it is only a dream, it is the warmest, the happiest I have felt in years. I would stay in his imagination forever if I did not have other loves and duties. So I influence him the only way our vows allow us.

"My love," I say, "we need to talk."

Verse 19
Captor and Captive

I admired her courage as she followed me up the hill, always just out of reach of the broom. We moved like a pair of fencers, measuring each other's reach, staying close enough to threaten but not close enough to be struck with ease.

Her eyes flickered as we crested the path and Nag came into view. I couldn't take my gaze off of my opponent, but I knew without looking that my horse stood as I had left him, head hanging low and listless, leg cocked to take the weight off the shoeless hoof.

I wasn't sure of her look, but I sensed approbation that made me defensive. As much as I wanted to water and feed my suffering horse, Rhoan had to take priority. Without turning, without breaking the gaze and posture that held my captive at bay, I pulled my sword from the scabbard on my saddle. I wanted my bow, too, but couldn't risk the time or attention it would take to retrieve and string it.

With the sword now in my hand, I tossed her the broom, wondering if she would be foolish enough to attack. But she didn't, just nodded and turned back down the path, the point of my sword a hand-span from her shoulder blades. As we walked I began to hum, constructing the sounds I needed in the back of my throat.

A hundred worries flitted through my head on that slow walk down. What if she had lied about the layout of the cavern hidden below? About the number of people there? Would the sword-point at her back be enough to hold her to her promise, or would she betray me, guessing correctly that I wouldn't stab her in the back?

The song I was attempting was untried. I had changed my appearance before, but never to the extent of trying to make myself disappear, to become invisible against grey-brown rocks. Why did I only think of these songs when I needed them? Practice would surely have been a good thing. But then, I hadn't sung a spell since the one that killed Doniver. That thought nearly blocked my throat.

She glanced behind her. I nodded, and she kept walking, head down, dragging her broom behind her. I hoped she was a singer — that the sound of a ditty coming down the path would be nothing new to ears below.

The cave mouth became visible beneath an outcropping of sandy cliff. I had a moment to admire how beautifully hidden it was before she turned back to me again. Those brown eyes grew wide, letting me know that I had blended into the colour of sand and stone more effectively than a chameleon. She reached a hand toward me, and I touched it with my sand-coloured sword, urging her on.

I flattened against the wall, closing the distance between us. No matter how well hidden, my form would certainly show against the light from the cave mouth. Stepping in time with her feet, I pressed closer still, hoping to become nothing more than her shadow as she rounded the turn into the cavern. I swallowed, forcing my heart back down from my throat as she stepped away, casually, smoothly, and crossed the cave to lean the broom against the far wall. I stayed where I was, taking in details as fast as I could. The cave didn't stretch far back, but there was a cleft in the far wall, which looked as if it had been enlarged by human tools.

She glanced back to where I stood, then turned, slowly looking around a half circle. Either she couldn't see me, or she was an excellent actress. My voice had gone quiet now. I had no idea how long the effects of my singing would last, so there was no time to waste. I stepped to the middle of the floor, reaching out to touch her again and motion her onward with my sword tip.

The gap in the back wall was as wide as a double door and just tall enough to fit a horse. In fact, I could smell horses and see their tracks as I passed through. An evenlamp burned high on the wall. *Expensive lighting for outlaws and bandits*, I thought as I stepped close to the girl, hiding in her shadow once more. The passageway sloped downward, with small stepped ridges cut into it every so often, human and hoof prints evident in the dusty ground.

"I'm not expected down there," she murmured in her accented Ilmarin. "My arrival will cause more alarm. You should go on your own."

I suppressed the tiny nervous laugh in my throat. "And the minute I'm away, you'll shout and warn them? No, I like you within measure of my sword."

Her eyes went hard.

She walked with what seemed like deliberate, taunting slowness, forcing my own steps to slow to her pace. My sword arm ached from holding it extended, its point two hand-spans from the centre of her back. My thighs ached too from maintaining the soft quiet footfalls and bent knees that kept me hidden behind her and ready to spring.

As we reached the bottom of the spiralling tunnel, I lengthened my step and touched her back with a reminding sword. She flinched and froze. I put my hand on her shoulder and saw by the way her eyes had to search for my face that my charm was still working. My sword-point the spurs, the cautioning hand on her shoulder the reins, we proceeded, stopping just as the edge of the room below came into view.

I left her there and inched farther around the curving wall, my sword still pointing back at her. It was risky: with my eyes off her, she could easily step past the blade and wrestle the sword from me. I only hoped that she had not had those instincts pounded into her by merciless weapons masters like I had.

The smell of horses had been growing stronger as we descended, but nonetheless, what I saw astounded me. A score of looseboxes lined the long rectangular hall. All were empty save one, in which Rhoan's mare was quietly chewing hay. She looked up, pricked her ears in my direction, and nickered.

Fortunately there seemed to be no human present.

I motioned the girl forward again, let her lead me past the empty stalls and out to the surprising daylight coming from the half doors at the end. And here I was more astounded.

Before me lay a grassy enclosure bounded by the riverbank on one side and a semicircle of steep cliff walls on the other. A dozen or so fine-boned desert horses, still half shaggy from the winter, grazed one half of the field, which was roped off with stakes.

The setting sun painted the rock walls brilliant ochre but had already left the ground in shade. Nonetheless I shrank back into the stable, unsure of my camouflage in this changed light. Around the rock walls, several doors had been cut, and above them windows, like so many swallows' nests. What I had envisioned as a small group of bandits appeared to be an entire keep's worth.

I pulled my captive back into the shelter of the barn. "Which way to my friend?" I asked.

This was a good question, but a foolish time to be asking it. I should have found out before coming down here. My sword was poking into the ragged clothes bundled about her midriff, and my left hand pulled at her collar harder than it had to. She looked uncomfortable, and with good cause. My fear, and my anger at myself, made me rash.

Instead of answering me, she glanced to her left. A man walked in, whistling, still lacing up his breeks. He may not have been able to see me well, but he didn't have to. Her posture, bent nearly double over the tip of my sword, pulled forward by her collar, was enough.

"Kîan?" he asked, his voice strangely accented and only mildly concerned. "What are you doing down here?"

All of a sudden, the close distance I'd maintained to the girl became a liability. I pushed her away, and she staggered backward while I darted behind the large grain bins, hoping her movement was enough to detract from my own.

But her eyes were still on me.

"There!" she pointed at the bins, running to move down the corridor. "Intruder—she's armed."

The man dropped to a defensive crouch and pulled a falchion from his waistband. They couldn't see me, I could tell, hidden behind the bins as I was, but he blocked the way out of the stable, and she blocked the way back up the tunnel.

I could run. I was fast and small and could slip past her, perhaps without them even seeing me clearly. But she reasoned that out and swung open one stall door, then the one opposite. Suddenly the corridor was much narrower.

She was brave, I thought, standing there unarmed, knowing I held a sword, using her body as a barricade. Did she know I lacked the heart to run her through? The man was my bigger problem. He called out, "Intruder," in a voice that echoed off the rock walls and caused Talwis to snort and stomp in her stall.

I glanced around, desperate for a way out, but saw only the obvious one. Bursting from behind the bins, I barrelled into the stall door the girl had opened, ducking under her outstretched arm and knocking her aside with an elbow to the chin. And then something, the door perhaps, hit me on the back of the head.

There was no moment of slow awakening from a dream, no luxury of groggy coming to, to piece together where I was and what happened. The sudden slap of cold water in my face jolted me awake and ran down my spine like the terror that washed through me.

I surged to my feet and tumbled over immediately, brought down more by the wave of nausea than the cords that held my ankles and wrists.

Someone toed me over, and the desert-baked face of a legendary Sandhorn raider filled my vision, haloed by light from the still-blue sky.

He spoke in Ilmarin. "I'm going to untie your feet. Run, an' I'll knock you cold again. Understand?"

I nodded, swallowing the bile that kept threatening to rise. Even that small movement made my head pound. I tried to make my limbs steady while he undid the cords at my feet, but my body wouldn't stop shivering.

He took me by the elbow to force or to help me to stand, I wasn't sure which. But with my feet beneath me once more, my stomach rebelled, and the meagre travel rations I had eaten that day spewed onto the dirt. I would have followed to the ground myself if I hadn't been suspended by the man's grip on my elbow.

He made no comment nor offered any more than that single hand's support, waiting silently for me to finish retching.

At last I stood, unable even to wipe the bile from my lips, and stumbled in the direction his guiding hand pushed me.

We entered through the largest of the sand-coloured doors set in the cliff wall. I was expecting a dark and low-ceilinged cave, but instead found a tall dome of a room supported by occasional sandstone pillars and airily lit by windows and evenlamps. Mosaic tiles in sparkling blues and golds paved the floor and decorated the pillars in waving bands of colour. In the centre rose a small fountain decorated in the same blue stone, gurgling with water that teased my dry nostrils and bile-scorched throat.

As my captor led me past, I forced out a one-word request. "Water."

"Soon," he replied, pushing me along into the darker recesses of the vaulted room.

As my eyes adjusted, they made contact with Rhoan's one good one. His other was shockingly swollen, and the side of his face was red with blood. I bit back a cry of dismay, not wanting to give my captor even that much satisfaction.

Rhoan was seated on the ground, his hands tied behind his back like mine, a large and many-scarred man squatting behind him. Opposite, a number of grey- and brown-clad men and women sat on rugs and cushions on the mosaic floor.

Between him and them, on the only chair in the room, was a woman. She was dressed no differently than the others, in layers of loose desert-coloured cloth, but it was evident she was the leader here. She sat upright but relaxed, her hand resting on the arm of the backless chair. The dark eyes that burned in her sun-worn face were as penetrating and alert as Angeley's at her most perceptive, but more forbidding by far. With a start, I realized they reminded me of the wolf-stare of Goffree's grandmother, the Lady Taerysh.

She spoke in a sharp burst of Ilvanin. Though I could read the language, I'd seldom heard it spoken, and could catch almost none of the words in her rapid dialect.

The man at my elbow answered and then told me, "Sit," nudging me toward Rhoan.

I knelt beside him, our legs touching. Never had I felt so glad for human contact.

My captor continued to talk to his leader in Ilvanin as he fetched a cup from a small table and dipped it in the stone basin that seemed formed from the back wall. He tipped it to my mouth, holding the back of my head while I drank. Much of the water ran down my chin, but I swallowed enough to mute the taste of vomit and quench my parched lips.

"And who is this?" the woman asked at last, in Ilmarin far cleaner and smoother than the man's.

"My daughter," Rhoan answered, shifting his weight against me in what I took for a request to let him do the talking.

But there was no talking to do, for the woman's question was directed to the other side of the room.

The girl I had fought answered in clear, slow Ilvanin I could follow, describing my attack on her.

"... one more horse. No more tracks," she finished.

She looked at me then, her eyes challenging me to respond, to prove I understood her. I stared blankly back, hoping my expression gave nothing away.

They did not treat us badly, or at least not as badly as one would expect from bandits. The bloody cut above Rhoan's eye was shallow, and a dark-haired woman cleaned and treated it with small quick fingers. We were given food, drink, a room with a bed, very little explanation, and a guard at the door.

As soon as we were alone, I turned and hissed at Rhoan. "What happened?"

He removed the wet compress he'd been told to press to his forehead, exposing stitches still too dark and bloody for me to gaze on easily.

"Well," he drawled as I looked away, "I seem to be having a spot of difficulty remembering, but near as I can put together, I found a path down the side of the cliff ... and hit my head."

"On a broom handle. Wielded by a girl."

He looked remorseful. "The outdoors is not my forte. A girl at the top of a castle stair with a broom I could manage." I had no doubt he could. "I plead sunstroke and fatigue." He applied the compress to his head again. "She blended in beautifully with the sand and rocks, though. Did she capture you the same way?"

"No. I captured her. I made it all the way down here, looking for you." My eyes narrowed. "Before she hit me on the back of the head with a stall door."

"Ah, well. Then I shouldn't feel ashamed to have fallen before a veritable mistress of the broom and door."

As if on cue, the door opened to let in the subject of our discussion, who came bearing a tray of food.

"I am sorry," she said in accented Ilmarin. "For your head." She was looking at Rhoan, not me, even though my head ached fiercely from the stall door.

Rhoan gave his most charming smile. "'Tis nothing. How could I hold a grudge over such a tiny scratch?"

I would, I thought.

Ignoring his charm, she turned to me. "Your horse," she said with blatant disapproval, "is lame."

Shame washed over me, erasing all my anger and fear. "I know," I replied. "I need to see him."

She shook her head. "We will look after him." From the look on her face, she clearly thought he would be far better off in their hands, and at the moment, I was in no position to argue.

Lᴀᴜʀᴇsᴀ's Cʜᴏʀᴜs

"Look, Mama." Irdina toddles up to her mother's knee, her chubby hands extended. Nestled between pink fingers are two pieces of eggshell, still joined by a strand of membrane. A thrush's egg, greenish and speckled.

Lauresa smoothes her skirts across her knees, and Irdina carefully deposits the shell on the blue velvet table her mother has created. She looks up, her hazel eyes troubled.

"What happen to de baby bird, Mama?"

"What do you think happened, Irdina?" asks Lauresa, ruffling the child's curly russet hair.

"Did it get et by somefing?"

It shocks Lauresa, seasoned parent that she is, that this is the first conclusion her youngest daughter would come to. *How much of the violence of the world has crept into the haven of this castle?* she wonders, looking over at her father. He is dozing in this chair in the sunny courtyard, his still-healing injuries hidden, a picture of homey peace.

"No, love. I think it just hatched, and the mama bird pushed the empty shell out of the nest."

Irdina's face clears like the sun. "She doesn't want it anymore?"

Lauresa smiles. "No, it's done its job, and her baby's safe. I think you can keep it." It is not really an untruth; she is simply ignoring the many other possible fates of the shell's inhabitant.

Branwen comes into the courtyard, followed closely by their older sister Lauriana. Always the louder of the twins, Branwen calls out the moment she spots their mother.

"Look! We found more!"

Her hands are full of a collection of shell fragments that she empties onto Lauresa's lap like a constellation of blue-green and ivory stars.

Her cries awaken Chanist from his doze, and his three younger granddaughters tumble onto his lap, talking at once, the fates of baby birds forgotten.

First they discard their shells, thinks Lauresa, *and if they survive crows and cuckoos and prowling cats, their parents will soon push them out and hope they fly.*

Allaigna and Allenry, are they ready to fly?

It seems such a short while since each of them was safe, enclosed within her like a chick in its shell. How could eleven years have flown so fast?

It is Allaigna she worries about most, even though she is the eldest. Allenry, along with her other daughters, seems hardier, more resilient than her thin, pale firstborn. But she is clever, if wilful, and strong for her size. And she will be under the care of her grandfather. Lauresa looks over at Chanist, who is bouncing all three younger granddaughters on his knee at once and laughing louder than any of them. Surely no harm will come to Allaigna and Allenry under the care of the Prince.

Yet the unease is still there. She remembers her own childhood and warm sunny moments such as this, but also much longer stretches of time where she saw neither her father nor her stepmother except from a distance, when she was brought up almost entirely by her nurse Dennein. Lauresa stands, chilled despite the warm sun, and walks the perimeter of the small courtyard, rubbing her arms for warmth. Some part of the cold nights she spent in the Valnirata Greatwood has never left her body, and it is the one thing for which she has not forgiven her father.

She argued for this. She was the one who wanted Allenry to go to Brandishear rather than to Aleran. She convinced herself she was acting in Allaigna's best interest in sending her too. Is it only a mother's heart, clinging to its firstborn so selfishly, which causes this pain? Or some worse, deeper foreboding? She wishes she were truly prescient, like her mother, and could separate maternal anxiety from justified fear. Or at least that she could talk to her mother. But Angeley has left Teillai now that Chanist is well, and will not return till after he has left, taking Lauresa's two eldest fledglings with him.

It is so easy, so natural to fall into Einavar's arms, long-lost lovers once more. But she catches herself before sinking into the embrace, stiffens, and pushes back so they almost spring apart, repulsed like a pair of matching lodestones.

She glances at him, but her eyes drop away and focus instead on brushing some twigs from the forest ride off of the sleeve of her coat.

"Thank you," she says at last, looking, she hopes, as cool as a house cat, "for coming."

His eyes, as ever, are unfathomable. She wonders, if they had a life together instead of awkward intermittent meetings, would she be able to read the face of her daughter's father, to tell when those eyes were glad, affronted, aloof, or angry?

What seems like a small sigh escapes him. "Princess," he says, though she is no longer one, "so long as I am able, I will always come at your call."

She turns her attention to her other sleeve, avoiding those eyes. "It isn't for my sake." She glances up, trying to see relief or disappointment in his face, though she hardly knows which of the two she'd prefer. "Allaigna is going to Rheran."

At last some expression—surprise, concern, anger—flashes in the grey eyes.

She continues, hesitant, apologetic. "As a page, in my father's court."

No longer unreadable, the frown is deep between his eyes. "After all he did to you, you'd send your daughter back into his hands?"

Anger flashes within her, a necessary counter to meet and repel his. "All he did? He was the most loving father a girl could demand, when he was there." *Which is far more than either you or*

Allenis can claim, she thinks, but does not say. For she is not so angry as to wound. Not when she needs him.

But his face opens again and she sees the wound there, words or no. His anger melts, replaced by guilt, which makes her want to reach out to him once more.

It is sorrow and concern in his voice now. "But he used you——"

"As he thought he had to. He used me badly, yes. As a princess, and a pawn, and a tool for propaganda. Princes must always place their realms before their hearts."

She sees the anger rising in him again. "Perhaps if princes followed their hearts more often than their ambition, the Ilmar would be a better place."

She has to——she cannot help reaching for his hand. It is cold, the fingers tense and hard. She holds it in both of hers and looks fully into his eyes. "Allaigna will be no pawn. No one except her grandfather will even know who she is. She's of no political use to anyone there."

"So why does he want her?"

"Can you find it in your heart to believe that he, too, might want the best for her?"

"I believe he does nothing that doesn't serve his political ends——somehow."

She sighs. "Then can you at least concede that her best interests and his ends might be entwined? None of us is a perfect parent, Einavar. Not you, not me, nor my father——"

"Why have you called me here, Lauresa?" he interrupts. "You are not seeking my opinion, and certainly not my permission, since I have none that can affect you."

It is true the decision has been made, and Einavar's voice, for better or worse, has no sway. "Your understanding," she says.

"And perhaps, if necessary, your forgiveness."

Why did she say that? If she is so sure, as her mother is so sure, that Allaigna will be safe in Brandishear, why is there a lump forming in her throat?

He is smiling now, but it is a small and bitter smile. "For sending my only daughter to the man I hate most in the world?"

She squeezes his hand hard, as if she could force her will into him that way. "Don't hate him, Einavar. For my sake, or for Allaigna's. We both love him. At least be happy for her."

"Is this what she wants?"

"At eleven? Did you know what you truly wanted at eleven? But she wants to try."

And now the real reason for summoning him, the one she has barely acknowledged to herself, surfaces. "But ... the Bastion is large, and Rheran larger still. Could you ..." She looks at him in his road-worn ranger's garb and knows he will hate this request. "Could you find a position in the Bastion? At least while your daughter is there?"

He laughs outright. "Your father would no more have me in the Household Guard than he would Caradar Halobrelia."

The name of her father's and her nation's greatest enemy makes her flinch despite herself. He reaches out, brushes the hair from Lauresa's forehead, and cradles the side of her face.

"But I have friends in the Guard still. And I will contrive to be in Rheran, if not the Bastion, as often as I can.

"I'll watch out for her, Lauresa. As I've always done."

He kisses her forehead and pulls her close. She rests her head on his shoulder, and they stay there in the springtime clearing, two parents, holding their worry between them.

Verse 20
The Sage Clan

Despite the knot of shame and fear in my gut, I slept, and soundly.

In the morning, we were brought before the council of the Sage Clan of the Sidharen people, as we soon learned they were called. We were asked many questions, which we answered with reasonable honesty save for those regarding my true identity. Even the fact that I'd accidentally killed a man we did not hide, for it provided the only reasonable excuse for us having ventured into the Sandhorn. And perhaps, I thought, outlaws might sympathize with me.

The outlaws of the Sandhorn, I'd been taught, were roving parasitic bands of Ilvani and Ilmari, too brutal and vicious to be tolerated in either society. They lived off the wealth and blood of unwary travellers along the Clearwater Way and ships that came too close to the coast of the peninsula.

These people were hardened, certainly, their bodies and minds weathered by the harsh desert life. But they were not uncivilized. This was an established community, a village or keep, as it were, carved from the very walls of the canyon. There was order, hierarchy, animal husbandry, and, judging from the beautiful mosaics, art. None of it was new or rough.

We were treated with suspicion but not cruelty. After telling our story, we were returned to our room, where we waited till the girl came back with a midday meal.

"Nag," I asked. "My horse. Has your farrier seen him?" I had no idea if they had a blacksmith here, but they had stables, so someone must know how to trim hooves at least.

"His feet are weak and brittle," she said with contempt. "He hasn't enough hoof left to nail a shoe to."

I was despondent but unsurprised. Once that shoe had come off, the desert sand and rocks had been unmerciful. "Can he put weight on it?"

She cocked her head as if unsure of the meaning of my words.

I reworded my question. "Can he stand square?" If he couldn't put weight on it, the situation was far more serious. His other front hoof would bear all the weight for weeks while his hoof grew, putting him at risk for lameness in the good foot. I felt my eyes start to water despite myself.

She cocked her head the other way, weighing, then held up a hand. "I will return."

Rhoan and I looked at each other as the door shut. He shrugged. "At least they seem concerned about our beasts. And the food is good."

He sat on the bed and took one of the two bowls and a piece of bread, digging into the thick barley stew. Last night's dish of roasted root vegetables had been palatable, and I was still hungry enough not to object to the strange-smelling spices this meal presented. I found myself eating despite my usual prejudices toward foreign food.

"What will we do?" I asked. "There're two of us. We could overpower her."

He snorted, coughed, and spat a mouthful of stew back into his bowl. "Did that desert sun bake your brains, lass? Why on earth would we do that?"

"How else will we get out of here?"

"First of all," he replied, fastidiously wiping up stray bits of barley from the rim of his bowl, "tell me why we should."

"Why …?" My mouth hung open for a moment. "Because we're prisoners!"

"Prisoners, or guests?"

Now I looked at him as if he was the one with sunstroke. "She hit you on the head and dragged you down here. Then she hit me too!"

He waggled a finger. "Ah, ah, you're forgetting the part where you attacked her and forced your way down."

"How else was I supposed to find you!" I dropped my voice, which had started escalating.

"You could have asked her."

I was stunned. Asked her? And lose my element of surprise? "But she hit you! And dragged you away!"

"And how did you know that? Ah, yes, you read the tracks. Yes, you're right—she hit me when I surprised her. My appearance at the top of the path took her quite off-guard. Woke her from a daydream, I'd warrant. And yes, she hit me with the broom she'd been waiting to use to wipe away the tracks of the hunting party that was due back. She called to her comrades, who passed me into the care of a healer. She returned, chastened, to sweep the path again."

At which point I'd attacked her. I could feel heat rising to my cheekbones. I looked at my bowl, feigning interest in my food. If we were prisoners here, it was my fault.

The door opened again, and the girl came in. I couldn't meet her eyes either.

"Give me your hands," she said, "and I'll take you to your horses." Her eyes flicked to Rhoan. "One at a time."

I held out my hands, and she tied a cord around one wrist then the other. I wanted to protest that I was hardly going to leave without Rhoan, but she had little reason to trust me.

The humiliation of being led out into the courtyard like a hound on a leash was only what I deserved, I told myself, but it was still hard to take. I walked head down so as not to even see if anyone else was present to witness our procession.

"My name is Allaigna," I said as we entered the welcome dimness of the stable.

"I know," she replied, sparking a tiny bit of irritation. We had said as much at our interview this morning. Didn't the girl recognize an invitation to conversation when she heard one? I'd never met anyone more silent and stoic than myself, and it rankled.

"And what should I call you?" I asked, putting on what courtly charm as I could still muster.

"Kîan."

Well, this wasn't going to be easy. We arrived at the stall where Nag was housed, and he nickered, alleviating the need for more awkward conversation.

"Oh, sweetheart," I whispered, and lifted my tied hands up to his muzzle. "I don't have anything for you."

His upper lip inspected my hands disappointedly, then he reached his nose forward to meet mine. I drank in his breath, the most welcoming scent in the world, and scratched the underside of his jaw.

Peering over the stall door, I couldn't see his foot in the dim light.

I turned to Kîan. "Please," I said, holding my wrists out. "I'd like to look at his foot."

She narrowed her eyes, considering. Nag reached over my shoulder and nuzzled my ear. It seemed to sway her. She undid the cord binding my hands and opened the stall door with a warning look in her eyes.

"Thank you," I said, and slipped into the stall.

I felt my way down Nag's leg. He lifted his foot into my waiting hands, and I was surprised to find his hoof covered in leather. Someone had fitted a boot to his foot. I put the hoof back on the ground. He put his weight on it carefully, but at least he was weighting it. I breathed a sigh of relief and began untying the laces.

As my eyes adjusted to the dim light, I could see as well as feel. The boot had been packed with matted hair—horse or goat—and wedged to even out the missing chunk of his hoof wall. I tied it back on, hoping my knots were as secure as those I'd undone.

Kîan was standing in the stall doorway, arms crossed, a bemused expression on her face.

"Thank you," I said, "whoever did this."

"You're welcome," she replied. "It was the stable master. I helped."

I really didn't want her to tie my wrists again, but I held them out nonetheless. "I'm sorry," I said, "for jumping you yesterday. I . . . I read the tracks and got the wrong idea."

She stuck out her lower lip, weighing my sincerity with a long look. She was taller, and looked down her broad nose at me. "I'm sorry I hit him too. It would have saved me a lot of trouble to simply talk."

I nodded.

She made no move to retie my hands, so I let them drift quietly back to my sides.

"I should take you back to your room," she said, and turned her back, letting me walk out of the stall.

Each day we stayed with the Sidharen, we enjoyed a little more freedom. Although a tough and secretive people, they were not the wild outlaws I had been taught to fear. They fed us and tended our horses with wary courtesy while we recovered. Nag's hoof wall needed to grow and the bruise on his sole had to heal before he could take me anywhere. I wasn't any closer to finding my father, but at least I was hidden from the world.

"Are there more people like you?" I asked Kîan as we made our slow way from the pump to the stable, burdened by two buckets of precious water each. "Here, in the Sandhorn, I mean." I set the buckets down, conscious of every slosh and splash.

With practised ease, she emptied hers into the larger bucket in Talwis's stall, losing not a drop in the process.

"There are five Sidharen clans," she replied, watching with a critical eye as I filled Nag's bucket.

"And you all live like this?" I waved my hand, vaguely indicating the whole of the cave-dwelling community clustered around this break in the gorge.

She shook her head. "The Snake and Fox clans are nomads. Osprey clan lives in the Zerai seafort. The Rose clan holds the remains of Br'nath, the Sidharen capital of old."

"Of old. How old?"

"I am of the eighty-first generation since the fall of Sidhen."

I ran the calculation in my head. If a generation was twenty or twenty-five years, that was anywhere between sixteen hundred and two thousand years ago—more, if the Sidharen were related to the long-lived, late-marrying Ilvani. Either way, her people dated from before our current calendar even started. How was it that these people had been living in the Sandhorn for all the Ilmar's history, and no one knew?

"We are taught," I said slowly, "that the Sandhorn is peopled only by outlaws."

She gave me a long look. "And we are taught that the Ilmar is full of violent, warring factions who cannot seem to live with one another." I blushed, remembering the violence of our first encounter. "After all, that is who you send us."

We picked up our buckets and headed back to the pump. "We don't send them to you," I argued, "just away from us." I blushed deeper as I realized what spurious reasoning that was.

"Your outcasts and villains come to us," she replied. "Some die in the desert, others live by preying on you as you travel the roads and coasts between your principalities. Those who think to prey on us do not live." She worked the pump handle, refilling our buckets. "Some join us. My father," she added, "was a soldier for your Prince once."

My heart skidded and stumbled. She was about my age, and clearly had Ilvani blood. But no—that would be a coincidence far beyond the realm of probability.

"How did he come here?" I asked.

"He was shot and left for dead on the Clearwater Way when his party was attacked by a band of those outlaws you send us." There was no bitterness in her voice, despite the words. "My mother found him, cared for him, and ... well, had me."

It was so much a mirror image of my own parents' story it took my breath away. I busied myself with filling buckets, lost in the swirl of water.

"Did he return to the Ilmar?" I asked at last, preparing to feel kinship with another bastard child.

"Of course not." She looked shocked. "You've met him. Gerran, the stable master." She picked up her buckets and headed to the field, where the Sage Clan's horses grazed. She looked back at me as if the pails of water weighed nothing. "No one ever leaves."

I followed, my shoulders stretched and aching already. I was lost in my own thoughts. What if my parents had decided to stay together? To run away from their lives and responsibilities? They may well have ended up here. And I would be a different person, with a simpler life. Without a man's death on my hands. I poured water into the large trough, stirring up tiny insects that had settled there for a drink. I shook my head. I could blame my mother for all but the last. Doniver's death was on my conscience alone.

The horses wandered over at the sound of fresh water and checked us for treats. I had nothing, but I pulled some grass from behind the trough, where even long noses couldn't reach, and offered it to a soft-eyed chestnut mare. I paused, scratching her behind the ears.

This little green valley was a gem hidden in the uncut rough stone of the desert. I could see why Kîan's father would have wanted to stay. But her words troubled me.

"What do you mean, no one ever leaves?" I asked as we headed back to the pump yet again.

She looked apologetic. "Our people have lived in secret for eighty generations. How could we do that if outsiders came and went?"

When the clearmoon had waxed full, the clan leader, Duinir, asked the question we all needed answered. "What is to be done with you?" We knew far too much about their lives, their location, their habits to simply walk back out to civilization. And remaining here with the Sidharen was not part of my life's plan.

"My word," suggested Rhoan, "as a bard and lore master, is my honour. You may trust it with any secret."

"That may be so," replied Duinir a little drily, "but a slight bit more surety than your honour is needed. A blood oath," she continued. "And should you break it, we will find you and claim your daughter, either as a blood debt if any of us is harmed, or as one of our own. Your life as well would be forfeit, of course."

The likelihood they could collect on such a debt was small once we were safely away from the Sandhorn, but still …

Rhoan's eyes hardened. "My life you may have, but my daughter's —"

"Is not his to give," I interrupted. I squashed his protest with a look.

"I am Allaigna Leisana Andreg, daughter of the Duchess Lauresa Irdaign Andreg of Teillai, granddaughter of Prince High Chanist of Brandishear."

A ripple went around the room.

"I will take your oath, and I will be surety for us both." I held out my left hand. "But not with you, madam. With your daughter."

"No!" It was not Duinir but Kîan's father who stood, shaking the low table laid out with bowls and pitchers. They danced and threatened to spill. "These two have lied to us at every turn. My daughter will not trade oaths with one such as this."

"Father!" Kîan grabbed him by the wrist. When she couldn't pull him back to the cushions on the floor, she used his arm to pull herself up. "I believe her."

She turned to look at me, her deep brown eyes entreating me not to prove her wrong. "The ring she wears. It has her name."

My ring? The only ring I wore was the one fashioned of vines of twisted silver. It had appeared on my pillow on my twelfth birthfeast, those first lonely nights in Rheran. I still didn't know from whom it had come, but my hunch was my grandfather.

Kîan stepped over to me and held her hand out. I had no idea what game she was playing, but my instinct for once was to trust. I screwed the ring off my middle finger, feeling the intricate leaves and nodules of the design as if for the first time.

She brought it to her father. "See," she said. "Look at the bumps on the vines. They are Oran runes." Even though I couldn't see my ring from where I sat, I knew the pattern as well as the finger I wore it on. The vines had tiny bumps and nicks along their length, ones I'd always taken for part of the design. Not for the ancient pre-Imperial system of messages.

She was spelling out loud. "I … G … N … A. Allaigna." She continued to recite more letters, coming up with 'Leisana'. But she wasn't done. "B … R … A … N … D … I … S."

A chill ran up my spine. I'd never given myself that name. And yet someone had. Could it really have been my grandfather, speaking his surname in ancient runes?

There was another murmur around the room, and Kîan's father had turned as grey as the desert sand.

"The Oran runes never lie," stated Kîan. "I trust her, and I will take her oath."

Irdaign's Chorus

Aster is exhausted, her flanks heaving, her grey coat dark with sweat and the mud of the road when we reach the gates of Teillai. I force myself to bring her to a walk, though I want to gallop all the way to Osthegn's door. Each slow step on the way up the high road is an agony of wasted time, but no matter my haste and concern for my family, I won't founder the mare.

At last I am within the castle walls. I toss the reins to a sleep-fuddled Wulf with hurried instructions regarding Aster's care. They are unnecessary. He will cool her properly, apply liniment, and feed her a warm mash before turning her in.

I sing a lullaby as I creep into my daughter's bedchamber, making sure her large family continues to sleep. It breaks my heart to see them all lying here in the great bed: Irdina and Branwen snuggled one each under Lauresa's arms, Lauriana in turn nestled next to Branwen, and Allaigna, in her prickly way, maintaining an elbow's distance between herself and the warm mass of her sisters and mother. Even Allenry and the fosterling Darras seem more comfortable in their shared trundle bed than Allaigna does.

I burn the room's image into my mind. It is the last time they will sleep thus, as a family, and I note the moment for them.

I whisper the words in Allaigna's ear that will wake her, glad at least her physical distance keeps her from jostling her sister awake.

I leave, head to my workroom, and wait for her to come with her questions.

By the time Allaigna and I have finished placing the enchantment upon the ring, I am as exhausted as my horse was earlier in the evening, but I am satisfied. Allaigna is less so. I cannot answer her question as to why she needs to give her brother this ring with its subtle ensorcellment that will someday prevent bloodshed between them. The images of foresight are never clear — they show what will pass, but never why. But also I will not tell her, because I do not want her to think any more ill of her brother than she already may.

I do not know for certain what will cause the rift between them, though the fault lines in the ground have been there since his birth. I only know that it will occur and must be mended — or at least bridged — for the sake of the people of Aerach. And for my grandchildren.

My weariness is not just from tonight's spellwork. I tried so very hard to twist the ropes of Fate — to send Allenry and Allaigna both to Rheran for his sake as well as hers. But though fate is my confidante, it is not my friend. Despite my machinations, Andreg learned of the plans to send Allenry to Brandishear and vetoed them, ensuring instead that my grandson will receive his education in the poisonous court of Vishod. I am under no illusions about Chanist's court either, but that one at least I know, and I have safeguards and informants still there from my time as Princess.

It seems I will be spending more time in Aleran now, for the sake of my grandson, and at cost to my daughter and other granddaughters. If I am honest, the feeling in my heart is not just concern, but resentment at the bitter hand of fate.

Lauresa, unsurprisingly, does not take the news well.

"Will you hang the messenger?" I snap, my own fatigue and emotions overriding my calm. "I have done all — all, I say — within my power to make things otherwise. What more would you have me do?"

"We will send him with Father anyway." She is no longer shouting, but the steel-hard will behind her gaze is more dangerous by far.

"No." My will is as hard as hers. Though she is lady within this castle, and I but a nurse, I am mother once more. "You will not."

"What could he possibly do?" She is full of contempt for her husband. "Sail after them and fetch Allenry home? Risk starting a conflict between Aerach and Brandishear?"

I reply as softly, as calmly, as I am able. "That would not start the war. The war would start the minute Chanist rode out these gates with your son."

"He wouldn't." There is doubt in her eyes.

My voice is low, threatening. "Your husband is a fine politician and diplomat, but there are some things over which his political sense would not prevail. He prizes his son beyond all else, Lauresa. Beyond his career, his cousin Vishod's wishes, and beyond you."

There is affront in her eyes as she is caught, though not startled, by the truth.

"Right now, I would fear not only for the Ilmar treaty, but for your life. And if that does not sway you, think of your daughters at least."

Verse 21

Ghosts

It rained that night, a rarity in that part of the world, a quick and heavy thunderstorm that sent torrents of water pooling down into the Sage Clan's hold. It delayed our departure by another day, for although the morning dawned bright and fine, the path up the side of the gorge would be soft and treacherous until the sun had baked it again.

Amid the flurry of activity, such as rolling away rain barrels for later use, diverting runoff, and mending shutters and awnings, Kîan's father, Gerran, sought me out.

"I apologize," he said, as we rested on the shady side of the enclosure, "for my outburst last night. I had no right to call your words into question."

I looked up at the sun-worn face and away again, not used to accepting apologies from my elders. "It's all right," I said. "I know I don't look much like a duke's daughter right now."

He shook his head. "It's not your paternal lineage I was questioning." I looked up at him again, but this time it was he who would not meet my eyes. "Lauresa of Brandishear died fifteen years ago, not twenty leagues from here."

"She's alive, I assure you. Or was two months ago," I insisted, puzzling at the vague suspicion hovering just out of reach.

He sank his back against the cool rock wall and put his face in his hands. I heard him murmur something and realized his shoulders were shaking. Then it occurred to me that he was not speaking the strange pidgin Ilvanin dialect used by the Sage Clan but perfect, fluid court Ilmarin, with a southern accent, no less. Hope flared in my chest, but I suppressed it.

"You were ..." I said, putting together the pieces that made most sense. "You were part of my mother's escort on her wedding journey." He didn't respond, merely continued to hold his head, his body quivering. "But they all died. Shot down by raiders' arrows. Only my mother survived. All the world knows that." *Though*, I continued silently, *hardly anyone knows how or why.*

He lifted a face wet with tears. "I was wounded." He pulled open the neck of his shirt to show an ugly scar below his right collarbone. "The arrow knocked me from my horse, and the fall left me unconscious. Duinir found me, saved my life, and brought me here. There was no one else left alive."

"Did you not hear how Lauresa of Brandishear turned up a fortnight later in Aerach, and the wedding went as planned?"

He gave a minimal shake of the head, his eyes focussed somewhere in the past. "We don't receive your heralds or broadsheets here. The less contact we have with the world, the safer we are."

For all these fifteen years, he had believed himself the only survivor. And so did my mother. "And you've been here ever since?" It was a foolish question. I followed it with more. "Do you miss it? Court life? Civilization?"

He had regained his composure. "I was only a few years older than you when I came here. Of course I missed it at first. But I was on my way to a new and unknown life in Aerach anyway. With Ceilaf and the Princess dead"—he cleared his throat, composure not fully established—"there was little for me to return to."

"No family?"

"My father was more liberal with the rod than with family feeling. My mother lived in her cups and hadn't missed me since I'd left for Rheran."

"So they think you dead still?"

He shrugged, and I felt for those parents the way I still didn't for mine.

"I'm glad she lived," he said quietly. "How did she do it?"

I hesitated, wondering whether to give the official story or the true one. But why muddy the myth with truth? "She was rescued by Valnirati after the raiders attacked."

His eyes narrowed. "That's the story, is it? Even though the arrow Duinir pulled from my shoulder was Ilvan, not Sidharen? I have it still. I may have slept through most of the attack, but I saw the shots that hit Anwerra before mine hit me. They came from Ilvan longbows. No horsebow could reach us from cover that far away."

It was a good thing for the myth, then, that Gerran had stayed silent in the Sandhorn ever since.

"You're right," I said at last. "It is a story, but it stopped a war. It was not one of the Valnirati who saved her. He was a traveller, part Ilvani. I'm riding these parts to find him." I didn't say he was my father. Gerran could read between the lines if he wanted, but his thoughts were elsewhere.

"So," he mused, "if the attackers were not who they were made out to be, and neither were the rescuers, it makes you wonder who else might not be what they seemed."

Before I could ask him to pursue the thought further, he straightened, running his hands through his hair. "But I am well beyond the politics of the Ilmar now." He gave me a long, searching look, as if seeing me for the first time. "I should get back to work."

The bandaged wound on my hand throbbed as I curried Nag's coat, but I relished the pain. It made each brush stroke retribution for the pain I'd inflicted on my horse. Though his eyes had brightened, his ribs were painfully visible underneath the sunburnt brown of his once-black coat. And he still hesitated to put weight on his near fore hoof. They used no shoes here among the Sidharen, but they had trimmed and packed his cracked hoof expertly. I cursed myself for my neglect, for even venturing this way on a horse overdue for shoeing, causing injury to Rhoan, to my horse … for risking all our lives in this reckless, unprepared sortie into the Sandhorn.

But had I not, I would not have learned what so few know about the Sidharen people. Raiders and bandits, yes, but what other way is there of living on this barren land? And I'd uncovered another kernel of truth in my mother's history, though I could tell no one, for I was sworn to secrecy by a blood oath. I paused in my grooming and adjusted the bandage wrapped around my left palm. Neither could I tell of the histories Rhoan and I had learned, of the civilization which once flourished here. I thought of the blue vase still wrapped in a grain bag, of how it came to be in that retreating waterhole, and what other treasures of the past might hide there.

A bump on my shoulder woke me from my reverie. It was Nag, reminding me to continue grooming. I rested my face in the hollow in front of his shoulder, heartbroken, knowing what I must do. His sweet horsey smell comforted me, but made that decision all the harder.

I removed the blue glass urn from the grain bag. I dusted the vessel with my hands, feeling the sand-scoured outer surface and the smooth interior now washed clean. The colours were muted, softened through age, but no less beautiful for all that. Even in the dim light of the stable, the blue seemed to reflect endless sky and water.

It was a mystery and a clue all in one. I longed to know when and how this thing of beauty had ended up buried in a desert watering hole, but even I had to admit that not all puzzles have a solution. And even if this one did, it might have to wait. For the present is more important than the past, and flesh and blood dearer than stone or steel or glass. It was not the hardest thing I had to give up.

Kîan entered the stall without announcing herself. She still seemed wary around me, standing with one foot on the threshold. Her left hand, the one sporting a bandage to match my own, rested on the top of the stall door as if ready to slam it closed.

"It's time," she said in her accented Ilmarin, her brown eyes deep and unreadable.

"Kîan," I said, unsure how to begin, cradling the jar against my belly. "Would you …" My throat tightened, trying to prevent me from making this terrible offer. I argued with it, forcing the words out. "Would you sell me a horse? Any one, as long as it's sound."

Her eyes widened with interest or shock, but she said nothing.

"In exchange for this?" I placed the ancient vessel in her hands.

It was clear she knew some of its value, for she handled it with reverence before placing it on the shelf across the aisle.

"Allaigna, you are my oath-sister now. I cannot sell you a horse." My mouth opened to protest, but she continued, "I can only give you one."

I blushed, overwhelmed at this unexpected generosity, picked up the vase, and put it back in her hands.

"Then I give you this. It's as old as your people. I think you may be the best one to care for it, and" — my eyes suddenly betrayed me, bursting with tears — "and to look after Nag."

Lauresa's Chorus

Lauresa watches her daughter's thin, fragile-seeming form dwindle as Soot's jiggy pony trot carries her away. After the first brief wave, Allaigna hasn't turned to look back. She won't, Lauresa knows. It's not in her character, for she doesn't like to show fear or pain or loss, or even affection.

Lauresa feels the growing distance like a rope anchored in her chest, pulling ever tighter, threatening to break or to yank her heart out.

And then, at last, when the girl and pony are almost too small to see, there is a bend in that straight form, a waver as she twists and maybe, just maybe, turns to look. Lauresa can't be sure, for her eyes have filled with water for the hundredth time today.

Her mother is beside her, properly deferential in her public role as servant, but standing near enough that Lauresa can feel the warmth from her, a shelter from the spring breeze that makes her shiver.

"She is strong. Stronger than you think," murmurs Angeley.

A small spark of anger kindles in Lauresa. *Does she think I don't know my own daughter?*

Though she doesn't want to admit it, she is not worried about how Allaigna will cope. She is worried about how she will cope without her eldest daughter. Not because of the reluctant help Allaigna gives. Because of the hole her absence creates in Lauresa's already wounded heart.

Irdaign turns to her daughter with a weary gaze.

"I have scried her already today, dear. All is well, and the charms I have woven will tell me if she is ever in peril."

Lauresa continues to pace nervously back and forth within the small confines of the workroom. "But I can't help feeling it."

Irdaign sighs and rubs her temples. "I wish you had had some proper grounding in the Sight."

Lauresa's anger, always so quick to spark these days, surfaces. "And whose fault is it that I don't?"

"Mine." Irdaign's reply is resigned and unemotional.

How could you? Lauresa thinks, hardly for the first time. *How could you walk away from me?* But she realizes — and with each realization, more deeply — how hard it must have been. Tears, just like anger, are quick to the surface these days. Since there is no one here but the two of them, Lauresa can do what she has done far too few times in her life, and let her mother hold her.

"I think," says Irdaign, when the tears have slowed, "you should go to Aleran instead of me this time."

Lauresa looks up, wiping her eyes, reordering her face. "I can't possibly leave. The children ... the household ..."

"Will all survive a se'ennight without you. Honestly. You deserve a visit. How many times have you been to your nation's capital? Twice, three times in a dozen years? You can go with

Allenis and Allenry. It will make Allenry feel better to have you there, even if he'll never admit it."

Lauresa feels a sudden pang of guilt. In her sorrow over Allaigna's absence, she has all but forgotten her son will soon be leaving for a month or more as his father's page.

Her heart lifts at last at the thought of escaping Teillai's walls and assuaging some of her motherly guilt in one simple action.

Out of breath, giddy with wine and dancing, Lauresa gratefully resumes her seat beside Allenis when her latest dancing partner releases her hand.

Prince Vishod leans over, his salamander-black eyes alert and intense in his ageing face, to speak to her husband.

"You've kept your lovely wife away from my court too long, cousin. See how she keeps my courtiers on their toes? I think in future, all my summons to Teillai shall include her."

Lauresa smiles, gracious and flattered by the compliment. "Nothing would please me more, Your Highness. It is an honour and a delight to be here." She surprises herself by meaning it.

Andreg is mild and relaxed, happy with his wife's courtly skills, and if he is jealous over the attention shown her by the courtiers, he hides it entirely.

Lauresa has had only one sip of well-watered wine to refresh herself when another shadow comes between her and the glittering hall. It is a man of youngish build, though gently weathered about the face: a messenger, perhaps? He drops to one knee before the Prince.

"Apologies, Highness, for missing the banquet."

Vishod waves him to his feet with a gnarled hand. "Accepted, Sir Piers. Now get to your feet so you can bow to the Duchess, whom you have so rudely missed meeting."

"Your Grace," says the newcomer, taking her hand after his bow, "tales of your beauty have failed to live up to reality."

She smiles as he kisses her hand, not yet tired of adding to her long list of admirers.

Lauresa collapses into the thrice-stuffed bed in her apartments at Vishod's court. Aleran may not be as cultured as Rheran, but it doesn't stint on comfort, at least.

Her legs, arms, and back all ache from a long day hawking with a small group of Aleran lords and ladies. Their conversation was mostly court gossip, in much of which Lauresa is unversed, but she found it stimulating anyway. Not the content of the talk, but the exchange of wit. The only disappointing aspect of the day was the absence of Sir Piers, who had planned the outing in the first instance. Still, she is grateful to have been included.

As she debates whether to call for her maid to help her change or to just toss her boots off and roll into bed in her riding clothes, there is a knock on the chamber door.

It is Sir Piers's page, offering his master's apologies and wondering if Lauresa will join him and a few other members of the hawking party for a belated stirrup cup in the west garden.

She almost declines. Her feet have no desire to bear weight again so soon. But Allenis is not yet back from his garrison tour, and there is precious little for her to do here: no children to worry about, no household to run. So she might as well spend her evenings out.

She gives the page her response, and summons the maid to help her dress and redo her hair.

When she finally comes down to the west garden, the early summer sun has just disappeared behind the walls, and only two people other than Piers himself remain at the impromptu party.

He kisses her hand and apologizes earnestly for his absence during the day. It is too much coming from such a schooled courtier.

"Not at all, Sir Piers," she replies. "I am grateful enough to have been asked. It was an enchanting, if tiring, diversion."

"Nevertheless, your Grace, it was the height of rudeness, for which I can only beg forgiveness and understanding for the obligations of my work."

She laughs, because she knows her laugh puts men at ease. "It is all forgiven and more. Let's speak no more of it. But tell me," she asks, spreading her skirts to settle on a stone bench beside the rose arbour, "what is the work you do?"

"Very dull, and not worth talking about. I am an envoy for the Prince."

"Dull? Hardly so. I'm sure you must travel extensively."

He passes her a goblet of wine punch that his page has brought on a tray, and toasts her with his own. "Travel is many leagues of saddle sores and seasickness to attend dull meetings with foreign functionaries. The only bright spot," he says, touching his goblet to hers, "is the brief opportunity to mingle with lively minds and beautiful faces. Imagine finding one here at home—I only wish I could stay longer."

Lauresa finds she is blushing like a girl and scolds herself for feeling enchanted by this practised diplomat. "And yet, in all your travels, you have never come to Teillai?"

"The Duke is closer than any to his cousin Vishod," says Piers, revealing his intimacy with the Prince by lack of titling. "My skills are never needed there."

"A pity," says Lauresa, blushing again when she realizes she has said it out loud.

"Indeed," he smiles. "Perhaps you could induce an argument between your husband and the Prince to give him an excuse to send me. A mission close to home and in such lovely surroundings would be a pleasant change."

"I think the earth would split asunder before those two fell out," laughs Lauresa. "But please, do not hesitate to use Osthegn as a way post in your travels."

He smiles, toasts her, and promises to never again pass through Werrancross without travelling inland to Teillai.

To stop her blushes, Lauresa throws out more questions, hardly caring about the answer. "And where have you been most recently?"

"A long round trip, all by ship. Up to Adamiel's court, if you can call it a court, in Holc. Across the sea to Elalantar, and finally to Rheran before returning home, my satchel of missives growing in weight the whole time."

Her heart stutters at the mention of Brandishear's capital, once her home and now host to her eldest daughter. The weight of sadness is so thick and sudden, it is hard to breathe.

"Tell me," she says, not wanting to know but unable not to ask, "What news is there from Brandishear?"

He looks steadily at her for a long breath, wondering perhaps at her sudden seriousness. "Your father is well, lady," he says softly. "But you must know that yourself, having seen him so recently."

Her eyes widen. No one outside of Teillai's walls was to have known of his visit and convalescence there.

"Forgive me," he says for the second time that night. "That was overly familiar of me. It is in the nature of my work to know these things, but rest assured very few others do."

She chooses to ignore her discomfort at this revelation. "Nonetheless, you have seen him more recently than I. Please," she reiterates, "I would have all the news you can spare."

She has never been so happy to see them, these youngest three who tumble into her arms the minute her feet touch the ground. They are only a fortnight older but seem to have grown so big she cannot encompass them all in one hug. They are like a bouquet of varied sunflowers: Lauriana with her red-gold hair the tallest, and Irdina and Branwen, flaxen and dark chestnut, crowding up from beneath.

"I've missed you so much, my darlings," she says as she kisses each one on the top of the head, "and you will have to tell me all that has happened while I was gone. But first I need to see to poor old Peri, who has carried me all the way from Aleran."

"I'll do that, Mama," says Lauriana, seeming grown-up for her seven years, clearly relishing her new status as eldest with both Allaigna and Allenry gone from the castle. "Wulf will help me," she adds, serious, wise, and motherly, before Lauresa can point out that her middle daughter is still far too short to reach Peri's tall back.

Lauresa sees, perhaps for the first time, that the child who bears the root of her own name is in fact a small looking-glass version of herself. It brings a pang of joy and sorrow both to the spot behind her breastbone.

When her husband and son return to Teillai a fortnight later, they do not disrupt the quiet harmony of the household as she anticipated. Now that Allenry has been away from her, she has somehow been released from the duties of motherhood and need only enjoy its benefits. Allenry is just turning eight, and he too seems to have grown since she left him in Vishod's court a mere half-moon ago. He is courteous to her and loving at the same time, as if he misses his mother's lap but is too shy to reclaim it. He adds bouquets of flowers to the breakfast trays he brings to her, and seems to seek her out when before he would never bother. Without his eldest sister around with whom to carp and snipe, he is kinder to his younger sisters too, and spends as much time laughing and playing with Lauriana as he does with his foster brother Darras. In fact, the three of them take to spending afternoons together, and the boys teach Lauriana to shoot a bow and arrow, and challenge her to ever more daring feats aboard Allaigna's old pony, Soot.

Allenis is softer as well. With Allenry under his fatherly wing and Allaigna absent, there is no tension between Lauresa and her husband over the upbringing or fate of their children.

She wonders, not for the first time, whether the tension whenever they discuss Allaigna is because he knows. Or perhaps her worry over protecting her cuckoo child causes her to feel as taut as a strung bow whenever her eldest is near her husband. Without Allaigna, the tension is released. She feels guilty to be relieved, and misses her daughter even more.

And so a year passes in this fashion while the household runs smoothly and the children thrive and laugh and grow. Allenry is gone more than half the time with his father, but his visits back are all the more sweet for it. Glimpses in her mother's scrying dish show Allaigna flourishing in the court of Rheran, where Lauresa herself grew up, and her daughter's letters comfort her in their factual, unemotional tone.

Lauresa takes two more trips to Aleran's court that year and draws visitors back to Teillai in return. Osthegn no longer feels like such an isolated, if comfortable, backwater; and Lauresa stretches her chatelaine's muscles by preparing more entertainments and feasts than ever before.

With this intercourse between the two cities, it does not require a falling-out between Aleran and Teillai to bring the diplomat, Sir Piers, to Osthegn's door.

On his first visit, in the chill days of late autumn, Lauresa rides to the hunt for the first time in years with her husband and his guest. It is an exhilarating diversion, almost sufficient to assuage her sadness. They have a feast of venison in honour of Allaigna's twelfth year, despite her absence.

The diplomat's second visit is a stopping point only on his return from Brandishear in the spring. Allenis is away, and it is neither the season for hunting nor for festivities. Instead it is three days of talk both gay and serious that feeds Lauresa's mind and sticks in her memory. It is time of a different shape, colour, and taste, and it flavours her palate with longing for more.

Irdaign's Chorus

The glow is back in my daughter's eyes, and I am delighted and troubled. I have not seen her so relaxed, so charming, so vivacious in more years than I can remember. Perhaps ever. There is a court once more around her, and courtiers to enliven it.

But I am wary of the Duke. He does not seem outwardly displeased that his home has of a sudden become a social hub for Aerach's gentry, but I know he is not comfortable with it. He was always tense, always gruff around me, but in this last year he has become so almost all the time he is home.

And then there is the spectre of adultery. Lauresa has been nothing but proper around her admiring courtiers, but I can feel the warmth of sexual interest emanating from them all, like stallions around a mare not quite in heat, and I know she feels it too. She smiles, flirts, allows them to sit ever closer to her on garden benches and fireside trestles, touches them longer and more often on the arm or shoulder, and leans closer to talk beneath the noise of the hall. She does this to him, the diplomat, especially.

Would I be less worried if the Sight had not already shown me one grandchild yet to come? Does it matter if the child is Allenis's or another's? The laws of Fate are not swayed by our morals and customs, our petty standards.

Should I intervene? Or have I already?

I find Lauresa in the garden with Sir Piers. They are in deep discussion of the new hybrid roses from Brandishear, planted last autumn and flourishing now in Teillai's soil.

"Your Grace." I curtsy. Sometimes it is harder, not easier, to do after all these years of pretence. "Lauriana has had a fall."

Lauresa blanches, the high colour washed from her cheeks in a wave of maternal concern. I hurry to reassure her. "She's fine. Just a sprained wrist. She's in my room, resting."

"You must excuse me." She disengages, retreating across the garden. "How did it happen?"

"I'm not sure, your Grace." I am sure, but I'll let Lauriana tell her mother that she was standing on the pony's bare back and cantering over ditches in the field. "She was riding Soot."

Lauresa's brow clenches. "She's too young for that pony," she mutters, and turns to the gate before remembering her manners. "Sir Piers, my apologies for deserting you thus. But my . . . nurse, Angeley, is far better versed in matters of horticulture than I. She can answer your questions easily." And with that, she is gone, leaving the diplomat and me alone in the garden.

"I suspect, good sir," I say with a curtsy, "you have little interest in what I might have to say about plants."

He tips his head, smiling. "Why, there are many blossoms in this castle I would have your opinion on, mistress."

I am sure there are, I think. Sir Piers is a studied diplomat, it is true, but it is his nature, not his art, that makes him a success at his trade. And his natural charm makes me wary of him.

"I'm sure I couldn't add a thing to the knowledge of one so travelled as you, good sir." Couldn't, or wouldn't.

With his knife, he plucks a rose from the bush. It is past full bloom, the outer petals beginning to drop, and he has done the gardener a good turn in removing it. But the presumption rankles nonetheless.

He brings it to his nose, fingering the soft velvet of the outer petals. "I sense, Mistress Angeley, that you don't like me much."

He holds out the rose, a faded peace offering. Oh, he is very good, remembering the name of a domestic servant with a contrite yet casual look in his eye.

I accept the rose, allowing myself for one brief moment to assume the grace and dignity of my former royal status before lowering my gaze once more. "It is not for me to love you or not, sir. Only to serve my mistress and her children."

"Ah, why then, your duty and my delight have a common centre in service to your mistress."

It is a bold statement. He has as much said that he would recruit me in courting my daughter. But I have given him all the help I will. He shall have to rely on his own fate to aid him further.

At the thought of Fate, a dizzy wash of Sight slaps against me, causing me to sway. He takes my elbow, assists me to the bench, and his touch burns the images into my senses till I am forced to face what I have always known.

He is not just a diplomat, but a spy. But for whom, I still don't know.

Verse 22
Crossroads

The following morning, as we tightened the girths on our saddles and double-checked the ties on our saddlebags, Kîan and her father led another horse into the stables. We had said our formal good-byes to Duinir and her clan in the courtyard, but I appreciated the opportunity for a more private farewell to my oath-sister.

"Milask," Gerran said, addressing not us but our guide. "A change of plan. I'll take your mount. Help Kîan saddle hers." There was no please or thank-you in the order, but I guessed as life-mate of the clan leader, Gerran had no need to be polite.

Milask, however, frowned and spat. "Duinir herself ordered me to see to them."

"And, as I said, there's been a change of plan." Gerran's Ilvanin wasn't as polished as his native courtly Ilmarin, but he delivered the line with authority. "You can go and question my wife yourself, or you can make yourself useful and help her daughter so we are not delayed."

Milask's eyes narrowed with doubt, but he spat again and stalked to the saddle racks. "As you wish, *brianth.*" The Ilvan word for *outlander* came out like a curse.

Gerran led us up the winding dirt ramp out of the stronghold at a quick jog. I was breathing hard when we emerged from the cave entrance and winded by the time we reached the upper lip of the gorge. "Up, let's go," he said, vaulting onto the saddle of Milask's horse. The stirrups were too short for his legs, but he didn't pause to adjust them, instead wrapping his calves around the horse's sides and squeezing her into a canter. I was still swinging my leg over my mare's back as she gave a jump start and bolted after the other horse. By the time I'd found my stirrups and sorted my reins, we were in full gallop behind Gerran, with Rhoan and Kîan pounding beside me.

We galloped for at least half a league before Gerran pulled his horse back to a trot, looking back over his shoulder. "That should be enough of a lead," he shouted, slowing yet again to a walk. "Kîan, keep watch. If you spot dust, shout."

I looked back but saw nothing behind us but our own dust, drifting sideways across the already-hot desert.

"Great woolly dags, man, what was that?" gasped Rhoan, nearly as breathless as his panting mare. "'Safe conduct', she said. Not a breakneck race!"

Gerran looked back over his shoulder. "Keep moving. We'll walk a quarter bell then trot. Unless we see we're followed." He turned his gaze to Rhoan. "That was getting you a head start from Milask, Duinir's best assassin."

Despite the growing heat of the day, cold enveloped my ribs. I looked at Kîan, who didn't meet my eyes.

"That's all a blood oath is worth to your wife?" growled Rhoan.

"That's how much the safety of her people ... and her daughter ... are worth to her." His gaze moved to me. "You would have been better to insist Duinir take the blood oath with you. She'd never have let you leave, but you would have lived."

"So she let her daughter take the oath, then sent an assassin to dispatch us. Would Kîan ever have known?" asked Rhoan.

"Of course not," replied Gerran. "What kind of mother do you take her for?"

I couldn't suppress a derisive cough.

Gerran continued. "I love my wife and my adopted people. But I couldn't let them kill Lauresa's daughter. No matter the risk."

"There is no risk!" I nearly yelled. "I took a blood oath. I, at least, intend to honour that."

"As do I," said Kîan softly. She looked at me, blinking back desert dust. "I didn't know. Please believe me."

"Why bring your daughter into this?" asked Rhoan. "If she was none the wiser, why not just replace Milask and leave her without this terrible knowledge?"

Gerran's face creased as if in pain. "I don't doubt my wife loves me. But I also know she wouldn't let that love stand in the way of protecting her people. Her love for Kîan, though — that may stop her from hunting us down with arrows, at least."

Rhoan and I looked at one another. Gerran was using his daughter as a shield. The debt I felt crash onto my shoulders was staggering.

"The horses have rested," said Gerran. "We need to trot."

The scent of hot pines reached me first, an outflow wind coming down from the Kelerin plateau. The horses noticed it too, pricking their ears and quickening their steps at the distant promise of shade and forage.

My heart still lurched every time I looked over the delicate curved ears of my chestnut mare and saw her red mane instead of Nag's shaggy, sunburnt black neck. Laldi was an easy ride, with a floaty trot and rocking-horse canter, soft in the mouth and light to the legs. But I missed the feel of Nag beneath my saddle, no matter how bone-shaking his gaits.

I looked up at Rhoan. I had to look up, for Laldi was shorter than Talwis. That irked me too. The cut on the side of Rhoan's face was healing well, and he looked almost normal again, though he was apparently lost in thought … or sleeping.

"We're almost there," I murmured, to see if he was awake or not.

Kîan, whose ears seemed as sharp as mine, turned in the saddle. "Did you doubt me when I said we would reach it by nightfall?"

I was almost affronted by my oath-sister's tone until I realized it was her own anxiety making her seem sharp. Pleased with myself for this insight, I responded with a smile worthy of Garæthiel.

"Never for a moment, sister."

Rhoan roused himself from his doze. "The path is clear from here. You don't need to accompany us further. You've done more than enough," he added.

"We'll take you all the way," came Gerran's voice. "Out of our lands."

We hadn't been pursued, or at least not visibly. I wondered, though, who might be tracking us.

"What will happen," I asked Kîan, nudging my mare to catch up with hers, "when you go back?"

She shrugged, but the glance she turned toward her father was apprehensive. "I don't know. My parents have never had cause to fight before."

"Your father." I paused, thinking of his words about arrows. "Will he be safe?"

Gerran pushed his mount up on the other side of Kîan's and looked across at me. "Duinir is harsh, but not vindictive. Would she have had me shot to ensure you didn't escape to spread word of us? To free Kîan from the blood oath? Yes. Will we fight when I return? Most certainly. And no"—he put his hand on his daughter's knee, looking fondly at her—"it will not be for the first time. But I will face no real peril from her."

There was an emphasis on the last word that Kîan and I both caught. "Milask, Szu, Fedorind …" she murmured. "Mother's guard."

"Have never liked me, and will love me less now," Gerran answered her in Ilvanin. "But your mother does. It's enough."

I could hear the unsaid worries beneath his words. What troubles had I caused, political and familial, for my new blood sister and this long-ago friend of my mother's?

"You could come with us," I said, catching myself off-guard with the hope carried in my voice.

Kîan's eyes darted up, reflecting, I think, the same hope. But her father shook his head.

"I'm part of the Sage Clan now," he said. "I no longer have a life in the larger world. And Kîan would be no safer in your lands than you are in ours."

The pang of disappointment I felt surprised me. "Why not?" I turned to her. "You could easily pass for one of us. Your Ilmarin is nearly perfect. And," I added with a heavy heart, "you have committed no crimes."

"I am of the Sandhorn. That is crime enough in your people's eyes."

No. No, it's not, I wanted to argue. *We have courts of law and processes for finding guilt and innocence.* But the reminder of courts froze my blood. I wanted to spin on my haunches and flee back to the Sage Clan. I was a murderer, so I might as well live the life of an outlaw. Morran Rhoan ... he would surely be better off without me.

Except he had fled White Tooth the same time I had. If there was any implication of murder, it would be upon both of us. I would not let him face that alone, guiltless as he was. Nor could I ask him to hide with me in the Sandhorn for the rest of his days. We were stuck together.

I fingered the pendant around my neck. The leather talisman Glaignen had given me so many years ago was smooth from years spent against my skin, but the embossed tooling was clear and familiar to the touch. The raven side was outward, protecting me — or so Glaignen had said — from scrying eyes. I twisted it back and forth in my fingers, wondering whether to turn the side bearing the foal outward. I wanted so badly to hear Angeley's voice, to ask her advice, to be a child once more.

But opening myself to scrying could let others know where I was as well. I wasn't well-versed in the magic, but I felt this at least to be true. So for now I continued with my raven outward, forcing myself to be alone, independent, grown-up.

We parted where the thin track headed up into the pine-dotted hills of the plateau.

"Gleoran is half a league that way." Kîan pointed into the low-hung sun.

We didn't hug, Kîan and I. Our bond was more weighty, more formal than that, and neither of us was the hugging type. But we clasped hands, the healing wounds on our palms pressed together once more, our left hands embracing them both. I felt I was bidding farewell, but not goodbye, to a friend and an ally.

LAURESA'S CHORUS

Her dreams take her to Rheran almost every night. Most often it is her daughter who populates them, but also her father, her siblings, her cousin Genissa, and her aunt Taerysh. They vary in ages through the dreams, as does she: sometimes young, sometimes old, but most often as she remembers them from her adolescence.

Einavar is there as well, but his face is more fluid than most, fading out and reappearing: at Ceilaf's side, as his squire, in the *keaugh* as her lover, as the changing face she has seen far too few times since then. In the dreams she can feel his touch on her arm, her shoulder, her waist. And always she wakes up hungry for more.

She is puzzled by this newly discovered appetite. Is it just that her youngest have grown older, have weaned themselves from her, leaving her mind and body available for other interests? Or is it the absence of her two eldest, the feeling that her nest has shrunk, that makes her want to fill it once more?

She shudders. No, she is done with babies. Five is more than enough for any woman, and she has no wish to feel the aching back of pregnancy or the bondage of nursing babes ever again. But even as she thinks it, her breasts tingle with the ache of absent milk. She shakes her head, scolding her traitor body.

The distraction of another visit from Sir Piers would be welcome if not for the letters he carries from her father and daughter. Allaigna fares well—so well, in fact, she will continue for another year in Rheran's court. It is not unexpected. Lauresa has always known Allaigna would have the ability to rise within the court should she apply herself, and she is proud of her daughter. But there was a selfish hope that Allaigna wouldn't like it, would choose to come home instead. And, selfish sentimental woman that she is, Lauresa cannot stop the tears.

"Your Grace?" Sir Piers has re-entered the solar. He stops when he sees Lauresa's damp face, then hurries to produce a kerchief from his sleeve. "Forgive the intrusion, my lady. I did not know the missives I carried were ill tidings."

She shakes her head. "I'm just a fool whose mother's heart should be proud, not sad."

"It is strength, not weakness, for a mother to have a tender heart," he says, smiling and seating himself beside her on the divan. "I miss my only daughter with all my heart, and wish I could bring her with me."

Lauresa is surprised. He has never mentioned a wife or family before. He tells her of the Brandishear woman he loved. "She died, alas, bringing our child into the world. The girl lives with her grandparents in Cadauwen, and though they bear me no love, I at least visit her on my travels to and from princes."

It makes him more human, safer somehow. Lauresa leans against him, and they sit in the long spring dusk, missing their daughters.

Sir Piers has only departed by a matter of hours when a second messenger arrives. This time it is her mother.

"In the usual place," she murmurs. "Midday. Tomorrow."

Lauresa is speechless. Einavar? Here? Now? She is both angry and curious, for is he not supposed to be in Rheran, watching their daughter's interests?

The weather is foul the next day, and she curses the need to meet in the forest. Not because of the weather — a hurricane could not keep her away — but because it makes it hard to find an excuse to ride out. So she makes a show of ill temper throughout the morning, and by noon the household is relieved to see her cool her ire in the downpour.

She is sodden and shivering by the time she reaches the spring, and as glad to see Einavar's tent as she is to see the man himself.

There is less emotion from either of them than she would have expected. They embrace briefly. He helps her out of her sodden cloak and wraps a blanket around her shoulders while she huddles by the small pot of coals that edges the chill away.

She opens her arm, invites him in, and he slips his warm body beside hers. They sit as easily as any long-married couple while she sips hot wine.

"Why?" she asks at last.

He hesitates. "An assignment I couldn't say no to."

"Couldn't? And what of Allaigna? You know she's not coming home yet."

He nods. "I had heard." He looks at her, then away, apologetic. "I am not able to keep as close an eye on her as you — as we both — would like. But I have no reason to doubt her safety or her happiness within the Bastion's walls at the moment."

Lauresa nods, sagging against him, accepting that all her worry will change nothing.

He reaches across, moves the wet hair from her cheek. She shivers at the sudden cold air that moves around them.

"But what of you? Are you well?"

Lauresa is surprised. "Very. Why do you ask?"

Troubled grey eyes pin hers for a moment before he looks away, shrugging. "I dreamed of you. Three, maybe four nights in a row."

She tenses, shifting and suddenly alert.

"That is not so unusual," he continues. "I dream often of you." He looks at her again, a half smile on his thin lips, a glint in his eye. "But this time it was the same every night. I could hear you calling me. By name. My true name."

Lauresa shivers again but smiles, and kisses him to avoid pondering the meaning of dreams.

Irdaign's Chorus

I hold Lauriana in my arms as sobs judder through her small body. There is a hesitant knock on the door. I raise my voice over the heart-turning sounds and bid Darras enter.

His too-pale lashes can't hide the fact he too has been crying, despite the grave and stoic face he presents. He has a bunch of flowers in his hand: poppies, cornflowers, and lavender that I suspect have come from my gardens. I forgive him.

"Laur … I … I'm sorry. About Soot."

I feel Lauriana stiffen in my arms, aware of this new witness. She wrenches free from my lap.

"Get out!" she screams at him.

She snatches the proffered flowers and hurls them at him, littering my workroom with multi-coloured detritus.

"It's your fault," she hisses, her exquisite face twisted into a mottled red mask. "You and my brother."

Poor Darras retreats under the onslaught, blinking away more tears from his eyes.

It is not his fault, of course. Allenry is always the ringleader in every game, contest, or adventure those three engage in. And it is Lauriana's own fault she rode the pony hard then turned him out, hot and sweaty, onto lush grass.

I put a restraining hand on her shoulder. "Your brothers are not at fault, Lauriana."

There is a flicker of gratitude in Darras's eyes. Not so much for absolving him, but for pluralizing 'brothers'. It is a reminder to them both that though he is a fosterling, Darras is part of the family.

She shrugs off my hand in a gesture so like her older sister's it makes me want to laugh. But I realize with sadness that this is a superficial similarity. Where Allaigna would be wracked by guilt over laming her pony, it is Lauriana's pride that is wounded most after the tongue-lashing she received from both parents in front of Allenry and Darras.

"I hate you!" she spits at Darras, and runs from the room, leaving behind a broken-hearted boy whose only desire is to belong. He turns to me, the hopeless pain in his pale eyes breaking my heart.

"Allaigna will be so sad," he says.

The pony must be put down, so badly is he foundered. I agonize over whether to tell Allaigna. Her mother insists we not write of it, to spare her the pain. But I waver, wondering how many lies of omission she will tolerate from us in the end.

I do write of it in my next letter, which I entrust to Sir Piers, who is most conveniently stopping by yet again en route to Brandishear. But the letter has another purpose. I sing a verse into its writing, subtle and, I hope, not easily detected. It is similar to the charm on Allaigna's pendant, allowing me to scry more easily upon whoever bears the letter. I am curious about this Sir Piers, and would follow his movements more closely.

As I finish writing, Darras knocks once more on my workroom door. He has a small paper packet in his hands, tied with string and sealed with a messy glob of wax. The letters 'DR' have been scratched into it. House Raen is not wealthy enough to spare a signet ring for its heir.

"It's for Allaigna," he says, thrusting the packet at me with hands that tremble ever so slightly.

I raise an eyebrow, smile gently, and finger the seal. "What is it, Darras?" The court at Rheran is most particular about what enters the castle gates these days. I should, in all honesty, look inside.

His pale skin turns scarlet. "It's … a lock of Soot's mane, ma'am."

He is lying, and he is not. The packet does indeed feel like a braid of hair. But the ink on the inside of the paper is what he doesn't want me to see.

No matter. I will sing a divining song over it before passing it on to Piers. That will ensure no magic, poison, or prohibited substance is carried to Rheran. And then I will place my seal on the whole bundle. The words he's written can stay between them.

I give him a brief, motherly hug, for which he is almost too old. He melts into it nonetheless.

"Darras," I say, "you are a good and true brother." I feel him swell and warm with acceptance. As I let him go, though, I feel ambivalence. "One day she will thank you for your kind heart."

And I recognize what the ambivalence in that kind heart is: even at the tender age of eleven, the regard it feels is more than fraternal.

The wet heat of the summer air rises from my skin and chills me, though there is no breeze to shift the languid trees of the inner yard. Disturbed, I place my pruning scissors and the bundles of fresh sage into my basket and stand, casting my gaze around the courtyard like a hound that has lost a scent.

There is nothing: no one present, no change in weather, nor, when I look with extra vision, no hint of charm or any other magic to disrupt the surroundings. There is no premonition, no fluttering warnings from the Sight. Why am I so perturbed in the absence of any threat?

Absence. That is it. She is gone. The tiny corner of my mind that has been monitoring, distantly aware of Allaigna's joys, sorrows, pain, pride, worries, and wants, has gone silent.

Thoughts of the worst sort ricochet through my heart. There was no warning, no moment of fear or pain to signal an accident. It is unthinkable that she could die in her sleep, in the middle of the day, so young and healthy. And with no warning from my inner eye.

I cross to the fish trough, fighting these thoughts and the panic that keeps me from focussing. The glaring sun overhead gives no subtle shadows within the water to work with, and I am unable to summon even the beginnings of a strong scrying charm to find her. I leave the garden for my workshop and, with trembling hands, fill my bowl.

And then I feel it: a tugging at the back of my head, as if someone is looking over my shoulder.

"Allaigna," I whisper to the water, calling her.

There is someone there, but not her. It is a mind I've touched before, so long ago and so different now. Yet unmistakable.

"Glaignen."

And the contact is broken with a sound like wine spilled on cobblestones and the same sudden, deep absence.

I am partly reassured. It can be no coincidence that Allaigna's sudden absence is paired with an attempt by one of our people to scry me. She is there, somehow, with him. But I must know why, and what it means.

It is well past summer's late nightfall before my repeated attempts to contact Nourd succeed. She is tired, irascible, and seems to have trouble seeing me in the shimmering water of her bowl. It makes her hard to hold onto.

"The girl is fine." She waves a hand, making her disappear from view for another agonizing moment. "Glaignen saw her today."

Another memory flits back, and I recall that Glaignen fashioned the pendant she wears, the one that makes it easier to see her in the scrying bowl.

"Is he there? Glaignen?" My anxiety makes me forgo courtesies that even I, Nourd's former pupil and long-time friend, should observe.

She gestures and wavers from sight again, but when the image re-forms, it is clear and strong, Glaignen's face appearing behind her shoulder.

"Good even, Grandmother," he says, the Leisanmira term of respect sounding harsh and discordant.

I have never had the pleasure of being addressed so by my own grandchildren. To have it come from this young man, who is no doubt responsible for my current inability to sense Allaigna, galls.

I bite my cheek to refrain from snapping. "You saw Allaigna today?"

"I did, Grandmother," he nods. "She seemed well and in good spirits."

He is lying, I feel sure, but from such a distance I cannot tell why. "Has she removed the pendant you gave her?"

His chin tips sideways a fraction, though his pleasant smile remains. "No, Grandmother. She has simply turned it over."

"Over."

The angle of his head increases. "To the raven side. It seemed prudent, amid the eyes and ears of the court, to prevent unwanted scrying."

He is right, of course, but the words hit me like a stonebow ball to the chest. That I never examined the pendant enough to notice the reverse charm embedded on the other side was bad enough. I spare a scrap of admiration for the skill of the boy who crafted it at so young an age. But unwanted scrying could refer to mine, and that hurts more than I'd imagined possible.

I lash out, not at the cool polite face of Glaignen, but at Nourd, my old friend. "You must make her turn it around, Nourd."

The old woman's face is impassive. "Why?"

"You've seen as many glimpses as I have. You of all people know how important she is to the Ilmar. To us all."

"I have seen as much or more than you, Irdaign." Her voice is as harsh and dry as a crow's. "And I have more faith in the workings of Fate. I've seen she is important, yes. And I trust she will live and thrive to fulfill that destiny. Do you, arrogant child, think you are Fate's only agent? That all must fall on your shoulders to oversee, and guide, and meddle?"

Nourd leans closer to her bowl so her eyes block out all else. Cloudy with age as they are, they are no less piercing.

"What could you do, from there in Aerach anyway, to protect her? She doesn't need a nurse anymore, Irdaign. Let her grow up."

In fury I throw my silver bowl over, sending water slapping against the floor, my workbench, and my carefully written notes and dried herbs, wishing she were not right.

Verse 23
Responsibility

Gleoran, though not as busy as Werrancross, is a large enough frontier town that Rhoan and I decided it was worth the risk of finding an inn for the night. It no longer felt safe to work as travelling entertainers, so we kept to ourselves. Even though I was of Brandishear blood and had spent a year and a half in its capital, I felt alien in this town. The language was the same, and the customs were the same; under the treaty, Brandishear and Aerach might as well be the same nation. And yet it felt like a vast ocean, not a mere sandy desert twenty leagues wide, separated me from my homeland.

As we sat in the low-raftered common room of the inn, beneath the false ceiling of smoke, I found myself fingering my pendant again, longing to turn it over, to gaze into a pool of fresh water and see if I could hear Angeley's voice calling me.

But I let it drop back inside my shirt, conscious in the dark room of its pearly pink glow and suddenly frightened of drawing attention from the other tenants of the room or from the Mage Guard. I remembered clearly how much more present those black-robed policemen of all things arcane were here in my grandfather's realm than back home in Aerach. I didn't think so small a magic as this would call their notice, but I couldn't be sure. And the Mage Guard were more active in border towns.

I could feel Rhoan's question before he asked it. I'd been waiting for it for days.

"So where next?"

Why ask me, I wanted to say. *You're the adult. I'm just a child.* I dearly wanted to turn responsibility over to him, or to anyone. But I was barely a child, despite my unfinished form. I was old enough to be betrothed, to have killed a man, to have taken my fate into my own hands. I might as well shoulder the full responsibility. Till now I had been running from the lies my mother had told me, from the life demanded of me, and from the life I'd taken. It was time I started heading *to* somewhere.

Wandering the countryside and hoping to stumble upon my father wasn't working, and I wondered that I'd ever pretended it might. I needed someone who had travelled the borders and knew the Ilvani, and I berated myself for not having thought of her before. I recalled her words to me: "If you ever have need of me, you have but to ask." I had forgotten that promise for years. She could be stationed anywhere, but she was in the Ranger corps and eventually could be found. I looked up into Rhoan's eyes, wondering how he would react, and wondering too why he'd never asked this of me himself.

"We're going to find Rhiadne."

It was not the reaction I'd expected. I'd expected a smile, or some sign of happiness at the prospect of seeing his long-lost love, perhaps. But there was barely a blink. A flicker of something passed behind his eyes, but the rest of his normally expressive face held a mask-like stillness. He took a long drink from his tankard and slowly, fastidiously wiped the foam from his lips with his travel-stained lace cuff.

"Will she know aught about your father, do you think?"

Taken aback by his cold reaction, I stuttered slightly. "Sh-she's a captain in the Rangers. Who else knows as much about the comings and goings of people in the Ilmar?"

"Indeed. And are not the Rangers the ones we've been avoiding the last few weeks?"

"Yes, but ..." I paused, trying to find words to express the muddle in my head. "But Rhiadne would never ... I mean, she would understand. She wouldn't turn us over. Not me. Not you?" That, at least, should have been a certainty, not a question.

"I hope not. At least the girl I knew would not. But I would not ask her not to. Would you ask her to compromise her position by aiding us?"

My heart dropped into my belly. Would I? The old me would have. The child of privilege who felt the world existed to serve her. It rankled that I hadn't recognized the jeopardy I would place her in. That it had taken Rhoan to point it out.

"Of course not." I sank farther into my chair, defeated. A lump began to coagulate in my throat as another thought took hold. "I can't—" I paused, swallowing back the lump. "I can't ask you to take any more risk for me either." The smoke had lowered, watering my vision and obscuring his features. I continued. "We should separate. You're not on any of my family's handbills. And we don't even know that anyone is looking for Doniver's ... killer."

He said nothing, his face unreadable behind the smoky veil.

I coughed, my throat stinging. "I need air," I mumbled, heading for the inn's rear doors.

The smell of the midden heap at the back of the building was sharp enough to blast the remnants of smoke from my nostrils but did nothing to prevent the continual watering of my eyes. Where to go then, I wondered, if not to Rhiadne? I couldn't conjure up places in this strange country, only names and faces. Garæthiel, Glaignen, Goff. Chal. Even Fîal. It was not my father I wanted, but friends. But what friend could I trust, and what friends would not be in danger from my presence?

I felt small, childish, and alone.

I drew the curved dagger that had once belonged to my father from the top of my boot. The clearmoon was beginning to spill watery light into the stable yard, washing away the dim orange from the inn behind me and replacing it with monochrome hues.

It made the knife look stranger, more alien, and even more deadly. The light was insufficient to see the intricate carvings on the haft, but I could feel them, familiar now to me after sleeping night after night with the knife beneath my pillow. The dagger was more familiar than my sword or maybe even my bow. It was as familiar as the handle of the knife I ate and prepared my food with, as familiar as the reins of Nag's bridle. *Not Nag's anymore*, I corrected myself, fighting with the tightness in my throat once again. And yet, as intimately as I knew the strange weapon, I was no closer to knowing its owner. If there were clues to his identity in this artefact, they were opaque to me, and all my travel and trials had been the aimless wanderings of an errant child.

Aimless, but not harmless. For I'd lamed my horse, killed a man, and caused no end of hardship to Morran Rhoan. I had done some small good too, I appealed to my sterner conscience. I'd shut down the boar-baiting operation, given Raddick his family lands back, and made an alliance of sorts with the people of the Sandhorn. That last, I felt, was rare and new.

So did it matter if I was no closer to finding my father? Could I not walk away from this quest and start my life from here?

I turned the dagger over in my hands. It would feel like giving up. The knife held no visible hints to my father's identity or locale, but it was still my only clue. And it might mean more to others. It had lived hidden in my boot top too long.

I felt a hand on my shoulder and turned to look up into the warm eyes of Rhoan. I knew from my mother's description that my sire was tall and dark-haired like Rhoan. I could only hope he was as kind.

"Will you carry a message for me?" I asked. "To Rhiadne?"

He nodded sadly, hopefully. "Where will you wait for her?" he responded, knowing already what the message would ask.

I hadn't thought that far. The only place in Brandishear I knew was Rheran. It was also the only place large enough to hide me.

I searched my memory for a suitable inn. I had never set foot in one when I was there, so I relied on memories of the signs hanging in the street. "At the Red Horse, near Brônagate." I had no idea what the place was like on the inside, but the image of the red horse, my Grandfather's sigil, on a green sign hanging against the blue skies and white stone of Rheran was clear in my head. "Leave word there for ... for Deil Taran." It was Ilvanin for 'little crow'. "And I will check daily for messages."

Rhoan nodded, neither protesting nor questioning, and it made me suspicious.

"You *will* do this? You aren't planning to merely follow me?"

He was full of wounded innocence. "My word is my troth, Allaigna. If I give it, you may trust it."

I narrowed my eyes. "But you haven't given it yet."

He sighed. "Yes, all right. I was planning to follow you."

I was touched, reassured, and irritated.

"But," he continued, "while you were out here … breathing the night air," he said, wrinkling his nose at the yard's clinging odour, "I made arrangements for you to travel with a caravan to Rheran."

I was furious. How did he know where I'd go before I knew myself? It was almost enough to make me change my plans to spite him. But how could I? It was too convenient, too reassuringly safe, too bloody thoughtful of him.

He smiled. "I know it will cramp your style, sticking to the plodding pace of draught animals, but you'll have food, a place to sleep, and" — the smile grew wider — "the family has pledged to see my daughter safe to her aunt in the city."

"Aunt?" I asked.

"A friend of mine in Rheran. I'll write you a letter of introduction."

I was fuming inside, overcome by irritation that he had arranged all this in so short a time and that it made far too much sense to refuse. And then another of his words struck me.

"Family?" I said. "Is this not a merchant van?"

"Far better." The irritating smile came again as he led me back into the tavern.

"Mistress Dourva," he said as we pulled up three-legged stools beside the table. "This is my daughter, Merri."

I was taken off-guard by her masses of ginger-gold hair, caught back with ribbons, and her eyes. They were green not blue, but nonetheless so like my grandmother's that I had no doubt this woman was Leisanmira.

I took her hand and bowed respectfully, terrified and awkward yet somehow glad to be with my grandmother's people.

Lauresa's Chorus

It's all Lauresa can do, when her mother tells her Allaigna's ship has docked at Werrancross, not to saddle a horse and head out to meet it.

But her belly is heavy once more — a weight she thought she'd never bear again — and she wouldn't last one quarter of the ride. Instead she stares out the window of the ladychamber at the huge oaken gates of the courtyard, and waits for her daughter to appear.

Her fingers tap impatiently on the taut drum of her abdomen as she tries not to resent this new child of hers. She knows she will love it, bless it, and die for it once she looks into its newborn eyes. But for now it is so very hard not to curse the pregnancy that has hurled her back into the role of a broodmare.

But this time it is so much worse. This time Allenis knows it is not his.

If he had reacted with anger, with violence even, it would have been so much more reassuring. The impassive calm with which he greeted the news was chilling. He was no colder than usual, and more or less considerate, as if being a cuckold were a mild and common thing for him.

Which makes her wonder whether he also knows the truth about Allaigna.

She thought she was done worrying about her eldest with Allaigna safely tucked away in Rheran, far from the scrutiny of Andreg as she grows more and more unlike him. But now she is coming home in quiet disgrace that, while not public, is indication enough she is not safe in Rheran either.

Despite her fears, despite her worry for both her cuckoo children, she is ecstatic to be so close to seeing her daughter's lovely face again.

She has barely left the ladychamber and its view of the gates all day, despite the many things she should be attending to for the feast tonight. Instead Angeley is looking after that in her superbly efficient manner. Lauresa feels guilt in allowing her mother to take hold of the chatelaine's keys once more, until she remembers that pregnancy is an ideal excuse to shirk responsibility. She pats her belly, relieved to have some small gratitude to owe this child.

She spots her. The oak gates that have stood so sullenly shut all day now frame between their half-moon lintels the lone figure of a woman, hooded and cloaked against the steady rain.

Lauresa rises from the window seat so swiftly she has to stop, hold the wall, and breathe till her blood rights itself. She tries to keep a steady pace down the corridor, to not skitter down the stairs like one of her daughters, restraining herself to walk in a frame that will not topple her over or cause more pain to her aching pelvis.

If Angeley has gone to stand before the gates, then it is a certainty Allaigna is not too far on the other side.

Curse the woman, why didn't she let me know? thinks Lauresa.

Her mother's look is mild and knowing as always, though there is a glimmer of concealed joy behind it.

"You shouldn't be out in the rain uncloaked, Lauresa." She doesn't use the charade term 'your Grace' any longer when there is no one around to hear it. "You know you're more prone to colds when you're pregnant."

She doesn't want to, but can't stop herself from snapping at her mother. "She's *my* daughter. I want to hug her first."

Angeley's eyes glint like blue metal for a heartbeat, and then she tips her head. "But of course, your Grace." And she takes a step back as the great gates begin to swing open.

It is of course not her daughter who rides through first, but the ranger who has accompanied her.

He dismounts and kneels before Lauresa, proffering the pad of missives he carries from Brandishear. Courtesy dictates she cannot ignore him, no matter how her gaze is drawn to the slim almost-woman behind him.

She accepts the parcel, barely hearing the ranger's words, until she realizes her own name has been spoken. At last her startled eyes meet his. It is no ranger at all, but Sir Piers, with a new beard and short-cropped hair.

She hasn't seen him in months — nearly six, to be precise — and her eyes follow his widening ones to her obvious belly.

Why he is disguised as a ranger, she doesn't know. Why he was chosen to accompany her daughter, she wants to know. But right now all she can do is flash a silent burst of anger and resentment at him. The look causes him to pull back and release her hand.

"Stay the night," she commands under her breath. "We shall talk … later."

One more reason to resent him now burns beneath her breastbone for, in the intervening time, Allaigna has slipped from her horse and run into her grandmother's arms.

Angeley's hug is fierce and brief. She pulls away, half turning Allaigna toward her mother. Allaigna doesn't seem to notice the belly, for her grey eyes are on Lauresa's face, brimming with tears. At last, Lauresa is able to clasp her daughter to her breast and hold her as if she will never let go.

Irdaign's Chorus

She is back, and though my heart aches for the pain and humiliation that has returned her, I can't help the joy that rises in me. It almost masks the hurt of her coolness toward me.

She is an adolescent, and my mind knows it is normal and necessary for her to separate herself from her family. I had expected outbursts of tears and other such turmoil as comes with the age. But her calm reserve is altogether more disturbing. She is pleasant and courteous to all, and no less so to me. There is no hint of her true feeling beneath that courtly mask, and I cannot help but wonder what it is she is hiding.

But what do I know? I missed these years of Lauresa's and have no grandmotherly wisdom in this regard.

Lauresa, too, is wounded by her daughter's reserve, but maintains her own cool distance, perhaps afraid of pushing Allaigna further away. And so the three of us dance around one another in a stately pavan, Lauresa and I holding masks over our faces of motherly concern. Allaigna's mask is nearly perfect, but beneath it I fear a roiling anger.

VERSE 24
BLOOD TIES

The caravan departed Gleoran in the orange hours of early morning. Rhoan rode with me to the outskirts of town, where the wagons were rolling into place amid eddies of children, dogs, and goats.

Our shadows stretched toward them, two black spearheads reaching for the colourful melee. I reined in before my shadow horse's ears touched the nearest van. I didn't want to say goodbye with other eyes around.

I didn't want to say goodbye at all, no matter that this parting had been my choice. I had set out looking for a father, and though I hadn't found my own, here was one who had all the qualities I could hope for. But would he even want a daughter? I wondered. Especially one who'd caused him so much trouble? I fought back the water in my eyes, tried to look at him, and failed.

"Allaigna." He so seldom used my name it almost came as a shock. "You don't have to, you know. Go alone."

I shook my head. I would not go through these arguments again, especially when he might win. It was all too tempting to turn away, to go with him and become a travelling singer in earnest, or ask him to come to Rheran with me. And I refused to change my mind.

"If you ever change your mind," he echoed my thoughts, "send word. I have no home to offer, but you will always be welcome to travel with me."

I managed to look at him at last, sideways, with the rising sun bouncing circles and shafts of light around his head.

"Thank you," I whispered. It was an inadequate phrase to encompass all I had to thank him for, but it was what I could manage. So I repeated it, reaching out from the saddle to embrace him before our horses shifted away again.

I wiped my eyes on my sleeve, reordering my face as I approached the caravans, unsure where to ride or who to ask. There was no sign of Dourva, but she was probably in one of the wagons. I took a deep breath and approached the nearest outrider. Facing the maddened sow hadn't been as frightening as this.

"Pardon me." I hated how high, thin, and girl-like my voice sounded. "I've arranged with Mistress Dourva to ride with you—"

The young man turned in his saddle, squinting into the morning sun. I looked down at my saddlebow, nervously adjusting my reins. "I'm—"

"Allaigna?" asked the rider.

I looked up. His face was half-shadowed by the hand he held against the sun's glare, but I recognized the smiling eyes and fox-red hair, two years taller and broader though he was.

"Glaignen?" I stuttered, amazed. Why had it not crossed my mind that he could quite logically be here with a gipsy van? I hadn't seen Glaignen since I'd stabbed my cousin Goff defending him in the streets of Rheran. That act had sent me home to Teillai in disgrace and cost me my place in my grandfather's court. At least I had only wounded Goff. So much smaller a crime than the one that rested across my shoulders now. "Not Allaigna. I go by Merri these days."

He wasn't listening. He was off his horse and on one knee beside mine. He placed one hand on my stirrup, the other on his heart.

"My oath, sister, if you'll have it, is too many years coming."

"Get up," I hissed as eyes started to turn toward us.

He stood, so much taller now that his head came to my elbow, but he did not let go of my stirrup.

"I'm happy to see you too," I muttered, confounded by his obeisance—and by his grown-up and admittedly handsome face gazing up at mine. "But I am not travelling under my own name. Please … I beg you, can you keep my secret?"

This seemed to trouble him. "I owe you my life—"

"You don't," I interrupted, more and more uncomfortable with the attention we were drawing.

"And I have given you my oath. The Leisanmira do not keep secrets amongst themselves. But I will forsake my clan ties if you ask it."

I shook my head, horrified. "No! I don't ask it!" The sudden tumble of words and oaths dizzied me, and I wanted to flee. I turned my horse's head away. "I'll just go." Though with that turning, I was surprised to feel my heart lurch and want to stay.

Glaignen caught my rein.

"Wait, Allaigna … Merri."

I held, softened by his use of my false name.

"There are no secrets amongst us, but we never let one slip beyond us. Whatever reasons you may have for forsaking your name, you are one of us. By blood, and by my oath. Your secrets are safe with us."

There was a warmth in my chest that threatened to make me cry again. I wanted to relax into the promised safety. I wanted — but was afraid — to release caution.

"Will you at least come and visit my grandmother again? She is old and never leaves her caravan, but it would do her heart good to see you."

I looked with trepidation at the painted wagon I knew to be Nourd's, but I nodded, unable to say no to the welcoming green eyes below me.

As I followed Glaignen to Nourd's wagon, I felt myself shrinking back to the reluctant nine-year-old I was when I first set foot on that step. Even though I no longer needed a hand up, Glaignen was there, as he had been half a decade ago, with a light and gallant touch on my fingertips, pulling me in behind him.

"Grandmother," he said. "It is Allaigna."

There was no surprise in her reaction. She sat at her table as if she'd been waiting there forever. I shivered. Of course there was no surprise. To Nourd, as to my own grandmother, the future is an open book. She tapped the table with her palm.

"Welcome," came that pebbled voice. "Sit." And then, "Glaignen, you may go."

I turned to look at him, terrified of being left on my own with Nourd. But he smiled, gave a reassuring squeeze of the fingers he still held, and winked before stepping back out into the golden morning sun.

The caravan seemed dark and airless when the door closed, and my heart was hammering as I sat once more at Nourd's table. Her eyes were different, a paler blue clouded with age.

"Come closer," she barked. "Let me see you."

I leaned over the table, nearer the small evenlamp. The flesh-starved fingers of her gnarled hands shot out on either side of my face, pinioning me like a mouse in the claws of a falcon. I didn't dare move or breathe as the bony fingertips walked across my face.

How ironic, I thought, for one with the Sight to lose her vision. As if she could hear my thoughts, she spoke again.

"I see light and dark, but little else with my eyes these days. It has only made the Sight clearer." She dropped her hands. "Why are you here, Allaigna?"

I wanted to shoot back that she should already know that. I shivered again when I realized she already did; my answer was part of a test.

"I'm looking for my father," I replied as evenly as I could, eschewing the padding of courtesy.

"Why?"

I blinked. It was a question I'd never asked myself.

"To ... to find out who I am."

"You already know that. You are Irdaign's granddaughter and Lauresa's daughter. You're a privileged brat of the nobility, but you carry your grandmother's blood."

I bristled. "And what of my father's blood—does that not matter at all?"

"Oh, it matters very much, young Brandis. It matters what you do with it."

I bit back a reply, momentarily confused by her calling me by the name of Brandishear's hero. But of course it was also my grandfather's surname.

She continued. "You don't need to find out who you are. You need to find out who you will be. The bowl." She pointed a bent finger at the brass bowl sitting high on a shelf.

I remembered the bowl. I remembered looking into its water-filled surface as a child and seeing things I neither understood nor wanted to see. I stood reluctantly and retrieved it. Its sand-scoured surface was thick with dust.

"Wipe it out," she commanded, handing me a faded turquoise scarf, "and fill it." She pointed at the ewer of water on the table.

Reluctant or not, I felt compelled to obey, cleaning off the layers of dust, polishing the dull yellow surface, and at last filling it with rippling clear water.

"I can't use it anymore," she whispered in a hoarse voice that seemed almost sad. "And I don't need to. With the world gone dark for me, I see more than I ever did. But I miss its beauty."

It was beautiful. The scouring pattern created mesmerizing whorls and spirals of gold light that scintillated through the water, even in the dimness of the cabin.

"But," she continued, "I can help you."

My heart was pounding by now, quailing in unreasoned terror at the thought of looking in those waters once more.

"Come." She put her hands out, palms up, on either side of the bowl. "It will show you what you need. Maybe it will even show you your father."

The look on her face was a challenge. Clearly she thought my father would not appear in those waters. That was all the dare I needed.

Straddling the three-legged stool, I put my hands into hers and, like I'd seen Angeley do so many times before, blew into the water.

When at last I let go, my limbs were trembling, my body soaked in sweat, and my breath coming in short gasps.

No, I thought. *I cannot. I will not.*

Furious, I glared at the old woman. "So — that's it? My future? As if I have no choice?"

"There are always choices." Her voice seemed softer, younger now. "The responsibility, to accept or decline, is always yours. The future is never fixed until it has happened — and even then is subject to interpretation."

"Why me?" I hissed, the anger still burning hot. And the unspoken resentment: *Why have you shown this to me? Why have you burdened me with the future, like you and my grandmother have been burdened?*

"Why not you? Is there anyone better, more fit? Your brother, perhaps? Goffree? There are many options."

Not them, I thought. *Neither is fit.* But I didn't say it aloud. Instead I issued another challenge. "You said it would show me what I need. I saw nothing to give me direction."

"Nothing?" she asked, her clouded eyes mild.

A memory flicked back of a man silhouetted against a purple, storm-fraught sky. I couldn't see his face. Only the background was visible: the high west tower of the Bastion.

I paused on the step of Nourd's caravan, blinking in the harsh morning light that sparkled from the wet brass bowl I held.

It was heavy in my hands, empty of water now but filled with the weight of foreboding. I wanted to let it fall, with all its portents, there on the roadside. Or better, to fling it away. I imagined it sailing through the cloudless sky, flashing in the sun, flinging diamond drops of water in its wake. But I knew I could not. My rebellious heart was still no match for the sense of duty and responsibility trained into me.

I hugged the offending object to my chest, crossing the short-cropped grass almost furtively to where Glaignen stood holding both our horses.

His eyes widened slightly at the sight of the bowl, or perhaps at my glowering face, but he said nothing. I opened my saddlebag to find room for the bowl and then paused, turning it over in my hands.

"This should be yours," I said thoughtfully, congratulating myself already on handing off the unwanted gift. "I don't have the Sight. I can't use it, but you—"

He held up both hands in refusal. "Nor do I."

I shook my head, puzzled. "But you do. I remember …"

"No longer," he smiled, no trace of regret in his eyes. "It's rare in boys to begin with. And unlike womenfolk, who age into it, it fades in us when we grow up."

"I'm sorry—"

"Don't be. It's a gift, and a useful one at that. But it's also—"

"A burden," I finished for him.

"Aye." He put his hands around the bowl, not taking it from me but rather holding it in my hands. "One I'd take back if I could. But its time with me is over."

"I don't want it," I whispered, not sure if I meant the bowl, the Sight, or the destiny I'd seen.

"You will cope," he replied, gently pushing the vessel back against my chest.

I nodded dumbly, feeling dread seep into me as if from the scoured brass.

"We'd best mount up," he said. "The vans are moving."

Indeed, the colourful wagons had started their creaky roll forward, shifting into line on the road. Our horses swung their hindquarters nervously, anxious not to be left behind. I put the bowl in my saddlebag and mounted as my pretty Sandbred mare danced beneath me.

Lauresa's Chorus

He comes to the garden this time, just as he did so many years ago. It is riskier by far, for Andreg is home, but Lauresa is too pregnant, and the weather too foul, to ride out.

It is dark. What little light the moon may have cast is muffled by the omnipresent cloud of late Verrist. Fortunately her feet know the stone pathways so well she has no need of light. And it is the sound of his breath and his scent of leather, horse, and birch leaves that lets her know he is there beneath the bare-limbed plum tree.

Their hands find one another in the darkness, his cold from waiting here, hers warm from the heat of the great hall. They kiss lightly, briefly, with the soft touch of friends, though her heart can't help stirring with faint warmth.

"How are you?" he asks, the banality of the question belied by the grip he still has on her fingers. He turns, angling so the meagre light from the tower windows falls on her face.

"Well enough," she answers.

"And Allaigna?"

She hesitates. "Grown. Grown-up. Beyond her thirteen years."

He frowns. "Is she ..." He can't seem to finish his question.

Lauresa shakes her head. "She is happy enough to be home now, I think. Despite the shame of banishment."

The grip on her hands becomes painful. "How could he? His own granddaughter!"

She wrests a hand free, placing it on his mouth. "What choice did he have? Don't bear him any more grudges."

He takes back her fingers, turning them over, and presses them to his lips distractedly. "I can't help it, Lauresa."

She sighs, shakes her head, and rests it on his shoulder, having long ago given up this argument. He will always bear her father a grudge.

"Are you going to tell me why you've come?"

"Why? For my daughter's thirteenth birthfeast, of course." She can hear the smile in his voice and is glad, at least, there is no bitterness.

He moves away, and she can hear jingling from beneath his cloak. "I hear she's getting a new mount. Perhaps you can give her this as well." He places something over Lauresa's wrist. From the weight, she guesses it to be a bridle.

"How did you know?" she asks as her fingers feel the soft braided leather of the reins and work their way down to the smooth light metal of what can only be an Ilvan-forged bit.

"My horse is stabled at the ostler's. I saw the pony there."

Lauresa thinks briefly, sadly of Daewen, his faithful black mare who died many years back. She has never since asked him about the horse he rides now, for what mount could possibly compare?

He is still talking. "Your husband has, at least, fine taste in horseflesh."

She shakes her head. "I'm sure our head groom picked out the mare." Though she is confident Angeley had a hand in it as well.

It is his turn to put a hand over her mouth now, for he hears the footsteps on the gravel before she does. It is Piers, lanthorn in hand, just outside the door to the keep.

"Lauresa?" he calls, and waits.

She is silent, frozen in the shadow of Einavar's cloak.

Piers calls once more, then turns and heads back inside.

"I should go back in," she says, shivering with sudden tension. "I've been missed."

Einavar doesn't look at her, his eyes still trained on the door through which Piers retreated. Nor does he let go her hand.

"Who is that?" he asks. "And why does he call you by name?"

She is nervous suddenly at the tone of his voice. "Sir Piers," she replies, wondering why her own voice is cracked and girlish. "He's a diplomat from Aleran. The one who brought Allaigna home."

Einavar looks down at her, and though his face is utterly shadowed, she can feel the edge in his eyes. "Allaigna was sent home with a ranger of the Fifth by the name of Caradon. And that was him."

The cooled sweat on her neck turns to instant ice. She opens her mouth, but can hardly speak the question.

"Then Piers is ..."

"Not whom he pretends to be. Or Caradon is not. Or neither."

She is dizzy and feels like vomiting, though it's been months since she has. As she sags, his arms come around her for support.

"Find out," she whispers, her voice clogged with fears. "Can you find out who he really is?"

His voice in turn is hard and clear. "I will. But you must tell me all you know of him: his movements, associates. And whose confidence he is in."

She nods. "I will. But not now." The fact that others are looking for her is only an excuse, but one she latches onto, giving herself a desperately needed reprieve in which to think. "Tomorrow. Here. At the same time." It is beyond risky, but her mind is too panicked to make other plans.

She throws her arms around his neck and kisses him good-bye. It is only then, in the dark, he notices the round weight of her belly.

He stops her, a hand on her abdomen.

"Lauresa … I …" It is his voice now that is bottled, and she knows he is counting the moons since their last meeting. "I didn't know. Forgive me."

"Forgive you?" she asks, regaining composure. "For what?" She turns and walks a few steps away. "Till tomorrow, my love."

Irdaign's Chorus

Newborn Vardry has fed and fallen asleep on his mother's chest, exhausted after the work of coming into the world. The maids have cleaned up, stoked the fire and left, and Lauresa too is drifting off to sleep. I lean over to kiss them both before pulling shut the curtains around the bed.

As I walk down the stairs to my workshop, I begin to compose the message in my head that I must send to the Duke. I wonder too if I should be sending another message to Piers, or to Einavar, but Lauresa will not tell me which, and so they will both remain uninformed.

I meet Allaigna on the bottom step. She is dressed in riding clothes, and is damp from the persistent drizzle outside. Her eyes have lost their passive calm for once.

"She has had it?" she asks.

"Him," I correct with a smile. "His name is Vardry."

She frowns. "That's an Aleran name."

I am annoyed Allaigna has noticed this obvious detail while I have not.

"Well, your father is cousin to Vishod. He has every right to it."

Allaigna looks thoughtful. "I wonder what Allenry will think." Her eyes narrow, and she seems older, suddenly, than her thirteen years. "Can I see him?"

I am surprised yet again by the question. I stop myself from saying no, that Lauresa must rest. Any interest Allaigna has in her siblings is not to be thwarted. It is a sudden thought that feels like the nagging of Sight.

"Go on—quietly. They may be sleeping. But have a peek."

The Duke returns early, a full two weeks before the birthfeast. There is ambivalence in his eyes when he rides into the yard, and I have a dull certainty that he knows the babe is not his.

And yet when he has little Vardry in his arms, his face lights with happiness as the tiny fingers catch his beard, and for the first time in all these years I feel a kind of love for my daughter's husband.

Allenry is all scowls, though. I want to laugh and ruffle his hair, reassure him he is still his father's heir and favourite, but even at nine and a half, he thinks he is too grown-up for the caresses of his nurse.

Allaigna, with her well-honed instinct for irritating her brother, coos and fusses over the baby, making much of his royal name and exclaiming on his resemblance to the Duke. I motion Allenry from the room before he says something that will get him in trouble.

"Come to my workshop, love. I have something to show you."

Away from the room of cooing relatives, his grumpiness eases and he lets down his grown-up demeanour, his legs swinging as he perches on the high stool, waiting for a treat. I pass him a candied violet from the jar I keep on the top shelf.

Next, I lift down what looks like a coil of dried meat. "Do you know what this is?"

He shakes his head.

"It's your brother's cord, where he was attached to your mother."

He reaches out to touch it but recoils in horror. I hold his hand, place the cord on it.

"Have you heard of a sooth brother? We Leisanmira believe that the cord that links us to our mothers has powerful protective magic, and that those who carry the cord of another are protected by it ... and bound to look after its first owner."

I take it back. "I was going to give this to Allaigna. But ... do you think you are old enough for the responsibility?"

His brown eyes are wide and solemn, but he doesn't hesitate to stretch out his hand to take it back.

Verse 25
Broken Ties

Glaignen kept me amiable company as my horse pranced and fretted behind the slow wagons. I wanted to relax and enjoy the ride on this beautiful late spring morning, a fine horse beneath me and a handsome young man beside me. But I felt chains around my heart, anchored with the weights that rode in Nourd's caravan ahead of us. The light was too bright, the mare's pace too jiggly, and I felt my head pound with every stride.

I answered Glaignen's pleasant attempts at conversation with the briefest of replies, my eyes cast down at my horse's neck, the tension running through my back and hands making her all the more choppy and difficult.

Waves of nausea began sloshing in my stomach, and when the caravan stopped at noon to let the horses rest, I retreated beyond the roadside and threw up my breakfast into the bushes. I stayed there, resting my head on my knees even while the van started to move again.

Glaignen, of course, came to find me.

"Go on ahead," I told him. "I'll catch up."

"What do you take me for, that I'd leave a maid in distress by the roadside?" His words were light-hearted, but I could hear concern beneath them, which only annoyed me.

"Please. Just go." I didn't want to throw up again in front of him.

Instead he swung down from his horse and sat beside me.

"Two can catch up as easily as one. I'll wait for you to be feeling better."

If my head hadn't hurt so much, I would have yelled. Instead I gritted my teeth, kept my voice low. "Thank you. But I don't want company."

The hand he placed on my back made my soft shirt feel like a horsehair blanket on my oversensitive skin. I shrugged it off, trying not to vomit again or to cry with the throbbing pain in my head. I reached into my shirt and pulled out the eversweet posy I kept with my pendant, but even that sharp clean smell would not clear my head.

I heard his breath, felt it like a hot desert wind.

"You still wear it."

He meant the pendant. The one he'd given me five years before at the Autumn Fair, when we'd first met. That was the first time I'd had a headache like this one, and sudden suspicion filled my head. I tore it off my neck, its absence feeling cold and naked on my skin.

I wanted none of it: no gipsy magic that chained me to prophecy and made my head ache.

I scrambled onto my horse's back, reached into the saddlebag, and pulled out the bowl. My throat was too full of tears to speak, to explain, to apologize, or even to breathe.

I spurred my horse, and as she filled the air with dust, I threw the bowl to him. It looked just as I had imagined, spinning and flashing in the sun as I galloped away south.

He followed me for some time, I think, but my desert mare was faster and could run longer than his draught cross. As I fled from friends, obligations, and responsibilities, the Valnirata Greatwood edged my vision to the left: a deep green ribbon both mysterious and frightening, which called to me like the Eastern forest had at home.

But to the right, the rich fertile fields of Brandishear opened, welcoming and warm, also my home by birthright. Through the gilded haze of nostalgia, the two years I'd lived there seemed the best of my life.

The two landscapes pulled on me equally, leaving me no place to go but straight ahead. I'd never travelled in Brandishear and knew only Rheran and its environs. But Rhiadne was stationed on the south-eastern border. And Morran Rhoan was heading there to find her. The thought of them both made my heart beat a little slower and my stomach unclench.

And then I stopped, jerking my mare to a rude halt from her ground-covering trot. *No.* I didn't need another family. I already had one father too many, and if I couldn't find my real one, I wanted no other. As for the rest of them — well, I'd had enough of the tangled weave of love and lies. I scratched the mare on the withers to apologize for my inconsiderate hands and turned her west, toward Rheran. She was the only company I needed on this road, and hers the only pace I wanted to keep.

Lᴀᴜʀᴇsᴀ's Cʜᴏʀᴜs

Lauresa lifts bundles of clothes from the footlocker, her fingers slipping past cold layers of cloth, releasing old and familiar scents. It has been a long time since these folds have been disturbed.

She feels Allaigna's suspicious, accusing eye on the back of her neck, icier than the spring air in the unheated room. But it is more than cold that makes her shiver. It's been many, many years since she has opened the false bottom of the chest, and never with a witness. She fumbles, grasps the blade end in error, and slices a thin line across her forefinger.

The pain and welling blood is a good excuse for the tears just waiting, but her daughter looks on with an impassive lack of sympathy as Lauresa pauses to suck the blood from the wound. At last she takes the carved handle with her left hand and places it in her lap, as if the cold of it burns her.

"This was his. It's all I have of him. Except you."

She's not sure why she's showing it to Allaigna, this blade with all its dangerous connotations. As proof, perhaps, so her cold-eyed daughter will believe her now that she's told the truth at last.

And it does seem to have an effect. Allaigna, who listened stone-faced to the story of how she came to be, now erupts in angry tears.

"How could you," she screeches. "How could you lie to me so long?"

Lauresa reaches out one hand to touch, placate, soothe her daughter, but Allaigna steps back, an expression of revulsion on her face.

"To protect you, my love," Lauresa says, lowering her voice pleadingly. "How would your father react if he knew he had a"—she stops herself from saying those labels that have taunted her all these years: cuckoo, bastard—"another man's child in his house?"

"He's not my father," Allaigna hisses, but she lowers her voice nonetheless.

The venom in the tone makes Lauresa wish Allaigna were yelling still.

In her thoughts that night, she is back in the Valnirata Great-wood. In the warmth of the *keaugh*, bundled together in a disarray of blankets and discarded clothes, she notices the blade lying beside her boot.

She leans across him, her breast brushing his chin, and he takes the opportunity for a playful nip while his arm snakes around her, holding her back. She squirms past anyway and closes her fingers on the tip of the blade, careful not to cut herself on the sharp steel.

"It's beautiful," she muses, lying back on the bed and holding it up to the lamplight. "But cruel, and wicked-looking too."

His hand closes over hers and lowers the dagger.

"I'd rather you didn't hold it like that. Even at arm's length, it could pierce those lovely ribs if you dropped it." He emphasizes his words by kissing her lower ribs.

She wriggles, refusing to be distracted. "Oughtn't it have a scabbard, then?"

He shakes his head. "It is an Ilvani blood blade. They are never sheathed except in the body of an enemy."

"That must make treaties difficult. Ilmar tradition demands parties at negotiations lay their sheathed weapons on the table."

"You would never bring this to parley. Each one is forged for a particular task. And once that task is done, it is never used again."

She shivers. It would have been a blade such as this that Caradar Halobrelia used to carve his mark on her grandfa-ther's corpse.

"And what was this one made for?"

He shakes his head. "I am not sure. It belonged to my father's father's mother. It never completed its task, or so we believe. But whomever it was forged to kill is likely long dead by now. And, as I've said before, I am not as superstitious as my father's people. To me, it's a knife. To others it may mean more."

"If it's just a knife, then, why not have a scabbard made?"

He kisses her. "Why don't you do that?" He puts it in her hands.

Lauresa wakes to little Vardry's impatient cooing and snugs him to her breast. She drifts back to sleep as he nurses, aware dawn is only just showing, and she has another hour of sleep at least before the twins and Lauriana begin to stir.

But something stops her from settling back. A feeling of disturbance, something in the air that smells not quite right.

When Vardry's head lolls and he rolls to his back, milk dribbling from his mouth, she eases up onto one elbow, slowly and awkwardly extricating herself from bedclothes and children without awakening the latter.

Once outside the bed, she recognizes the scent of lavender just before she sees the open footlocker, its contents of carefully stacked clothes and herbs scattered on the floor. She doesn't need to look inside to know the false bottom is open and the dagger missing.

Not bothering with slippers or a robe, she rushes out of the room, bare feet hardly noticing the cold stone of the uncarpeted corridor. Anger keeps her warm as she strides toward the north tower and Allainga's private chamber.

She doesn't knock; she just walks in with a righteous maternal fury she has seldom summoned. But the room is empty. The first place she looks is under the pillows: it's where Allaigna used to hide things from her as a child. Next, she looks under the bed, and in the table beside it. When she opens Allaigna's chest, though, her fury is washed away in a wave of foreboding.

She doesn't keep track of her daughter's personal possessions anymore — not since she left to become a page. But Lauresa is certain the locker should have more clothes in it. The wardrobe too, is emptier than it should be. Most notably of Allaigna's tall boots and her heavy woollen cloak.

She rushes to the window, throwing open the shutters, but the room looks east, and not into the courtyard as hers does.

The sprint down the stairs, out the main doors, across the courtyard, and into the stalls seems interminable. The rooster is just crowing, and bleary-eyed Wulf is climbing down from his chamber in the loft, answering the hungry whickering of the horses.

She ignores him, rushes to Nag's stall, and cannot help her scream when she sees it empty.

Jrdaign's Chorus

I wake and know she is gone. The inevitability of this moment has haunted me all her life, and all Lauresa's too. All I want is to turn back time, to have one more day, or hour, even. Not for the first time, I curse my uneven Sight that told me she will and must leave home this second time, but did not tell me when.

I hear Lauresa's bare feet slapping the stone floor as she rushes past my rooms. I want to stop her, take her in my arms and warn her that she will not find her daughter within the castle walls; but I know I cannot reach her in time. Instead I will wait, and let her tell me the news.

To spend the time, I pour water into my scrying dish, though I know the task is hopeless. Allaigna has kept her pendant turned around since she came back two years ago, and I have little hope of finding her unless she is in some peril or thinking of me.

She knows now who I am, of this I'm sure. She has done since she came back. And yet she's made no admission, nor acknowledged in any way, that I am her grandmother. That would hurt far more if I didn't deserve it. Someday she may forgive her mother and me for the lies we've told her, but that will be a long time coming.

Despite my doubt, I do see her. Nag is a darker smudge on the dark grey road. The view is high and far away, but I can tell she is at least an hour gone from Teillai.

"Leave the road," I whisper, wondering why she hasn't thought of it herself. And she does, slowing Nag to a walk and turning east through farmers' fields.

I breathe a sigh of relief, wondering if she has for once heeded my advice or simply come to her own conclusions.

I hear Lauresa's wail of despair, even though the shutters of my window are closed, and I meet her partway down the stair.

She collapses into me, her words coming out in shaky sobs that lose themselves in my chest. She is standing one step below me, and as I hold her, my heart aches: not for the granddaughter who would never let me hold her thus, but for my daughter, whose years at this height I missed.

I kiss the top of her head and realize that despite her adult scent and the perfume she wears, her hair still carries a lingering hint of its baby smell. It is too much for me. The tears start down my face.

"Come, Lauresa," I whisper into the sobbing shaking head, and lead her into my room.

She protests as I urge her to sit, but accepts the cup of tea I pour. "I must rouse the guard—send out the rangers—"

"Hush. I'll attend to that. Stay here, drink." I sing the last few words, and she does.

I hurry out to the stables to control the damage already done.

Wulf is in nearly as much distress as Lauresa and has already saddled two horses and roused his father, Master Baredh, and the kennel master. I silently applaud and curse his initiative, for he's made my job more difficult.

I planned for years what to do when Allaigna finally ran away from home. I had the pieces of a cover story almost in place: an illness sending her to the healers in Aleran. But it has happened too soon, and now I have too many people panicked.

I do what I would rather not. I sing a charm on all these witnesses.

It is a strain, and it almost doesn't work on the veteran Baredh. I will have to frequently reinforce it on all these people in the days and weeks that come, but for now, I seem to have convinced them to forget Lauresa's scream and ignore the missing horse.

Feeling exhausted and unclean, I head back to my chambers, where Lauresa is asleep, thanks to the tea.

She will be furious with me yet again for foreseeing this event and not warning her. But I know the workings of Fate well enough to know she would not have been able to prevent it. And I know as well that she should not. There is much Allaigna will accomplish in this terrifying, risky flight from home. And some of it will alter the course of history.

Eventually we will send out search parties. I have bought my granddaughter some time, though, and I hope it will be enough.

There is still much to be done, but for now I curl my tired body around that of my daughter and will myself back to sleep, guiltily enjoying the physical comfort of mothering, despite Lauresa's distress.

Verse 26
Token

A summer rain was falling as I walked up Rheran's high street. It
was not cold, but damp and dispiriting nonetheless. I had stabled
my mare at the Red Horse Inn, where I'd agreed to meet Rhoan,
but had left no message nor taken a room. I was filled with an
uneasy restlessness, light and directionless. I found myself at
one point in front of Goff's grandmother's house, wondering
if I should inquire within. But we'd not parted as friends two
years ago, and regrets over my recent encounter with Glaignen
clouded my thoughts.

And then there was Fraell Edris. I could take my dagger to
her — see if she, with all her sword lore and contacts, could
trace its descent. Or Garæthiel. I could send a message to the
Bastion to see if she or Fîal would care to meet me. But the
Bastion seemed most frightful of all, its grey stone base rising
wet and grim from the crown of Rheran Hill.

I turned back down Clealla Way, away from the high street,
and found the Greenling Hostel. It was an overflow barracks
used when Brandishear's troops were called in and could not
all be housed in the Bastion. Between times, many rangers and

troops on leave preferred it to quartering in the castle anyway. It was closer to the nightlife of the city and less scrutinized than the entries into the well-guarded Prince's seat.

For some reason it appealed to me as well, better than the well-appointed inn frequented by visitors to the city. The presence of my mare at the Red Horse would tell Rhoan or Glaignen I'd arrived safely. But I paid in advance and left no other address. When I decided to meet either of them again, it would be on my terms.

My money was running low, so I agreed to sing in the evenings at the Greenling to pay for my bed, leaving my weapons with the hosteller for security. I had been there four or five nights, singing in the evenings and reacquainting myself with the roads and alleys of Rheran by day, with no sign of either Glaignen or Rhoan. I don't know if I was disappointed or relieved to delay all contact with people I knew, but I checked back on my horse daily, just long enough to groom her and give her a last-season's apple or carrot ends from the Greenling's kitchen.

I left the hostel that morning, carrot tops in hand, after retrieving my father's dagger from the innkeep. I didn't wear my sword but decided, after an encounter with drunken youths the day before, that a small show of arms was prudent.

With the dagger thrust prominently through my belt, I stepped into the already hot morning only to be jerked roughly back into the dark of the hostel by an arm through mine. I yelped in surprise before a hand was clamped over my mouth. I reached for the dagger, but it was across my body, and my other arm was twisted upward so painfully I had no choice but to follow.

"Sh," said a voice in my ear. "Apologies, but you shouldn't go outside with that."

I looked up and over my shoulder, my eyes readjusting to the dim light once more. I recognized the man. He'd been in the hostel a few nights already while I'd performed, chatting with friends, carousing with a chestnut-haired woman who was obviously more than a friend. I could see the emblem on his cloak—a Brandishear Ranger—and began to squirm.

"Hst! I won't hurt you! Stop fighting me and sit down."

He pushed me not so gently into a chair and sat down beside me, boxing me in a corner between a table, a wall, and him. My dagger, I noticed, was in his hands. I opened my mouth to protest and he shushed me again.

"Where did you get this?" he asked.

There was such urgency, such menace in his question that I didn't dare dissemble.

"It ... it was my mother's."

"Was?" His fingers spasmed on the handle of the knife, clenching it with whitened knuckles so the tip curved toward me.

I flinched backward, pressing into the corner.

"Is?" I amended.

"And your mother is of what house?"

I swallowed, unable to comprehend the question at first. Like an idiot I finally stuttered out, "She's not. Not Ilvani."

"You do know it's death for an Ilmari to carry a blade such as this?"

I stayed silent, staring into his cold-eyed glare like a rodent facing a hawk.

"If you believe that sort of thing," he added, releasing the dagger so it spun on the table, settling with its handle pointed toward me. "I do know any self-respecting *dreimar* would kill you just for touching it."

A small flame of defiance rose up in me. "Not that it's any of your business, but my father gave it to her."

"And where did he get it?"

"I don't know. I … I'd like to find him and ask." I looked up into the chilly eyes, not daring to question or hope that this man, the first to know something about the weapon, might know something of my father as well.

He shook his head slowly. "Best not, child. Do you know what this is?" He didn't wait for an answer. "An Ilvani blood blade. No two are alike." He traced the intricate carvings with a long finger. "Each one is forged for a particular vengeance. This one has already been used."

I shivered. "How do you know?"

He ignored the question. "If this was your father's, then he stole it. Take it back if you would, but if I were you, I'd keep it hidden. Even here in Rheran's walls, there are those who would kill you just for looking at it."

My hand hovered over it as if the grip would brand me. I breathed, let my fingers settle on it. It didn't burn at all but felt cool and familiar in my hand.

"Stolen or not, it's all I have of him," I said.

"Oh, I doubt that," he said, smiling. It was no more than an upward twitch of the corner of his rod-straight mouth, but it softened his face, made it almost handsome in a thin and weathered way. "I'm sure you have something of him. His eyes, perhaps. His chin? His hair?"

I wanted to know more — to find out what this stranger knew of the knife — but I couldn't find a way to ask.

"Did you assault me just to issue this warning, sir?" I asked instead, as I tucked the knife back into its old, hidden spot beneath my tunic.

Another twitch of a smile. "No one makes a career singing in barracks on purpose. You seem … to lack direction." He pushed away from the table and stood. "In two day's time there will be what we nicely call a recruitment drive. Most of the idle youth of the city will find opportunities to serve their Prince. I'd suggest you leave by then if you don't wish to be press-ganged into the infantry."

I thought at first he mistook me for a boy, then remembered again we were in Brandishear, where women also could be pressed into military service.

"Or," he continued, leaning down to place a round wooden token on the table, "show them my chit and you'll be posted to the Sixth Rangers. It's not an easy life, but it's better than that of a foot soldier … or a beggar."

I sat, turning the token over in my fingers after he left. It was stamped with BRVI on one side and the mark of a raven's head — the emblem of the Sixth Rangers, I guessed — on the other. I thought of my pendant, the one I'd ripped from my neck a mere two weeks before, with its red foal and black raven. I'd abandoned my posy, my pendant, and my home. All I had left were my weapons: sword, bow, and dagger. I had forsaken magic and the bends and twists of prophecy. Why not turn to the simple life of a ranger? Spend time in the forests and wilds that had called to me all my life? I'd be alone for the most part, but when in company, I'd be with others like Rhiadne, my most admired mentor. And then there was the stranger who had more, perhaps, to teach me of the knife I carried.

Or I could wait for Glaignen or Rhoan. Either of whom would take me back like family. Or take me back to my family, if I asked.

I knelt in the courtyard of the Bastion, one of at least two hundred new recruits, and made my oath once more to my grandfather. I kept my head down, not wanting to meet his eyes in case he recognized me, then rose and made my way through the throng to join my captain.

❧ ❧

Allaigna's Song concludes with *Chorale*,
due out from Pulp Literature Press in 2021

❧ ❧

Acknowledgements

Much like childbirth, the second time around is both easier and more difficult with book releases. On the one hand, you know how to do it. On the other, your attention and energy are divided between making a new baby and dealing with the ever-increasing complexities that come with the first one. In my case those complexities were not just looking after *Overture*, but also guiding the release of three novels by other people, and the quarterly magazine from Pulp Literature Press. Which is a roundabout way of saying that this book, which I had originally promised you, dear readers, as an early-2019 release, is a year late.

Fortunately books fare far better than babies when ridiculously post-term, and *Aria*'s long gestation hasn't harmed her a whit — perhaps it has even improved her. I am indebted to the many midwives and doulas who have helped along the way. Mel Anastasiou and Susan Pieters have listened to this tale and offered gentle guidance from its beginning; Amanda Bidnall is the genius copy editor and layout designer who makes my prose exponentially more readable; and Mary Rykov, Jessica Fabrizius, Alana Krider, and Genevieve Wynand have between them caught more typos than any single manuscript should have a right to possess. Once again I am indebted to Melissa Mary Duncan for her beautiful cover artwork — this time produced with an injured hand — and to Kate Landels for the cover design based on Kris Sayer's work for *Overture*.

Thanks remain due to Scott Fitzgerald Gray, whose land of the Ilmar must be looking less and less recognizable under my pen. And of course I couldn't do any of this without the support of the love of my life, Chris Richardson, who remains my biggest fan … short perhaps of Margot Landels, who has been waiting most impatiently for this book. Sorry, Mum. I'll try to get the next one out faster. To the rest of my wonderful readers, thank you for your enthusiasm, encouragement, and patience while this long-overdue novel gestated. My goal is to give birth to the final book within a year and a half. Wish me luck!

JM Landels, February 2020

About the Author

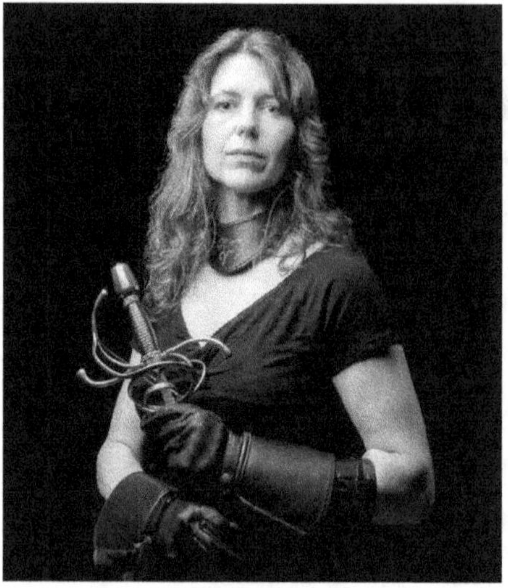

photo by Mark Feenstra

In addition to her work as a writer, editor, artist, and publisher, JM Landels teaches swordplay and riding—sometimes both at the same time—in Langley, BC. She draws on this experience, as well as her time as a rock musician and childbirth educator, to inform her fantasy trilogy, Allaigna's Song. She is currently working on a new series, La Bergère, featuring a shepherdess-turned-spy in seventeenth-century France.